Emma Blair was born in Glasgow and now lives in Devon. She is the author of many bestselling novels including *Scarlet Ribbons* and *Flower of Scotland*, both of which were shortlisted for the Romantic Novelist of the Year Award.

For more information about the author, visit www.emma-blair.com

'Pure heart-tugging, page-turning satisfaction' *The Bookseller*

ARROWS OF DESIRE

Emma Blair

sphere

SPHERE

First published in Great Britain in 2008 by Sphere
This paperback edition published in 2008 by Sphere

A CIP catalogue record for this book
is available from the British Library.

ISBN 978-0-7515-3987-5

Typeset in Adobe Garamond by Palimpsest Book Production Limited,
Grangemouth, Stirlingshire

Printed and bound in Great Britain by Clays Ltd, St Ives plc

Sphere
An imprint of
Little, Brown Book Group
100 Victoria Embankment
London EC4Y 0DY

An Hachette Livre UK Company
www.hachettelivre.co.uk

www.littlebrown.co.uk

For Bree

Bring me my bow of burning gold!
Bring me my arrows of desire!

'Jerusalem', by William Blake

Chapter 1

Beth frowned, then looked up from her midday meal. 'Do you hear something?' she asked after a few seconds.

Her brother Roy paused with his fork halfway to his mouth. 'Like what?'

Beth shook her head. 'It's gone now, but I could have sworn . . .' She trailed off, and addressed herself again to her plate. Dinner was mince and potatoes, one of her favourites, except the mince just hadn't had the same taste to it since the war started eighteen months ago. It was far more fatty and gristly then it had been. Still, she was thankful the family had it at all, meat being a commodity that was becoming scarcer and scarcer with every passing week.

'*I* can hear it now, a sort of thumping noise,' declared Cissie, Beth and Roy's mother, the third and final person at the table.

Beth was intrigued. Crossing to the window, she raised it and leaned out.

1

The bitter March wind stung her face, while behind her Roy exclaimed as a draught swirled round the room. There it was again, a thumping noise carried by the wind from what seemed a fair way off.

That's odd, she mused: it sounded like blasting she'd once heard. Perhaps some old buildings were being blown up?

'Shut that bloody window!' Roy complained.

'Come here and see what you make of it,' Beth called to him over her shoulder.

'I'm not hanging out of a window like some old gossip,' Roy retorted. Snorting, he pushed his plate away and began to light a cigarette.

Suddenly a new sound intruded, and the steady drone of a plane's engines filled the room, building up to such an intensity that Cissie, whose hearing had always been acute, was forced to clap her hands over her ears.

'What bloody madman's that!' Roy shouted angrily, coming to his feet. A few quick strides brought him alongside Beth and then he too was leaning out of the window.

The plane appeared over the surrounding rooftops, so low Beth felt she could've reached up and touched it. Green, with a white underbelly, it roared overhead while both she and Roy gaped. Then it was gone, the sound of its engines gradually receding.

Beth knew now what that far-off thumping noise was. Glasgow was being bombed for the first time ever.

Roy pulled himself back into the room to stare at his mother. 'A Jerry. I saw the bastard's markings plain as day.'

Cissie bit her lip. 'They'll be going for the docks.'

'Aye, that'll be it right enough,' Roy muttered thoughtfully.

'What'll we do?' Cissie asked him, for with her husband Andrew away in the army, Roy was acting head of the family.

'What we've been told to do when this happened, go down to the shelter,' Roy replied, for the city had long known it would eventually be a bombing target. The only question had been when. Cissie rose from the table and hurried through to the hallway for her coat.

'I'd better get back to the hospital. They might need me,' Beth declared. She was a trainee nurse at the nearby Victoria Infirmary.

'The hell with that!' Roy retorted. 'You'll take Ma down to the shelter and stay there with her until this raid's over.'

'But it's my duty . . .' Beth started to say, only to be cut short.

'It's your duty to look after Ma, not to mention staying alive. You'll do as I say, Beth, and no buts about it.'

Beth glared at her older brother. It infuriated her when he treated her as a child and not the nineteen-year-old she was.

Cissie hurried back into the room carrying Beth's cape. 'Roy's right. You could well get yourself killed going out on the streets when there's a raid in progress. No one at the hospital would thank you for that, I'm sure.'

Grudgingly Beth acquiesced, knowing them to be right. Suddenly the air raid siren burst into life, its ululating wail originating from the local ARP post.

'They're a bit sodding late.' Roy gave a short barking laugh. 'Typical!'

On the landing outside they ran into old Mrs McGurk from next door. She lived alone, her man being long dead and her family now grown up with homes of their own. Cissie linked arms with her, and together they clattered downstairs with Beth and Roy bringing up the rear.

Mrs Carmichael, who stayed at the bottom left hand side of the close, or communal stairway, was standing at the door crying while Mrs Todd, another neighbour in the close, tried to comfort her.

'It's her weans at school. She's worried sick about them,' Mrs Todd explained.

'They'll be all right. The teachers will have taken them to the basement which, I can assure you, having seen it myself when my two were pupils, is a far safer place for them than our shelter. You have my word on that, hen,' Cissie told her.

Mrs Carmichael's tear-stained face brightened a little. 'I hadn't thought of that,' she said huskily.

'There's a Primus and fresh water in the shelter, so let's away in and brew ourselves a cuppa,' Mrs Todd proposed.

'Good idea!' exclaimed Mrs McGurk, who'd never been known to turn down a cup of tea and a natter. She led the way to the back green where the brick and concrete shelter was situated.

Beth was about to follow her mother and the others when she realised that Roy was making for the front of the close and the street beyond. 'Where are you off to?' she demanded.

'Work. Where do you think?'

'But what about the raid?'

A stubborn look settled on his face. 'No damn Jerry's going to get me into a shelter. That's for you womenfolk.'

Beth just had to laugh. 'It's not all right for me to get killed, but it is for you. Is that it?'

'It's a male thing, lass. Can you understand that?'

'You're an awfy man,' Beth replied, shaking her head, for although she often found her brother exasperating in the extreme, she also greatly admired him.

'Away with you, I'll be fine. Only the good die young and I'm certainly not one of those.'

'Well, that's true enough,' she agreed.

He shook his fist at her in mock anger. Then, striding out into the street, he disappeared from view.

In the back green Beth paused to listen, but the wind had shifted so she could no longer hear the thumping sounds. High in the sky she could make out two tiny specks that were certainly aeroplanes, but she had no idea to which side they belonged. Opening the shelter's door she slipped inside, blinking at the sudden change from bright daylight to soft candlelight.

The shelter was in two sections, the partition being a brick wall running down the middle with a hole in its centre which allowed people to pass from one section to the other. Each section had its own entrance door.

Beth's section was supposed to cater for the three flats, or houses as they were always called, up her side of the close, the other section for the opposite side. But in practice, air raid drills having been a regular occurrence during the past year, the families tended to use whichever section they found themselves in.

Cissie, Mrs McGurk, Mrs Carmichael and Mrs Todd

were sitting on boxes round a Primus which Cissie was coaxing alight. Mrs McGurk, as was her wont, was chattering away nineteen to the dozen. It was gloomy, spooky almost, inside the shelter, with shadows flickering on the ceiling and walls. It was also extremely cold, so Beth was glad of her thick nurse's cape.

'Tea up in a minute or two,' Cissie informed her as she joined the huddled group.

Unfortunately, no one had thought to bring milk, but cups, spoons and sugar were on hand and these Mrs Todd now set out. The tea when poured was thick and strong, and once sugared was absolutely delicious. Beth was raising her cup for a first sip when a curly head was stuck through the hole in the partition. The head belonged to Edgar Martin, eldest son of the family who lived opposite the Carmichaels.

'Is that tea we smell?' he enquired.

'No, it's just your imagination, son,' Mrs McGurk instantly retorted, causing Mrs Todd to snigger.

'Och, don't be such a tease, Edna. After all, it's not as though he's a laddie still. He's a piper in the army now, don't forget,' said Cissie. And indeed, Edgar was in the uniform of the Glasgow Royals which he'd joined six months previously.

'Just me having a wee bit fun. No offence meant.' Mrs McGurk smiled at Edgar, who replied that none had been taken.

It was true that for a moment Mrs McGurk had forgotten that Edgar was all grown up. She'd thought of him then, as she often did, as the wee boy who used to whoop up and down the close playing cowboys and

Indians. And who'd once – his father had leathered his backside for it – put a handful of stink bombs through her letter box, the smell from which, despite repeated applications of disinfectant, had lingered for months afterwards.

'There are some cups through there. Bring them here and I'll brew up a fresh pot for you,' Cissie told Edgar.

'That's awful kind of you, Mrs Somerville,' Edgar beamed in reply, and withdrew his head back into the other section.

When the fresh pot had masked, Cissie poured, then told Beth to put the cups on to a tray and take them through.

Beth discovered Edgar sitting round a sputtering candle with three young men his own age, all of whom were in the uniform of the Royals. The four of them rose at her approach.

There were several other neighbours in that section, and they were also treated to a cuppa. Beth was about to make her way back to her mother when Edgar asked if she'd sit with them for a moment or two as he'd like her to meet his pals, all of whom were in the band with him.

Jacko was tiny, even for a Glaswegian, with flaming red hair and a long pointed nose. He spoke with a very thick guttural accent which placed him as coming from one of the really rough working class areas.

'And this is Teddy Ramsay. He and I were in the Boys' Brigade together and joined the Royals within a week of one another,' Edgar informed Beth, introducing her to the second young man.

Teddy solemnly shook Beth by the hand, but didn't say anything. The shy type, she thought.

The third young man was called Ron, and there was certainly nothing shy about him. 'You're a right smasher,' he declared, which caused Beth to laugh, and Edgar to frown warningly at him.

'Watch that one, he's quite the ladies' man. Wherever he goes he leaves a trail of broken hearts behind,' Jacko grinned.

'Not true!' Ron protested.

'Och, away with you, you're known throughout the regiment for it,' persisted Jacko.

Ron pulled a long face. 'Honestly, it's a case of give a dog a bad name,' he assured Beth.

'I doubt that,' she replied with a chuckle.

Jacko produced a packet of Pasha. 'Would you like a ciggie, Beth?' he asked.

She stared at the packet, as though making a decision. Finally she nodded. 'Thank you, don't mind if I do.'

As Jacko helped her to a light, Edgar declared in astonishment, 'When did you start that? All the years I've known you I've never seen you with a cigarette before.'

Beth smiled sheepishly. 'In actual fact I've been smoking for a while, but I have to be careful. My brother Roy would give me what for if he ever caught me at it. He thinks smoking and drinking are unladylike.'

'I'll bet he smokes like a chimney and drinks like a fish himself,' Teddy Ramsay commented, speaking for the first time.

'That's right. How did you know?'

Teddy smiled at her. 'I've noticed in the past that those who lay down hard and fast rules for others are usually the worst offenders themselves.'

This Teddy was a thinker, Beth mused. She liked that.

'How's your da? Have you heard recently?' Edgar asked.

Beth shook her head. 'The last letter we got was over two months ago, and that said precious little after the censor had got through with it. He was well at the time, which is the main thing, and somewhere tropical. At least that was the impression we got.'

Edgar explained to the others. 'Her da's with the Black Watch.'

'They're a good bunch, the Watch,' Ron enthused. 'And they've got a damn fine band.'

'Aye, that's right enough,' Jacko confirmed.

Beth stared off into the darkness, thinking about her da. He was relatively young still, only forty-three. A fine figure of a man with exceptionally broad shoulders that came from humping dozens of coal bags every day, the job he'd been doing since leaving school. He'd been a skinny runt then, he'd often told her, but a couple of years on the coal cart had soon altered that. She and he were close in that special way daughters often were with their fathers.

It worried her silly to think of him off fighting, a subject consciously referred to as little as possible at home. Da had gone off to war, and Da would come home again when it was all over. That's the way it would be.

'A penny for them?' Teddy asked.

Beth came out of her reverie to regard Teddy slightly quizzically. He was different from the others, more mature somehow, more in control of himself. 'I wasn't thinking about anything in particular,' she lied. Then, coming to her feet, she said, 'I'd better get back. It's been nice meeting and talking to you, lads. I've enjoyed it.'

Edgar was opening his mouth to reply when suddenly there was a terrific explosion. Beth screamed as she was thrown backwards and landed heavily on the concrete floor. She was vaguely aware that the shelter had been plunged into total darkness – the candles must have been blown out. Brick dust filled the air.

Confusion reigned as she groggily struggled into a kneeling position. Must get to Ma, she told herself. Coughing and choking, she stumbled in the direction of the connecting hole. At last her groping hands found it, and she was through.

'Ma? Are you all right?' she called.

'I'm over here.'

Beth sighed with relief, and made her way towards her mother's voice.

'What in God's name happened?' demanded Mrs McGurk.

'We must have been bombed,' replied Mrs Todd.

Beth reached Cissie, and they fell into one another's arms.

'Here we are!' cried Mrs Todd jubilantly, and a match flared into life. A very dishevelled Mrs Todd was revealed holding the match in one hand, a candle in the other.

'Oh, no!' exclaimed Cissie when the light from the candle lit up their section.

Mrs Carmichael was lying prostrate, a trickle of blood flowing from her mouth, her open eyes already glazing. Beth knew even before she touched her that Mrs Carmichael was dead.

'Is she . . .' whispered Mrs McGurk.

Beth nodded. 'I'm afraid so.

Mrs McGurk sobbed while Mrs Todd chewed a finger. 'Those poor weans of hers,' Cissie choked.

'And her poor husband,' added Mrs McGurk.

'Beth, come quickly!' shouted Edgar, appearing in the hole.

Instantly Beth was back on her feet and hurrying towards his outstretched hand.

At first she thought it was Ron who needed her attention, for he was clutching his arm, but when he saw her making for him he shook his head. 'Never mind me. Have a look at Teddy,' he said.

Jacko held a candle over Teddy, who was stretched out on the floor, his face the colour of milk. For a dreadful moment Beth thought he too had been killed; then she saw that, mercifully, he was still breathing.

'I think he hit the wall. At least, he was slumped against it when I pulled him away,' Jacko volunteered.

'I need more light,' Beth said, squatting beside Teddy. Quickly she ran her hands over him, starting with his lower legs and working her way up. She grunted acknowledgement as second and third candles were brought to bear.

As far as she could tell, none of Teddy's bones were broken, but internally? He would need a proper doctor's examination to find out about that.

The back of his head was sticky with blood, and he groaned when she lightly touched him there. Glancing up, she found Edgar, Ron and Jacko staring apprehensively at her. To Edgar she said quickly, 'He needs an ambulance. Run to the telephone kiosk at the end of the street and ring through to the Victoria. Tell them it's an emergency.'

'I'm on my way,' Edgar replied, handing Jacko the candle he was holding.

'Is anyone else hurt in here?' Beth called out.

No one was, so Beth turned her attention to Ron. 'Let's have a look at that arm of yours then,' she said.

'I think it's broken,' he muttered.

And he was correct, as Beth's gently probing fingers soon discovered. 'A plaster cast for this and you'll soon be right as rain again,' she told him.

'Will it affect my playing?' he asked anxiously.

'I shouldn't think so. Your fingers will be stiff for some time after the cast comes off, as will the arm itself. But exercise will soon cure that.' Someone had produced a bandage, and as she spoke she was wrapping it round him, binding his arm to his body, which was the best she could do in the circumstances.

Teddy groaned, turning his head sharply to one side and then the other. Beth knelt by his side again and smoothed his brow, which was cold and clammy. She recalled there were some blankets in the shelter some-where and asked Jacko to find them and bring her one.

When Teddy was tucked up and as comfortable as she could make him she returned to the other section, where she told Cissie that Edgar had gone to call an ambulance for Teddy. Then she shouted through to Jacko to bring another blanket, to cover Mrs Carmichael's body.

'Can I go back to my house now?' asked Mrs Todd who, judging by her expression, had gone into shock.

Beth guided her to a box and sat her down. 'Not yet, Mrs Todd. None of us must return till the all-clear sounds.'

'Oh, aye. Aye, of course, that's right.' Mrs Todd turned her head away and began to cry.

'I'll look after her,' Cissie offered. Kneeling, she took Mrs Todd in her arms.

Ron appeared in the hole and beckoned to Beth. 'I've just had a dekko outside and guess what? We weren't bombed at all. It's a Jerry plane that's come down and hit the tenements at the back of here. You should see the mess. It's complete devastation.'

'Then I must go out there. I'll be able to help,' Beth replied at once. Passing again into the other section, she crossed to Teddy, who was still unconscious. She noted that his breathing had become a lot easier, which was a good sign.

'You stay with Teddy,' she said to Ron. 'If his condition changes before the ambulance arrives, come and get me. Don't worry if he gives the occasional moan or groan, but if his colour alters for the worse, or he starts to thrash about, then come for me as quickly as you can.'

'Understood.' He nodded.

'And what about me?' Jacko demanded.

'If it's as bad as Ron says out there they'll need every pair of hands they can get.'

'Right!' Jacko acknowledged. Together, he and Beth headed for the section door.

Outside, Beth led the way round the bin enclosures to the palings separating the back greens from those of the tenements that backed on to them. Only the palings weren't there any more. Nor were the tenements.

'Oh, my God!' breathed Beth, staring at the smoking, and in some parts blazing, piles of rubble. The German

13

plane had hit the line of buildings lengthways, bringing down the lot of them.

'Look!' exclaimed Jacko, pointing.

It was an amazing sight. Right in the middle of the rubble stood a fireplace with a pair of china dogs on either side of the mantelpiece. It was incredible to think that those fragile ornaments had survived the impact while all else around them had been reduced to smithereens.

In what had been the living room of a family named Walker were the twisted remains of the plane's fuselage. They could see the tailpiece a little further off.

'Heinkel 111, I think,' Jacko commented.

Firemen were already on the scene, as were ARP wardens. The latter were frantically tearing at a mound of brick, metal and jagged chunks of concrete. Beth and Jacko hurried over to them, and a warden said to Jacko, 'Get stuck in here, Jim. There are folk underneath.'

Beth worked alongside Jacko, heaving away the smaller bits of debris, and they were told that this particular mound of rubble hadn't been part of the tenements but rather one of the shelters belonging to them. It had been blown apart by the explosion when the plane's fuel tank had gone up.

Beth glanced across at the shelter she'd been in, and shuddered. Rotten athlete though she was, even she could have hit it with a thrown tennis ball. Why, if the German plane had been even . . . The picture conjured up in her mind didn't bear dwelling on.

Jacko pulled a block of concrete away to expose a piece of severed leg. Moments later a middle-aged woman was revealed, her face covered in blood.

Beth knelt by the woman and unbuckled her uniform belt. She tied a tourniquet round the stump, then called out for something with which to do the same on the woman's other leg, which was open to the bone behind the knee. A warden, looking as though he might throw up at any moment, handed her his tie.

Off in the distance a bell started to clang, announcing the approach of another fire engine.

The woman with the severed leg was a goner, Beth was sure. She was mumbling to herself, her voice cracked and filled with pain, and bending over her Beth could hear 'Harry ... Harry ... Harry ...' repeated over and over again.

'Here, nurse!' shouted one of the wardens.

Beth recognised the baby as wee Sandy Taggart. His mother's name was Alison, and his father Alex was away serving in the Navy. Sandy was smiling and sucking his thumb, not a mark on him.

The second fire engine arrived and with it a dozen more firemen. Although the all-clear had not yet sounded, other men were appearing out of adjacent shelters to lend their muscle to the excavations.

Edgar ran up to say an ambulance was on its way. 'Jesus wept!' he exclaimed, gazing about him in awe. It was he who, a few minutes later, uncovered the body of Alison Taggart, who'd been crushed to death beneath a slab of concrete. Eventually the bodies of fourteen more people were found.

When she returned to the woman with the severed leg, Beth discovered that she'd passed on. Beth had seen her round and about often enough, but had never known her name. Poor Harry – no doubt he was the woman's husband; she was wearing a wedding ring.

A retired bus driver called Mr Reid was the only adult survivor of the blown-up shelter. When Beth examined him all he could talk about was his favourite pipe, lost and presumably smashed among the debris.

'Twenty years and more I've had that briar, twenty years and more!' he said to Beth, eyes glistening with anger behind their rheum.

Apart from a few lacerations he was fine, but Beth insisted he would have to go to hospital anyway, just to be on the safe side.

'Twenty years and more!' he called after her, shaking his head in despair.

Beth held Sandy Taggart in the crook of her arm, where he gurgled contentedly. She stared up at the sky, but it was devoid of planes; nor could she hear the far-off thumping noise of the bombing. The raid must still be going on, she told herself, as the all-clear still hadn't been given. Where is that ambulance, she wondered, and as if in answer suddenly heard the distinctive clamour of its bell.

She stopped a warden and asked if there were any people buried underneath the tenement rubble. He replied that he didn't think so, enquiries at the other shelters serving the tenements having indicated that everyone had gone there when the air raid warning sounded. Still, they would go through the rubble as best they could to confirm that was the case.

Beth wasn't worried about Cissie. Her ma would cope all right. The best thing she could do now was to get back to the Victoria as soon as possible, which she would do travelling in the ambulance.

When it arrived, Jacko led two of the men to the shelter where Teddy was, and a few minutes later they reappeared carrying Teddy on a stretcher. Jacko was still with them, as were Ron and Mrs Todd.

Beth, carrying Sandy Taggart, was the last to climb into the vehicle before the doors slammed shut behind her. Seconds later, its bell once more clamouring, the ambulance jolted forward.

They'd almost reached the hospital before she realised she'd forgotten to say goodbye to Jacko.

Chapter 2

Just after tea ten days later, Beth was in the bathroom washing her hair, after which she intended to have a good long soak in the bath.

She was thinking about Miss Kettle, the new ward sister, already nicknamed Genghis Khan by the girls, when she heard a knock on the front door. She presumed it would be one of the neighbours, who were forever popping in to have a natter with Cissie, or borrow something, or both. It was a surprise to her therefore when, a few seconds later, Roy shouted from the hallway, 'Beth, you've got a visitor!'

Must be Eileen McCallum from two closes down returning the book she'd lent her, she thought. 'Is it Eileen?' she shouted back.

'No, a chap called Teddy Ramsay. Says he's here to thank you for what you did when that Jerry plane came down.'

Teddy Ramsay! Now there was a turn-up for the book. She'd visited him once when he was in the Victoria, but the second time she'd gone to see how he was getting along he'd already been discharged. 'I'll be through in a couple of minutes,' she called, and began furiously rinsing.

She towelled her hair as dry as she could, then combed it. Rats' tails, she thought angrily. Damn the man for coming at such an inconvenient time. She had no make-up on, and was in her dressing gown with hardly a stitch underneath. She looked awful.

Poking her head out into the hallway, she heard Roy talking in the living room, presumably to Teddy. A quick peep showed her that the living room door was drawn to so she wouldn't be seen going past. Well, that was something, at least.

Tiptoeing, she reached her bedroom and hurried inside. She was wriggling into her slip when Roy called out, 'Beth, where are you? What's keeping you? Mr Ramsay's waiting.'

There was a hint of laughter in his voice which betrayed the fact that he was deliberately teasing her. 'Bugger!' she swore softly. Sounding as casual as she could, she called back, 'I'll be right there. Keep Mr Ramsay entertained, will you?'

There was no time for a proper make-up, so she made do with only lipstick. Quickly she smoothed down her dress and checked that the seams of her last pair of stockings were straight.

Teddy rose to his feet when she entered the living room, although Roy stayed firmly in his chair. Knowing her brother, she'd have been flabbergasted if he'd done otherwise.

'I hope you don't mind me dropping by like this but

I wanted to thank you again for what you did for me that day.' Teddy smiled.

'Your thank you at the hospital was enough,' Beth replied, her tone frosty. They stared at one another, and it was Teddy who dropped his gaze first. Now why had she done that? Beth wondered. For on her part it had been more of a glare than a stare.

'Och, sit down, the pair of you, you're cluttering up the place,' Cissie piped up from the rear of the room where she was curled up on the couch knitting.

Teddy sat, then immediately got up again. Crossing to where he had left his coat, he reached into a pocket to produce a box of chocolates. 'Just a wee token,' he murmured to Beth as he handed it to her.

'Are those real? I haven't seen real chocolates for God knows how long!' Cissie exclaimed.

'Oh, they're real all right,' Teddy assured her.

'I don't know where you got them from but they must have cost you all your ration coupons,' said Beth, touched by the gesture, but also, for some reason she couldn't understand, angered by it.

'Not to worry about that. I don't have a sweet tooth myself,' Teddy replied.

Roy realised that Teddy's glass was empty. 'You'll have another dram,' he declared, lurching to his feet. 'Mr Ramsay brought a half-bottle with him as well,' he explained to Beth, refilling Teddy's glass, then his own.

'How's the head?' Beth asked Teddy.

He grinned ruefully and rubbed the back of it. 'I'm still getting headaches, but they're not nearly as bad as they were. The doctor said they could go on for some months.'

Beth was desperate for a cigarette, but was unable to light up because of Roy's presence. 'You could easily have suffered a very bad fracture, or split your skull wide open. And if part of the skull had been pushed inward to puncture the brain itself, well . . .' She trailed off and raised her eyebrows.

'Dead,' Teddy stated.

'Or worse,' she said.

'How so?' Roy queried, frowning.

'He could've been reduced to a vegetable.' Beth spelt it out.

'Yes, I was lucky,' Teddy acknowledged in a low voice.

'Beth mentioned you when she got in later that night. How long were you unconscious for?' Roy asked.

'A little over two hours. I had them worried, apparently, but then I just woke up and that was that.'

'So why the headaches?'

Beth explained. 'They often go with concussion. Real blinders which gradually, as the doctors told Mr Ramsay, fade away.'

'What's all this Mr Ramsay nonsense? Call me Teddy, please?' He smiled.

It was Roy who'd started the Mr Ramsay business and she'd carried on with it because she hadn't wanted to seem over-familiar. 'If you like,' she said, and popped a chocolate into her mouth, thinking how gauche she must be appearing.

'That was an awful raid. Two raids, really, as they came back the following day. According to the papers, Clydebank has been more or less levelled,' Cissie put in.

Teddy nodded. 'I read that.'

Cissie went on, 'They're saying now it was the big yards down there the Jerries were after, and not the docks at all.'

'The planes that came over here must've been lost,' said Roy.

'Aye, they must've been,' Teddy agreed.

A hiatus followed during which Teddy played with his glass while Roy stared at him. Beth desperately racked her brains trying to think of something, anything, to say.

'If you and Edgar were pals as boys does that mean you come from round here?' she asked eventually, shooting her brother a dark look, which he studiously ignored. Sod! she thought. He could be doing a lot more to put Teddy at his ease.

And then she was angry again. Angry with Teddy for turning up on the doorstep without any warning. Angry with Roy for just being Roy. And angry with herself, probably most of all, because she must be looking a mess with her half-dried hair and no proper make-up on. That and the fact she just wasn't coping with the situation at all.

'I do,' Teddy replied, and named a street about a quarter of a mile away.

'Posh houses those,' Roy commented.

'They're not all that different from these,' Teddy answered.

'Get away with you. You know they're better. A better quality of house, a better class of people. Professional as opposed to workers.'

Teddy was aware he was on dangerous ground. Roy was prodding, seeming to want some sort of verbal dust-up. He decided to try to steer the conversation in a slightly different direction. 'Edgar and I met in the Boys' Brigade. Even at twelve we were both daft on the pipes,' he explained.

'I love the pipes. The sound of them never fails to send shivers up and down my spine,' Cissie enthused.

'Are you a good piper?' Beth asked.

'All right, I suppose. I'd like to be better.'

'What school did you go to then?' Roy queried.

'Princess Park.'

'So it wasn't Glasgow Academy or one of the other fancy ones?'

Roy had taken a dislike to Teddy, Beth thought. Or there again, maybe he hadn't. You just never knew with Roy.

'No, one of the ordinary everyday Corporation schools. And what about yourself?'

'Beth and I both went to Stonefield Street.'

Pointedly, Cissie said, 'I wouldn't refuse a chocolate if offered, Beth. Or do you intend keeping them all to yourself?' She snaffled three when the box was handed to her.

'Sorry if I caught you washing your hair,' Teddy apologised to Beth.

'That's all right.'

'Perhaps I shouldn't have come in?'

'Don't be silly. I'm glad you did,' she lied.

Their smiles became strained. 'More whisky?' Roy said, so explosively it almost caused Beth to leap out of her chair. He topped up Teddy's glass. 'When did you join the Royals, then?'

'Seven months ago.'

'Easy number, the pipe band, I should think.'

Teddy blinked, then stiffened slightly. 'What do you mean by that?'

'Just that it must be a lot easier than being a rank and file squaddie.'

Teddy replied carefully, 'We're always there in the thick of the fighting, I can assure you.'

'Oh, no doubt! I'm sure! Don't take me the wrong way.' Innocence was written all over Roy's face.

'It may interest you to know that pipers often go into battle armed with nothing more than their pipes. And of course we do double up as stretcher-bearers,' Teddy went on.

'But you haven't seen action yourself yet?'

'No, not yet.'

Roy put on a serious expression, and nodded several times as though what Teddy had just admitted to was of great significance.

Teddy fought to bring his irritation under control. 'I gather your *father* is in the Black Watch,' he said, staring hard at Roy.

Beth caught the implication. 'Roy's exempt,' she said hastily, then wondered what on earth she was doing defending her brother, which made her angry again.

'Oh?' Teddy prompted.

Roy made no move to explain, so it was left to Beth to elaborate. 'He works at Dixon's Blazes, the big steel-making complex.'

'I know it.'

'I'm a puddler.' Roy sat back waiting for Teddy to ask him what a puddler was, only Teddy didn't.

'And what about you before you joined up?' Cissie asked.

'I was training to be a quantity surveyor.'

'A quantity surveyor, eh? Marvellous job, that, I understand. Well paid, too.' Cissie looked impressed.

'How long have you left before you qualify?' Beth enquired.

'Two years.'

Suddenly all Teddy wanted was to get out of there, away from the strained atmosphere and Roy's rudeness. It had been a mistake to come. He finished his drink, slowly so that it didn't seem he was rushing, or being rushed. Then he came to his feet. 'Thank you for your hospitality, but I must be getting on my way now. I'm due back in barracks.'

'And where are they?' asked Beth, rising when he did.

'Over the river, just north of the London Road.'

Roy swung his legs round and placed his feet halfway up the side of the fireplace. 'Come back any time,' he invited unconvincingly.

'All the best with your puddling then,' Teddy said at the living room door, slurring the word ever so slightly so that it came out as 'piddling'. A point up to me, he thought, as Roy's face creased into a frown.

Cissie called out her goodbyes and Beth ushered Teddy into the hallway. 'I can see myself out,' he said, but she told him she wouldn't dream of it.

On the landing he gave her a sort of combination wave and salute, thanking her again for what she'd done for him in the shelter. His boots clattered on the stairs as he took them two at a time.

Beth closed the front door and leaned against it, her stomach churning. What a fiasco that had been! Everything that could've gone wrong had, and she was just as much to blame as Roy. Clenching her hands, she made her way back to the living room where she found Roy polishing off the remains of the half-bottle.

'I must say I thought he was a very nice young man. Pity you didn't give him more encouragement,' Cissie admonished her.

'I can take him or leave him,' Beth replied, trying to appear indifferent.

'I quite liked him as well, considering he's an obvious Tory,' Roy drawled.

'You certainly didn't give that impression,' Beth snapped.

Roy once again assumed an expression of innocence. 'Didn't I?' he exclaimed, looking as though butter wouldn't melt in his mouth.

'You know very well you didn't!'

'If he doesn't mean anything to you then it hardly matters,' Roy said craftily.

Beth wanted to scream. To drum her feet on the floor. To slap Roy silly.

'I agree with Beth. You were a bit hard on the young chap,' Cissie rebuked her son.

'He was a right boor,' Beth added scathingly.

Roy's response was to smile and drink more whisky.

'I wonder how you'd feel if we acted like that towards your Margaret?' Beth said. Margaret was Roy's girlfriend.

'Margaret can give as good as she gets. That's one of the reasons I like her.'

'Poor lassie. Does she really appreciate what she's getting herself into, I ask myself?'

'Beth, that's enough of that,' Cissie warned her.

'Oh, I'm supposed to watch what I say, but he can say what he likes. Is that it?'

'Roy's a man. There are different rules for them.'

'Then it's unfair.'

'Life is,' Roy smirked.

'There are times when I hate you,' Beth spat.

'Beth!' Cissie exclaimed, visibly shocked.

'He wasn't your type, anyway. Far too high-falutin'. Did you hear the way he spoke? So proper he almost sounded like an Englishman.'

'Who are you to say who's right and who's wrong for me?' Beth demanded.

'I'm your brother.'

'So?'

'So I have a very *large* say in the matter.'

Beth's eyes blazed with fury. 'Only till I'm twenty-one or Da gets home. After that it's none of your business.'

'He wasn't your type,' Roy persisted. 'And if Da was here he'd tell you the same thing.'

'If Da was here he would've been polite to Teddy, for Da's a gentleman. Unlike some I could name.'

'You mean Da's soft, especially where you're concerned.'

'I won't have your father spoken about like that,' Cissie chipped in, sudden steel in her voice.

'It's true enough, though, you can't deny it.' Roy glared at Beth.

Beth shook her head. 'No, Roy, it's Da who's strong and you who's soft. Da doesn't have to prove himself every five minutes.'

'You mean I do?' Roy thundered.

Beth groped for words. She knew in her heart and mind what she meant, but the actual words which would explain it were eluding her. 'I'm going for that bath now,' she declared instead, picking up the box of chocolates Teddy had given her. At the door she rounded on Roy. 'I pity your Margaret. She must have done something really awful to deserve you.'

For a moment Beth thought he was going to leap out of his chair at her. Then, all of a sudden, as was often the case with him, his mood changed. Holding out a hand he wriggled his fingers, the prelude to a game they'd played as children which consisted of his chasing her and tickling her when he caught her.

Beth was out of the door in a flash, being ticklish in the extreme, and Roy's laughter, loud and mocking, followed her down the hallway.

While the bath was running she sat on the lavatory and munched her way through the chocolates that were left. It made her feel a whole lot better, although she couldn't have said why.

It was a real pea-souper, fog so thick you could've almost cut it with a knife. Beth coughed, and drew her scarf further up round her mouth. She was dog tired, having just come off the night shift. All she could think of was getting a bite to eat and then falling into bed to sleep the sleep of the totally exhausted. Around her figures flitted in and out of the fog, people off to their work, bent, just as she herself was, against the cruel April cold.

It was with a sigh of relief that she turned into her

close and hurried upstairs. Cissie would have porage waiting for her: just the ticket for a morning like this.

She hung up her cape and scarf. 'Cooee, I'm home!' she called out.

She found her mother in the living room, sitting at the table with Roy across from her. She frowned at her brother. 'What are you still doing here? You'll be late for work!'

He swivelled his face in her direction, and what she saw there caused her heart to skip a beat. Something dreadful had happened.

'Da?' she queried tremulously.

'Oh, lass,' Cissie choked. Picking up a piece of yellow paper, she held it out to Beth.

Numbly Beth stared at the paper, which she could see was a telegram. WE REGRET TO INFORM YOU . . . KILLED IN ACTION . . .

Beth pulled out a chair and sat between Cissie and Roy. Cissie whispered, 'It came about half an hour ago. There was a knock on the door and I opened it thinking it was you home early and forgotten your key. Only it wasn't you. It was a telegram boy with that.' Cissie paused, then went on, 'The wee fellow couldn't look me in the face when I gave him a tip. I think they must know which ones come from the War Department.'

A completely stricken Roy reached out and took Beth's hand. He opened his mouth to say something, but no words came. Instead he squeezed her fingers tightly.

'Oh, my bonny man,' Cissie whispered, and suddenly seemed to collapse in on herself.

Beth was instantly on her feet and round holding her

29

mother by the shoulders. Cissie's body was convulsed by sob after racking sob.

'I'll make a cup of tea,' Roy muttered. Rising stiffly, he made his way through to the kitchen.

Beth stared after him in astonishment. She'd never known her brother do anything which could even vaguely be termed women's work before. It was a revelation he even knew how to boil water.

'I think I'd like to lie down,' Cissie jerked out.

Beth murmured words of comfort, for her own sake as well as her mother's.

In her bedroom Cissie sat on the edge of the bed while Beth helped her off with her shoes. 'Do you want me to get the doctor?' Beth asked.

Cissie shook her head.

'Are you sure, Ma?'

'Aye, I'm certain.'

Cissie slipped under the quilt to lie staring up at the ceiling. She was forty-two years of age but at that moment she looked much older. And terribly alone.

Beth had forced herself to come to the dance in the nurses' home. It was a month now since the telegram had arrived informing them that Da had been killed, and during that time she hadn't been over the door other than to go to work.

Now she was actually at the dance she found she was rather enjoying it. The music was good, albeit only a gramophone and not a live band, and she'd been on the floor three times so far. But, probably because she hadn't been either particularly enthusiastic or communicative, her partners had all let her go at the end of one record.

She gazed around her, not all that interested but sizing up the talent anyway. There were a lot of uniforms about, the Highland Light Infantry and Argyle and Sutherland predominating. The last she'd heard the Argyles were barracked in Stirling Castle, so these lads must have come down especially for the dance.

She started as a hand touched the bare flesh of her arm. 'Hello. I recognised you from across the room.' Teddy Ramsay smiled tentatively.

'Oh, hello.' She smiled back.

'It's nice to see you again.'

'And you.'

His smile faded to be replaced by an expression of sadness. 'I heard about your father. I am sorry.'

'Thank you,' she said quietly.

He could see she didn't want to talk about it, so he changed the subject. 'Would you like to dance? Or as they put it in some parts of this fair city of ours, are you for up?'

'I am.'

It was a slow number, a waltz, which suited them both fine. He wasn't a bad dancer, she thought after a while. In fact he wasn't bad at all!

'I must apologise for that night you called in on us,' she said in a small voice.

Teddy prised them apart slightly so he could stare down at her. 'It was my fault, appearing out of the blue as I did. I should've known better.'

'No, no, my behaviour was unforgivable. So was Roy's. Mind you, he's usually like that, but I'm not. It was just . . . well you caught me completely on the wrong foot.

I was pleased you'd come, but furious you chose the time you did.'

'I understand.'

'Am I forgiven?'

He nodded, then gave a sudden barking laugh. 'I nearly offered you a cigarette when I was there. I only remembered at the last moment what you'd said in the shelter about Roy not allowing you to smoke.'

'I'll tell you what, I wouldn't refuse that cigarette if you were to offer it now.' She smiled.

'Then let's find a couple of seats.'

Later they danced some more, smoked some more, and talked virtually non-stop, finding they had a great deal in common, but at half past ten Beth reluctantly declared she had to go as she was on early in the morning.

'Can I walk you home?' he asked hopefully.

'Please. I'd like that.' Very much, she thought.

Once they'd retrieved their coats and got outside he slipped his hand into hers. In response, she manoeuvred her fingers so they curled round his.

At the close mouth he was suddenly shy. So, with a smile, she drew him into the rear of the entry and kissed him. He kissed her back, and then they took it in turn to kiss one another.

There could be no doubt about it. As the local expression went, they'd clicked.

Chapter 3

His Majesty King George the Sixth stood on a dais in the centre of George Square. He was dressed in the uniform of Commander-in-chief of the Glasgow Royals, whose bicentenary this march-past was celebrating. It was 3 September 1941, the second anniversary of the declaration of war.

The crowd was massive, thousands spilling out as far as Ingram Street in the south, and Parliamentary Road in the north. From her vantage point on the steps of the City Chambers Beth could see the king quite clearly. She wished Queen Elizabeth had been with him, but apparently the queen had another engagement somewhere in England.

'Listen!' Eileen McCallum exclaimed, tugging at Beth's sleeve.

And there it was, the far-off skirl of the pipes announcing the approach of the regiment.

'Not long now,' Eileen said excitedly.

The king was smaller and slighter than Beth had

imagined. She felt, seeing him in the flesh for the first time, that he was the sort of man a woman would instinctively want to mother. What a heavy load this war must be for him. Thank God for Churchill. Roy hated Churchill because he was a Tory, but Beth was convinced he was the man the country needed in these dire times.

And then suddenly the regimental band appeared, a braw sight in their blue bonnets sporting the white cockade, their kilts swinging rhythmically in unison. The king came to attention and saluted as a great roar went up from the crowd, for the Royals were nearly all Glasgow boys whose relations these were watching them.

Beth looked frantically for Teddy, and eventually spotted him in the fifth row behind the big drum. Edgar and Jacko were on his left, Ron on his right. Beth fairly swelled up inside with pride, until she felt she must surely burst. And then the band was gone, its music fading into the distance.

'Oh, I envy you! You've got one there as handsome as they come,' Eileen McCallum enthused.

'Aye, he's not bad,' Beth acknowledged with a smile.

'When are you seeing him again?'

'Sunday. We're going on a picnic. Providing the weather keeps up, that is.'

The regiment was past now, the tramp of their boots fading just as the band's music had done.

'The king! The king's leaving!' someone shouted.

Beth and Eileen cheered and waved with the rest of the crowd as His Majesty entered his official car and was driven off.

* * *

Sunday dawned bright and sunny, much to Beth's relief, as she was really looking forward to this picnic. She made some sandwiches and a flask of tea for dinner. It wasn't much, but it was all the household could spare.

Roy was at Margaret's when Teddy arrived on the dot of eleven, so he exchanged a few pleasantries with Cissie before escorting Beth downstairs. The pair headed for the nearest red bus stop several streets away. 'I thought we'd go to Waterfoot,' Teddy said. 'Have you ever been there?'

Beth shook her head.

'You'll like it. There's a river, a weir and lots of grass. Very countrified.'

'Have you taken many girls to this place?' Beth teased him.

'Only two or three hundred,' he replied, laughing.

'Ach, away with you,' she riposted, and dug him in the ribs with an elbow.

They spoke little during the journey, content just to be in each other's company. Beth couldn't remember when she'd been so happy.

On arriving at Waterfoot they found a number of people already there, so decided to walk upriver, away from the weir, which seemed to be the centre of attraction. The spot they finally chose, where they would be completely alone, was an idyllic one. Here, screened by wild rhododendron bushes, Beth laid out their picnic.

Teddy had brought several bottles of beer which they drank with the sandwiches, leaving the tea till later. Beth was feeling slightly tipsy by the time she lay back to stare up at the buttercup-yellow sun high overhead. Closing her eyes, she let the heat beat against her face.

'I could take a fortnight of this no bother,' she murmured, listening to a bird singing somewhere among the rhododendrons.

'Beth?'

'Hmm?'

He lay down beside her and touched a hot cheek.

'That's nice,' she breathed.

He traced a line down the cheek, then along her neck. She stiffened fractionally when he cupped a breast. With his other hand he undid several buttons of her blouse. His breathing was tight and very controlled as he slipped his fingers inside.

'Beth?'

She opened her eyes to find his face only inches from hers.

'I love you,' he said.

She tried to reply, but before she could do so his lips were crushing hers, his tongue filling her mouth.

'I know you do. And I love you too,' she whispered when the kiss was over.

The hand left her breast to slide down the length of her body, then began to creep back upwards.

'No!' she exclaimed suddenly, and pushed him away. Panting slightly, she sat up and brushed the hair away from her sweat-streaked face. 'Could I have a cigarette please?' she asked, refastening the buttons of her blouse.

'Why?' He fumbled for his packet.

She drew smoke deep into her lungs, watching two butterflies flitting to and fro.

'Are you scared someone might appear?'

She shook her head.

'Then what, Beth? I want you so much, and this is the first opportunity we've had to—'

'I want you too,' she cut in. 'But I won't make love until I'm married. I'll have a ring on my finger and a piece of paper in my possession before that happens.'

Teddy drank off what remained of his beer. Then he gazed through slitted eyes at the ground as though seeing something profound there.

'Well?' she prompted.

'I'd marry you tomorrow if it wasn't for the war. We might only have known each other a relatively short time, but believe me, under normal circumstances I would've proposed to you before now. But the circumstances aren't normal – far from it. It wouldn't be fair to either of us, particularly you, to get married the way things are.'

'I see,' she replied, a sinking feeling inside her.

'Do you? The regiment's going abroad soon, and that means action. I've thought about it carefully, and if I'm going to be killed I have absolutely no intention of leaving a young widow behind. Or, worse still, a young widow with a child.'

'There's news of the regiment going overseas then?' she asked quickly.

'There have been rumours flying around for weeks now. The Royals have been slowly built back up to strength since Dunkirk, and now we're raring to get back into the midst of things. As you know, the HLI are already gone, embarked from the Tail of the Bank at the end of last week. We're certain the Royals are next.'

She stared at him, her face filled with concern. 'Do you think you'll be gone for long?'

'It could be years,' he replied gravely.

'Despite that, and what you say about its being especially unfair to me, I would still marry you if you asked me,' Beth said quietly.

Teddy ran his fingers through his hair. 'How can you say that after what happened to your father?'

Ashen, she turned away.

'Beth, I'm in a *Scottish* regiment,' he went on. 'As was your dad. We Scots have a great reputation for our prowess in the field, and because of that we're nearly always chucked in where the water's deepest. The Camerons, the Gordons, the Argyles, the HLI, the Black Watch, the Royals and so on have a list of battle honours as long as your arm. Twice as long as your arm! And by God it has cost them dear in the number of their fallen. Do you see the point I'm making?'

'You're saying you don't think you'll survive the war?'

'I'm saying I don't rate my chances very highly. Who knows how long the war might go on for? Or how many major engagements the Royals will be involved in. Why, we lost eighty-two per cent of our chaps in France. Eighty-two per cent! That's even worse, though only just, than what we suffered at the Somme.'

Beth rose and crossed to where water bubbled out from the earth and scooped up a handful. Ice cold, it made her skin tighten and tingle as she splashed it against her face. What had started out as a perfect day had turned sour. Or perhaps turned sour wasn't the right phrase. Taken on grim dimensions might be a better way of putting it.

'I'm sorry,' he said.

'So am I.'

He cleared his throat, then lit another cigarette. 'By the way, I was wondering if you'd like to come to tea on either Wednesday or Thursday? I can arrange it so I can get off then. What about you?'

'I'm on a late Thursday so it will have to be Wednesday. Do you mean tea at your house to meet your folks?'

'Not only them but my elder brother Steve who's coming home on leave.'

This was the first Beth had heard of a brother; up until then she had thought that Teddy was an only child. 'Is he also in the army?'

Teddy chuckled. 'Not Steve! Nothing so mundane as square-bashing for him. He's in the RAF flying Spits. Shot down eight Jerries during the Battle of Britain and was shot down twice himself. He's quite a character.'

'Is he much older than you?'

Teddy paused to think. 'He's, er . . . twenty-four now.'

'Same age as Roy,' Beth said.

'Well, he's not at all like Roy. Not in the least.'

'Roy isn't that bad,' Beth protested. 'I know he has a lot of adverse points, but he has good ones as well.'

Teddy smiled. 'I'll take your word on that. And you'll come Wednesday?'

'I'll look forward to it.'

'I'll pick you up at the hospital's main gate and we'll walk back together.'

A lump of emotion swelled in her throat. 'You're a lovely man, Teddy.'

'You're not all that difficult to put up with either.'

She came to him and put her arms round his neck. 'How long do you think the regiment's got, then?'

'Days as opposed to weeks, I'd say. But that's only a guess.'

'Not long, darling.'

'No.'

She was tempted to give in, desperately so. But surrendering her virginity was such a big step to take, especially as she'd always sworn to herself that she'd only part with it in her marriage bed. She'd known several girls who'd been caught out whose lives had been ruined as a result. She didn't want that happening to her; nor would she let it. 'You can still kiss me. There's no ban on that.' She smiled.

'I'm glad to hear it.'

The kiss was different from all their previous ones, having something sombre about it.

When it was over they packed up and headed home. Again, they hardly spoke a word during the journey but this time it was for quite different reasons.

The tenements in the street where the Ramsays lived were of a deep red, almost maroon, coloured sandstone. There were neat hedges round the front gardens, the gardens themselves being well tended and cared for. Roy had been right in saying a better class of people lived here; you could feel it even before you walked into the front close. The very building itself exuded the fact.

'You're not nervous, I hope?' Teddy smiled.

'Why should I be? I've nothing to be ashamed about,' Beth retorted.

'That wasn't what I meant at all. Of course you've nothing to be ashamed about. It would be bad manners on my part to bring you here if you had.'

Beth blushed, realising she'd over-reacted. 'Let's away up then,' she said.

Outside the Ramsays' front door she made Teddy wait before opening it while she indulged in a last-minute check-up in her compact mirror. Her hair was tidy and newly washed, her face devoid of make-up as she was wearing her uniform.

'Right,' she announced, hoisting what she hoped didn't look too false a smile on to her face.

It was something of a shock to discover the Ramsays were far older than her own parents. She judged them both to be in their early sixties, which meant they'd had Teddy and his brother fairly late on in life.

Mrs Ramsay was tiny and fat with twinkling blue eyes. 'It's a pleasure to meet you at last,' she enthused, grasping Beth's hand firmly in her own.

Beth later found out that Mr Ramsay was a bank manager and that's exactly what he looked like. Tufts of grey hair stuck out of his ears and nose, reminding Beth of a genial garden gnome.

'Where's Steve?' Teddy queried.

'Gone out for a few minutes to get some tobacco,' his mother explained. Then, to Beth, 'Disgusting habit, smoking. Being a nurse you don't yourself, I'm sure?'

'Just the occasional one to be sociable,' Beth tactfully replied.

Mrs Ramsay declared she'd put the kettle on and bustled out of the room. When she'd gone Mr Ramsay invited Beth to take a chair, and sat down facing her.

The room they were in was obviously the one reserved for special occasions and honoured visitors. There were antimacassars on all the chairs and the sofa, and a huge aspidistra dominated the window. Despite the continuing good September weather there was a hint of mustiness in the air which Beth took to mean the room hadn't been fired for quite some time.

A door banged, followed by footsteps in the hall outside. 'That'll be Steve now,' Mr Ramsay declared, his face lighting up.

They heard Steve talking to his mother, and then he breezed into the room.

'Enter Biggles,' Teddy teased him.

Beth couldn't help laughing, for Biggles described Steve to a T. He was wearing a leather flying jacket and a white silk scarf – jacket and scarf when the weather was positively Indian! – and a pipe was clenched firmly between his teeth.

'Now now, little brother, don't take the Michael,' Steve retorted good-humouredly, wagging an admonishing finger at Teddy. He then advanced on Beth, paused for a second in front of her, smiled, and bowed.

Beth gaped at him. No one had ever bowed to her before. In Glasgow that sort of thing was simply unheard of. She gaped even more when he lifted her right hand and lightly kissed it.

'I told you he was a card.' Teddy grinned.

Too sure of himself by half, Beth thought, and somehow not transparently honest the way Teddy was. If he'd been a bell she'd have bet her wage packet on his producing a false note when struck.

'I'm Steve, the black sheep of the family,' he declared disarmingly.

'Surely not,' she said politely.

'A great disappointment to my parents. Isn't that so, Father?'

'Not at all, as you well know, son.'

Steve released Beth's hand, laughing as he did so. Crossing to Teddy he put an arm round his brother's shoulders. 'He's a good lad, the best there is. I hope you appreciate that.'

'Steve!' Teddy exclaimed, turning puce.

'This one's got a mind, a bit of the old grey matter. If the army had any sense, which it hasn't, it would give him a commission instead of letting him waste his time with those godawful bagpipes.'

'Language.' Mr Ramsay frowned.

'I like the pipes,' Teddy protested.

'And so do I,' Beth added.

'Sticking up for you already, that's a good sign.' Steve nodded. 'He was top of the class, you know, unlike me. I was always somewhere down at the bottom.'

'Only because that's where the best-looking girls were. You told me that yourself,' Teddy reminded him.

Steve laughed again. 'That did have something to do with it, I confess, but not all that much. Academic brilliance was never exactly my forte, whereas it is yours.'

Mrs Ramsay entered pushing a trolley heaped high with plates of scones and other home baking. Beth ogled a mound of fresh strawberry jam.

'We have a friend who has a big garden in the country,' Mrs Ramsay explained. 'That's where I get my fruit from.'

'But the sugar it takes to make jam!' Beth exclaimed.

'I keep getting these parcels, you see,' Mrs Ramsay replied guiltily.

'You mean from abroad?'

'No, from England.'

'I have connections down there. You might call it one of the perks of being a hero,' Steve declared in an offhand manner.

Hero! The arrogance of the man was unbelievable. He might well be a hero but it was in awful taste for him to say so. Beth decided she didn't like Steve Ramsay one little bit.

'So between Steve and our friend in the country we do better than most.' Mrs Ramsay blushed.

'Good luck to you then,' Beth replied, and meant it. If you could get a little extra then why the hell not? To turn it down would be just plain stupid.

'You're the first lassie Teddy has ever brought home,' Mrs Ramsay said to Beth during tea. 'And now you've found your way here we hope you won't be a stranger. Even when he's away we'd be delighted if you dropped by from time to time.'

'So I'm the first, am I?' Beth smiled.

'Honestly!' Teddy exclaimed. 'If I'd known you were all dying to give away my secrets I'd never have brought her.'

'Any definite date for your going away yet, son?' Mrs Ramsay asked in a strained voice.

He shook his head. 'But it'll be soon. You can bank on it.'

'Lucky fellow. He'll probably end up somewhere we'd all give our eye teeth to be. Wouldn't mind a touch of the Mediterraneans or Africas myself, I can tell you,' Steve enthused.

Insensitive sod, Beth thought. Couldn't he see how anxious his parents were? And here he was making a joke of something that to them was very serious indeed.

'What did you think of my big brother then?' Teddy asked later as he was walking Beth home.

Beth laughed briefly. 'I don't know how you can call him that when he's actually smaller than you!' At five feet six or seven Steve was several inches shorter than Teddy.

'It's just an expression, as you well know. Why, you use it yourself,' Teddy retorted.

'I know – I'm sorry. I suppose I was just having a bit of a dig at him. If you want the truth, I thought him far too cocky for his own good. I kept getting the urge to go over and slap him.'

Teddy nodded. 'I know what you mean. He's always been a bit like that – extroverted, I suppose – but it's got a lot worse since he joined the RAF. Perhaps it's the crowd he's mixing with down there. Or again, it could be connected with the flying itself. I asked him about the flying once, but he wouldn't talk about it. Flatly refused. But honestly, underneath all that slick chat there's one helluva nice chap.'

'Maybe so,' Beth murmured, quite unconvinced. She changed the subject, not having the least desire to discuss Steve Ramsay any further.

Beth was giving Mr McPherson a blanket bath when Sister Kettle appeared round the screen. 'How are you this morning then, Mr McPherson?'

'Not so bad, considering,' he replied with a smile.

'Your op's been put down for the day after tomorrow. So it'll soon be all over with.'

'Oh, that's grand!' He was suffering from an ulcerated stomach, at least part of which would have to be removed.

Sister turned her attention to Beth. 'There's a telephone call for you in my office, Nurse Somerville. The man on the other end says it's an emergency,' she snapped in a voice as cold as a Siberian winter.

Beth was alarmed. A phone call? Private calls to the ward were strictly forbidden. It had better be a real emergency or she'd be for the high jump – Genghis Khan would see to that.

'On you go then!' Sister snapped, taking Beth's place at Mr McPherson's bedside.

Beth gave Sister a quick nod, and fled from behind the screen, going as fast up the ward as she could without actually running.

'Hello?' she said into the phone.

'Beth, it's Teddy. I've got some news.'

A few minutes later Sister Kettle entered her office to find Beth staring out of the window. 'Well, nurse, what was that all about?' she asked in the same Siberian tone of voice.

Beth's eyes were moist when she turned round. 'It was my boyfriend, Sister. I'm sorry he rang here but it was to say goodbye. His regiment's sailing from the Clyde in just over two hours' time. Apparently it was sprung on them late last night and they were immediately confined to barracks. He's only just been able to get the use of a telephone.'

'I see.' Sister nodded, her fierce expression softening. Beth waited. If a punishment was to be meted out she'd be told now. 'Which regiment is he with?'

'The Royals.'

Sister glanced at the upside-down watch she wore on the left breast pocket of her uniform. It was just before noon, which meant Beth had another five and a half hours of her shift left. 'He's sailing in a little over two hours, you say?'

'Yes, Sister, from Windmillcroft Quay.'

'Hmm!' Sister looked thoughtful.

Here it comes, Beth thought. Probably an extra week on nights, or a month being solely responsible for the bedpans.

'Do you know the Samaritan Hospital?' Sister suddenly barked out.

Beth was taken completely by surprise. 'Yes, I do.'

'Well, I have a friend at the Samaritan, a sister I trained with. There are several bits and pieces I'm having trouble getting hold of here which I happen to know she has in stock. I shall ring and ask her to lend me what she can and inform her that you will be picking them up.' Sister Kettle paused, and assumed a particularly fierce expression. 'Get started immediately. And, as these things can often take longer than we might think, I shan't expect to see you back here till tomorrow.'

Beth looked blank. Was she really hearing this?

'Do I make myself clear, nurse?' Sister added in a level tone of voice.

A lump rose in Beth's throat. What a smasher Genghis Khan had turned out to be after all. 'Crystal clear, Sister.'

'Hop to it then.'

Sister snorted after Beth had gone. She must be mad, she told herself. She couldn't imagine a sister in her young days doing what she'd just done.

Then she smiled. That was one of the nice things about being boss: you could break the rules. And Nurse Somerville rushing off to say goodbye properly to her boyfriend was ever so romantic.

She returned to the ward feeling better than she'd done for a long time.

The warship was grey and squat, its bow already pointed downriver towards the sea. Directly above it a great many gulls of various varieties wheeled and cried raucously, and as Beth hurried towards it over the cobbles several army lorries that had been parked by the gangplank simultaneously roared into life and trundled off.

Beth could see a number of sailors moving purposefully about the ship. Aft there was a large group of soldiers standing chatting and laughing, and she feared that she might be too late and Teddy was already aboard and below deck.

There were a hundred or so civilians on the quayside, and one of them started waving at her. 'Beth!' he called out.

It was Mr Ramsay, with Mrs Ramsay by his side. 'Is Teddy already aboard?' Beth asked anxiously when she joined them.

'We don't think so. But that's only a guess, as we're not long here ourselves,' Mr Ramsay told her.

'I hope Teddy got it right and this is the correct quay.

There are several ships taking the regiment wherever it's going, and they're all leaving from different quays,' Mrs Ramsay fretted.

As though to underscore her point, from somewhere downriver came the distinctive whoop-whoop of a warship, followed by the deep-throated reply of a tug.

'Where's Steve?' Beth asked. Teddy's brother was conspicuous by his absence.

'He'd already gone out with an old pal when Teddy rang. I've no idea where,' said Mrs Ramsay.

'He'll be upset to have missed this,' Mr Ramsay added. Then, grasping his wife's arm, he said, 'Here are some more lorries, dear. Teddy might be on one of these.'

Beth counted fourteen lorries as the convoy drew up in a line. Almost instantly they began disgorging their passengers.

'Andy!' a woman shouted.

'Graeme!' another woman yelled.

More and more voices were raised in recognition as people rushed over to the milling soldiers to embrace and be embraced in turn. An officer and two sergeants started herding their charges up the gangplank, turning a blind eye for as long as they could to those who had someone there to see them off.

Beth scanned the mêlée yet again, but of Teddy there was no sign. 'Are you the last lot?' she asked a passing squaddie.

'Sorry, I've no idea.'

A tug hove into view, closing on the warship's far side. Departure was obviously imminent. The lorries moved off and finally, after cajoling from the officer and sergeants, the last stragglers went aboard. There were now definite signs of activity on the bridge.

Beth glanced downriver to see a warship already out in mid-channel. One of its tugs broke away and headed back for the ship in front of her.

'He must have already been on board after all,' said Mr Ramsay, shaking his head in despair.

'Or else he did give us the wrong quay,' Mrs Ramsay added, again voicing a possibility that had worried her since their arrival.

'Over there!' Beth exclaimed, pointing to where two more lorries had suddenly appeared.

'Please God,' Mrs Ramsay whispered to herself.

As all the previous lorries had done, the new arrivals stopped beside the gangplank. When Beth saw that the first man out was carrying a pipe case she knew that this must be the band and that Teddy would be among them. Sure enough, Jacko jumped out of the rear of the second lorry. And after him came Ron and Edgar, followed by Teddy.

Beth raised a hand, but didn't shout. Teddy spotted her straight away, his astonished expression quickly changing to one of sheer delight.

'Come on, lads, aboard the Navy's lovely boat as soon as you can!' a pipe major called out, striding up and down glancing threateningly about him.

'Oh, son, we were starting to think we'd missed you,' Mrs Ramsay cried when Teddy joined them.

The conversation was stilted. No one quite knew what to say.

'I thought you were stuck at the hospital?' Teddy said to Beth.

'I was, but then Sister proved she really has a heart and not the swinging brick we all thought. The pretext is I'm out doing an errand for her.'

Teddy took Beth's hand. 'You will write, won't you?'

She'd already promised she would on the telephone. 'Of course. As often as I can.'

'And so will I.'

'Come along there!' the pipe major yelled, glaring at the bandsmen mingling with the civilians.

'I'll have to go,' Teddy said tightly.

'Well, all the best, and look after yourself,' said Mr Ramsay.

Father and son stared at one another, then emotion overcame Teddy and he swept his father into his arms and hugged him. On being released Mr Ramsay harumphed and turned away, but not before Beth had glimpsed a film of moisture over his eyes.

'Mind you change your socks and underwear regularly, and if your plumbing gets bunged up remember to drink some nice hot cabbage water. That'll see you right again,' Mrs Ramsay instructed her son.

'I will, Mum. Don't you worry about me.'

'I won't worry. I've been through all this before with your brother,' Mrs Ramsay replied, her voice quavering. A child of four could've told she was lying about not worrying.

'God bless you, Mum,' Teddy croaked, kissing her on both cheeks.

'Let's be having you, Ramsay. And you too, Farrell!' the pipe major bellowed.

'Coming, Pipe Major!'

Mr Ramsay squeezed his wife's arm. 'You and I will just walk over this way a wee bit,' he suggested.

She was about to protest, then realised her husband was letting Teddy have a few last private moments with Beth. 'Oh, aye, right you are.' Together the pair of them moved off.

'I love you, Beth. Don't ever forget that,' Teddy said earnestly.

'And I love you too.'

'When this is all over and the peace is signed you'll have that bit of paper. I promise you.'

'I'll hold you to that.'

'It'll break my heart if you don't.'

He kissed her, and she nestled in the crook of his arm.

At the stern of the ship a sailor cast off the extreme aft line. Teddy picked up his pipe box and heaved it on to a shoulder, then ran up the gangplank with the pipe major right behind him. They were no sooner on deck than the gangplank started to be hauled aboard. Teddy joined Jacko, Ron and Edgar at the ship's side, the four of them waving to Beth and the Ramsays, who waved furiously back. The ship drew away from the quayside, pulled into the centre of the river by tugs fore and aft. Eventually the tugs were cast loose and the warship crept slowly forward.

The friends and relatives had fallen silent, standing together in a sombre knot watching the squat warship, like some grey ghost, make its way down to the sea.

'That's that then,' Mr Ramsay said quietly when the ship finally vanished from view.

'Oh, my baby!' Mrs Ramsay choked. Mr Ramsay took

her in his arms, making soothing noises as he tried to comfort her.

'Teddy will be back all right. I just know it,' Beth declared.

The knot of people began to break up and disperse. Beth declined the Ramsays' offer of a cup of tea, thinking it best they be on their own. As she walked in the direction of her tram stop a strange sensation came over her, which when she recognised it surprised her greatly. For the life of her she couldn't think why she should suddenly be feeling free.

Chapter 4

S he had to knock three times before Mr Carmichael answered his door, although she knew him to be at home because she'd seen a light on.

'Oh, it's yourself, Beth. Come away in.'

He was unshaven and haggard beneath the bristles. His eyes had a peculiar dead quality about them, as though their inner light had been switched off.

'Are the children in bed?' Beth queried.

'And asleep half an hour since,' he replied, ushering her into the living room.

The dirty tea dishes were still on the table, as were the breakfast ones. 'Sorry if it's a bit of a tip, but I haven't got round to clearing up yet,' Mr Carmichael apologised.

He was a completely changed man since his wife had been killed, Beth reflected. Once he'd been great fun, always laughing and joking, a natural entertainer. The man now standing before her was a shadow of his former self.

'I dropped by with some sweets from the hospital.

'Several American parcels came our way and I couldn't help but think of your two, so I've brought them a bagful of bits and pieces.'

'That's very kind of you. They'll appreciate it, you can be sure,' Mr Carmichael said as she placed the bag on the mantelpiece.

'And how are you getting along?'

'Och, fine. The neighbours have been very helpful since . . . since.' He swallowed. 'Since what happened. There's always someone will take the children to school and look after them at night until I get home. And my mother comes over as often as she can, which is a big help.'

Beth took off her coat. 'Being here I might as well give you a hand myself. I'll get stuck into these dishes,' she declared, lifting plates from the table.

'That's right good of you, lass. But are you sure you've got the time?'

'Won't take more than a couple of minutes. So why don't you just put your feet up and relax? You've no doubt had a hard day.'

'I feel so drained of late, I've hardly any energy at all,' he muttered.

'I think that's understandable in the circumstances,' she said sympathetically. It wasn't extra energy he needed, but more of a will to carry on. He must have been very much in love with his wife, she thought.

She boiled the kettle, then set to at the sink. When she returned to the living room, having put all the dishes tidily away, she found Mr Carmichael staring vacantly into an empty fireplace.

55

She touched him on the shoulder. 'Anything else I can do for you?'

'Aye, lass, if you wouldn't mind?'

'Just say.' She smiled.

He asked her to sit down, looking startled for a moment when she did so on the chair facing him. Beth realised it must have been Mrs Carmichael's chair.

She started to rise, but he hastily told her not to. 'It's the unexpected things that get you at times. It's difficult to explain.'

'I understand.'

He glanced across at the door. 'There are occasions when I'm sitting here at night and I forget she's gone. God alone knows how often I've looked up at that door expecting her to walk through it, or started to call out thinking she's in another room. Then I remember and . . . it sort of hits you all over again. That's when it's really bad.'

Beth nodded, and waited.

Finally he went on. 'It's almost certain I'll be going on night shift soon. Probably in a couple of weeks or so. What I've decided is to move the children to their gran's, with me staying there as well.'

'Does that mean they'll have to change schools?'

He shook his head. 'No, that's going to be all right. My mother's is still within striking distance.'

'So how long are you going to be on night shift for?'

'Your guess is as good as mine, Beth. And, to tell you the truth, I won't be in that much of a hurry to come off it. Night shift will suit me down to the ground – or I should say suit my current frame of mind. But with us away it does mean this place is going to be left empty, which is something of a worry.'

'Have you considered giving it up altogether and staying at your mother's permanently?' Beth asked.

'That would be the sensible thing to do, I suppose. It's just . . .' He broke off to stare about him. 'There are so many happy memories here that I'm loath to let the house go. It may be that after a while I'll want to come back and would bitterly regret it if I couldn't. So, for the foreseeable future anyway, I'd like to keep my options open.'

'And where do I come in, Mr Carmichael?'

'If I give you the key when we go, would you pop in once or twice a week to make sure everything's as it should be? No burst pipes, that sort of thing. The weather will be turning shortly and the house will need to be kept well fired, especially when winter proper sets in. I could send you money for coal.' He paused to give her a rueful smile. 'Would that be too much of an imposition?'

'Not at all. It'll be my pleasure to look after the house. In fact, it could be to my advantage.'

'How so?'

'I'm still studying for exams at the hospital, which means I need peace and quiet. And to be quite frank with you, my brother can be a noisy sod in the evenings. So coming here would give me a nice bolthole. In other words, I might be doing you a favour but you'd also be doing one for me.'

'Then it's agreed.' Mr Carmichael nodded, relieved. He said he would write out his mother's address and give it to her when he handed over the key, so that Beth could forward any mail.

Beth mounted the stairs to her own house delighted that things had turned out as they had. It was going to be marvellous to have what was virtually a place of her own to get on with her studies.

It was a Saturday afternoon late the following January when Beth and Cissie arrived home from town to find Roy and his girlfriend Margaret waiting for them, the pair of them looking extremely smug and self-satisfied.

'I could murder a cup of tea,' Cissie groaned, sinking into the nearest chair.

Beth leaned against the wall. 'It was just awful in Sauchiehall Street. At least half of Glasgow must've been there.'

'I'll put the kettle on,' said Margaret, jumping to her feet.

'Wait a minute, pet. Don't you think we should give them the news first?' Roy asked.

'And what news is that?' Cissie demanded, eyes narrowing.

'Will you tell them or will I?' said Roy.

Margaret blushed. 'I think you'd better.'

He took a deep breath. 'We've agreed to get engaged. I'll be buying the ring next week.'

'Congratulations!' Beth exclaimed. Grabbing Margaret, she gave her a big hug.

'Well well well, son! I am pleased. You've got yourself a right fine lassie there whom I'll be proud to have as my daughter-in-law.' Cissie beamed.

'When are you going to get married?' Beth enquired.

'Hold on a minute!' Roy protested. 'Let's get ourselves engaged first.'

'Next year sometime, I should think. And it'll be in a church, that I can assure you. There'll be none of this registry nonsense for us,' said Margaret.

Beth, knowing Margaret and her family to be great churchgoers, wouldn't have expected anything else. She also knew that although Roy might be pulling a face right now, underneath it all he would be secretly pleased at the prospect of a church wedding. The pomp and circumstance, and his own casting in a central role, would be right up his street.

Abruptly, Roy stood up. 'I'll tell you what! We'll have an engagement party, a proper one in a hall. What do you think of that idea, pet?'

'Absolutely splendid,' Margaret enthused.

'Right, we'll do it then. And I'll make all the arrangements personally as I'm the best organiser at that sort of thing.'

'He's so modest, my brother,' Beth commented scathingly.

'You can say that again!' Margaret agreed. Then she and Beth went through to the kitchen, the pair of them chattering nineteen to the dozen about the sort of wedding dress Margaret had in mind, and how difficult it was going to be to get suitable material for it.

As parties went, Beth considered it to be a complete flop. The band Roy had hired was positively geriatric – they might have been playing for a wake rather than an engagement. And Margaret's people were a sour-looking bunch. With the single exception of an uncle who was obviously straining at the leash, all of them were stiff, starchy and self-righteous. Roy, done up like a dog's dinner, was on the floor with Margaret, who was wearing an orange-coloured dress which did nothing for her whatever.

Beth sipped the sweet sherry she was holding, thinking it awful muck. She'd much have preferred whisky, but Roy would've had a canary had she started drinking that. As it was, she was lucky to have been allowed sherry.

All their own relatives and close friends had come, but although they'd started out in a jovial humour, the good mood had now evaporated thanks to Margaret's lot, who seemed to have cornered the market in disapproving stares. Beth saw Margaret's mother have a whispered word with her husband, who then glanced in her direction. He's going to ask me to dance! she thought, appalled at the prospect. The man had 'bore' written all over him. I must escape, she told herself, and promptly headed off.

Outside in the corridor she sighed with relief. If only she wasn't Roy's sister she could've made some excuse and gone home, but that was impossible. Roy would never forgive her, and nor would Cissie.

Wheechs and other sounds of merriment came from nearby, and she decided there must be another party in progress in an adjoining hall. She finished her sherry and wondered how long she could hang on here before she would have to go back. Just as she was thinking, reluctantly, that she ought to be moving, the door marked Gents opened and a chap emerged.

'Well, look who it is!' he exclaimed in surprise.

For a moment she didn't recognise him, probably because he was dressed very differently from when they'd last met. 'Oh! Hello.'

Steve Ramsay smiled at her. 'How are you keeping, then?'

'Fine. And you?'

'Mustn't grumble. My folks were talking about you just the other day. They're disappointed you haven't been to see them since Teddy left.'

'I've meant to, tell them. It's just . . . well, things have been so hectic at the hospital.' It was true enough, but only up to a point. She *had* fully intended to go and see the Ramsays, but somehow had never got round to it. She decided to change the subject. 'So what are you doing back in Glasgow? Not more leave so soon, surely.'

'I've been posted up here, to an aerodrome called Langbank. It came with my promotion to squadron leader.'

'Congratulations.'

'Thank you. The big advantage of Langbank is that I can see the folks regularly, which pleases them immensely, as you can imagine.' He glanced down at her empty glass. 'Another drink?'

'I'd prefer a cigarette, but I haven't brought any with me.'

He produced a packet of Black Cat. 'Be my guest.'

Beth hesitated. This corridor was far too close for comfort to the hall where Roy was. 'Is there a back door? I could use a breath of fresh air,' she lied.

'I saw something earlier. Just follow me.'

It was a side exit which opened out on to a dirty and rubbish-strewn alleyway. She accepted the cigarette and lit up, drawing the smoke deep into her lungs.

'Are you still writing to dear Teddy?' Steve asked in what she thought was rather a patronising tone of voice.

'Of course! Why do you think I'd have stopped?' she snapped back, marvelling at the capacity Steve had for irritating her.

'No need to get heated. It was a straightforward question.'

'It was the implication.'

'There wasn't one, I assure you.'

She raised a disbelieving eyebrow.

'On my word of honour, Beth,' he declared, crossing his heart. 'My God, you are touchy.'

She dropped her cigarette and trod on it. 'I must get back. They'll be wondering where I am.'

'Don't go, not yet. Please?'

'There's no reason for me to stay.'

'There would be if I got us both that other drink. Now what about it, Beth? I really would like to talk to you a bit more.'

Another drink – a *decent* drink – would be nice. And she'd only had a couple of puffs of the cigarette. 'Is there any whisky through in your party?'

'Bottles of it. Don't ask where they came from, but they're there. A large one?'

'With water.'

'Coming right up.'

'And can I have another cigarette?'

He gave a low laugh. 'You can have the packet if you want.'

'No, one'll do.'

She watched his retreating back till he vanished round a corner. He might be bumptious and arrogant but he did have a certain charm, a cavalier quality Teddy lacked.

Teddy was strictly a feet on the ground, salt of the earth, no nonsense type, whereas Steve was of the stuff buccaneers and . . . she laughed to herself . . . heroes were made of. Suddenly her mood changed and she frowned. How could she be comparing the two? Teddy was by far the better human being, reliable through and through. And what more could you ask for than that? Steve probably had a dozen or so girls running after him, all at the same time.

Her thoughts were interrupted by the tread of feet behind her. 'That was quick!' she exclaimed, turning round. Her jaw dropped when she saw it wasn't Steve, but Roy. He was glowering at her, a thunderous expression contorting his features.

'They were asking after you so I said I'd come and find out what you were up to.'

There was no point in trying to hide the cigarette as he'd already seen it. She'd gone cold all over, but was determined not to be intimidated. She should have made a stand before now.

'I'm nineteen – almost twenty,' she said. 'Old enough to smoke if I choose.'

His nostrils flared and his eyes narrowed. Beth realised that he was fairly far gone with drink. She knew then that standing up to him was a mistake, but she'd committed herself and pride, or sheer stubbornness, wouldn't let her back down now.

'Put the fag out,' he commanded.

She lifted her chin. 'No.'

She saw the hand coming but was too slow to evade it, and cried out with shock and pain as his palm smacked hard against her cheek. Staggering backwards, she went banging into the exit door.

'What's going on here?' Steve's voice came from behind Roy.

Roy lumbered round to eye the two glasses of whisky Steve was carrying. 'I think it's me should be asking that.'

Steve glanced past Roy to Beth. 'Are you all right?'

Beth nodded.

'So who's this then?'

'My brother Roy.'

Steve returned his attention to Roy, who was considerably taller and broader than he was. 'Why did you hit her?' he demanded.

'That's certainly no fucking business of yours,' Roy replied, and swept Steve aside with his arm. Steve, stumbling, tried to retain his balance, while the two glasses of whisky went flying.

Beth cried out a second time as Roy grabbed her by the hair. 'We'll sort this out when we get home tonight,' he snarled.

Roy grunted as Steve's punch screwed into his kidneys. His legs buckled under him when the edge of Steve's hand slammed into his neck, and he flopped to his knees. He started to come to his feet again, and Steve's third blow took him full on the nose. Blood sprayed in a crimson fountain, covering Roy's face and the front of his shirt, and he blinked rapidly, trying to get the blood out of his eyes. Then he lashed out with a savage kick which would probably have broken Steve's leg if it had connected, but Steve danced out the way, replying with a kick of his own to Roy's ribcage.

Roy grimaced with pain, knowing that at least one of his ribs had been staved in. With a roar he launched himself at Steve, who somehow eluded him at the last possible moment. His momentum carried him straight into a wall, which he hit head first.

'Enough!' Beth yelled. 'Enough, for pity's sake!'

Steve took a pace backwards. Roy, on hands and knees, his face a bloody mask, glared groggily up at him.

'Please go now, Steve,' Beth said.

'I'm sorry about this, Beth, but it was hardly my fault.'

'Just go, Steve, before it starts up again.' She knew Roy would never give in while there was breath in his body. Steve nodded and, without taking his eyes off Roy, retreated down the corridor a considerable way before turning and striding off.

Beth slumped, her heart hammering so hard her breasts were quivering from it. What a fiasco! And what on earth was Roy going to say when he returned to the party!

'Let's try and get you cleaned up a bit,' she suggested as he came to his feet.

'Lucky for that wee shit he didn't stay or I'd have murdered him,' Roy spat out.

From where she'd been standing it had looked as though the murdering had been going the other way, which said an awful lot for Steve as Roy, even when drunk, was hardly a pushover. In fact, drunk or sober, he was a pretty hard case.

'I noticed a stairway on the way out here,' Beth said. 'You can tell Margaret and the others you tripped and fell down it. I'll back up your story.'

Roy's reply to that was to head to the Gents, leaving

her to reflect that although the party might have started off as a boring non-event it certainly wouldn't be ending that way.

Next day Beth took a different route home from the hospital in order to call on Steve and apologise for Roy's behaviour. She found him outside his close working on a motorbike whose engine he was in the process of stripping down.

'Well, if it isn't Florence Nightingale.' He smiled at her from the pavement where he was sitting.

'I came to say sorry about last night. It really was awful of Roy.'

'Is he always like that?'

'Believe it or not he can be quite sweet at times, but he does have this phobia about women smoking and drinking. Thinks it's dreadful and completely unladylike. I suppose you could say he hit me because he cares for me.'

'That's rather Irish, but I take your point.'

'You broke three of his ribs and he had to go to Casualty after the party. We told everyone he'd fallen down some stairs.'

'I only hope the ribs cause him a great deal of pain. I never could stand a bully, caring or otherwise.'

Beth thought that was a perfect point to terminate the conversation. 'Anyway, thanks for coming to my rescue. It was appreciated.'

'Any time.'

She made to move away and he bent again to the engine, various parts of which were neatly laid out before him. On a sudden whim she crossed to the bike and ran a hand lovingly over its maroon petrol tank.

'Do you like motorbikes?' Steve asked curiously.

'I think they're absolutely marvellous. If I was a man I'd have one. A big machine like yours.'

He scrambled to his feet and joined her. 'This is a Norton, as you can see. A real beauty. If she's tuned just right I can get a hundred out of her.'

'Wow!' she exclaimed, eyes opening wide.

'I used to ride bikes for a living, you know. Did Teddy mention that?'

Beth shook her head.

'Before the war started I was over in Canada for twenty months. I only came back in order to join up. I began riding professionally here, then in Canada I rode in a sort of bike circus. Stunting, death-defying leaps, that sort of thing.'

'I'm impressed.'

'Have you been on many bikes yourself?'

'A few. I had a boyfriend who had one, far smaller than yours, but exciting all the same. I've never been on a machine this size.'

'Then we'll have to remedy that. When would you like to go for a spin?'

'Do you mean it?'

He laughed. 'I never make an offer unless I mean it. Now when are you free?'

'I have all day Thursday off.'

'So Thursday it is. I'll take you down to the coast and you can give those aching nurse's feet of yours a paddle in salt water. There's nothing better for the feet than salt water, I'm told.'

'That would be really smashing. Except what about petrol? Will you be able to get enough?'

He gave her a conspiratorial wink. 'Remember Mother's sugar? I'm a dab hand at getting things which are rationed and in short supply. Petrol will be no problem whatever.'

'I'll look forward to it, then.'

'So will I. What time shall I call round for you?'

Thinking of Roy, she said that she'd come here rather than have Steve pick her up. At the time they agreed Roy would be at work, but it was best to be on the safe side. Roy was a man to hold a grudge.

'And don't forget to wear something extra warm. The wind'll go through you like a knife on that pillion,' was Steve's parting shot.

As an elated Beth walked away a thrill ran through her at the prospect of sitting astride that gorgeous machine at a hundred miles an hour.

He was ready waiting for her when she arrived dead on the dot, wearing his Biggles outfit including the white silk scarf. He handed her a crash helmet and said he hoped it fitted, which it did. Then they climbed aboard.

The Norton roared into life, and excitement sent shivers coursing up and down her spine. 'Hang on now!' Steve shouted over his shoulder.

She gripped him tightly round the waist, giving an involuntary gasp as the motorbike leapt forward, her nostrils filled with the intoxicating smells of engine oil and leather.

They encountered very little traffic as they made their way through the south Glasgow suburbs, but Steve kept the speed down all the same. Once away from Glasgow, however, it was another matter entirely. He let rip.

Beth was absolutely petrified, while at the same time thoroughly enjoying herself. She had every confidence in Steve's ability to drive the Norton, sensing he was the complete master of it. Here was a man who understood the very essence of motorbikes, and machinery in general. The bike he was driving had become an extension of himself, like another arm or leg, responding at the lightning speed of thought to whatever he commanded. She realised then that Steve must be a superb pilot, for he would surely handle a plane with the same ease and expertise with which he drove a motorbike.

They bypassed Port Glasgow and sped through Greenock before they cut back again, heading for Inverkip and Wemyss Bay. They had gone several miles before Steve brought the Norton to a halt beside a beach which sloped gently down to the sea.

Beth slipped from the pillion, feeling slightly ethereal. She was still covered in goose pimples, as she'd been throughout the entire ride.

'Well?' Steve queried.

She shook her head. 'I haven't got the words to describe that. All I can really say is that I wasn't disappointed.'

Steve threw his helmet down on the sand. Sitting, he pulled out a pipe and lit up. 'Go and have your paddle,' he said to her through a haze of curling blue smoke.

And she would, too, she thought. She took off the short boots she was wearing, and a thick pair of Roy's socks. Her stockings were next on the list, and she paused to glance across at Steve, thinking he'd have the decency to turn away. Instead he gave her a wicked smile and kept on looking.

Oh, to hell with him! she decided. He must've seen dozens of women take their stockings off. And so, making a bold front of it, she pulled up her skirt and started to remove them.

The sand squished between her toes as she ran down to the sea. The grey-green water was freezing, filled with rolling and bursting whitecaps, but what else could she expect at this time of year? Even at the height of summer it could be bitterly cold.

Freezing maybe, but it did feel good. Purifying, you might say. She exclaimed as a surge of wave went up her legs almost to mid-thigh. It showed just how wild the sea was, as the water she was standing in was only ankle deep.

A couple of minutes were enough. Running back up the beach she fell panting beside Steve. 'That was terrific,' she gasped.

She lit a cigarette, and for a short while they sat in silence enjoying the scenery. A wind had sprung up, whipping salt spume against their faces, which they found both refreshing and exhilarating.

'Why this particular spot? Have you been here before?' Beth asked eventually.

He used the stem of his pipe to point inland. 'Langbank is just over there. If I've got time, and there's daylight left, I often come to this beach after a patrol. I find it extremely relaxing.'

She recalled that Langbank was the name of the aerodrome where he was now stationed. 'Is your squadron part of Glasgow's defences?'

He shook his head. 'I'm not on fighters any more. I moved over to Stirlings when I was transferred here. They're bombers.'

'Not quite as glamorous as being a Spitfire pilot. Does that upset you?' There was just a hint of malice in her voice.

He gave her a long, straight look which caused her to redden and glance away, angry with herself for not being able to hold his gaze.

'Our job at Langbank is to protect British and Allied shipping and sink any U-boats we might come across, plus harry and destroy any enemy warships we encounter. I consider that to be a damned worthwhile job.'

Chastened, she reached between her legs to make some squiggles in the sand. 'Was it purely because of your promotion that you were transferred to Langbank?'

'No, there was more to it than promotion. A lot of the chaps there are young and relatively inexperienced, so the powers that be decided some experience should be imported. And I was it.'

Suddenly he was on his feet, a hand shielding his eyes as he gazed out to sea.

'What is it?' she demanded.

'It's one of ours, and she's in a bad way.'

Beth jumped up. Squinting, she gazed into the far distance, trying to locate the plane he was referring to. What she spotted was a mere dot with a feather of smoke trailing behind.

'God, your eyesight's good,' she muttered.

They watched the plane come closer and closer, all the while continuing to lose height. The smoke could now be seen to be black and acrid and coming from the port wing, half of which was missing. Yellow and orange flames flickered and danced from the one remaining port engine.

'B for Baker. Charlie Forbes,' Steve stated through gritted teeth.

The broiling whitecaps were only twenty or so feet below the Stirling's landing gear as it headed straight towards them.

'Down!' Steve yelled. Grabbing Beth by the arm, he threw her flat on the sand. A maelstrom of air whistled and eddied all around them as the Stirling flashed overhead.

'Let's go,' Steve said urgently, pulling Beth upright again.

'Where to?'

'The 'drome.'

Beth hastily picked up her boots and stockings and Roy's socks, stuffing the latter into a pocket. There was no time to put the boots on as Steve was already astride the Norton, impatient to get going. Holding her boots and helmet in one hand she jumped up behind him, and instantly they were away. So precarious was her hold on Steve's waist that she thought she was going to have to discard the boots and helmet, but somehow she managed to hang on to them. It was with enormous relief that she saw the aerodrome loom up ahead.

B for Baker, as Steve had known would be the case, was still circling while the firefighters on the ground hurriedly got their apparatus ready. Baker was now so low that her wheels were occasionally skimming the high grass that grew hereabouts.

There were no sentries on the gate as the Norton screeched through, coming to a spine-jolting halt beside a cluster of huts. RAF personnel were rushing in all directions, but with apparent purpose. First one fire engine and then another trundled over to the edge of the area where the planes took off and landed, the aerodrome not having a proper runway as such. When the fire engines were in position a Very light burst above them in a green flaring ball.

'Easy does it, Charlie. Easy does it,' Steve said quietly, his face white, drawn and etched with worry.

B for Baker's wheels kissed the ground and for the space of a few seconds the plane ran straight and true. All too soon, though, what was left of the port wing slewed round so that the plane started to spin in a slithering circular movement.

Beth covered her eyes, not wanting to watch, yet compelled to peep through the cracks between her fingers. Quite out of control now, the plane spun round and round. Steve prayed she wasn't going to flip on to her back, for if she did that it was almost a certainty that what fuel she had left would explode, incinerating Charlie Forbes and his crew in the process. Steve had witnessed that horror many times, and had once narrowly escaped such a death himself.

Baker finally scrunched to a stop. The moment she'd done so the two fire engines were racing towards her, as were many other personnel.

'Not over yet,' Steve muttered to Beth.

A figure tumbled out of Baker, followed by another and another, all of whom were immediately dragged away.

'Come on, Charlie lad!' Steve urged.

A fourth figure came tumbling out and, after an agonising delay, a fifth.

'The buggers made it!' Steve breathed in relief. He groped for his pipe and stuck it unlit into his mouth.

Looking down, Beth saw that her feet were cut and bloody from the hectic ride from the beach. Still, now was hardly the time to complain about some minor abrasions. She put on Roy's socks and her boots – the stockings would have to wait till later.

Steve turned to her and smiled. 'After Charlie makes his report he and his crew will be going in for a drink. Would you care to join them?'

'I'd love to. But I'd appreciate being able to tidy myself up first.'

Steve took her to a ladies' lavatory. There were several on the 'drome as it had WAAFs numbered amongst its personnel, and Beth was able to sort herself out to her satisfaction.

'Are you sure it's all right me being here?' she asked, on re-joining Steve.

'Too late now if it isn't,' he replied with a shrug. 'As the French would say, it's a fait accompli.'

Charlie Forbes was already at the bar when they got there and downing a pint as though it were water. 'I really needed that,' he declared, having drained the last drop.

'The lengths some people will go to just to get noticed,' Steve joked, putting on an expression of mock disapproval and shaking his head.

Charlie laughed. 'And who's this then?' he asked, indicating Beth.

Introductions were made, after which Steve ordered a round for Beth and himself plus the members of B for Baker's crew. There were several higher-ranking officers present, but Beth could see that Steve was the natural leader and focus of attention. All the aircrew congregated round him.

'Damn careless of you to lose an engine and half a wing like that,' he teased Charlie in a bantering tone.

'Fog did it!' Ruarhi McNaughton, Charlie's co-pilot, piped up.

'Fog?' Steve queried, pretending surprise.

'Fog it was,' Charlie corroborated.

'*Just* fog?'

'Well, that and a German battleship we came close as dammit to ramming,' Charlie declared, delivering the punchline and filling the room with laughter.

'Any idea which one?'

'Not a clue. We only saw it for a couple of seconds and then we were past it.'

'Still long enough for their gunners to score at least one hit on you,' Steve replied, smiling lazily.

'The gunners were already at their posts when we came on the big lady. I mean, they had to be. Even the Jerries aren't that fast.'

'Why were you flying at such a low altitude anyway?'

'We'd spotted a U-boat some minutes earlier in a clear patch and were hoping to come on it again. Not very likely in the circumstances, I grant you, but we felt it was worth the effort.'

'There's your answer then. You saw the U-boat and they also saw you. So no doubt they radioed the fact of your presence to the battleship, which is why her gunners were already manning their guns.'

The room had fallen strangely quiet. All eyes were on Steve, who now finished his drink and placed the empty glass on the bar.

'Did I do wrong going so low?' Charlie asked.

'Yes. You were asking for it and came within a whisker of getting it. If Baker had gone down it would've been your fault.'

Charlie bit his lip.

'But we all have to learn and those of us who keep on surviving are the ones who don't make the same mistakes twice. In fog the golden rule, except in the most unusual of circumstances, is keep as high an altitude as possible.'

Charlie nodded. 'I'll remember that.'

Steve gently punched him on the arm, and then steered Beth towards the door. As they reached it a hubbub of voices broke out behind them.

'They think a lot of you,' Beth said when the door was closed behind them.

'And so they should. I am a Battle of Britain hero, after all.'

This time she could see he was sending himself up, and she laughed.

'Would you like to look over my bus?' he asked.

'Bus?'

'My Stirling. O for Oboe.'

'I'd enjoy that very much,' she said enthusiastically.

He led her round behind some of the huts and across to where three Stirlings were drawn up in a line. O for Oboe was the first they came to.

The fuselage was smaller inside, more compact, than she'd expected. The smell of machine oil was so heavy it almost clogged her nostrils. 'Follow me.' Steve led the way up the four-sectioned fuselage to the cockpit.

It was like walking uphill, Beth thought. The plane's nose projected upward at a considerable angle when it was on the ground. She passed several turrets, each housing, so Steve informed her, a twin Browning machine gun. The cockpit canopy was latticed, many small windows making up a whole. Peering out, she found herself staring at a massive propeller blade.

'What do you think of Baby?' Steve smiled.

'She has character.'

'But don't you think she's beautiful?'

Beth laughed. Only a man could describe this blunt-nosed monster as that. 'Yes I do,' she agreed, and listened patiently while Steve, his eyes blazing with enthusiasm, rattled off a host of facts and figures, all of which she forgot the moment after he'd uttered them.

'Can I sit in your seat?' she asked when he finally ran out of breath.

Steve settled in the co-pilot's seat beside her. There were so many switches, levers, clocks and knobs that she marvelled that anyone could remember what they were all for. She thought of B for Baker limping home with an engine and half a wing gone. 'What's it like out there? Out in the Atlantic?' she asked.

Steve took the stick in his hands and held it gently. It was some time before he replied, and when he did it was in a strange, hollow sort of voice. 'You can go for days, weeks sometimes, without making a sighting, friendly or otherwise. Life becomes reduced to the inside of this cockpit, the ocean, the sky and the horizon.' He paused, his features darkening. When he eventually went on it was in a whisper.

'It's the horizon I find most fascinating, because it represents the unknown. The ocean and sky I can see, but the horizon? Who knows from one minute to the next what's going to appear over it coming straight in your direction?'

He took a deep breath and exhaled very slowly, as though trying to purge himself of something. Suddenly he was an entirely different Steve Ramsay from the one Beth had known up until that moment. His face contorted, his expression becoming one of extreme anguish and fear. It dawned on Beth that the boast of being a hero was all sheer bravado, as were the arrogance and bumptiousness. It was a front the real Steve Ramsay had erected to help him cope with the terrible things that could happen to him on active service.

The expression vanished, and he was his usual bouncy self once more. He grinned at her, and she smiled back. She'd asked a question, and the answer had completely rocked her.

'How about a cup of coffee and some sandwiches before we start for home?' he suggested brightly.

'Smashing.'

Thoughtfully, she followed him back down the fuselage.

Chapter 5

Beth laid her head back on Mr Carmichael's sofa and closed tired eyes. The text book she'd been engrossed in for the past two hours lay open on her lap. Within minutes she began to drift off to sleep.

She started at the sound of a rap on the outside door. Now who could that be? she wondered. Cissie?

But it wasn't her mother, it was Steve holding an aromatic newspaper bundle in one hand and a bottle in the other. Her stomach lurched at the sight of him.

'Congratulations! You've just won a couple of fish suppers and some gin,' he grinned.

She quickly ushered him inside, not wanting his voice, or to be precise *their* voices, heard on the landing. 'To what do I owe the honour?' she asked casually.

'O for Oboe's having her engines completely overhauled, which will take at least until tomorrow afternoon. When I realised I had this evening free I had the bright idea of coming to Glasgow to see you. Hope you don't mind?'

She didn't reply. Instead, she went through to the

kitchen, with him trailing behind, to hunt out plates and cutlery.

'Have you been upstairs?' she asked, unearthing knives and forks from a drawer.

He shook his head. 'The last thing I want is to cause trouble between you and your brother. No, I thought I'd try the hospital, hoping you'd be on a late duty. I was going to walk you home when you came off. Maybe even buy you a cup of tea or a drink somewhere.'

'Jesus!' Beth exclaimed. 'Sister will kill me if you went wandering on to the ward.'

'I was the very soul of discretion itself,' he assured her. 'I waited outside the ward doors till I could nab one of the nurses. She told me you weren't on.'

Beth breathed a sigh of relief. 'So how did you know I'd be here?'

'I didn't. But I remembered you telling me about coming downstairs once or twice a week to do some studying. So I thought I'd chance my luck.'

'Two fish suppers. What if I hadn't been here?'

'I'm not totally daft, Beth. I came round first, went into the back green and looked up at the window. When I saw a light I knew it had to be you so trotted off to the chippie. The gin I already had.'

'You should've been a detective,' she mocked, placing the packets of fish and chips on the plates she'd found. They went through to the living room where Steve poured them both hefty measures from the gin bottle.

'No mixer, but I'm afraid you can't have everything in life,' he said.

The gin on its own tasted horrible, but she drank it

anyway. It was a potent mixture, fish and chips and neat gin, she reflected. By the time she'd finished her drink her head was light and woozy, though not disagreeably so. She allowed him to pour her another.

She was delving into her fish when she glanced up to find him staring at her in a way that made her insides contract. A warm flush started at her neck and spread rapidly downwards.

'Have you been busy?' he enquired. It was the first time they'd seen one another since he'd taken her out on the Norton.

The croak in his voice and that look gave it away. He'd been thinking just as much about her as she had about him. Not in a platonic way, either.

'The ward's been bedlam. And then of course there are my exams, which are getting closer and closer.'

'When are they?'

'In six weeks.'

'Will you pass?'

She shrugged. 'With a bit of luck. And how have things been with you?'

'Lots of dull and dreary patrols.'

'No battleships?'

'No battleships. Not even a little one.'

This was all wrong, she thought. It was Teddy she loved. If she had any sense she'd tell Steve to leave as soon as he'd finished eating. But she knew she wouldn't. Since being in the cockpit of O for Oboe and the subsequent ride home she'd desperately wanted to see him again. And now here he was. And he was still looking at her in that disconcerting way.

She sipped some gin, grimacing a little as it burned a passage down her throat. She found she was sweating, though whether from the alcohol or the blazing fire she couldn't say. Then she realised her agitation was caused by neither. The reason was the pure emotion welling and surging within her.

He was talking again, but somehow she couldn't tune into what he was saying. She heard herself replying, a jumble of words she thought. Yet, judging from his expression, they seemed to be making sense to him.

She became fascinated by his mouth, the way it opened and closed as he ate. His lips gleamed tender pink in the reflected glow of the fire.

Suddenly he was out of his chair and she was in his arms, the lips that had so fascinated her pressing against hers. His tongue was deep inside her mouth.

'Wait,' he whispered. He crossed to the light switch and flipped it off, and the room was plunged into a darkness filled with weird flickering reflections thrown out by the burning coal.

A hand was on her blouse, unbuttoning it, the blouse falling away to be followed by her bra.

'Oh, Beth!' he breathed.

This was the time to stop. He mustn't be allowed to go any further. She'd promised herself time and time again that she wouldn't give up her virginity until she was married, the possessor of a ring and a piece of paper.

Her skirt dropped to the floor as hands slid under her knickers. 'A ring and a piece of paper,' she mumbled. But he didn't hear.

He laid her down, and she stretched out catlike before the fire feeling deliciously wanton.

Was this the result of the drink? she wondered. The answer was no. It was because of Steve himself. Pure and simple.

Afterwards she slept. When she woke he was sitting staring at her, smoking a cigarette. Smiling, he handed it to her.

She sat up also, thinking she might now be embarrassed by her nakedness. But she wasn't. 'When I first met you I disliked you intensely,' she told him quietly.

'Funny how things work out, isn't it?'

'Yes, isn't it?'

They regarded one another in silence, the only noises to be heard being the sputtering of the coal and the steady tick-tock of the clock on the mantelpiece. There was a word pregnant between them, and when Beth flicked the remains of the cigarette into the fire Steve finally spoke it.

'Teddy,' he said.

'Are you regretting what's just happened?' she asked.

He shook his head.

'Neither am I.'

'Good. But that still leaves my brother. He should be told if we're to continue seeing one another. That's only fair.'

'Yes,' she whispered.

It was strange, she thought, turning to gaze into the depths of the fire. When she and Teddy had been together she'd genuinely believed she'd loved him. But she hadn't. Love, when it did strike, was a revelation. All else was counterfeit and could be seen clearly as such. It was Steve she was in love with. She knew that now with a certainty that went as deep as her femininity.

'I'll write to him tomorrow,' Steve said.

A solitary tear oozed from Beth's left eye. Poor Teddy. He was going to be so hurt.

'Don't you think it should be me who breaks it to him?' she asked over her shoulder.

'I'm his brother.'

'And I'm the woman he loves.'

Steve reflected on that. 'In which case maybe we should both write.'

She nodded her agreement. Sweeping a stray wisp of hair away from her face, she suddenly asked, 'Have you slept with many women?'

'What a question at a time like this!'

'Have you?' she persisted.

'Positively hundreds! I've even had them two and three at a time!' he joked.

'I'm being serious.'

'Well, how would you feel if I asked you how many men *you'd* slept with?'

'That's just it,' she replied quietly. 'There's only been one, and that was about twenty minutes ago.' She turned to meet his questioning gaze and he saw the truth of what she'd just said written plainly on her face.

Reaching out, he touched her arm. 'Are you working this weekend?'

'No.'

'As Oboe's undergoing a major service it would be relatively easy for me to claim something isn't right about the finished job, which means I could be free over the weekend. How about you and I going away together and spending it in an hotel?'

'You mean as Mr and Mrs Smith?' She grinned. 'I'd probably burst out giggling when you signed the register.'

'No you won't. Now what do you say?'

'A dirty weekend sounds so sordid, don't you think?'

His face fell. 'If you'd rather not, I quite understand.'

She kept him on the hook for a few seconds more. 'Have you any particular hotel in mind?'

He smiled.

Beth stood at the window staring out. The scenery was breathtaking, a highland landscape filled with rock, heather, moss and mountains. In the far distance was a twinkling silver river in which, Steve had told her, salmon and trout could be caught.

She closed her eyes and sighed. It had been the most marvellous two days. Everything had been simply perfect.

It was ridiculous really, but after only such a short time she now couldn't imagine life without Steve. He was well and truly her fate, as the girls at school had always said of the man they'd eventually meet and fall in love with. She smiled. It was an expression she hadn't thought of for donkey's. Her fate. Yes, there could be no doubt about it. That's precisely what Steve was.

A glance at her watch told her there were still several hours till tea, after which she and Steve would be starting back on the Norton. Steve was outside now checking over his beloved machine prior to the journey.

She decided to take a shower. The shower facility in

the bathroom attached to their double bedroom had been a totally new and novel experience for her. Slipping out of her clothes, she padded through and turned on the cascading water.

She closed her eyes and luxuriated in the hot droplets pummelling her skin, making her feel vibrantly alive. When she opened them again it was to find Steve staring at her.

'I didn't hear you come in.'

He smiled slowly, then started to strip.

'You're covered in oil,' she protested when he joined her.

'Then the shower's the best place for me.'

She wriggled as he fondled her breasts. 'This isn't decent, you know.'

His expression changed to become serious. 'I just can't believe I've found you.'

'Nor I you.'

'Ever since we arrived here I've kept thinking it's all a dream and that any moment I'm going to wake up and find myself back at Langbank.' He stroked her sodden hair, then ran his fingers through it. 'I have a week's leave due to me which I can probably arrange for next month. What do you say we use it to drive to Gretna Green?'

Her mouth was suddenly dry. And, despite the heat of the cubicle, she shivered. 'Is that a proposal, Steve Ramsay?'

'The only one I've ever made.'

She wanted to laugh, sing, shout and dance all at the same time. She also felt vaguely sick.

'Well?'

'Where will we live?'

'We'll sort that problem out when we come to it. So, what's your answer?'

'Of course I'll marry you.'

He swept her into his arms and for a moment they stood stock still, like entwined graven images.

'I wonder what's for tea?' he mused aloud.

He was roaring with laughter as, towel in hand, she chased him from the bathroom.

Beth stood in the teeming rain by the Langside Monument, where they'd agreed to meet. It was a foul day to choose to drive to Gretna. Steve had been joking when he mentioned it, Gretna Green being the traditional destination for runaway English couples who wouldn't have been able to marry south of the border, but Beth thought it would be ever so romantic to elope, and the idea had stuck.

A peep at her watch told her Steve was a few minutes late, which was unlike him, as he was usually very punctual. Probably some sort of hitch with the Norton, she thought. Motorbikes could be temperamental in weather like this.

It had been sheer hell for her to get this time away from the hospital. In the end she'd managed it, though it was going to cost her dear in late shifts, night shifts and working weekends. And she'd had to lie to Cissie and Roy, telling them she was off on a wee holiday break with a pal from an adjoining ward. Roy would be furious when he found out the truth of the matter. Fortunately, by then it would be far too late for him to do anything about it.

Lightning flickered overhead, followed by crashing thunder. An old van drove by splashing water in all directions, but of Steve and his motorbike there was still no sign.

When he was twenty minutes late by her watch she began to get really worried. What in the name of the Wee Man was holding him up? The only thing she could think of was that something had gone seriously wrong with the Norton and that even now he was frantically trying to repair it.

That had to be the case, she told herself. Unless, for some reason or other, he'd been detained in Langbank the previous night when he'd been due to drive to his parents'. At last, much to her relief, a motorbike came over the crest of the hill heading towards her. Only it wasn't Steve. Nor was it even a Norton. She watched the motorbike round the monument and speed off in another direction.

Her mood plummeted. Maybe he'd had cold feet and was giving her a dissy, as a disappointment by being stood up was called locally. She went chill inside and a sort of numbness started to creep over her. He wouldn't do that, would he? Not her lovely Steve! Biting her lip, she began pacing up and down.

When it reached forty minutes past the appointed time she became convinced he wasn't coming. Feeling angry, stupid, and very alone, she picked up her holdall and headed homewards.

She was so engrossed in her emotions she failed to hear the Norton till it was almost beside her. 'Oh, Steve, you've come after all!' she cried, launching herself at him the moment the bike stopped at the kerb. She buried her face in his leather jacket, drinking in the smell of him and telling herself she must've been mad to doubt him.

Steve pushed her to arm's length and lifted his goggles up on to his forehead.

'I really believed you weren't coming,' she laughed. But

then she noticed how drawn and haggard he was, his cheeks sunken, his lips pale and bloodless. His eyes . . . oh, his eyes! 'What's happened, Steve?'

'I was just about to walk out of the door when the telegram arrived. From the War Department.'

Beth's hand flew up to her mouth. 'Teddy?'

'Aye. Missing in action.'

'So he isn't dead then?' she said quickly.

Steve shook his head. 'I really don't know. Father seems to think he is while Mother is taking the telegram literally. The two of them are in a right old state, as you can well imagine, which is why I'm late.' He laid a hand on her shoulder. 'I have to go back to them, Beth. I just can't go off and leave them as they are.'

'I understand. Yes, of course you must go back to them.'

'What a mess!' he exclaimed, drawing her to him again and holding her close.

Beth's mind was whirling. Poor Teddy! She saw him clearly as he'd been that day on Windmillcroft Quay, remembering how he, Edgar, Ron and Jacko had stood side by side waving to her and the Ramsays as their warship steamed off down the Clyde. A lump filled her throat, a lump so big she thought she might choke on it.

'Will I drive you to your street?' Steve offered.

'No, I prefer to walk. I need time to make up a story to tell Ma when I get home. But listen, can I call round to your place in a little while? Or would I be in the way?'

'I'm sure Mother and Father will be pleased to see you. It is natural for you to visit, after all. As far as they're concerned, you're still Teddy's lassie. I'll tell them I bumped into you and that's how you know.'

'You haven't explained about us then?'

He shook his head. 'Rather cowardly of me, I'm afraid. I was putting it off till we returned from Gretna.'

She kissed his bloodless lips. 'I love you, Steve,' she whispered.

'And I love you.'

She stood watching him till he reached the bottom of the hill and turned out of sight. Then, picking up her holdall, she trudged after him.

A little over two hours later Steve answered her knock, and led the way to the living room. Mrs Ramsay had very obviously been crying. Her eyes were red-rimmed and bleary, while Mr Ramsay had the fixed, staring expression of someone in shock.

'I was just going through the family album,' Mrs Ramsay told Beth tremulously, indicating the open album on her lap. 'Looking for photos of Teddy as a boy. There's one here of the four of us taken on holiday at Eyemouth. Teddy would've been eight . . .'

'Ten,' Mr Ramsay interrupted, still staring ahead of him. 'The lad was ten.'

'Ten then,' Mrs Ramsay conceded, turning her head away.

'Will you have a drink, Beth?' Steve asked, pointing to a bottle of whisky standing on the sideboard.

She hesitated; it was awfully early yet. But considering the circumstances . . . 'Just a small one.'

Mr Ramsay picked up the glass before him and drained it. 'I'll have another, please, Steve.'

'You appreciate Teddy's only missing.' Mrs Ramsay

smiled at Beth. The smile had a curious stretched, wavering quality about it. 'Which doesn't mean to say the worst has happened.'

'No,' Beth agreed, accepting her drink from Steve. 'Did the telegram say anything apart from that?'

'Just that he's missing,' Mrs Ramsay repeated, her smile stretching further than ever.

'The lad's dead, Ellie,' Mr Ramsay said heavily.

'Don't say that, dear!' his wife exclaimed, her face filling with terror.

Mr Ramsay suddenly turned his attention to Beth, the first time he'd acknowledged her since she'd entered the room. 'During the Great War, which I fought in, missing in action meant they couldn't account for the body. It happened a lot in trench warfare, you know. Men blown into a thousand bits. Others drowned in mud, disappearing for ever into that grey, slimy muck. Autumn and spring were the worst for mud. One wrong step and you'd had it.'

'Please, dear,' Mrs Ramsay whimpered.

'Aye, I think that's enough of that, Dad.'

'I had a friend,' Mr Ramsay persisted, although now he was talking more to himself than to Beth and the others. 'A chap called Jam Roll Robertson. One day, so the story went, Jam Roll was standing talking to an English officer when out of the blue a shell landed right on top of them. When the smoke cleared there was no more Jam Roll or English officer. Not even the tiniest trace of them. It was as though someone had waved a magic wand and they'd completely disappeared. I believe Jam Roll's wife got a telegram saying *he* was missing in action.'

'I think . . . I think I'd like to lie down under the quilt for a wee while,' Mrs Ramsay croaked.

'I'll help you through, Mum.'

'Jam Roll Robertson,' Mr Ramsay mused, shaking his head. 'I haven't thought about him in years.'

'It might be a good idea for you to lie down too,' Beth suggested.

Mr Ramsay didn't reply.

'Dad, Beth's talking to you,' Steve prompted.

'Eh? What's that?'

Beth repeated herself.

'Och no, I'm fine here.'

'I'm sure Mrs Ramsay would appreciate the company.'

Mr Ramsay looked at his wife, and nodded. Rising, he crossed and took her in his arms. Like two lost children they shuffled from the room, Steve bringing up the rear.

Despite the early hour Beth poured herself another whisky, a hefty one this time. She noticed her hand was shaking as she picked up the glass.

When Steve returned he offered her a cigarette and they both lit up. 'Do you think I should get the doctor in?' he asked.

'I'd recommend it. They probably both ought to be kept on sedatives for a day or two.'

They smoked the rest of their cigarettes in silence, and then Beth left. Outside, the rain had stopped and the sun was breaking through the rapidly dispersing clouds. It was going to be a fine day after all, she thought. But not for her.

Chapter 6

Beth pressed button A, which put her through to Langbank, and asked the female voice on the other end if it was possible to speak to Squadron Leader Ramsay. She was told to hang on.

'Hello?'

'Steve, it's me. Guess what?'

'What?'

'I've passed my exams and am now fully qualified. How about that, eh?'

He laughed. 'Fabulous news. I am pleased for you.'

'The results came in this morning and the first thing I did on reaching the hospital was apply for a staff nurse's job. I've an excellent chance of getting it too.'

'Well, I think this calls for a bit of a celebration. How about getting your glad rags on on Saturday night and we'll do the town?'

'That would be smashing, Steve.'

'I'll meet you beside the monument at—'

'No,' she cut in sharply. 'Anywhere else, but not there.'

They arranged the rendezvous and then hung up. Not the monument, she thought grimly. She would never meet anyone there again.

Everybody loves a Saturday night, so the words of the song went, and they could've been written with Glasgow particularly in mind. Saturday was *the* big night for people to go out and play.

Arm in arm Steve and Beth strolled along Sauchiehall Street, heading for a dance hall they both liked at Charing Cross. The pavements were packed with folk toing and froing, many of them, like Steve, in uniform.

'A drink first, then the jigging?' Steve suggested. Beth agreed, so they turned down a side street and made for a pub which looked as though it might be relatively quiet.

Beth sat at a table already littered with empty glasses while Steve went up to the bar. There were no spirits available so he returned with a sweet stout for Beth and a pint for himself.

'Here's up your kilt with a wire brush!' he toasted, causing Beth to splutter into her stout.

'That's disgusting.'

'But an idea all the same.' He winked.

'Ten of them from the Royals,' a voice declared. 'Crucified to trees with bayonets. You've never seen anything like it in your life. It was horrendous.'

Beth and Steve stared at one another, then turned to look at the man who'd just spoken. A soldier wearing the insignia of the East Lothians, an Edinburgh regiment, he was talking to three other men who were all civilians.

'One chap in my platoon spewed up at the sight, and

I can tell you I wasn't far off it myself. God, they're bastards, those Japs.' The soldier paused for a swallow of beer. 'Thank Christ my mob got out before the surrender. Who knows what the Nips will do to those poor sods they've got their hands on now.'

Steve and Beth rose and crossed to the soldier. 'Excuse me, but I couldn't help but overhear just now,' Steve said.

'Oh aye?'

'It's of interest to me because I have a brother in the Royals who's been reported missing in action.'

The soldier dropped his gaze to stare into his pint. 'I'm sorry, pal.'

'Were you talking about Singapore?'

The soldier nodded. 'The Royals engaged the Nips up country. It was one helluva scrap, but the lads didn't really have a chance. In fact, the odds against them were so heavy they didn't have a hope.'

'You did say crucified?' Beth's voice shook.

'Aye, I did.'

'Dear God,' she whispered.

'The Japs aren't like us. They're just not civilised.'

Steve thanked the soldier for the information, and he and Beth returned to their seats. 'At least we now know where Teddy was,' Steve murmured.

In her mind's eye Beth had a clear picture of men pinned to trees with bayonets through their hands and feet. 'Dear God!' she repeated, and shook her head.

'There were thousands taken when Singapore fell. Teddy could be one of them.'

'If he was, surely the army wouldn't have reported him missing? They must know who the Japs have got.'

Steve passed a hand over his forehead. 'I feel so guilty.'

'Because of me?'

'I know I shouldn't, but I do. If only Teddy had been here it would all have been so different.'

'How do you mean?'

'I'd have told him about us face to face.'

'If Teddy had still been here I'd never have gone to Langbank with you that day and what happened between us wouldn't have done,' she pointed out.

She wondered about Ron and Jacko. Were they dead? Or had they been amongst the captured, and those who'd surrendered, now in Japanese prisoner of war camps? Edgar Martin was definitely dead. His mother, who lived across the landing from the Carmichaels, had received a telegram informing her so the day after the Ramsays had received theirs.

'I think we have to accept Teddy isn't coming back,' she said.

'Yes.'

'I just hope . . .' She trailed off, suddenly aware of a presence by her side. Looking up, she found herself staring into Roy's contorted features.

For a moment or two it didn't click with Steve who Roy was. Then he remembered him.

'So you're at it again, you wee runt,' Roy snarled.

'What are you on about?'

Roy stabbed a finger at Beth's glass. 'Booze, and fags no doubt as well. What else do you have in mind, I ask myself?'

Steve slowly rose to confront him. 'I don't want any trouble, not right now. So why don't you just move on?'

Roy grinned. 'Yellow with it, eh?'

A muscle twitched in Steve's cheek as his hands clenched into fists.

'She's coming home with me.' Roy nodded at Beth.

'No I'm not.'

'You'll do as you're told,' he spat back. 'I'm not having a sister of mine sitting in a public bar like some common bloody tart.'

'I think you've said quite enough,' Steve said quietly.

'Why don't you fuck off!'

Steve's entire body jerked as though he'd been punched. It was a struggle, but he somehow managed to keep himself under control when all he really wanted to do was knock Roy flying.

'I'm not doing anything wrong, Roy,' Beth hissed. 'I'm twenty years old. Not some wee lassie still at school.'

'Are you coming home under your own steam or do I have to drag you?' Roy retorted.

'Lay a finger on her and I promise you you'll regret it.'

Roy laughed. 'Just because you were lucky once . . .'

'I wasn't lucky. I was the better man. As it would give me great pleasure to prove to you again.'

Roy stuck out his chest. 'Shall we step into the street, then?'

'No, please!' Beth said. 'I'll come home with you if I have to.'

'You'll do no such thing,' Steve said to her. Then, to Roy: 'If you and I are going to fight we'll do it here, where everyone can see. And you know why?'

Roy blinked.

'Because when I beat the shit out of you I want others

to have a good laugh at your expense, which they'll most certainly do as I'm only a wee runt, as you put it. Let me tell you something else, Roy. Glasgow is a very small city in some ways so I should be very surprised if at least half your workmates didn't already know what happened when you report to work on Monday morning.'

Roy glared, but now there was uncertainty in his eyes. Uncertainty and fear. Not fear of Steve himself, but of being publicly humiliated. If Steve *were* to beat him in front of other people it would take years to live down. And Steve *had* already bested him once. He'd put that down to luck on Steve's part. But what if he was wrong and Steve was the better man in a fight? He couldn't chance it. He would have to back off.

'Well, what's it to be?' Steve asked softly.

It was one of the hardest things Roy had ever done. Turning, he walked stiff-legged to the door and disappeared outside. Steve sat down and shook his head.

'I'm sorry about that,' Beth said.

'It's hardly your fault you have a brother like him.'

Beth shuddered. Despite the heat of the pub she was cold all over. 'I'll tell you this – he may not have actually hated you before, but he will now.'

As if in defiance of Roy, Steve pulled out a packet of cigarettes and offered her one. 'I shouldn't have gone that far with him, not when I intend marrying his sister. Only his timing couldn't have been worse, coming as it did directly after what that soldier told us.'

Beth finished her drink. 'I don't fancy going to the dancing now, Steve. What's happened tonight has put me completely off the idea.'

They made their way back out into the night, where they decided to walk until it was time to go home.

'When are we going to get married, Steve?' Beth asked, glancing at his face.

'I think it's only decent and proper to let a few months go by. It just wouldn't be right otherwise.'

'So when then?'

'Let's leave it till the summer, eh? July or August, by which time I'll be able to wangle another full week off. What about you?'

'Once we finalise the date I'll work something round it.'

'That's agreed, then.' He smiled and squeezed her hand.

They walked a little way in silence, he thinking how changed Sauchiehall Street was since the imposition of the blackout. It was a ghost of its former well lit, dazzling self.

'Steve?'

He brought his attention back to her. 'Yes?'

'Once we're married we should have a place of our own. I mean, I know you'll be at Langbank most of the time, but you do manage through fairly often.'

'I've already done something about that. I came into a lump sum on my twenty-first which will be just enough to buy and furnish a bungalow. I thought King's Park would be nice.'

'A bungalow!' she breathed.

'I thought you'd like the idea.'

'Like it? I love it!' Not caring who saw, she stopped and kissed him on the lips.

'I've made enquiries and there's nothing on the market just now,' Steve continued. 'But the moment something comes up I'll be notified and we can go and see if it suits.'

A bungalow! Beth couldn't get over it. In her wildest dreams she'd never imagined herself living in one of those. And King's Park was such a posh address. Why, one of the specialists at the hospital lived there!

'Do you think that'll be soon?' she asked excitedly.

'We'll just have to keep our fingers crossed.'

Roy was waiting for her in the living room, as Beth had known he would be. Cissie was sitting at the table looking irritated, having guessed correctly that the two of them had already been arguing.

'I forbid you to see that man again,' Roy declared without preamble.

Beth took a deep breath, and crossed to the mantelpiece to stare in the mirror hanging above it. She was undoubtedly a woman in love: all the signs there for anyone capable of reading them. The sparkle in her eyes, the flush to her cheeks. A sort of inner satisfaction and well-being that positively radiated from her.

'You hear me, lady?' Roy demanded.

She turned to face him. 'I used to have a great deal of respect for you, Roy. Oh, you had your faults, but so do we all. Now? That respect's gone, right out of the window. I think you've made a complete fool of yourself over Steve.'

Roy started to rise. 'You won't speak to me like that . . .'

'Don't hit her!' Cissie interjected.

Roy stopped half in, half out of his chair. 'You heard how she spoke to me.'

'Aye, I did. And I know Beth, so there must've been a

reason behind it. She was never cheeky or disrespectful in her life.'

Roy sank back into his chair. 'If I say she won't see him again then that's the way it's going to be.'

'You can't make me give him up,' Beth protested.

'I can. I'm now the head of this house and you'll do as I tell you, otherwise—'

'Otherwise what?' Beth cut in. 'You'll throw me out. Is that it?'

'Just so.'

'Well, I'll be leaving soon enough. Steve and I are going to be married.'

'Beth!' Cissie exclaimed.

Roy snorted. 'I'll believe that when it happens. I know his type, the ones with a plum in their mouth. When he goes out with a lassie like you it's for one thing only. And I wouldn't be at all surprised if he isn't getting it already.'

'How can you say such a thing about Steve? You've never even spoken to him apart from shouting at him.'

'Has he proposed?' Cissie asked.

'He has.'

'You're engaged then, I take it?' Roy sneered.

'Yes, I suppose you could say that.'

'So where's the ring, eh? Come on, show it to us. Show us your engagement ring.'

Neither she nor Steve had thought of a ring. The way things had worked out, an official engagement, or engagement ring, had just never entered into their plans.

'I haven't got one yet.'

'I see.' Roy smirked.

'No you don't at all!' retorted Beth, angry and frustrated at his seemingly having caught her out.

'And while we're talking about respect,' Roy went on, 'let me tell you, that one has none where you're concerned. If he did, he wouldn't be taking you into a pub to be seen drinking and smoking like some common floozy.'

'That's nonsense. There's nothing wrong with smoking and drinking in moderation.'

'*Not* for a woman!'

'You're right out of the Ark so you are,' she replied scornfully.

'I have standards, Beth, and if they're old-fashioned then so am I. But they're good standards.'

'And a little one-sided if you ask me. I'm not supposed to smoke, drink or do anything like that. And why? Because I'm a woman. I don't see those selfsame standards applying to you and your sex. You can do what you like and you're just thought of as a bit of a lad. Let a female try to enjoy herself and instantly she's a Jezebel.'

'That's how life is.'

'Then I don't agree with it and it's high time that way of life was changed.'

'You're speaking like a loose woman,' Roy snarled.

'She's speaking sense,' Cissie chipped in.

Roy regarded his mother with astonishment. 'You surely don't agree with her?'

'Up to a point I do. I think nowadays women should be given a wee bit more rein. It's the twentieth century, after all, not the nineteenth. Besides, some of the young girls today are only doing in public what their mothers and grandmothers did in private. I call that more honest myself.'

Roy gaped at her. 'But the Church . . .'

'The Church is run by men, *for* men, and always has been. And if I may say so, son, you know very little about women. Though that's hardly uncommon amongst the men of this city.'

Roy was completely nonplussed, but Beth was amazed and delighted at having found an ally in her mother. Cissie had never given even the slightest hint that she held such views prior to this occasion.

'I still don't think he'll marry you,' Roy persisted.

'He will. As you'll see.'

'When's the ceremony going to be, then?'

She'd be damned if she was going to tell him her plans, so she remained silent.

'You mark my words, he's after only one thing,' Roy reiterated.

'Beth's been well brought up. I trust her not to make a mistake,' Cissie stated.

'It'll be the last mistake she makes round here if she does.'

'Ma, if Da was still alive and at home, would he allow me to smoke now I'm twenty?'

Cissie's gaze flicked from Beth to Roy, then back again to Beth. 'I believe he would, lass. Mind you, never in the street. That's just not the done thing.'

Seeing the look on Beth's face, Roy sat bolt upright. 'You wouldn't dare!'

Beth couldn't resist it. Snapping open her handbag, she pulled out a packet of five, lit up, and blew a long stream of blue smoke straight at Roy.

'Goodnight all,' she declared airily, and left the room.

A little later Cissie knocked the door of her bedroom. 'Beth? Beth, are you awake?'

Shutting her eyes, she pretended to be asleep. She heard the bedroom door open, then close again, and then the sound of Cissie padding away down the hallway.

Her mother would be wanting to find out all about Steve, and to talk about him and the forthcoming marriage, but Beth had already decided to keep the details of their plans from Cissie as well as from Roy. That way there'd be no nastiness or unpleasantness before the event. Cissie might have surprised her with some liberal beliefs earlier on, but she knew her mother disapproved of register office weddings.

June weather in Scotland, as Beth knew to her cost, is often very different from that in England, where the month is traditionally associated with sun, heat and long hazy days. But in Glasgow the June of 1942 was after the English model, sun cracking the skies from dawn to dusk.

Beth, now Staff Nurse Somerville, was tucking in Mrs Rennie's sheets when a wave of nausea suddenly came over her, causing her to stagger and clutch on to the side of the bed.

'Are you all right, Staff?' Sister McKeown queried, appearing beside her.

Beth touched her forehead to discover it was clammy and covered in cold perspiration. 'I'll be fine in a moment.'

'I think you'd better come with me,' Sister McKeown declared, taking her by the arm. In her office Sister sat Beth down and fetched her a glass of water. 'What's brought this on then?'

'I've no idea, but it's not the first time it's happened.

I've been having these attacks regularly for the past couple of weeks.'

'I don't like the sound of that at all.' Sister frowned.

'They soon pass.'

'That's hardly the point, Staff, as you should well realise. Have you seen your doctor?'

'No,' Beth admitted reluctantly.

'Then I think you should. In fact I insist you do. Or would you prefer to see one of the hospital doctors? I can arrange that easily enough for you. Say an afternoon later this week?'

'Maybe that would be best,' Beth agreed.

'You leave it to me. I'll attend to it. Now, how about a nice cup of tea? It's almost your break anyway.'

While Sister put the kettle on Beth wondered with dread if she'd developed something really terrible, like a tumour perhaps, or . . . Her mind whirled with possibilities, each more horrific than the last.

Dandy – so called because he always wore a bow tie – McAllister was a tall, thin, gangling man with sandy-coloured hair and a beak of a nose. He was the senior registrar on Sister McKeown's ward, which was a medical one. He and Beth were in the examination room, and she was describing to him the attacks she'd been having.

He listened attentively, then told her to strip to the waist and gave her a thorough sounding, back and front. Then he asked her to take off her bra.

Beth was a little embarrassed by this request, but did as she was told, sitting up primly when she was ready for him.

Dandy stared at her right nipple, asking if it was tender

when he touched it. She confirmed that it was. Next he probed the underside of her breast, enquiring if that was also tender.

'Yes,' she replied, fear rapidly mounting in her. My God, he's going to tell me I've got breast cancer! she thought, appalled at the prospect.

Giving a grunt, Dandy crossed to the sink where he started to wash his hands. 'You can get dressed again,' he said over his shoulder. 'I'll need a sample for verification.'

'Then you're pretty certain what it is?'

'Oh aye. The sample's just a formality.'

Heart pounding, she buttoned her apron into place. 'Is it breast cancer?'

He looked at her in astonishment. 'No, it's nothing like that. You're pregnant, Beth. About ten, maybe twelve weeks, I'd say.'

She was stunned. Of all the things she'd thought of she'd never considered pregnancy. And yet, of course, it was the most natural, and obvious, explanation.

She gave Dandy a sideways glance. The pair of them had a good, jokey relationship on the ward, though it would be stretching it to call them friends. Reasonably close colleagues might be a better way of putting it. 'Do you have to report this?' she asked quietly.

'You'd rather I didn't?'

She nodded. 'Please, Dandy.'

'In that case you'd better forget about the sample. That would have to be entered with your name.'

'Thank you,' she whispered.

'There are certain people I know who could help if you're—'

'I'm going to be married very shortly,' she cut in.

He smiled. 'Then there isn't a problem.'

'That's right,' she confirmed. 'And in the meantime you'll keep this to yourself?'

'I'll tell Sister you've picked up a germ which'll take your system a few weeks to clear. That will give you an alibi for further dizzy attacks and whatever.'

'Thanks, Dandy. You're a pal.'

After Dandy had gone she sat on for a moment or two, trying to analyse her emotions. It didn't take her long to decide that what she felt was a combination of fear and jubilation. The fear stemmed from her uncertainty about how Steve would react to the news, but there was nothing uncertain about the jubilation.

She was having a baby!

Chapter 7

That evening Beth stood deep in thought staring out of her bedroom window. It was six weeks yet till she and Steve were due to go down to Gretna, which meant, if she was ten or twelve weeks gone now, she'd be sixteen or eighteen by the time of the wedding.

Putting a finger into her mouth she worried the nail. If only Steve was here to talk things over! But he was on duty for another fortnight, and it was unlikely that he'd manage through to Glasgow during that time. The good weather was keeping the squadron in the air sometimes up to eighteen hours a day.

She considered waiting till it was well dark then nipping to the nearest public telephone box and trying to ring Steve. But, on reflection, she decided against doing so. Breaking her news by telephone just didn't seem right somehow, particularly if there were people about at his end and they couldn't discuss the matter freely.

A letter was the answer. She'd write it immediately and post it first thing in the morning.

Sitting on the edge of her bed, she started to write. *Dear expectant Daddy* ... She prayed she hadn't misjudged his sense of humour.

She hadn't. When his reply came by return it began *Dear Preggy and bun in the oven* ... Beth sighed with relief.

The letter was short. He was delighted by her news and would talk to her about it the day after next, which he knew to be her regular day off. He was coming through to Glasgow, having a surprise in store for her. He went on to say where he'd meet her and at what time. He ended with lots of kisses and a special large one for the bun.

She read his letter six times during the course of the day, thinking on each occasion how much she loved that man, and how much she would love his child – *their* child – when it came.

Beth arrived early to find Steve already waiting. He swung her into his arms, and she laughed with sheer joy.

'How did you manage the time off?' she queried when he finally released her.

He tapped his cheekbone beneath his left eye. 'Ask no questions, get no lies.'

'Idiot!'

He looked tired, she thought; worn at the edges. His skin had a greyish tinge to it. 'You're overdoing things,' she admonished him, straightening his crooked tie.

'There's a war on, or hadn't you noticed?' he teased.

'I'd noticed all right.'

He put his arm round her waist. 'I am pleased, Beth, tremendously so.'

Emotion welled up in her. As there was no one to over-hear, she told him about her dizzy spells and the bout of vomiting that had struck the previous evening. He expressed concern, saying he wished he could be with her when such things happened, but then their conversation was interrupted by the arrival of a 4A bus, which Steve declared to be theirs. Beth knew then what his surprise was. The 4A went to King's Park.

'So what do you think we should do, then?' Beth asked after they'd paid their fares.

'I won't be able to manage through to Glasgow again before we're due to go to Gretna – things are just too hectic at the moment. On the other hand, there is a padre on the 'drome who'll happily help us out. You'd simply have to come to Langbank for a couple of days. There's a pub not all that far away where you could stay, and we'd fit in the ceremony when we could.'

Beth screwed up her nose.

'It's either that or wait till the week we've planned. I can't see any other alternative.'

She glanced down at her figure. How long before she started showing? That was the big question. Should she take a gamble and hold out for Gretna, or settle for the ceremony at Langbank?

'Suits me either way.' Steve smiled.

She snuggled up to him. 'If we do go to Gretna it would help if I could move in with your parents when we got back. That way I wouldn't have to worry about Roy. If I stay on at home it won't take him long to work out, even if he hadn't beforehand, that I was already preg-nant when I got married.'

'Don't concern yourself about Roy. I'll sort him out if there's any problem,' Steve replied grimly. 'But I think your suggestion's a good one. You can sleep in my bed till we get the problem of a house sorted out. Mother will enjoy that, and so will the old man – once they've got over the shock of us getting married, that is.'

Beth made a decision. It was just under six weeks till Gretna Green. Surely she could disguise any changes in her figure for that time? She would have to give more thought to what she wore at home. As for her uniforms, letting out a few strategic seams would solve that problem. She smiled up at Steve.

'Let's leave our plans as they are.'

'Positive?'

'Positive,' she replied, squeezing his arm.

At the top of a hill from which Glasgow could be seen for miles around they got off the bus. On the other side of the road the park itself could be seen behind the single row of houses there.

'Well, you've guessed by now what the surprise is.' Steve grinned.

'I like the house already,' Beth enthused.

Steve held up a warning finger. 'Don't get too excited. It might not be at all suitable. And I can assure you, I'm not buying anything unless I'm convinced it's dead right for us.' He consulted a letter, then led her to a cream-coloured bungalow with a red-tiled roof.

The outside was absolutely gorgeous, Beth thought with delight. The front garden was laid to lawn with herbaceous borders, and a red chip path led up to the front door.

'The name of the owners is Mailer,' Steve said as he rang the bell. A few seconds later, a smiling Mrs Mailer answered and invited them in.

The first thing that struck Beth about the inside of the house was how friendly an atmosphere it had. It was almost as though a very warm, loving person had reached out and put an arm round her shoulders.

The sitting room was a dream, and Beth could just imagine herself spending long winter evenings there surrounded by a bevy of children. Steve shot her a glance behind Mrs Mailer's back which told her he liked the room just as much as she did.

The well-appointed kitchen was bigger than she would've thought for a house that size. The windows looked out on to a rear garden and a clump of firs in the park beyond.

There were two bedrooms, the master one only slightly smaller than the sitting room directly below. It had built-in wardrobes and a standing washbasin, and the carpet underfoot was fitted, the first Beth had ever encountered.

'My husband and I have been extremely happy here and are very sad to be leaving. But I'm afraid he's been transferred down to Newcastle. He's a scientist,' Mrs Mailer explained, her tone indicating quite clearly that she wouldn't be elaborating further on the nature of her husband's work.

A boffin, Beth thought. Tied up with something hush-hush.

'Curtains and carpets are included in the price,' Mrs Mailer added.

Downstairs again, Beth and Steve were offered tea,

which they politely declined. At the door Steve said he and Beth would discuss what they'd seen and let her know their decision.

Beth was so exhilarated she felt that if she flapped her arms she would take off. 'Well?' she demanded when they were clear of the house.

Steve's face broke into a huge grin. 'I thought it was bloody marvellous.'

'Can you afford it?'

'Oh aye. I wouldn't have bothered looking it over otherwise.'

She gripped his arm. 'Steve, that house is just us. I could actually see us in every room we went into. And what about the carpet in the master bedroom? How about that!'

His grin became a leer. 'It did give me ideas, I must confess.'

She punched him on the shoulder. 'Behave, now. It's a house we're talking about, not that sort of thing.'

'Will we buy it, then? I don't see us getting anything better at the price. I think we've landed on our feet first time.'

'Then let's go ahead,' she whispered.

'I'll make a telephone call from the first box we come to and get things rolling right away.' He walked a few steps further, then added, 'On one condition, though.'

She came to a halt. 'What's that?'

'You and I pay a visit to Mr Carmichael's house tonight before I drive back to Langbank. Just to check everything's as it should be, of course.'

'Of course!' she agreed demurely.

They were both laughing as they continued on their way.

Beth squatted in front of the lavatory with her head hanging over the bowl. When she decided there was no more to come she rose groaning to her feet and flushed the mess away.

Sitting on the seat, she wiped her face with a towel, noting that she was trembling all over. There were four and a half weeks remaining till she and Steve left for Gretna. She felt whacked out, and promised herself an extra early night. She waited till the trembling had stopped before opening the window to let the air circulate and take away the smell of sick.

Cissie was in the kitchen cooking tea when Beth went in. 'That tummy upset still bothering you?' she asked.

Beth nodded. 'I can't seem to shake it off. It's a really nasty one and no mistake.'

Cissie clucked sympathy.

'I'll set the table.' Beth turned to leave the kitchen.

'Beth lass?'

She paused. 'Yes, Ma?'

'When am I going to meet this young man of yours? If it's as serious between you as you say then I think I should.'

'Would you like me to bring him home?'

Cissie sighed. 'You know you can't do that while Roy feels the way he does about him.'

'It's your house, Ma.'

Cissie looked sad as she stirred the mince. 'That's not quite so, as you well know. Oh, sure the house is in my name, but Roy's the head of it now your da's gone. If he says your chap isn't welcome here, then he isn't, I'm afraid. But that doesn't mean I can't meet him outside somewhere.'

Beth had a sudden inspiration. 'You know that wee holiday I'm going on next month?'

Cissie nodded.

'Well, why don't I fix up something for when I get back?'

Cissie brightened, putting new energy into her stirring. 'I'd like that fine, lass.'

Beth went through to the living room. Cissie would meet Steve all right. Only it would be in their house in King's Park, the buying of which was now under way. She could just imagine Cissie's face when she showed her round. Especially when she saw that bedroom carpet!

Oh, what a coup it was going to be.

Steve had written, sending Beth money and saying they'd better get some bits and pieces together in readiness for moving in. Accordingly, she was visiting the Crown Showrooms, where she had set her heart on an oak tallboy that was even now under the hammer. She bid, then bid again. The only person bidding against her was a rather testy-looking gentleman in a black homburg

She wouldn't go any higher than this, she told herself, raising the bid yet again. But when Black Homburg topped her by two shillings she couldn't resist, and was thrilled to find that that was it for him. Positively fuming, Black Homburg folded his arms and glowered at the floor.

Flushed with victory, Beth heard the tallboy knocked

down to her. Next she was after a sofa that would look just perfect in the sitting room.

The letter containing Steve's cheque – another first for her as she'd never had a cheque before – also suggested that instead of merely spending their week solely in Gretna they might tour the surrounding countryside, staying in farmhouses, hotels, or whatever was available. She'd thought it a marvellous idea. But better still was the further suggestion that they return to Glasgow for the final night and book into the Central Hotel, one of Glasgow's best hotels, and possibly the grandest. A real honeymoon treat was how Steve had put it. He had added that you only got married once in your life, at least that was his intention, so why not splash out a little! There would be top quality champagne for the occasion: he'd see to it personally. Knowing Steve's ability to get hold of things as she did, she had no doubts whatever that top quality champagne there would be. Champagne of any sort would be yet another first for her.

'And now this delightful sofa inspired by Charles Rennie Mackintosh . . .' the auctioneer started.

Beth brought her attention back to matters in hand.

Mr Paterson stared in trepidation at the kidney dish Beth was carrying, only too well aware that underneath the covering cloth lay a syringe. Although he'd never have admitted it in a thousand years he was terrified of needles.

'Arm or bottom?'

'Arm,' Mr Paterson mumbled. Other patients had told him it was less painful in the bottom, but he hated the idea of young lassies seeing and doing things to his backside.

After his forthcoming operation he was sure he'd die of humiliation when it came to the dreaded blanket baths.

He glanced away when he saw the needle. God, you could spear a man to death with that!

Beth gave more injections than anyone else on the ward because she was so good at it. She had the touch, a patient had commented. Slide in. Slowly squeeze. Slide out, followed by a wee rub. 'Well, how was that?'

'Can I go back to listening to the wireless now?' he demanded in a bad-tempered tone.

'It's custard with skin on top for dinner afters,' Beth declared, and walked away. She thought he might have shown just a little gratitude considering the care she'd taken in giving him his jab. She knew he loathed custard, especially when it had skin on top, and that he had a very sweet tooth. What she'd just told him, which was quite untrue, would ruin his entire morning.

The face peering in through one of the glass-panelled ward doors was vaguely familiar. A doctor who'd worked on the ward? An ex-patient? Then she recognised the blue he was wearing as that of a Royal Air Force uniform. And with that recognition she placed him. The pilot of B for Baker, Charlie . . . Charlie . . . Forbes. Yes, that was it, Charlie Forbes. But what on earth was he doing here?

She opened the doors and stepped out into the corridor. 'Hello, Charlie. What are . . .' She got no further. His expression stopped her.

She put a hand on the wall to steady herself, her insides suddenly heaving with apprehension. 'What's happened?'

Charlie cleared his throat. 'It's Steve. He . . . er . . . Oboe got into trouble yesterday. Discovered a surfaced U-boat pack and sank two of them, and was badly strafed in the process. In fact, according to the crew, she was so badly shot up it was a miracle Steve managed to keep her airborne as long as he did.'

'The crew survived then?'

Charlie shifted uneasily from foot to foot. 'They bailed out close to Langbank. It was such a close-run thing two of them actually landed in the shallows. Oboe herself crashed into what used to be a golf course.'

'And Steve? Is he hurt?'

Charlie swallowed. 'Steve didn't make it, I'm afraid. Another minute airborne and he might have. But he didn't get it.'

It was like walking along the street, then suddenly finding you've plunged into an endless tunnel and you're falling . . . falling . . . Her hand instinctively went to her stomach where the baby was. A baby now without a father.

'If it hadn't been for Steve the entire crew would've been lost. All of them, with the exception of Steve, were wounded and would never have survived in the water.'

'A U-boat pack, you said?'

'Oboe sank two of them,' Charlie repeated.

'When was this?'

'Yesterday morning. We all knew you and he were going to get married . . .'

'A week today,' Beth choked. 'It was to happen a week today.'

'His parents will be notified officially but we thought, the lads, that one of us should come through and tell you personally. We all thought very highly of Steve, you see, though I'm sure you know that.'

'Yes,' she whispered. 'It was obvious that day I was at the 'drome.'

The ward doors opened and Sister McKeown poked her head out. 'When you've finished, Staff, I need you in here.' She was frowning.

'Thank you for coming, Charlie. I appreciate it.'

'He was a great flyer. One of the best.'

'Biggles,' Beth said, a tight smile stretching her mouth. Noting Charlie's look of incomprehension she explained, 'That's what his brother called him. Biggles. Because of the jacket, scarf and pipe.'

She glanced through the glass-panelled door to see Sister staring pointedly at her. 'Goodbye, Charlie. Good luck,' she said, and watched him walk away down the corridor. Then she turned and went back inside the ward.

'Really, Staff . . .' Sister McKeown began, only to trail off in confusion when Beth walked straight past her to the nurses' room. There she took her cape from its peg and draped it round her shoulders. Sister McKeown stood open-mouthed as she went past her to leave the ward.

'Well, really!' exclaimed Sister, who'd never known such a thing happen before.

For Beth everything was rather muddled and confused after that. There was a tram ride, a riverbank, and lots and lots of walking. When she did finally become aware of her surroundings again it was evening and she was standing beside Langside Monument.

She stared bitterly up at the grey stone edifice, thinking that this was where things had started to go sour for Steve and her. He'd been just about to walk out of the door, he'd said, when the telegram arrived. If only he'd left a few minutes earlier they'd have been off to Gretna on the Norton. She would've been Mrs Steve Ramsay several months ago. And the baby would be born . . . she gagged on the word . . . legitimate.

She made a fist which she pressed into her mouth. If only Teddy hadn't been killed. If only the telegram had arrived later. If only Steve hadn't met up with that U-boat pack. If only she wasn't pregnant . . . She checked herself on that last one. She musn't think like that. She wanted this baby, desperately. Her only regret was that it would be born in these circumstances.

She wondered whether Steve had been killed instantly. She'd forgotten to ask Charlie Forbes that. She prayed that he had – that an almighty explosion had obliterated him in the space of a heartbeat. The alternative was too dreadful to think about, although it happened to many pilots. Steve had once told her that. When the pilot was fully conscious and trapped as his plane turned into an inferno around him.

'Oh, please God,' she whispered, 'don't let that have happened to him.'

Beth let herself in quietly, snicking the front door shut behind her.

'Is that you, Beth? You're hours late. What kept you, lass?' Cissie called out.

Suddenly, as if a plug had been pulled, tears were streaming down her face while sobs rose choking in her throat. She flew to her bedroom, slamming the door and bolting it. Still wearing her cape she fell on her bed keening 'Steve . . . Steve . . . Steve . . .' over and over again.

'Beth! Beth, what's wrong?' The handle turned, and the door rattled. 'Please open it,' Cissie begged.

Beth snatched up the quilt and wrapped it round her head and shoulders. Her eyes were swollen, her cheeks red from emotion and tears. She was a woman demented.

'Beth, what is all this nonsense?' Roy shouted from the other side of the door.

The scream came from somewhere deep inside her: a hidden place; a terrible place. The epicentre of all hurt and pain.

The door splintered as it was ripped from its hinges. Roy came staggering into the room, having shouldered it open.

'Go away! Go away!' Beth shrieked.

'What in Christ's name has got into you?' he demanded, standing over her.

Cissie appeared from behind him to take Beth in comforting arms. 'There there, my bonny,' she crooned, stroking Beth's inflamed cheeks to try to calm her down.

Roy left the bedroom and returned a few moments later carrying a large glass of whisky. 'I was saving this, but she'd better have it.'

'That's a good lad, son,' Cissie approved, taking the glass. But Beth would have none of its contents. The very smell made her want to throw up.

'Waste not, want not,' Roy declared, taking the glass back from his mother and drinking it off himself.

Control was gradually returning to Beth now, the dementia receding like an ebbing red tide.

'Did something happen at the hospital?' Cissie asked.

Beth clutched her mother's hand, holding it so tightly that Cissie winced. 'Steve's been killed,' she jerked out.

'Oh, lamb!' Cissie whispered, her eyes filling with pity and understanding. Roy looked grim, but said nothing.

'And there's something else, Ma. Something I've got to tell you. Something you're not going to like.' Only she didn't have to say it, because Roy had already guessed.

'You're bloody up the spout!' he accused her, his voice quivering with rage.

'Not our Beth. You've got it all wrong.' Cissie smiled. 'Hasn't he, lass?'

'No.' The single word tiptoed from her mouth to land amongst them like an iron cannonball.

'I knew it. I knew that fancy-speaking wee bugger was getting it from you,' Roy hissed.

'We were to be married at Gretna Green next week.'

'I thought you were supposed to be off on holiday then?' Cissie seemed bemused.

Beth nodded. 'But with him.' And she explained how they'd been going to elope before, only to be stopped on the brink of departure by the arrival of the telegram saying Teddy was missing.

'I didn't realise your Steve was Teddy's brother.' Cissie was still struggling to take it in.

'I know of someone in the town,' Roy said through gritted teeth. 'It'll cost a few quid but to hell with that.'

Beth glanced up at him. 'What are you talking about?'

'A doctor. He'll sort you out and no one'll be any the wiser. I'll take the day off work tomorrow and we'll go in and see him. With a bit of luck he'll be able to do it more or less straight away.'

Beth shrugged herself free of Cissie and stood to face Roy. 'I'm going to have this baby,' she said quietly.

'Don't talk daft. That's impossible.'

'Why?'

'Because you're not married.'

She shook her head. 'I don't care.'

'You're not thinking straight, Beth.'

'Oh, yes, I am.'

He covered his eyes with a hand, and took a deep breath. When he removed his hand the rage had gone, replaced by a cold, detached, lethal air. 'I won't have a bastard born in this house, lady.'

'And I won't have an abortion.'

'Think of Ma. Think of what the neighbours are going to say. The finger-pointing. The talking behind our backs. The laughter. The ridicule.'

'I don't care what other people do or say,' Beth replied doggedly.

'Your da would've—' Cissie began, but Roy cut her off.

'Da's not here any more. I make the decisions now.'

Cissie bowed her head. 'It's a terrible disgrace,' she whispered.

'I can't let you have it, Beth,' Roy said flatly. 'There's Margaret and her family to consider.'

'Oh yes, the big churchgoers.' Beth smiled cynically. 'What was it Jesus said? Suffer little children to come unto me. I wasn't aware he differentiated between those born in wedlock and those born outside it.'

'Don't try to twist things,' Roy snapped.

'That's precisely what I'm not doing. On the contrary, I'm trying to clarify the situation. Isn't it the Church, or so many of the hypocrites who attend it, who twist things?

In other words, if I pretend what's happened hasn't, have an abortion, and continue to appear to be upright and pure, then that's all right, I'm still acceptable? Whereas if I don't commit murder, which abortion is as far as I'm concerned, and go ahead and have this little human being now inside me, and love and cherish it, itself a product of love, then I'm not acceptable.'

'You're better with words than me, always have been, but that doesn't alter matters. You'll go and see this doctor with me or else you're out. I completely wash my hands of you.'

'No, son!' Cissie exclaimed, anguished.

'You'll actually throw me out?' Beth said.

Roy nodded.

'Your own sister?'

'I warned you, Beth, repeatedly. I did everything I could to prevent this from happening. Now, one way or the other, you accept the consequences. The choice is up to you.'

'God must weep in his heaven when he hears and sees what's done in his name,' Beth said softly.

'You'd better pack a case.'

'Surely she can stay till morning, at least?' Cissie pleaded.

'I won't have a slut sharing my roof, and that's that.'

Beth laughed, amazed and astounded by his values, which were so double-sided as to border on the farcical. 'I used to think you were a big man. Well, now I can see I was wrong. Steve might have been small in size, but when it came to doing the right thing he was double – no, three times – the man you are. He wouldn't have gone by what neighbours, or his fiancée's sanctimonious family, thought. He'd have done what he considered to be right. Do you think what you're doing to me is that?'

Roy turned away, unable to keep looking her straight in the eye. 'I'll give you a few quid so you can book into an hotel tonight. After that you'll have to fend for yourself.'

'Take your few quid and stick it where you sit.'

'Beth! Don't be so crude,' Cissie admonished her.

Beth fixed her brother with a glare. 'And to think Steve was killed defending the likes of you. It makes me want to puke.'

Roy left the room.

Cissie took Beth in her arms and they stood hugging one another, Cissie crying while Beth wondered what on earth she was going to do. Finally she extricated herself and began to pack.

When she'd finished, and changed, she said goodbye to her sobbing mother. Going into the hallway she found Roy waiting for her with a hand outstretched.

'I'll have our key, please. And the Carmichaels'. You won't be needing either again.'

Moments later she was out in the street.

Chapter 8

Beth had never been in Matron's office before, and was sure she never would be again, for she knew why she'd been summoned here and what was coming. There was a primness about the room very much in keeping with the sort of person Matron was: everything neat, tidy and looking as though it might have been sterilised.

'Sit down, Somerville.' Matron had made a brisk entrance and seated herself behind her desk before she raised her eyes to stare disapprovingly at Beth. She came straight to the point. 'You're pregnant.'

It was August and Beth was five months gone. She was surprised she'd got away with it for so long, as it was now quite obvious she was expecting.

'Yes, I am.'

Matron frowned, her lips thinning into a downward curve. 'At least you aren't trying to deny it.'

Beth gave a low laugh. 'That would be pretty pointless, wouldn't you say? Anyone with half an eye in their head can see what's what.'

Matron didn't laugh back, but then she was the type of woman who rarely saw humour in any situation. 'You realise I have to dismiss you?'

Beth nodded. It was standard practice.

'Which is a pity, as you're a very good nurse.'

'Thank you.'

Matron leaned back in her chair to study Beth. 'Are you getting married?'

'No.'

'Do you know who the father is?'

That angered Beth. 'Of course I do.'

'Then why won't he marry you?'

'He's dead,' Beth said baldly.

'Oh, I'm sorry,' Matron muttered, a little of the wind taken out of her sails.

'We were to be married last month, only . . .' She trailed off. It still gave her incredible pain to think of Steve. 'He was killed first.'

'A soldier?'

'Royal Air Force pilot. A hero of the Battle of Britain. One of The Few.'

Matron opened the folder in front of her and read the top sheet of its contents. 'It states here that you recently moved into the nurses' home.'

'My brother threw me out of the house when he learned I was going to have a baby.'

'Your brother?'

'My father was killed last year fighting with the Black Watch.'

Matron chewed her lip. 'You haven't exactly had an easy time of it recently, have you?'

Beth didn't reply, mesmerised by the faint fluttering, like the moving wings of a butterfly, in her stomach. It was the first time she'd felt the baby. 'So when do I leave?' she asked, bringing her attention back to Matron.

'Friday at the latest. You'll have to vacate your room at the nurses' home at the same time, I'm afraid. Have you anywhere to go?'

Beth shook her head. 'Not yet. I have been looking for a place for several weeks now, knowing this interview was inevitable. So far I haven't had any luck.'

Matron closed the folder and pushed it to one side. 'What I can't understand is why a good girl, as you obviously are, allowed herself to get pregnant in the first place. If you were going to be married why not wait until then to sleep with him?'

Beth couldn't help but smile. She thought it was typical of a dried-up old spinster to ask such a question – a question of the mind and not the body. It was the question of a woman who'd never been so much in love that all else was swept aside, completely forgotten in an all-consuming blaze of passion that was its own master, acknowledging no other. 'We were in love,' she said simply.

'I presumed that. But couldn't you have waited?'

She could sit here all day trying to explain it, and Matron would never, could never, understand. The very fact that she had to ask the question told Beth so. 'I suppose people do things in wartime they wouldn't do otherwise.'

Matron nodded. That made sense to her. It didn't justify Somerville's behaviour, but it did make sense. 'Well, if it was absolutely essential for you to sleep with your young man, you should have taken precautions,' she said matter-of-factly.

'The best laid schemes of mice and lovers . . .' Beth paraphrased Robert Burns.

Matron wasn't quite sure what to make of that, so didn't comment. Instead, she explained the procedures Beth would have to go through when leaving the hospital, not all of which Beth took in.

The baby was moving again, and as far as Beth was concerned that was the most important thing in the world.

Beth sat in an austere anteroom twisting the brand new wedding ring she was wearing. This would be the sixth factor she'd been to see and she'd learned her lesson. Unmarried mothers, and unmarried mothers to be, just didn't figure in the scheme of things when it came to house allocations. So she'd decided to change her status to Mrs Ramsay, widow.

There was a fat woman facing her who might have been the original model for a certain line of seaside postcards. Beth couldn't help but smile to herself as the comparison occurred to her.

'I know he's got a house going today,' the woman whispered to her companion, a sly-looking middle-aged female whose face seemed to be set in a permanent shifty scowl.

'Is that a fact?' Slyboots replied, wriggling even closer to the fat woman.

'Oh aye! I had it off Mr Carruth the butcher. You know him with the funny leg over in Hagland Street?'

'I know him all right. It's always a couple of ounces under, never over with him.'

'Well, be that as it may,' Fatty steamrollered on. 'He hears all sorts in the shop, you see. And he told me personally that an old biddy round the corner from him kicked it a few days ago. The factor took possession of the key yesterday afternoon from her son down from Arbroath to bury his ma.'

'I'm desperate, just desperate, for a wee house of my own,' Slyboots stated. 'Ever since Vi, my sister's eldest, gave birth to twins there's been no peace in our place. I've got to get out or I'll be driven off my head so I will. I've never heard weans cry like them. Morning, noon and night with hardly a rest. And you can't move for nappies. The damn things are everywhere.'

'It can be a sore trial living with relatives right enough,' Fatty agreed, launching into a litany of her own problems, which seemed to be mainly to do with rats.

A house definitely available, Beth thought, having been earwigging. She just *had* to have it, for it was Thursday afternoon and tomorrow she was due to leave the hospital with nowhere to go. True enough, an old school pal had said she'd be welcome at their house for a few days, an offer she'd take up if she had to. But what she needed was a permanent solution to her problem.

'Next, please!' the receptionist called out, sticking her head round the door that connected the anteroom with the corridor beyond. Fatty started to lumber to her feet, but Beth was quicker.

'That's me,' she replied, and was through the door like a shot, leaving the fat woman gawping after her.

Mr McLure was a small, pasty-faced man with a bald

head and horn-rimmed glasses. He took Beth's form, which she'd filled out in the anteroom, and told her to sit.

Slowly he read the form through. Then he pursed his lips. 'You appreciate how bad the housing situation is in Glasgow nowadays, I presume?'

Beth nodded. 'I've been everywhere. You're my last hope.'

'Oh, dear me. I'm sure you're exaggerating!' He gave a thin, dry, reedy laugh.

Beth took out a handkerchief and started to wind and rewind it round her hands, allowing just a hint of moisture to creep into her eyes. 'I'm a nurse and my hospital is throwing me out on the street tomorrow because I'm expecting.'

'That is unfortunate.'

'My husband was killed last month. He was a hero, Mr McLure. One of The Few. The RAF transferred him back to Scotland earlier this year, which was when we met up again. We'd been orphans in the same orphanage, you see, and got married—'

'Orphans, eh?' Mr McLure broke in.

'Steve was an abandoned baby while my parents both died of TB when I was an infant. As I had no relatives who wanted me I ended up in the orphanage, where I was reared till I was old enough to leave and start training as a nurse.'

The tears were in full flow now. At the back of her mind it surprised her how easy she was finding it to mix lies with the truth. And what whoppers they were!

'I suppose Steve and I were always in love,' she went on, 'but we thought we'd never see one another again when he went off to join the RAF. When he reappeared out of the blue that was it. We went to Gretna Green and got married.'

'And then he was killed?'

'He was on U-boat patrol and came upon a surfaced pack of them. He managed to sink two of them before his plane was so badly shot up he had to break off the action. At that point he should have ditched, but his entire crew, apart from himself, was injured and he knew some of them would never survive in the water. So he brought his plane back to land and had them bail out there, only he didn't get a chance to follow them. Steve was killed when the plane crashed into what had been a golf course.'

'And his crew?'

'They all survived.'

'That's an awful story. And a terribly brave one,' Mr McLure declared, shaking his head. 'I have two sons in the army myself, you know.'

Beth's hanky was so sodden she could've wrung it out. Nor were the tears all crocodile ones, albeit they'd started out as such. There was too much truth in her tale for that. 'I hope your boys come through this in one piece.'

'Thank you, Mrs Ramsay. That's kind of you.'

She shuddered. 'If I'm homeless, Mr McLure, I'll have to throw myself on the authorities, which means they might take my baby away from me when the wee mite is finally born. I couldn't stand that – my baby being put into care, or an orphanage even. To go through what his mother and father had to. In fact I'd rather . . .' She broke off to bite her lip. 'No, I mustn't even think of that. It would be so wrong.'

Mr McLure looked at her in horror. Her implication wasn't lost on him.

'I'll take anything. Anything at all you can offer me,' she pleaded.

He cleared his throat. 'As it happens, you've struck lucky. I had a house come available yesterday, the first for three weeks. It's not much, mind you, a single end with stairhead closet—'

'I'll take it,' she interrupted.

'The rent's eight shillings a week. Can you afford that?'

'The rent's just fine. I'll be signing on the unemployment and I have a little money of my own put by. Combined, that should carry me over till I can find another job.'

'Like houses, jobs are hard to come by,' he pointed out.

'I'll find one. And the rent will be paid on the dot every week. You have my word on that. If I fall behind for even one week you can turf me out and I swear there won't be a squeak of protest on my part.'

He opened a drawer to take out a largish iron key. 'Number twenty-one Sweet Street. You have to pay two weeks in advance.'

She accepted the key, and handed over a pound note. He gave her her change, then filled out her rent book while she mopped her face as best she could with the sodden handkerchief.

'To be paid every Friday to my receptionist,' he said, laying the rent book in front of her. She picked it up, clutching it to her bosom as she thanked him profusely. He replied that he was only too pleased to be in a position to help. She had risen to leave when he said, 'Your husband sounds to have been quite a man, Mrs Ramsay. I wish I could've shaken his hand.'

As Beth passed through the anteroom on her way out, the fat woman glared furiously at her, but she didn't care. She had a house to herself and to bring her baby home to when it was born. That was all that mattered.

On leaving the factor's she caught a tram to Hagland Street, which was a short but busy thoroughfare lined with shops of all descriptions and a great many pubs. She found Sweet Street without difficulty.

It was an old, completely neglected street. Originally of grey stone, the tenements were now soot-blackened and crumbling. Several chimney pots leaned drunkenly, and from where she was standing she could see about a dozen broken windows either boarded up or blocked off with cardboard. Most of the children playing on the pavements and in the gutters were barefoot, although one little ragamuffin was making an incredible din as he clattered around in wooden clogs. The slum smell was all-pervasive: a combination of unwashed bodies, general dirt and squalor, human and animal excretions, and a certain unidentifiable something else which once smelt was never forgotten.

Beth had never lived in conditions such as these. She was working class, but she came from a decent neighbourhood. Outside No. 21 she glanced up to find an Irish-looking woman staring curiously back at her from the window out of which she was hanging watching the passing scene in the time-honoured tradition. The woman smiled, displaying a mouth with many missing teeth, and Beth smiled in return before hurrying into the close.

She climbed the filthy stairs to discover her single end, a one-roomed apartment, on the third flight. Then she went back down half a flight to have a look at the stairhead closet she'd be sharing with the three other households on her landing. What she saw was unsavoury to say the least.

The WC stank appallingly. The cistern was leaking, while the walls were so damp that the plaster came away when you touched it. Dropping her gaze, she noted a number of large black beetles scurrying round the bottom of the pedestal. She promised herself there and then she'd never put this WC to the use for which it was intended. Instead she'd get hold of a chamber pot and do her business in that, conveying the contents here to be flushed away.

Returning to her door, she inserted the iron key. It turned noisily in the rusty lock. The room was about fourteen feet square, with a sink and window at one end and a cavity bed at the other. Crossing to the window, she stared out on to what would've been a back green had the grass been allowed to grow, but was in fact a devastation of churned-up earth and scattered refuse. There were also some air raid shelters of a different design from those she was used to, these being smaller, with corrugated iron roofs.

An examination of the room's walls showed them to be dry, which was a tremendous relief. She'd been expecting the worst after the stairhead closet. Nor were there any beetles in evidence. There was a mattress on the bed, probably where the old biddy had died, which she'd get rid of at the first opportunity.

Beth stood in the centre of the room and gazed about her. Eight bob a week for this was daylight robbery. However, that was the way things were, and beggars, even paying ones, couldn't afford to be choosy. There were dozens of others who'd gladly snap this up at the price.

She thought through the items of furniture she'd bought at the Crown Showrooms, currently in storage, deciding what she'd keep and what she'd have re-auctioned. Sale of the latter would realise a few more pounds for her kitty, which would be most welcome in the circumstances.

She recalled seeing a café in Hagland Street with a sign in its window saying it had a public telephone. She'd go round there now and ring the Crown Showrooms to make the necessary arrangements. After that she'd return to the hospital to pack.

The café was reasonably neat and clean inside, appearing to be as much a cheap restaurant as a café. Beth bought coffee from the pleasant middle-aged woman behind the counter and took her cup over to a table, where she left it while she went to the telephone situated in an alcove at the rear.

As she was talking to the Crown Showrooms she saw a stoutish middle-aged man wearing an apron coming out of a door behind the counter. She was just hanging up when a scream rang out.

She and the couple were the only ones in the café. It was the woman who'd screamed, and Beth started running towards her when she saw a spurt of bright arterial blood

136

arc over the counter to fall spattering on the linoleum floor. The man was frozen, staring at his wife, who was clutching her wrist from which the blood was spurting.

Beth snatched up a tea towel as she ran behind the counter. Elbowing the man to one side, she quickly wound it round the woman's arm just above the wound, twisting it tighter and tighter to make a tourniquet.

'The knife somehow slipped,' the woman gasped. 'I was making sandwiches and it somehow sort of slipped.'

'Call an ambulance and tell them it's an emergency,' Beth said to the man. He just looked at her, his face filled with incomprehension. 'Call an ambulance,' she repeated.

When he neither replied or made to move she kicked him hard on the shin. 'Call an ambulance!' she yelled.

That had the desired effect, and he snapped out of it. 'Yes, of course. Understood,' he said. Turning, he ran back up the length of the café.

The spurting blood was reduced to a leak, then a dribble, and finally stopped altogether as Beth tied the tourniquet off.

'It's an awfully stupid thing to do. I feel quite ashamed at the trouble I'm causing,' the injured woman apologised. Beth let her rattle on while she used another tea towel to bind the actual wound itself. As she did so, the husband returned to announce that an ambulance was on its way.

'Good,' Beth replied. 'Now get me a blanket. The thickest one you've got.'

The doorbell tinkled to admit another customer, a man in working clothes and a cloth cap. 'What's to do then, Edna?' he asked the woman.

When the wrist was bound as neatly as Beth could manage, she called the worker round to help her, and together they assisted Edna to a hard-backed wooden chair at the nearest table. The husband, huffing and puffing, reappeared carrying a cream-coloured blanket which Beth wrapped round his wife, explaining that it was imperative for Edna to be kept warm.

'I'll keep an eye out for the ambulance,' the working man declared, and went back out into the street. The husband consoled Edna, who was now in shock, while Beth checked the wound every so often to ensure it hadn't started to bleed again. The ambulance seemed an awfully long time in coming, but eventually, much to Beth's relief, it could be heard approaching, its bell clamouring in the distance.

While the worker was guiding the ambulance to the right spot, Beth got Edna on to her feet and out on to the pavement. The husband locked up behind them.

Beth told the ambulancemen what had happened and what she'd done as they helped Edna into the rear of the vehicle and made her lie down on a stretcher bed. Her husband joined her in the ambulance, and one of the ambulancemen stayed with them while the other slammed the rear doors and ran round to the driving seat. Then, with a couple of children shouting and laughing behind it, the ambulance clanged off.

'If it's not one thing it's another,' the working man said to Beth, shaking his head. Beth agreed, thinking that she could certainly have done with that cup of coffee now. With a brief word of thanks, she headed for the nearest tramstop, and promptly forgot the incident.

*   *   *

It was two and a half weeks since Beth had moved into Sweet Street and in that time she had worked wonders with her single end. She'd got hold of some yellow distemper and had completely transformed the walls and ceiling, which together with her furniture gave the room a warm, cosy feel.

She was making girdle scones on the second-hand cooker she'd managed to acquire when there was a knock on the door. A glance at the clock told her that Cissie was right on time. Her mother had always been a great believer in punctuality, saying it was inbred in her generation.

Beth opened the door and gave Cissie a hug, which was warmly returned.

'Come away through, Ma.' Beth took her mother by the arm and drew her into the room.

Cissie nodded her approval while Beth hurried over to the cooker to attend to the scones. 'You've done well with it, lass.'

'It's amazing what a wee bit of elbow grease can do.'

'Don't belittle yourself. There's far more to making a place nice than that, as you well know.'

Beth helped her mother off with her coat and laid it on the cavity bed. 'Tea will be up in a jiffy.'

Cissie settled herself into a comfy chair. 'It fair relieved me to get your letter and know you were all right.'

'I knew you'd be worried.'

'I didn't sleep a night through till that letter arrived. It was a load off my mind to learn you'd got your own wee house and were settling in.'

'If I'd had my pick I certainly wouldn't have come to Maryhill. But I was lucky to get even this.'

'Aye, the housing shortage has been dreadful of late, which is why Roy and Margaret have decided they'll be living with me after they get married in February.'

'Why then?'

Cissie shrugged. 'I've no idea. Roy never said. He just came in and announced that was the date for it. He did ask my permission about moving Margaret in, mind you. I could hardly say no.'

'You did right, Ma.'

Cissie looked sad, and a little morose. 'I had hoped that when he got married he'd move out and you'd move back in. Not to be, it seems.'

'Would that really have worked, Ma? I mean, what about the neighbours?'

'They know now you're expecting.'

'Have any of them been nasty about it to you?'

Cissie shook her head. 'There have been a few veiled comments, though nothing you could call nasty. What beats me is how they found out. Roy and I have certainly never mentioned it to anyone.'

Beth gave a low laugh. 'That's easily answered. Quite a lot of the girls at the hospital knew I was expecting. It only takes one of them to open her mouth for it to spread like wildfire.'

'Aye, I'm sure that's right.' Cissie nodded.

Beth took the scones from the griddle and cut them in half. 'No butter, I'm afraid. Just some scrapings of marge.'

'It'll be a treat all the same. You always were a grand baker.'

Beth poured the tea and handed a cup to her mother,

with a scone. 'Before I forget, there are two things of mine I'd like from home. I'd be obliged if you'd bring them next time you come.'

'And what are they, lass?'

'One-eyed Suzie and my scraps.'

Cissie smiled. 'I won't forget.'

'Thanks, Ma.'

'So,' Cissie said, taking a deep breath. 'How are you within yourself?'

'Physically I'm blooming. Couldn't be better. But mentally . . . well, Steve and I might not have known one another all that long but I miss him as though we'd been married twenty years or more.'

'I appreciate how you feel,' Cissie said quietly. 'Your da and I never had much money, particularly those years he was idle when things were really bad. We had each other, though, and as long as that was so we felt we wanted for nothing. We had some right happy times together, many of them just sitting at home talking to one another after you and Roy had gone to bed.'

'Would you ever contemplate marrying again?' Beth queried. At forty-four Cissie was still a relatively young woman.

Cissie shook her head. 'Your da and I went through too much together for me to take another man. But then we had all those years of married life which you and Steve didn't. In other words, no matter how deeply you feel the loss of Steve now, you're the one who should be open to the idea of someone else in time.'

'Perhaps. In time, as you say, who knows what might happen?'

Cissie was satisfied. She'd come determined to make the point, and Beth's question had given her the perfect opportunity to do so. 'You haven't found a job then, I take it?'

'I've been out trying every day. In fact I was at a factory close by here early on this morning. It's the same old tale, though. If they do have something available they won't give it to a female who's pregnant.'

'So how are you managing?'

'I have my money from the unemployment. The rest comes from some furniture I sold which belonged to Steve and me. Also I was able to put a little by when I was at the hospital.'

'What happens if that runs out and you still haven't got a job?'

Beth pulled a face. 'I try not to even think about that.'

'Maybe I could—'

'No, Ma,' Beth cut in.

They stared at one another. 'Roy earns a decent wage packet,' Cissie said slowly.

But Beth was defiant. 'I won't take a penny piece that originates from him, and that's the end of it.'

'What he gives me in housekeeping is mine to use as I see fit.'

'No!'

Cissie sighed. 'Suit yourself then.' She'd been hoping Beth would accept a weekly contribution, but she should have known better. Beth was Beth.

'By the way,' Cissie went on. 'I was in the Co-op last week and couldn't help but overhear a conversation about a family who'd lost one son with the Royals and another with the air force.'

'And?' Beth prompted.

'Have you seen the Ramsays since Steve was killed?'

'No, for they didn't even know about Steve and me. Steve intended to tell them after we got married. As far as they were concerned I was still Teddy's girl – or had been up until Teddy's death, anyway.'

'Don't you think they should know they're going to have a grandchild?'

'Just what was it you heard, Ma?'

'That the father suffered a stroke on hearing about Steve and is now paralysed down one side. The mother's looking after him at home, though apparently she's not the woman she was, having faded away to almost nothing.'

'Teddy's death hit them hard. Steve's must've destroyed them.'

'So are you going to tell them about the baby?'

Beth thought about it then shook her head. 'A bastard on top of all their other problems? I don't see them being overjoyed by that news, somehow.'

Cissie finished her tea and laid her cup on the floor. 'I hope you've made the right decision. You know them, after all. I don't.'

When they kissed each other goodbye, Cissie said, 'I saw many things for you in life, Beth, but not this.'

Beth gave a wry smile. 'Neither did I, Ma. Neither did I.'

Chapter 9

Beth got off the tram in Hagland Street, being careful not to slip on the wet cobblestones as she made her way to the pavement. It had been raining non-stop for two days now.

She was in the depths of depression, feeling almost at the end of her tether. She had known it was going to be difficult finding a job, but that difficulty was turning out to be a sheer impossibility.

It was nothing to do with the social stigma of being pregnant and unmarried since to all intents and purposes she was Mrs Ramsay. It was the fact that she *was* expecting that was the stopping block. One look at her swollen belly and that was it. A little bit of polite chit-chat, to show willing, and she was back out of the door again.

Despair welled through her like a great black cloud. What in God's name was she going to do! She was down to the last pound of her own money and after that all she would have was her unemployment, which was not even enough to cover the rent.

She daren't throw herself on the mercy of the authorities. What she'd told Mr McLure was a real fear: if she went to them they might decide she was unfit to keep the baby when it was born. That nightmare had haunted her during the past few weeks.

She passed a hand over her face. Six months gone and every passing day lessening her chances of finding a job. There must be something available somewhere, she assured herself. There just had to be!

She jumped as thunder rolled overhead, close on the heels of a long streak of jagged lightning. The rain increased in intensity, bouncing back inches off the pavement. On the spur of the moment Beth decided to treat herself to a cup of coffee, and turned into the café where the woman had cut her wrist.

This time the place was busy, most of the tables occupied by people eating their dinner. 'Coffee, please,' she said, noticing that the woman behind the counter was still wearing a bandage round her wrist.

Several chaps glanced at her and self-consciously she touched her hair. I must look like a half-drowned cat, she thought. Not at all a pretty sight.

She paid for the coffee and smiled at the woman, who smiled in return. She was just about to go in search of a seat when the woman suddenly recognised her. 'It's you, isn't it, hen? The lass who helped me that day I cut myself?'

'You seem to be well recovered.'

The woman slapped Beth's money back in front of her. 'You're certainly not paying for the coffee, and that's a fact.'

'Why, thank you.'

'Now just you wait here a minute.' With that, the woman scooted through the door behind the counter. Edna, Beth recollected. That was the woman's name. It had come back to her now.

Edna reappeared with her husband, who was wiping his hands on his apron. His face was wreathed in smiles as he took hold of Beth's right hand and pumped it up and down. 'We've been hoping you'd come back so we could thank you proper like for what you did that day.'

'I'm only pleased I could help.'

'Edna would've died if it hadn't been for you. The doctor told me so at the hospital.'

'Are you a nurse?' Edna asked.

'I was until recently.'

The man nodded. 'That explains it, then. The doctor said you obviously knew what you were doing.'

'Would you care for something to eat with that coffee? A couple of fried eggs, perhaps, or we have some real mutton pies?' Edna said.

A *couple* of fried eggs! Why, eggs were like gold dust. And real mutton pies! She hadn't seen one of those in well over a year. 'I am rather peckish, now you come to mention it.'

'Right then. You sit down and leave it to me.' The man beamed and disappeared through the kitchen door again.

Beth sat at a table across from two working men. Both had grimy faces and hard, calloused hands, and one of them was slurping tea from his saucer. The tea-slurper's mate belched, pushed his plate aside and stood up. Within the space of a few minutes the café emptied, leaving Beth the sole remaining customer. 'They all work round about,'

Edna explained, joining Beth with two fresh cups of coffee. 'When are you due?'

'December. Just before Christmas.'

'You're new around here, aren't you? Colin and I had never seen you before the day of the accident.'

'I've only recently taken over a single end in Sweet Street.'

'Has your husband got himself a job in the area then?'

Beth glanced down into her coffee. 'My husband was killed two months ago. He was in the RAF.'

'Oh, I am sorry,' Edna sympathised. 'And you expecting and all. Isn't that a tragedy.'

'Yes,' Beth whispered.

'How long were you married for?'

'It would be just over seven months now,' Beth lied smoothly.

Edna shook her head. 'There have been lots of good blokes from this neighbourhood who went away and won't be coming back, many of them not even out of their teens. It's a crying shame, so it is.'

Colin appeared carrying a plate which he laid in front of Beth. On it were two fried eggs, four rashers of thickly cut bacon, three sausages and a quartered tomato. 'Would you like some bread and butter?' he asked.

'That would be absolutely smashing,' she replied with a grin. Butter on top of all this! Butter simply hadn't been available of late, not for love or money.

'Being in the trade we get things, you understand,' Edna explained as Colin went back behind the counter. 'And you certainly deserve a wee treat after what you did for me.'

'Hardly a wee treat. More a slap-up feast,' Beth declared,

tucking into eggs and bacon. She paused, fork halfway to her mouth, to stare in utter astonishment at the soup bowl filled to the brim with butter that Colin placed beside her plate, next to another plate on which were half a dozen slices of bread.

'The lassie's just lost her husband,' Edna told him.

His face creased with concern. 'I'm awfully sorry to hear that.'

'RAF,' Edna said.

'A Battle of Britain pilot,' Beth added automatically.

'Well, well,' Colin murmured, obviously impressed.

'I made Colin get rid of that knife. I couldn't bring myself to use it again after what happened,' Edna said. 'Gave me the willies even to look at it.'

'I made a present of it to the butcher down the street.' Colin nodded.

'How is the wrist?' Beth asked.

'I'm going to have a bit of a scar, but far better that than dead, eh?' Too late, she remembered Beth's recent bereavement. 'Oh, I am sorry!'

'That's all right.' Beth smiled.

'She's living in Sweet Street. A single end,' Edna informed her husband.

'Number twenty-one,' Beth elaborated.

'You must be in what was Granny Liddell's house,' Colin mused.

'An old biddy who passed away?'

'Aye, that's the place.'

Colin and Edna watched Beth as she polished off the remains of her meal, mopping up the yolk with bread, unwilling to waste any of it.

'Would you like some more?' Colin asked when she had finished. 'How about one of those mutton pies I mentioned?'

It was just too good an opportunity to pass up. 'Could I?'

'Coming right up.'

'We always wanted a family, but we were never blessed,' Edna sighed. 'Something you have to reconcile yourself to in the end, I suppose.'

Beth and Edna chatted about babies till Colin returned with the pie. The steam curling from the hole in its top gave off a tantalising aroma. 'The genuine, unadulterated article,' he declared. 'We know the baker – he's a long-standing pal of mine.'

'Hmm!' Beth murmured on taking her first mouthful. 'It's absolutely delicious. Exactly as I remember them from before the war.'

A serious expression settled on Colin's face. 'I completely seized up that time of the accident. I could see Edna was badly hurt but for some reason I couldn't move a muscle to help. Not until you shouted at me. If I'd been on my own she would've . . . right there in front of me . . .' He trailed off and shook his head. 'If there's ever anything I can do to try to repay what we owe you, all you need do is ask.'

Beth sat back fractionally to stare at him. 'There is one thing I'm desperately in need of.'

'What's that?'

'A job.' She indicated her swollen stomach. 'No one will entertain the idea of employing me because of this. And when I say I'm desperate I'm not exaggerating. At the moment I don't even have enough coming in to pay the rent.'

'A job?' Colin repeated. His eyes flicked from Beth to Edna and back again.

'Can you think of anyone who might be able to give me a start? I'm willing to do almost anything. And I'm a hard worker.' She laughed mirthlessly. 'That's something nurses learn early on, I can assure you.'

Edna nodded her approval, having already guessed what was in her husband's mind.

'We can get pretty frantic in here dinner times, that being by far our busiest period,' Colin said slowly. 'Up until now Edna and I have coped by ourselves. But an extra pair of hands would make things an awful lot easier. It's the serving up and clearing the plates away that takes the time and where we could use the help.'

'You could start an hour and a half before dinner time and assist the pair of us,' Edna chipped in. 'Then, after the dinner hour, you could do the same again, which would mean four hours a day, Monday to Saturday.'

Beth closed her eyes. Relief had temporarily drained all her energy, and she was suddenly totally exhausted.

'Are you sure that won't be too much for you in your condition?' Colin asked.

'No, no, I'll manage,' Beth replied quickly. 'What would the pay be?'

Colin pursed his lips while he thought about it. 'Would twelve and six be all right?'

'Och, don't be a meany. Add another bob,' Edna urged him.

Colin grinned. 'Thirteen and six then. Does that suit?'

'If the customers take a shine to you you'll pick up a tip or two on a Friday,' Edna said. 'Unfortunately it'll only be a few coppers, as being working folk they've hellish little to spare.'

'They seemed a friendly enough bunch from what I saw.'

'Oh, they are that. Salt of the earth. A lot of the men work at the gasworks nearby, others at the wee distillery up the street. The lassies are mostly employed by the munitions factory in Garscad Road.'

'I know the one you mean. I tried to get work there myself but they turned me down.'

'A munitions factory is hardly the place for a pregnant woman,' Colin said reprovingly.

Beth shrugged. 'As I told you, I've been desperate.'

'So when can you start?' Edna enquired.

'Would tomorrow be too soon?'

'Tomorrow would be just dandy,' said Colin. He extended his hand and he and Beth shook on it.

'There will be a free dinner for you every day after you've finished,' Edna added.

Beth glanced out of the café window to see rain still hammering down out of a now almost black sky. But as far as she was concerned the sun was shining brightly, and directly on to her.

Edna peered at her watch. 'Any moment now and the distillery chaps will be here. They're the closest so they're first in and last out. Next are the men from the gasworks, with the munitions lassies a few minutes after that.'

Beth hadn't thought she'd be nervous, but she was. She

wiped her palms on the sides of her apron while in her mind she went over everything she'd been told about menu and prices. The door banged open and half a dozen hungry-looking men came bursting in, scrambling for what they considered to be the best seats.

'Here we go,' Beth muttered to Edna. Fixing a smile on her face, she came out from behind the counter.

Ten minutes later the café was full. Beth took orders and dispensed meals as quickly as she could, but she failed to notice a late arrival, sitting at an out-of-the-way table, who was vainly trying to catch her attention.

'Fucking hell!' he growled. At six feet he was an exceptionally tall man by Glasgow standards, and was inevitably known to all and sundry as Tiny Tommy. 'Hey, you – the bloody waddling waitress!' he called out in a very loud voice.

Somebody laughed, while somebody else choked on what he'd been in the process of swallowing. The hum of conversation died, and everyone waited to see what would happen.

Beth stopped and glanced across to where the voice had come from to find Tiny Tommy glaring at her.

'I've been here so long my stomach's beginning to think my throat's been cut,' he complained belligerently.

Edna decided not to intervene. Beth had to learn to handle this sort of thing if she was to survive in the job.

Beth realised it was a make or break moment for her. Either she dominated the customers, or they ruled her, and which it was to be could well depend entirely on what she did next.

She considered just ignoring Tiny Tommy, but thought

better of it. A face to face confrontation was necessary here. She made her way over to his table. 'You bellowed?' she said sweetly.

'Fucking right. I want some dinner.'

She was well aware that every eye in the café was focused on her, every ear tuned in her direction. 'What can I get you then, you smooth-talking bastard?'

'Don't you speak to me like that!' he exclaimed, half rising out of his seat.

God, he was a big brute, she thought, and hard as nails with it. But she didn't back off or show any sign of fear. That would've been fatal. 'All right, if you afford me the same courtesy,' she replied quietly.

He grunted, and sank back into his seat. 'What's the scoff the day?'

'Spam fritters. Bubble and squeak. Toad in the hole.'

'What's in the toad?'

'Breadcrumbs.'

'No sausage meat?'

'Not even a sniff of it.'

'Spam fritters then. There *is* Spam in the fritters, I take it?'

She raised an eyebrow.

'All right, all right! Don't spoil it for me. Just serve up the fritters!'

She turned away, warm inside from the knowledge that she'd won. She was halfway back up the café when Tiny Tommy shouted after her.

'And you still bloody waddle!'

The café dissolved, but Beth didn't mind. This time the jibe had been good-natured – affectionate, almost.

She accentuated her waddling, swinging her hips provocatively, and earned a rousing cheer and a few handclaps.

'Nice bum,' Tiny Tommy whispered to his neighbour, who wholeheartedly agreed.

It was the Friday afternoon of Beth's first week at the café, and she was just about to sit down to her free dinner. Before doing so she wanted to find out how much she'd collected in tips.

From her apron pocket she took out a handful of small change, and then another, and placed both on the table in front of her. She started to count.

'How did you do?' Colin joined her, carrying a bowl of soup.

Eyes shining, she looked round at him. 'Five and ten.'

He whistled. 'That *is* good. They've obviously taken to you.'

'I got one sixpence. Believe it or not, from Tiny Tommy.' They burst out laughing together.

She was a success at the job, she told herself. There could be no doubt about it. Not when Tiny Tommy gave her a tanner.

The first explosion happened at a few minutes past midnight, waking Beth from a sound sleep. Groggily she brought herself into a leaning position, it being impossible to sit up in a cavity bed. A second explosion followed the first, this one close enough to cause the entire building to shake.

It must be a raid, she thought. Swinging her legs over the side of the bed, she reached for her coat, which doubled as a dressing gown. She shivered. It was the beginning of December and bitterly cold; snow had been threatening for over a week now.

She slipped on a pair of woolly socks she kept ready for getting up in the morning. Padding over to the window, she glanced at the sky, thinking she might see silhouettes of the attacking German planes. But there were no silhouettes, only a fierce red glow which reminded her of the glow often tinting the sky above the steelworks where her brother Roy worked.

A third explosion went off, a dull cracking sound which gave her a brief pain in both ears.

Confused, she decided it would be best to get dressed. Closing the blackout curtains, she crossed to the nearest gas lamp and lit it, but the lamp only stayed lit for a few moments before petering out and dying altogether. The gas was off. What a damned nuisance! As she struggled into her clothes, she heard the strident clang of a fire engine, then another, coming from what sounded like a different direction.

Normally she didn't mind at all being alone, but in these circumstances she found it both scary and worrying. She gritted her teeth as the baby kicked her hard. When she was dressed she hunted for a candle, then decided to have another look out of the window before lighting it. She made a chink in the blackout curtains and peered out. The sky was even redder than it had been, while over to the right licking flames were coming from a rooftop.

Beth lit the candle, then worried a nail. What best to do? Stay here, or go down to the street and try to find out what was going on?

The sound of talking came from the stairs, two female voices and a male one speaking in low, urgent tones. She decided to go out to ask if they knew what was happening. Since there were no blackout curtains on the stairhead windows she blew out her candle before opening the door, to be confronted by three huddled shapes on the landing.

'Hello? It's Mrs Ramsay. Who's that?'

'Mary O'Malley and her husband Seamus,' a female voice replied.

'And their daughter Kathleen,' a younger female voice added, clearly piqued at being omitted.

Mary O'Malley was the Irish woman who'd been hanging out of her window the day Beth had arrived in Sweet Street. She lived in the house across the landing from Beth, though they'd never spoken as such, only nodded politely to one another when passing in the close or in the street. The O'Malleys had a large brood of children of whom, at sixteen, Kathleen was the oldest.

'Is it a raid, do you know?' Beth asked.

'No, missus, it's nothing like that. I've had a word with the ARP warden and he told me these explosions are coming from the gasworks,' Seamus O'Malley replied in a thick Irish accent.

That explained why the gas was off, Beth thought. 'I saw flames—'

'The entire street up that way's afire,' Seamus cut in excitedly.

Beth pondered that piece of information. 'The distillery isn't far from there, is it?'

'Or the munitions factory,' said Kathleen.

Beth's mouth was suddenly bone dry. If the latter went

up the entire district would be devastated, with casualties running into thousands.

'Listen!' Kathleen exclaimed. Off in the distance could be heard the approaching clamour of more fire engines.

'The blessed saints protect us!' Mary O'Malley murmured, crossing herself.

Coming from a Presbyterian background Beth was somewhat discomfited by this blatant Popery. She thought it smacked of mumbo jumbo.

'Shouldn't we go to the shelters out back?' Kathleen queried.

'I've been wondering about that,' said Seamus.

'Well, you won't get me into one of them. I'd rather take my chances here or in the street,' Beth declared, and Mary nodded.

'I agree with Mrs Ramsay. For some reason or other I've never fancied those shelters myself.'

Another explosion went off, louder than any of the preceding ones. 'I think I'll go back downstairs and see what more I can learn,' said Seamus.

'Good idea. And I'd be obliged if you'd let me know what you find out,' said Beth.

'Certainly, missus.'

'Would you like to come into our house till Seamus gets back?' Mary suggested kindly.

Beth almost accepted, but decided against it. She wanted to be in her own home.

Chapter 10

Back indoors a sudden pain gnawed at Beth's insides. Indigestion, she thought. Putting a hand on the wall for support, she bent over from the waist, a trick that had usually relieved it in the past. Unfortunately, on this occasion it didn't. Straightening herself again she cursed the fact that she'd run out of anti-acid powder.

She relit her candle and staggered over to a chair. Clutching her belly, she sank down into it, groaning as the pain worsened. It was by far and away the worst attack of indigestion she'd ever had.

A little later, still clutching herself, she glanced at the clock, which told her it was a quarter to one. If she was going to be awake all night – and it certainly looked that way between her stomach and what was going on outside – she'd be shattered tomorrow for work.

A few minutes later there was a tap on the door. Lumbering to her feet she went and answered it.

Seamus O'Malley stood revealed. 'Quick, come inside,' Beth said, and then laughed despite her pain as a sudden thought struck her. 'I don't know why I'm worried about showing a light when there are buildings blazing.'

Seamus grinned at her. He was a fairly handsome man, if you liked that type, Beth thought. He had curly black hair, china-blue eyes and a thick drooping moustache. Tufts of hair protruded from his open-necked shirt and layered the backs of both hands. She judged him to be in his early forties.

'So what did you learn, Mr O'Malley?'

'Oh, Seamus please. Seeing as we're neighbours like.'

'Seamus it is, then.'

'That last explosion we heard wasn't gas but dynamite. The fire brigade have called in the army and they're the ones doing the dynamiting,' he explained.

'Why?'

'They're trying to stop the fire reaching the munitions factory by blowing up everything in its path.'

'And Sweet Street?'

'We're safe – at least for the moment. That might not be the case if the wind changes.'

'I see.'

'They've got bulldozers as well. I counted half a dozen of them clearing away the rubble of what's been dynamited.'

Beth gasped and stumbled. This new pain was completely different in quality from the indigestion one. It was as though her living flesh was being ripped apart.

Seamus took her by the elbow. 'Are you all right, missus?'

'Sit . . . must sit.'

He helped her to a chair, which she virtually collapsed into, her face lined with agony.

'Just hold on a tick,' Seamus said, and ran from the single end. He returned with Mary to find Beth doubled up in the chair, whimpering.

'Where does it hurt, me darling?' Mary asked, squatting beside Beth.

'Stomach . . . low down.'

'And what exactly does it feel like?'

Beth described the pain. Mary nodding knowingly. 'It's your time, that's for certain.'

'It can't be. I'm not due for another three weeks yet.'

Mary smiled. 'Babies aren't ruled by doctors' fancy calculations and what have you. They come when they're ready. Have your waters broken yet?'

Beth shook her head.

'Right then.' Rising, Mary turned to Seamus. 'Go find a telephone box and ring the hospital. Tell them we need an ambulance here as soon as possible. On your way out send Kathleen and Mo-Mo through. They can help me get Mrs Ramsay ready for the ambulance when it arrives.'

'I'm on my way.'

'Are you sure it's the baby?' Beth asked.

Mary laughed. 'I've had nine of me own so it's a subject I'm what you might call an expert on. There's very little about babies – getting them, having them, or bringing them up – that I don't know about.'

Suddenly Beth cried out, sweat breaking on her brow.

'Do you want to keep sitting there or would you prefer to lie on the bed?' Mary asked sympathetically.

Beth thought about it, and came to the conclusion that she wouldn't like to be in a confined space the way she felt now. 'I'll stay here.'

The door opened to admit Kathleen and Mo-Mo. The latter was fifteen, the next down from Kathleen, and extremely pretty in a wild, dark way. Her proper name was Maureen, but she'd been called Mo-Mo by Kathleen when they were both tiny and the nickname had stuck.

'Mrs Ramsay is going to have her baby so we'll be getting her ready for the ambulance,' Mary explained, before turning again to Beth. 'Now what things do you want to take with you? Just tell the girls here and they'll pack them for you nice as can be.'

Beth told them there was a suitcase under the bed, and gave them a list of the items she'd take with her and where they were to be found. 'What a night for it to happen,' she said to Mary, wincing as another explosion occurred. As the noise died away Mary looked thoughtful. Excusing herself, she said she'd be back in two flicks of a lamb's tail.

When she returned she said to Beth, 'I've just told the rest of the family to get some of our bits together. If we have to leave here tonight I don't want it to be with just what we stand up in. We might not have much but even a little is a sight better than nothing at all, and that's a fact.'

Beth was rapidly warming to the Irish woman. She wished she'd got to know her sooner. That she hadn't was entirely her own fault, since she had purposely kept her distance from the others living in and up the close.

There was a whooshing sound, like a monstrous roman candle going off.

'Merciful God in heaven. What's that!' Mary exclaimed. Hurrying to the window she made a chink in the blackout curtains and peered out. 'I can't see from here what it was.'

'Want me to run to the close mouth and find out?' Mo-Mo asked.

Mary considered and finally nodded her head. 'But see and take care, mind!' she called out as Mo-Mo left the room at a gallop.

'Is there anything I can get you?' Kathleen asked Beth.

'A drink of water, please.'

Kathleen held the cup to Beth's lips. The water was good, icy cold. She drank all that was in the cup and asked for more.

Mo-Mo returned wide-eyed. 'That was the distillery going up,' she announced. 'You can see it quite clearly from the corner. It's burning like a huge bonfire, crackling and roaring and shooting off sparks. The air's full of them – one landed in my hair and singed it.'

Beth and Mary exchanged glances, neither liking the sound of that at all, and Mary frowned. 'What's keeping himself?' She wet a towel at the sink and used it to wipe Beth's forehead and face. 'You're not worried about the birth, are you?'

Beth nodded.

'There's no call at all for that, Mrs Ramsay. You've got the sort of figure pops them out like a pea from a pod.'

'I haven't got very wide hips,' Beth murmured. It was something which had been bothering her during recent months.

Mary laughed. 'And that's the best way to be, sure enough! This child-bearing hips thing is an absolute nonsense. Women with those sorts of hips are the ones who inevitably have problems, while the skinnymalinks, the ones you'd think would have trouble, drop their babies no bother whatever.' Seeing that Beth was sceptical, she went on, 'I swear by blessed St Peter himself that what I've just told you is one hundred per cent true. Don't ask me why it's so, for I couldn't say, but true it is.'

'I never knew that.'

'It'll be as easy as one two three for you because you've got the perfect build for having children. As I said, I've had nine of my own so I know what I'm talking about.'

'Well, that's one load off my mind at least,' said Beth, convinced.

'Here's Da!' Mo-Mo exclaimed excitedly, having heard the distinctive clatter of his tackety boots on the stairs.

Kathleen opened the door and Seamus slipped inside. 'It's sheer pandemonium out there.'

'How long till the ambulance comes?' Mary asked.

'I couldn't get through to the hospital on the telephone so I've run there and back. It seems there isn't an ambulance available in all north Glasgow. Every single vehicle is already busy carting the injured away from the doings up the road.'

'So there have been a lot of casualties?' Beth asked.

'They thought the distillery was safe and didn't bother evacuating the people in the houses facing on to it. They say it's terrible up there. Human torches leaping out of windows . . .'

Mary's hand flew to her mouth. 'Holy Mary Mother of God!' She quickly crossed herself, Seamus and the two girls following suit.

'The doctor I spoke to at the hospital said if you want

to have your baby there the night, missus, you'll have to make your own way.'

'Of course.' Beth nodded, thinking of the carnage round the distillery. She shivered at the picture conjured up in her mind of human torches leaping out of windows, and couldn't help but remember how Steve had died. For what must have been the millionth time she prayed he'd not been burnt alive.

'I did my best, missus,' Seamus apologised.

'I'm sure you did. Thank you.'

'Do you think you can make it to the hospital?' Mary asked.

'I can certainly try, if I have a shoulder to lean on.'

Seamus came forward. 'You can have mine, missus.'

Beth smiled her gratitude. 'Has the wind changed at all?'

'No. Sweet Street is still safe, for the time being anyway.'

The hospital was about half a mile away. A hell of a distance for a woman already started in labour, Beth reflected. With Seamus and Mary's help she came to her feet, and Kathleen brought her her coat. 'If we can just take it slowly,' she murmured to Seamus.

Seamus picked up her suitcase and they went out on to the landing, Mary, Kathleen and Mo-Mo bringing up the rear.

'Good luck, Mrs Ramsay,' Mary said as Beth started to descend the inky stairs. She turned to reply and as she did so her waters broke and she was suddenly sodden at the crotch and down both legs. She started to cry.

Instantly Mary was by her side, puting an arm round her. 'What is it, me darling?'

Beth told her in a whisper.

Mary shook her head. 'The poor woman will never make it to the hospital the way she is now, and that's a fact,' she declared to Seamus. 'So it's inside again for her.'

With Mary's assistance Beth stumbled back up the stairs and into the welcome familiarity of her own home, where she flopped into the chair she'd just left.

'The way I see matters there's nothing else for it but to deliver the babba right here,' Mary said.

'But I can't—'

'Why not?' Mary cut in. 'There have been millions of babies brought into the world at home, you know. It isn't exactly a new idea.'

'But I had planned . . . the doctor . . .'

Mary squatted beside Beth to take one of her hands between her own. 'What you didn't plan was for half of Maryhill going up in flames at the same time. So I'm afraid you've no choice, Mrs Ramsay, none at all.'

Beth could see the Irish woman was right, no matter how much she might want it to be otherwise. 'You will stay and help?' she pleaded.

'Of course. The two lassies here and myself are only too pleased to do everything we can for you.'

Beth wiped away her tears. 'I'm putting you to so much trouble and we've only just met . . .'

'Och, away with that nonsense,' Mary interjected. 'That's what neighbours are for. I'm sure you'd do the same for me and mine if it was one of us needing a hand.' She came to her feet, suddenly all brisk and businesslike. 'First thing is for you to make yourself scarce, Seamus.

Away through and keep an eye on those holy terrors of ours. I'll call if I need you.'

Seamus gave Beth a broad, reassuring smile before leaving the room.

'Next thing is to get this place heated up. You've plenty of coal in the scuttle so there's no problem there. Mo-Mo, you set the fire. A nice big roasty one.'

Mo-Mo jumped to do her mother's bidding, while Kathleen looked expectantly for her instructions.

'We'll need hot water,' Mary declared.

'The gas is off,' Beth reminded her.

'That won't worry us too much. Have you got a large copper pan?'

Beth shook her head.

'You run through and get ours, Kathleen. And bring a couple of candles. We need more light here. The water is still on, I take it?'

'It was only a few minutes ago I gave Mrs Ramsay a drink.'

Mary strode over to the sink and turned the tap. 'May the angels be praised!' she exclaimed when water gushed out. Kathleen went off to get the pan and candles.

When she returned Mary filled the pan and put it to one side as a precaution in case the water did go off. The pair of them then stripped Beth's bed and dragged the mattress out on to the floor.

'Now, we can't use these sheets. They're far too good to be ruined,' Mary declared. Despite Beth's protests Kathleen was again despatched to the O'Malley house for a pair of 'old tatties', as Mary called them.

Suddenly Beth screamed and writhed in the chair. The pains were now regular, roughly forty-five seconds apart.

'Just as well you turned back when you did,' Mary said. 'For you're coming on so quickly now I doubt you'd have made the hospital. You'd probably have ended up having the poor babba on the pavement somewhere.'

She helped Beth out of her stockings and knickers and consigned both to the bin before sponging Beth's crotch and announcing her to be well dilated. Kathleen had meanwhile spread the 'old tatties' over the mattress on the floor. Beth thought she'd never seen a more patched and repaired pair of sheets.

Another massive explosion went off. Several knick-knacks Beth had on the mantelpiece fell to the floor where one of them shattered into pieces.

'That was closest yet,' Mo-Mo gulped.

'What happens if we're all told to evacuate?' Beth queried.

Mary's face suddenly creased into a smile. 'I'll tell you this, me darling, you'll be an absolute sensation when they carry you out on to the street. You can bet on that.'

Beth had to laugh. The thought of being carted out on to the street in the process of giving birth *was* very funny, even if it was humour of the black kind.

Mary pulled Beth to her feet and started taking off the rest of her clothes. Kathleen handed her a flannelette nightie she'd taken from the suitcase and Beth struggled into it. Then she lay on the mattress, enjoying the heat from the fire washing over her, while Mary had another look between her legs. She was continuing to dilate nicely, and in Mary's opinion the birth couldn't be all that far away.

Mo-Mo made tea and they all had a cup.

'What was he like, your husband who was killed?' Mo-Mo asked.

'How did you know that?' Beth queried in surprise.

'You hear things round about,' Mary answered for her daughter, shooting Mo-Mo a dark look.

It was to be expected that folk would be curious about her, Beth thought. She had made no secret of what had happened to Steve – quite the reverse. In a quiet voice she recounted the story she'd told the factor, McLure.

'That's ever so romantic,' Mo-Mo breathed when Beth was finished.

'There's nothing romantic about being left a widow so young,' Mary said, the tone of her voice reflecting a hard life. 'You have my sympathy so you do, Mrs Ramsay.'

'It's awfully sore,' Beth muttered through gritted teeth at the conclusion of another pain.

Mary dipped a fresh towel in the copper pan and washed down Beth's face and neck. 'The way things are going you won't have to suffer long. That babba's just bursting to get out.'

'It feels like me who's bursting.'

Mary drew off some water from the pan and took it to the sink where she scrubbed her hands for the third time, using carbolic soap.

Beth found herself wanting to bear down, which she did, placing her hands on the mattress to give herself more leverage. Her entire body was covered in sweat, and she noticed that her flesh had gone very white, as though all the blood had been drained out of it.

'You're doing lovely. Absolutely darling,' Mary encouraged her.

'Aaaahhh!' Beth yelled, pushing with all her might. 'Aaaahhh!'

'I can see the top of the babba's head,' Mary declared excitedly. Beth had time for a brief smile before yelling out again.

Minutes later the head slipped out, followed quickly by the shoulders. Beth pushed and pushed, drumming her heels as she did so.

'Almost there,' Mary whispered as the child's body, red, wrinkled and covered in vernix, started to slide into view.

She *was* bursting, Beth thought. She was going to split wide open. She was going to . . . 'Aaaarrrgh!' she screamed, a sound all jagged at the edges that seemed to shred her throat. Then it was over. The mass which had been part of her for so long had gone out of her, leaving her totally and utterly exhausted.

'Is everything all right?' she croaked.

'All his fingers and toes are there if that's what you mean,' Mary assured her, busy clearing stuff from the baby's throat.

His fingers and toes, Beth thought elatedly. It was a boy! What she'd secretly hoped and prayed for.

'Come on now, son,' Mary murmured, patting the baby quite sharply on the bottom. The infant gave a sudden spasm, and his ribcage began to move in and out. Opening his eyes, he stared in what looked like wonderment for a moment, then let out a lusty cry.

Mary, face covered in blood and other mess, swiftly wrapped him up warm and handed him to Beth, who immediately laid him on her breast. Mary glanced across at Kathleen and Mo-Mo. 'Between one thing and another you won't forget this night in a hurry, will you?'

Both girls shook their head.

'He's a wee smasher,' Mary said to Beth, beaming as she spoke.

Beth grasped the baby and held him up inches from her face. 'I'm going to call him Stephen after his father,' she said, smiling.

There was a soft rap on the door, and Mary answered it. When she returned she said to Beth, 'That was Seamus. He's been out checking the state of things and apparently the street's now definitely safe. Praise be to God!'

Beth closed her eyes and in her mind saw O for Oboe with Steve at the controls. Staring straight at her, he nodded his approval. Then Oboe was gone, disappeared into dense cloud.

The same cloud swirled round her as she drifted off to sleep.

Mary stayed the rest of the night. Kathleen brought through fresh clothes for her, and she dozed in the chair after she'd washed and changed. Just before seven a.m. she roused herself and returned to her own house to make the family breakfast.

Beth, wakened by Mary's departure, put Stephen to the breast. Much to her delight he was able to feed, which he did noisily and with great relish.

When the baby had finished Beth tried to get up, but found it too painful to do so. She ached tremendously, and there was some bruising on the insides of her thighs.

Mary came back with tea and toast for Beth, a toddler

she introduced as Michael clinging to her skirt. The rest of the family had gone off either to school or to work.

'Have you got a crib at all?' she asked.

Beth shook her head.

'You can have the loan of ours then. Sure it's hardly in the luxury class but it'll do the trick if you're not too fussy.'

'That's very kind of you.'

'Seamus was out at first light to see the damage done last night. He says it's terrible to behold. Piles of smoking rubble where yesterday there were streets.'

'The café in Hagland Street—'

'The place where you work?' Mary cut in.

'You know that, then.'

'That end of Hagland Street wasn't touched at all, though the top part was. Quite a lot of damage there, I believe.'

So Colin and Edna were safe. That was a great relief. 'Is there any chance of you dropping by there and telling the Moncurs what's happened to me?'

'No problem about that, me darling, no problem at all.'

Beth looked at Michael, who was busily picking his nose. A right wee scruff, she thought, and immediately felt ashamed of herself for thinking that of Mary's child after Mary had been so good to her. God alone knew what would've become of her if it hadn't been for Mary and her two girls. But he was a wee scruff none the less. She swore there and then that she'd somehow do better for her Stephen, although how she was going to manage such a thing was quite beyond her for the moment.

'Do you want to keep lying where you are or will I put the mattress back on the bed for you?' Mary asked.

'I think I'd like it back on the bed. I can't help you though, I'm afraid. I tried to get up earlier and found I couldn't.'

'I'll manage by myself. Don't you worry about that.'

'Me help, Ma,' Michael volunteered.

'There's a good son.' Mary beamed. 'With a big strong lad like yourself to help me it'll be no bother at all sure enough.'

Michael grinned from ear to ear, delighted by the compliment.

'We'll have to get you sitting up first,' Mary said to Beth, who carefully laid Stephen down beside her and with Mary's assistance made it to the nearest chair. 'It'll take a day or two, but you'll soon be over it.' Mary picked Stephen up and handed him to Beth. Michael was already tugging at the mattress.

Mary stripped off her 'old tatties', bundling them up and putting them to one side to go into the bin later. A little blood had seeped through on to the mattress, and she did her best to wash it off.

'I'll put the mattress into the cavity for you, but I suggest you don't get back on to it until it's dry. Do you want me to light a fire for you? That'll help it dry more quickly.'

Beth assented, and Mary started manhandling the mattress. The toddler was more of a hindrance than a help, but being the sort of person she was Mary wouldn't have dreamt of not letting him try to do his bit.

With the mattress finally in position Mary got down

to the fire. She was in the process of shovelling ashes from the grate when there was a knock on the door.

'Now who could that be?' Beth wondered aloud.

'Must be one of my lot back for some reason or other,' Mary said, coming off her haunches on to her feet. But it wasn't, as she discovered on answering the knock. It was Cissie.

'Ma!' Beth exclaimed on hearing her mother's voice.

'I was so worried.' Cissie hurried into the room. 'I heard all about it on the wireless—' She stopped short.

'This is Stephen. Your grandson,' Beth informed her. Eyes shining, she launched into the story of how Stephen had decided to come early, and how, if it hadn't been for her neighbour Mrs O'Malley here, she would've had the baby all on her own.

'In the name of the Wee Man!' Cissie exclaimed, aghast at the thought.

'I'll just get this fire going then leave you two to yourselves,' Mary said.

'Don't worry about the fire. I'll attend to it,' Cissie replied. 'I can't thank you enough for what you've done already.'

'I'll call into the café with your news and pop back later, if you'd like me to, that is?' Mary said to Beth.

'Please, Mary. I'd appreciate that.'

When Mary and Michael were gone, Cissie took Stephen from Beth and held him to her bosom, gently rocking him back and forth. 'And you had him right there on the floor?' she marvelled.

'On the mattress from the bed.'

'I wanted to come after hearing the first report of what

was happening on the wireless. Only Roy persuaded me not to.'

'I wish you had been here. I wanted you so badly.'

'If I'd known you were in labour nothing would've stopped me.'

'I know that, Ma.'

'Roy said you'd have sense enough to get out of harm's way, and I'd be endangering myself unnecessarily by coming to Maryhill.'

'You tell Roy there were human torches leaping out of windows. I'm sure a lot of them were sensible folk too,' Beth said.

Cissie had no answer to that, so she handed Stephen back to her daughter and set about making the fire. When its cheery glow was warming up the room, she handed Beth a brown paper parcel she'd brought with her.

Beth opened the parcel, and was delighted when its contents were revealed. 'One-eyed Suzie and my scrap album,' she exclaimed, fondly touching first one and then the other.

'You asked me to bring them next time I visited.'

'Thanks, Ma.'

'I also made it my business to find out about the Ramsays. It seems they're both more or less the same. He is still badly paralysed and she's continuing to look after him. Are you sure . . .'

'No.' Beth shook her head. 'And I won't change my mind.'

When Cissie had her coat and hat on and was ready to go, she kissed them both. 'Oh, Beth, I wish I could take you home with me,' she whispered with tears in her eyes.

'I can never go back there, Ma. You know that.'

'Aye, lass, I do. Though that doesn't stop me from wishing it otherwise.' Crossing to the mantelpiece, she placed three pound notes on it. 'Take care. And of that wee lad there. I'll be back within the next fortnight, I promise.'

'I'll look after him, don't you fear!' Beth called out in reply as the door snicked shut. She had never been more sincere in her life.

Beth got up the next day. To begin with she was woozy on her feet, but as the day wore on the weakness gradually disappeared till by evening she was beginning to feel something like her old self again.

The following afternoon she decided to go for a walk and view the damage for herself. Slipping on her coat, she wrapped Stephen tightly against her by means of a tartan shawl and set off.

Despite having had it described to her it was still a shock to see the carnage with her own eyes. Line upon line of buildings had been razed by dynamite and bulldozers; others were mere skeletons gutted by fire. The distillery was a charred shell of what it had been, while what remained of the gasworks looked like a toy that a child had angrily smashed to smithereens. The munitions factory stood bleakly alone, surrounded on all sides by rubble pushed into piles by bulldozers, far enough away from the factory to ensure that flames couldn't leap the distance between them.

Nobody knew yet what had sparked the original explosion at the gasworks. One theory, according to Mary, was sabotage. A second, and far more likely, explanation was that some silly bugger had been sneaking a fly smoke with inevitable and horrendous consequences. Over a hundred had died, nearly sixty of whom had lived in the houses facing the distillery.

Beth turned away from the devastation and slowly made her way down Linton Road. She wanted to reassure herself that the nursery where Stephen would shortly be going hadn't been damaged in any way.

'Oh, no!' she exclaimed when, on rounding a corner, she saw that the roof of the nursery had completely gone, along with an entire wall.

She slumped where she stood. This was an awful blow, for the nursery was the only one in all Maryhill.

She walked home in despair, and was coming up her landing when Mary's door swung open. 'I saw you from the window. So you've been out, then?'

'A little walk, and it has fair worn me out, I can tell you.'

'Do you fancy a cup of tea? Sure the kettle's singing its head off even now.'

Beth accepted the offer and went inside. How untidy the place was! she thought, then berated herself for being unkind. With eleven people occupying three rooms, what else could you expect? She sat down and undid her shawl, gently laying Stephen on the floor in front of her. He was smiling in his sleep, frothy bubbles on his lips. Her heart went out afresh to him – how she adored her wee son.

In a voice flat with worry and disappointment she told Mary about the nursery while Mary made the tea and nodded sympathetically from time to time. When Beth had finished she brought over the cups and sat down opposite her. Michael squatted beside his mother's chair and started sucking his thumb.

Mary was looking thoughtful. 'Aye, it's a problem for you right enough,' she said.

'Honest to God, it's just one thing after another. And now this.'

Mary gave a wry smile. 'Life can be like that. And it usually is, for all of us.'

'I'm sorry,' Beth apologised. 'Ever since we met I seem to have done nothing but involve you with my problems.'

'Think nothing of it. I've already told you, that's what neighbours are for.'

'Ma, I'm hungry,' Michael complained, still sucking his thumb.

Mary leaned down to ruffle his hair. 'You're a bottomless pit, so you are. Was it a piece and dripping you were after?'

Michael nodded vigorously.

'Then by all the holy saints that's what you'll be having.'

Michael came to his feet with a whoop to dance Red Indian style on the spot, while Mary took a pan loaf from the bread bin and cut off a thick slice. She spread it liberally with dripping and handed it to her son. 'There you are, then.

'Himself and I have nightmares about feeding this lot, I can tell you,' she confided to Beth. 'Kathleen and Mo-Mo are working, but the rest, with the exception of Michael here, are still at school and not bringing in. It's sheer hell making ends meet so it is.'

'What does Seamus do?'

'A rope-making factory. Damned hard work and little pay at the end of it. It's a crying sin what that man brings home with eleven mouths to feed in this house and all. Once Michael goes to school I'll be casting around for a wee part-time something. Anything that'll bring a few more bob into the place.'

Beth thought about it. Mary was excellent with children, that was obvious. What was more, Beth instinctively trusted her. 'It appears to me we both have a problem which perhaps we can solve by helping one another.'

Mary frowned. 'I'm not with you?'

'How much would you want for looking after Stephen while I'm at work?'

Mary rubbed her chin while regarding Beth thoughtfully. 'Now that's an idea.'

'How much?' Beth persisted.

'How much can you afford?'

Beth made a few rapid mental calculations, based on the presumption she'd be making as much in tips when she returned to the café. 'What would you say to a shilling a day, Monday to Saturday? That's six bob a week.'

'How many hours?'

'Four a day.'

Mary's face broke into a grin. 'Sure I'd have done it for nothing if you'd asked me, but I won't be refusing the cash. When do I start?'

'Just as soon as I can get Stephen weaned on to taking a bottle for the time I won't be around.'

Mary got down on her knees and smiled at Stephen. Although highly unlikely, he being only three days old, it seemed to Beth that Stephen smiled back.

A good omen, Beth thought. A very good one.

Chapter 11

He stood out because he was the only male customer in the club not in uniform. 'Scotch on the rocks.' He smiled at Beth.

It was nine months since she'd had Stephen, during which time she'd left the Moncurs' café in Hagland Street to move on to a far better paid job as bar manageress in a club called Bruce's Cave which catered exclusively – the owner being an expatriate Yank called Zenth – to American servicemen.

Mary was still looking after Stephen, and the pair were getting on famously. Kathleen worked at the club as a hostess, of which there were a number, and it was through her that Beth had got to hear of the manageress's job. Beth had always been good at figures and organising things. Mr Zenth had recognised her as a natural for the job and hired her there and then.

'We don't get many male civilians in here,' Beth said, laying the customer's drink in front of him.

'I guess not.'

He was shy, she thought. She found it appealing – it made a change from the usual brash American behaviour. She judged him to be in his late thirties, or possibly forty.

She moved away to serve some new arrivals, but returned to him when he beckoned her over for a refill. This time the dollar he handed her wasn't the usual greenback, as his previous one had been, but a Canadian bill.

'My error,' he apologised when Beth pointed it out to him. He took it back and exchanged it for an American one.

'Have you been to Canada?' she enquired.

He smiled. 'I *am* Canadian. This is the first time I've been abroad, if you discount a brief trip to the other side of Niagara Falls, that is.'

'My husband was over in Canada before the war. He was a rider in a sort of motorbike circus – stunting, death-defying leaps, that sort of thing.'

'No kidding!' the Canadian exclaimed. 'Say, what's his name? I might have seen him. I just adore those motorbike rodeos. I've never missed one that's come to the province.'

'Steve Ramsay.'

'Steve Ramsay?' the Canadian mused. 'You know, that does ring a bell. I'm sure I must've seen him.' The Canadian brought his full attention back to Beth. 'Did you say *was*?'

'He was killed a year last July flying for the RAF.'

'I'm sure sorry to hear that,' the Canadian sympathised quietly, speaking with sincerity.

'Do you ride motorbikes yourself?'

He shook his head. 'Always wanted to as a young man, but my father would never allow me to have one. Said they were instruments of the devil. Death on wheels.'

'They can be extremely dangerous.'

'So can crossing the street if you don't keep your wits about you. Hell! I remember saving up once for a brand new Norton I'd set my heart on—'

'That's what Steve had, a Norton,' Beth broke in excitedly. 'Over here, that is, not in Canada. He and I often went for rides on it.'

'You like bikes then?'

Beth nodded. 'I think they're smashing. I've certainly never experienced anything more thrilling than being on the pillion of that Norton.'

'Well well well.'

Beth was called away again. The club was so busy that she hadn't time to think about the Canadian for the next twenty minutes or so, and when she finally did look his way again it was to find he'd gone. His seat had been taken by a peroxided blonde who was laughing too loudly and unconvincingly, and when Beth glanced round the club there was no sign of him, either at the tables or on the dance floor.

Pity, that. She'd rather enjoyed chatting to him. And to think that he might have seen Steve ride over in Canada! Now that had been interesting to hear.

He was the first customer in when the club opened the following evening. He smiled at Beth and ordered Scotch on the rocks.

She was pleased to see him, and let it show. She said she'd have a tomato juice when he asked her what she'd like to drink.

'Nothing alcoholic. Or very rarely, anyway, when I'm on duty,' she explained.

'I didn't introduce myself last night. The name's Gene McKay,' he said, offering her his hand.

'That's Gene as in Autry, I take it?'

'That's right. Gene as in Autry and not Harlow,' he replied, and they both laughed.

'I'm Beth Ramsay.'

'Real pleased to meet you, Beth. Short for Elizabeth, I take it.'

She laughed again. Not only was he shy, but he had a sense of humour as well. Better and better. 'Correct.'

'Got too crowded for me last night. All that pushing and shoving, not to mention the jukebox. I could hardly hear myself think.'

'It's loud because the majority of customers prefer it that way. There are always lots of complaints if we turn it down.'

'Far too noisy for a country boy like me who's used to solitude and wide open spaces.'

'If you don't mind me asking, what do you do?'

'I'm a farmer. Mainly arable, though I do run a few cattle and have some timber. My farm's situated just outside the town of Stewarton in Ontario. Real good farming country round there.'

'McKay and Stewarton. Both Scots names?'

'My great-grandparents came from Scotland. They settled in Stewarton on account of there being already quite a Scottish community there. Stewarton itself was originally founded by some Scots from the Scottish Stewarton.'

'So what are you doing over here?'

He gave a wry grin. 'I don't suppose you've ever heard of Hadley's Volunteers?'

'No.'

'Well, in our part of Ontario it's traditional that the young men, in times of national conflict, join the Volunteers, the idea being that they'll be serving alongside friends, relatives and others from the area.'

'Are you over here to join them?'

Gene laughed. 'No. As a farmer I'm exempt. What I am here to do, along with a guy you haven't met yet called Theo Hasten, is meet up with the Volunteers to give them messages. You know – greetings and general all-round support from home.'

Beth looked blank. She'd never heard of this sort of thing before.

Gene went on to explain. 'I'm the president of the province's Farmers' League, while Theo is the president of the Bureau of Ontarian Industry – the BOI. Well, a few weeks back the League learned that the Volunteers had been pretty chewed up in action and suffered very heavy casualties. Naturally the League was real concerned about that and at a meeting it was suggested we make a gesture of support to the survivors as it was reckoned their morale must be really low. When we heard the Volunteers were due for some rest and recreation here in Scotland it was proposed I get over here to spend time with them. Being of Scottish ancestry I've always wanted to see Scotland so I agreed to the trip. When the BOI heard what we intended they insisted their president accompany me, which is how Theo and I come to be together.'

'I think it's a lovely idea,' Beth enthused. 'Two faces from home, talking about home things, having just come from there. Messages being hand-delivered . . .'

Gene grinned. 'I got a whole bag full of those.'

'So when do you meet up with the Volunteers?'

'They were supposed to be already in Scotland, at a place called the Isle of Arran, only they're not. There's been a hitch of some sort and now it'll be at least another week before they get there.'

'Who's running your farm for you in the meantime, then?'

'My twin sister Loretta, who knows as much about farming as I do.'

'And this Theo Hasten, why hasn't he come to the club with you?'

'He's been ill since we arrived. A stomach bug that started to affect him the last day aboard ship. But he wouldn't come here anyway as he's strictly temperance. Fanatically so.'

'He sounds boring.'

'He is as far as anything to do with alcohol is concerned. You only have to mention the word to get a ten-minute lecture.'

Beth poured Gene another Scotch, this one on the house. 'Where are you staying?'

'A little hotel off Sauchiehall Street.' He hesitated. 'Did I say that right?'

She laughed. 'Not quite. Close, though.'

'Well, a little hotel off there. It's OK, except they sure give you small portions at mealtimes.'

American eating habits were another thing Beth had learned about since coming to work at Bruce's Cave. She presumed Canadians ate the same way. 'That must be something of an eye-opener to you after what you've been used to.'

Gene held his hands up roughly a foot apart. 'At home I eat T-bone steaks this size at least two or three times a week.'

'That's more than a month's meat ration for an entire family here.'

Gene sighed. 'No offence meant, but no wonder so many folk look drawn and haggard. They just ain't getting enough to eat and that's a fact.'

'We're told it's healthier this way. Though I suspect that's only propaganda myself.'

They were interrupted by the appearance of another customer, and Beth moved off to serve him.

'Do you ever get a night off?' Gene asked her when she returned to the part of the bar where he was sitting.

'Yes. Sundays.'

'Then what about you and me having dinner together?'

A number of club customers had asked Beth out, but up until now she'd always turned them down, thinking it a wise policy not to mix business and pleasure. For Gene McKay, however, she decided to make an exception. 'All right.'

He beamed at her. 'What time will I pick you up?'

She didn't want him coming to Sweet Street. 'No. Let's meet somewhere. How about outside the Central Station? That should be easy enough for you to find. Does seven o'clock suit?'

'I'll be there, ready and waiting.'

'Then it's a date,' she declared, using the American expression.

A large party of army personnel arrived, followed by a group of air force people. The jukebox burst into raucous life, and for the next few minutes the bar staff worked flat out. When next Beth glanced across to where Gene had been sitting it was to find he'd done another of his disappearing acts.

Sunday was the day after next. She was looking forward to it.

The rain was pelting down as she hurried to the station. Hardly the best of starts, she thought, feeling a trickle of water run down the back of her neck.

There were about a dozen people standing at the front of the station, which was a favoured meeting place, but Gene wasn't one of them.

'Damn!' she muttered angrily. So much for him being ready and waiting.

But she'd misjudged him. Not being allowed to park in front of the station he'd done so across the road, and within seconds his sleek American car glided to a stop beside her. The passenger door swung open. 'Hop in,' he invited, giving her a smile.

'Where on earth did you get this from?' she asked as they drove away.

'The consulate. It belongs to them and they were kind enough to put it at my disposal while I'm here. Being a so-called VIP has its advantages.'

'I'll say. What make is it?'

'A Buick V8.'

'It's the first time I've ever been in an American car,' she said happily. Her burst of anger at thinking he was going to keep her hanging about in the rain had completely disappeared.

'Then sit back and enjoy the ride. So, where are we going?'

The restaurant she suggested was out at Anniesland on the road to devastated Clydebank, and called the Buttery. She knew about it because she'd heard customers at the club mention it favourably.

Gene ordered an expensive bottle of wine, then asked if steak was available. He had to settle for chops which proved to be tiny, if delicious. Beth felt she'd done a lot better in ordering stew. It consisted mainly of vegetables, with only the odd scrap of meat, but was tasty none the less.

'Tell me about your farm,' she said.

'Well, it's just over a thousand acres. Two hundred of timber, twenty-five of apple trees. What's left I grow wheat on. Or I should say Loretta and I do, as technically the farm's half hers. For the moment, anyway.'

'What do you mean, for the moment?'

His eyes took on a faraway look while a smile twitched the corners of his lips. 'I hope to be very shortly assuming overall ownership.'

'You mean buying your sister out?'

'In a manner of speaking.'

'Does she want to sell her half, is that it?'

'I didn't say I'd be actually buying, I said in a manner of speaking,' Gene replied somewhat mysteriously.

Beth couldn't make head or tail of this. What *did* he mean, then? She decided to change the subject as it was obvious he didn't want to continue with the present one.

'Didn't you tell me you also have some cattle?'

'A few hundred head which I intend selling off next

year. For the foreseeable future there's more money to be made from wheat.'

'I see.' Then, a moment or two later, 'If you're so keen on motorbikes why didn't you buy yourself one when you were older?'

'My father wouldn't let me.'

'But you're a grown man!' she exclaimed in astonishment.

'My father only died eighteen months ago. When he was alive you just never did what he didn't want you to. That's the sort of person he was.'

'What about your mother?'

'I never knew her. She died giving birth to Loretta and me. I don't think my father ever forgave us, although that's only a guess as he would never discuss the matter. But I can't see any other reason why he would've hated Loretta and me so much, and hate us he surely did.'

'He sounds awful.'

'He was, if you'll pardon the expression, a real chromium-plated son of a bitch who made my life hell.'

They sat in silence for a while. 'Did you say your great-grandparents came from the Scottish Stewarton?' Beth asked eventually.

Gene roused himself from the reverie he'd fallen into and shook his head. 'No, a place called Mauchline. Ever heard of it?'

'It's in Ayrshire, I think.'

'That's right. He was a farm labourer there, she a labourer's daughter.'

Beth listened with interest as Gene recounted his family history. He concluded by saying he had cousins somewhere in Saskatchewan, but he and Loretta were the only McKays left living in Ontario.

'Were you married long?' Gene asked over the cheese, an excellent croudie.

'Only a few months.'

He shook his head in sympathy and commiseration.

Beth stared at her plate. Then, suddenly smiling, she looked up at Gene. 'But he did leave me a son whom I'm very proud of.'

'A son, eh? How old is he?'

Beth told him about Stephen and Mary O'Malley and how it was thanks to Mary she was able to work. 'I fell on my feet there. I honestly don't know what I'd have done without her.' She went on to tell Gene about the night the gasworks had gone up and how the nursery she'd intended placing Stephen in had been destroyed as a result.

When they'd finished their meal Beth went outside to wait while Gene paid the bill. It had stopped raining, leaving the air crisp and clean-tasting.

Gene joined her and they got into the Buick. 'I'll take you home,' Gene said.

Beth was about to say that she'd prefer to be dropped somewhere, then decided against it. Perversely, she was now curious to find out what his reaction to Sweet Street would be.

When they reached her tenement Gene parked and glanced up at the building lowering over him. The street smell filtered into the car, making his nose twitch in disgust.

'Lovely area, don't you agree?' Beth smiled.

'It's . . . it's real nasty.'

Beth's smile widened. 'That's putting it rather mildly. But now you're here would you care to come up for a drink?'

'Do I get to meet your son?'

'Of course.'

'Then thank you.'

He came round to her side of the Buick and helped her out, a touch she appreciated. She took his hand to guide him up the stairs, which were in complete darkness.

Once inside her door she instructed him to stand still while she closed the curtains and lit the gas lamps. Then she invited him to help himself to a drink while she went through to the O'Malleys' for Stephen.

'Did you have a decent time then?' Mary demanded.

'I did. Absolutely smashing, actually.'

'We heard a car draw up outside. Is it his?' Mo-Mo asked.

Beth nodded. 'An American Buick.'

Mo-Mo's eyes grew large. 'Fancy that!'

Stephen was fast asleep, but he woke when Beth picked him up and started to cry. She made shushing noises.

'As usual he's been an angel itself,' Mary declared.

Beth said she'd see Mary in the morning for a natter and would tell her then all about the restaurant they'd been to. Then she returned to her own house and found Gene with a large glass of whisky in his hand.

'So this is the little guy, eh?' Gene said, smiling at Stephen, who, endearingly, smiled back.

'Strong,' Gene commented, having given Stephen a finger to hold which Stephen was now firmly gripping. 'Sturdy too. An athlete's build, I'd say.'

'A bit early to tell that.' Beth laughed. Gene was right, though: the child was well built.

Beth put Stephen into his cot and tucked him up before giving him a loving kiss on the forehead. 'He'll be off again in a couple of minutes.'

'I like what you've done to the room,' Gene commented, gesturing round it with his glass.

Beth helped herself to sherry. She was well stocked with alcohol, which she could get from the club at trade prices, and occasionally slipped Seamus O'Malley a bottle of Irish for which he was always tremendously grateful. It pleased her to be able to do it.

'I've done my best with what's available. Everything's so scarce in wartime, you'll appreciate.'

'You've got taste, and that's something you can't buy.'

'You're very kind.'

'Not in the least. I'm only saying what's fact.'

Beth sat down, and Gene followed suit. 'You like children, I take it?'

'Oh, yeah,' he replied softly.

'Yet you haven't married?'

He sipped his drink. 'I may be thirty-eight but I'm not quite over the hill. There's still time for that, I reckon.'

'From what you've said I presume your sister Loretta isn't married either?'

'She has aspirations in that direction, let's say.'

'She has a boyfriend, then?'

'Not the sort she'd marry. She's been having a relationship with an Indian for the past year. A guy who works on the farm, called Michael Fleetfoot.'

'An Indian!' Beth exclaimed. 'You mean a Red Indian?'

'Of the Tobacco tribe.'

Beth was intrigued, as her expression clearly showed. 'Why isn't he the sort Loretta would marry?'

'Because he *is* an Indian. White people don't marry Indians in our neck of the woods. It just isn't done.'

'Does she love him?'

'Hell no! But he's young and handsome. And I suppose good in the sack.' Gene regarded her thoughtfully. 'Does that offend you?'

Beth shook her head. 'Not in the least. On the contrary, I find it fascinating. But what about you? Have you got some Indian girl tucked away somewhere?'

'Nope. I've got no one tucked away anywhere.'

Beth was relieved to hear it, then told herself not to be silly. As soon as Gene had met up with the Volunteers he'd be going back to Canada and out of her life.

'Have you heard anything further about the Volunteers?' she asked.

'Not so far. Theo and I have to go to the consulate tomorrow and I'm hoping they'll have some news then.'

'And you've no idea what the hold-up is?'

'None at all, although I suspect it's probably something mundane like a transport problem. On the other hand it could be something else entirely.'

He finished his drink. Beth offered him another but he refused, saying he tried to be careful when driving, especially when it was someone else's car.

'As you work at night, what do you do during the day?' he enquired.

Beth shrugged. 'The normal things. I clean the house

every week. I shop. I take Stephen for walks in the pram . . .'

'In that case do you have anything special scheduled for the day after tomorrow?' he interrupted.

'Why, what do you have in mind?'

'I'd like to drive down to Mauchline and have a look around. What about you and Stephen coming along?'

The idea of a drive in the country appealed to Beth, particularly one with Gene. 'I'd have to make sure I was back in time to start work.'

'Then we'll leave nice and early so there's no hassle on that score. Are you up by eight?'

'I can be.'

'I'll call for you then.'

'Can you manage downstairs all right on your own?' she asked at the door.

'I'll be OK.'

For a moment she thought he was going to kiss her, but then he was gone, swallowed up by the inky darkness.

That night she dreamt of being made love to by a Red Indian in full warpaint and feathers. In the morning, she realised the Indian's face had been Gene's.

Chapter 12

She was already in her coat with Stephen on her lap when he arrived on the dot of eight. As she got into the car she spotted Mary, plus several other neighbours, peering down at them. She gave Mary a wave, and received an extremely enthusiastic one in return.

Soon Glasgow was left behind and they drove along surrounded by the green of the countryside. 'It's marvellous to get out of horrible Glasgow,' Beth commented.

'Yeah. It's such a filthy hole. Even the better areas are dirty.'

'There are worse places than Glasgow!' she retorted hotly, feeling it was all right for her to criticise Glasgow should she want to – she was a native after all – but not for a foreigner to do so.

'OK, OK. Don't blow your top.' Gene smiled.

She calmed down again, chiding herself for over-reacting. 'It's a funny thing. Glaswegians are forever running down their city, but underneath it all they love it dearly. It's difficult to describe. Glasgow isn't merely where they live, it's an actual part of them. Like an arm or a leg.'

'It's still dirty.'

'I can't deny that,' she acknowledged, laughing.

'My father always intended to pay Mauchline a visit one day,' Gene said, a little further on. 'It seemed he'd promised his father he would but never got round to it. I'll be the first of the McKays to return there since the great-grandparents left.'

'When we were talking about your father the other evening you mentioned he'd always made life difficult for you. How did he do that?'

Gene shot Beth a quick sideways glance. 'I told you I'm thirty-eight, right?'

She nodded.

'Well, up until the day he died he only gave me five dollars a week allowance. *And* I had to get my own clothes out of that.'

'Surely your family aren't hard up?'

'Not in the least. We do exceptionally well out of the farm, always have done. Whatever else my father was he was a damn fine farmer.'

Beth frowned. 'I thought you told me you once saved up for a Norton?'

'I did. With money I earned outside the farm. For years I've been going into Stewarton several evenings a week to do casual carpentry work. That's how I've been earning bucks on the side to pay for some of the things Father just wouldn't buy me or provide cash for.'

'If that was the case, why didn't you leave home?'

'Because if I'd done so I would've lost the farm. I had no intention of letting that happen.'

'What do you mean, lose the farm?'

'Father would've disinherited me and the whole shebang would've gone to Loretta. Well, I couldn't allow that, could I? That farm's got my blood, sweat and tears in it and it's mine. No one's going to take it away from me – or if they do it'll be over my dead body, so help me.'

Beth could tell from the vehemence of Gene's tone and the expression on his face that he meant every word of what he'd just said. 'Your father sounds quite a tyrant,' she commented.

'You know something, Beth? I can't remember him ever, not once, putting his arm round me, or being affectionate in any way.'

'He must've loved your mother very much. Was she also of Scottish ancestry?'

'No. Her people were French Canadian. When I was a kid I discovered a photograph of her which my father thrashed me for looking at. I'd gone into his room, you see, which was strictly forbidden. She was very dark, with black hair and eyes. I thought she had a lovely face, but a mean, spiteful mouth.'

'What else did he do to you?'

Gene laughed mirthlessly. 'You got a free couple of months? It would take me that long to recount all the rotten things he dreamt up.'

They arrived at Mauchline to find it a typical Scottish village of sturdy stone houses, each one looking as though it was regularly scrubbed both inside and out. Gene parked the Buick in the main street and they got out, Beth wrapping Stephen to her with her shawl. Slowly they wandered round the village and back to the car again.

'I wonder . . .' Gene mused.

'What?'

'The farm my great-grandfather worked on was owned by a family called Douglas and I'm wondering if their descendants still have it.'

'Ask someone and find out.'

They waited by the car until a fresh-faced country woman with unkempt hair happened along. 'The Douglas place? Oh aye. You'll find that about two miles along the Failford Road on the left hand side,' she said.

Gene established which was the Failford Road and thanked the woman, who walked on, turning several times out of curiosity to glance behind her.

'That must be it over there,' Gene declared shortly afterwards, indicating a small complex consisting of a farmhouse and various other buildings which had come into view on their left hand side. A little further on he swung the car off the road and they got out again.

Squatting, Gene picked up a handful of rich brown soil and sifted it through his fingers, nodding approval as he did so. 'Good land this,' he said to Beth.

'A better farm than yours, do you think?'

He smiled. 'Not a chance. Anyway, it's only a fraction the size of what Loretta and I have.'

He pulled out a pipe, startling Beth who'd never seen him with one before. She was instantly reminded of Steve, who'd also smoked one. Gene puffed his pipe while gazing long and hard at the surrounding fields and hedgerows.

'A penny for them?'

'I was just thinking if my great-grandparents hadn't gone to Canada it could be me working this land today. A labourer, just as he was.'

'Instead of which you own your own farm.'

'Only half of it . . . only half . . . as yet,' Gene murmured.

And rounding on Beth he gave her a beaming smile.

The following night at five to eleven Gene appeared unexpectedly at the club to tell Beth they were going back to her place when she was finished.

She laughed. 'Are we indeed!'

'I've got a surprise for you. A real louie of one, which I'll show you when we get there.'

'What is it, then?' she demanded, her interest roused.

'If I told you now it wouldn't be a surprise.'

'Oh, come on!'

He shook his head, declaring firmly she'd see the surprise when they got back and that was that. In the meantime he'd have a Scotch to be going on with.

On the stroke of midnight Beth closed the bar and started to cash up. Kathleen came over to moan that her feet were killing her, as she'd been on the dance floor most of the evening. She sighed with relief when Gene said she could have a lift home with him and Beth.

When they arrived in Sweet Street Gene took a cardboard box from the Buick's boot and carried it upstairs. Reaching her landing, Beth let Gene into the house then went through to the O'Malleys' to collect Stephen. When she returned to her own house it was to discover that

Gene had already closed the curtains and lit the gas lamps.

She laid Stephen in his cot and gently tucked him up, noticing again that the older he got the more like Steve he became.

'Was it a difficult birth?' Gene asked, coming to the other side of the cot.

'No. It was a fairly easy one,' she replied, thinking it was a rather strange question for a man to ask.

'If you were only a few months married when your husband was killed you must've gotten pregnant quickly?'

An even stranger thing to say, she thought. 'What are you driving at, Gene?'

'Nothing at all. Would you like your surprise now?'

'Oh, yes, please!'

He crossed over to the cardboard box he'd placed on the table and took out a paper bundle. 'Any ideas?'

'Not a one.'

He unwrapped the bundle to reveal its contents: two huge T-bone steaks.

Beth gasped. 'They're absolutely enormous. Where on earth did you get them from?'

'I had a word with the consul who had a word with the consulate chef.'

'I've never even seen a T-bone before.'

'Well, tonight's the night your taste buds get a real treat. Cooking T-bones is my speciality.'

'You cook?' Beth was amazed. It was completely outwith her experience for a man – apart from a professional such as Colin at the café – to do such a thing.

'And what's more I'm good at it. My spaghetti bolognese

is the talk of Stewarton, I'll have you know. Now, have you ever had broccoli before?'

She shook her head. 'What is it?'

'A green vegetable that goes perfectly with steak. It's served with a squeeze of lemon over it, or else melted butter. Which would you prefer? I've brought both.'

'I don't mind.'

'Then we'll have it with lemon, which I think is best. Now why don't you just sit down, light yourself a cigarette, and leave the rest to me. Oh! I nearly forgot.' He returned to the cardboard box to produce a tissue-wrapped bottle. 'Best French champagne. What do you say about that?'

'Lovely.' She smiled, remembering the champagne she'd once been promised by Steve.

Gene said he'd have to do the steaks individually as there wasn't enough room under the grill for both of them. Indeed, they were so large that one covered the entire grill pan, some of it even hanging down over the side.

'Let's have the champagne now,' Gene suggested. He popped the bottle's cork, which went flying off to land somewhere out of sight underneath the sink.

The champagne was tangy and rich. Absolutely gorgeous, Beth thought, taking a second sip. She was delighted to discover that the bubbles actually did tickle the inside of her nose.

The delicious smell of grilling steak filled the air. Combined with champagne, it made a heady mixture. 'Too bad we don't have any onions. I'd have loved fried onions with mine,' Beth said.

'I'll remember that for next time.'

She regarded him lazily through slitted cat eyes. He wasn't exactly a handsome man but he was certainly not ugly. His hair was dark brown and very shiny, and his nose was curved like the beak of a bird of prey. She couldn't pin down the specific colour of his dark eyes, as it was forever changing. His skin had a faint olive tinge about it, except at the chin where it was almost blue. In height he was average, a little taller than most Glaswegian men, and his shoulders were broad and muscular. His arms looked strong, and his voice was a pleasant baritone.

'Come and smell this,' he said, gesturing her over.

She joined him and poked her nose at the grill. He'd made some sort of sauce which he'd spread on top of the steak, and this was now starting to give off a rather spicy, mouth-watering aroma. She turned to him, the beginnings of a smile curling the corners of her lips, and suddenly their faces were only inches apart.

The smile died as she stared intently at him. He was staring intently back, and her stomach felt as if it had been transformed into a tunnel through which warm water was rushing.

Slowly he took her into his arms. Then he was kissing her, holding her tightly to him as he did so, and she was kissing him in return.

'Careful you don't burn the steak,' she said huskily when the embrace was over.

'I won't do that.'

Beth poured herself more champagne.

A few minutes past ten o'clock in the morning three days later there was a knock on Beth's door. Still wearing her dressing gown she answered it, thinking Mary had come for the usual morning blether. Instead she found a rather pale-faced Gene.

'Come away in,' she invited, ushering him through.

'I've hardly slept a wink all night,' he told her, flopping into the nearest chair.

'What's wrong with you?'

'There's nothing wrong with me. It's just that I spent all day yesterday with the Volunteers—'

'They've finally arrived, then!' she interjected excitedly.

Gene nodded. 'Theo and I were alerted as we were having breakfast. A car was laid on to take us to a place called Wemyss Bay, where we caught a boat for the Isle of Arran.' He paused for a moment. 'Jeez!' he choked. Shaking his head, he groped for his cigarettes.

'That bad, eh?'

'Reading about casualties, or even being told about them, is one thing. When you actually see them with your own eyes and hear a first-hand account of the stories they have to tell it becomes a whole different ball game.'

'So they had their casualties with them.'

'Yeah. There's a big mansion on the east side of the island that's been converted into a makeshift hospital. The other guys are in British accommodation close by.'

'Did you and Mr Hasten visiting them?'

'They were knocked out. I mean that. Really knocked out. A kid I know personally cried when he saw me. Bobby Sorenson's his name. He's nineteen years old and he's lost a leg. He told me he was the victim of a booby trap.'

'That's awful,' Beth sympathised.

'I've known that kid all his life. Why, I can remember the day he was born.'

'Did you find out where they'd been?'

'Sicily. They were part of the July invasion.'

'And what was the hold-up?'

'Well, it wasn't transport as I thought. They were waiting for all the wounded to be fit enough to travel.'

'What happens to them now?'

'The real bad casualties are being shipped home next week. The not so bad ones will be staying in Arran till they've recovered, when they'll rejoin the other Volunteers who by that time will be back in action.'

'Are you going to visit them again?'

'Yeah. Tomorrow.'

'Then what?' she asked, already knowing the answer.

'There's a convoy leaving Monday. Theo and I will be on it.'

A strained smile stretched her face as she rose to her feet. 'How about a cup of tea?'

'If things had been otherwise—'

'That's all right. I understand perfectly,' she cut in.

Doggedly he went on, 'I would have taken longer. Courted you properly.'

'I said I understand, Gene,' she snapped, busying herself at the sink filling the kettle.

'I appreciate we've only known each other a ridiculously short while, but in that time I've come to feel a great deal for you. Enough to ask you to marry me.'

She went very still. Water bubbled back out of the kettle to spill down its sides. 'Say that again.'

He came up behind her and put his hands on her

shoulders. 'You're the woman for me, Beth. I've known that almost right from the beginning. You would do me great honour if you'd agree to be my wife.'

She wasn't hearing this, she told herself. Except she was. Her mind whirled. She was confused, dumbfounded, and elated all at the same time. The unexpected proposal had quite taken her breath away.

He turned her round, then kissed her. 'Well?'

'I need a little time, Gene. That's only fair.'

'All right, but not too long. Monday's only five days away, after all, and there would be a lot of arranging in the meantime.'

'What about Stephen?'

'I'll treat him as my own son. You have my word on that.'

Then he kissed her again.

That evening before opening, a thoughtful Beth idly polished glasses behind the bar. She liked Gene and was very attracted to him as a man, but she wasn't in love with him. Perhaps . . . perhaps one day she would be. Not the same sort of love she'd had for Steve, but love all the same.

On the other hand, what was there for her here ? The house in Sweet Street might be pleasant inside, but the disgusting slum outside was a different matter entirely. It certainly wasn't the place she'd choose to bring up her child. Stephen was still a baby, but he wouldn't remain one much longer. All too soon he'd be a product of his environment: a dreadful slummie brat. The prospect filled her with dismay.

Then there was her job here at Bruce's Cave. Well paid and reasonably secure, it was true. But did she want to go on working in a dingy club when a brand new life was being offered her? A sort of life she could only now guess at, but one that had to be a great deal better than her present circumstances.

And what an opportunity it would be for Stephen! Fresh air. Oodles of good food. A farm to grow up on, surely heaven for any young lad. Especially one with a little bit of spunk about him, as Stephen was bound to have being Steve's son.

She'd be mad to turn Gene down, she decided. It was a chance she must grab firmly with both hands. She would have a husband who was a kind and caring man; Stephen a father who'd promised her he'd treat the boy as his own.

There was one fly in the ointment, however. If she accepted Gene's proposal she'd have to produce certain documents for their marriage and travel arrangements: a previous wedding certificate and Stephen's birth certificate. The first she didn't have; the second gave Stephen's surname as Somerville and not Ramsay.

She came to the conclusion that Gene would have to be told the truth, and the sooner the better. What happened after that was up to him.

The desk porter looked at Beth in astonishment. Glancing down at his watch, he raised an eyebrow.

'I appreciate how late it is. But the matter is extremely urgent,' Beth said. She had come to Gene's hotel straight from finishing at the club, and it was almost one o'clock in the morning.

'It's impossible for you to visit Mr McKay in his room. Hotel rules, you know. However, if you'll wait in the lounge I'll inform him you're here.'

Beth laid a florin in front of the porter, whose manner abruptly changed.

'Would Madam care for a pot of tea while she's speaking to Mr McKay?'

'That would be very nice. Thank you.'

'I'll arrange it, then.'

The hotel lounge was chintzy and smelt of stale cigarette smoke. There were some newspapers lying on a table, and Beth picked one up and read it absent-mindedly while she waited for Gene to appear. He came into the lounge wearing clothes that had obviously been thrown on, a tuft of hair standing straight up at the back of his head.

'What's happened?' he demanded.

'Nothing.' She offered him a cigarette. 'I promised you an answer as soon as I'd thought it through. And the answer is yes,' she said after they'd both lit up.

'Oh, Beth!'

'But before we go ahead there's something you have to know which might stop you wanting to marry me.'

They were interrupted at that point by the arrival of the tea. Beth told the porter just to leave the tray as she'd pour, and waited until he had gone before turning her attention back to Gene. 'I have no right to call myself Mrs Ramsay. Steve and I were never married,' she stated baldly. 'He was killed a week before we were due to be. To make matters easier for myself when I moved to Sweet Street I told people I was a widow, which isn't true. I'm an unmarried mother.'

Breaking eye contact with Gene, she picked up the teapot and poured. Slowly, she added sugar and milk to his cup and then to her own, giving him time to think. Then she took up her cup and sat back in her chair.

'I'm glad you told me,' Gene said.

'I wouldn't have if I hadn't had to. But I did.'

He nodded that he understood. 'If you like, when we get to Canada I'll keep up the pretence that you were married before. For Stephen's sake.'

There was a long pause. Finally she whispered, 'Thank you.'

'This tea's godawful,' he declared, grimacing into his cup. 'If I drive you home will you give me something stronger?'

'You're on.'

He took her hand in his as they headed for the door.

The next few days were fast and furious for Beth. If it hadn't been for Mary O'Malley on her side and Linal Cardy the Canadian consul on Gene's the whole thing would have been quite impossible, but make it they did, getting married by special licence on the Monday morning a few hours before their ship was due to sail.

Cissie came to the ceremony, as did Mary, Kathleen and young Michael. Colin and Edna Moncur also attended, along with several girls from the club whom Beth had been particularly friendly with.

Beth had briefly toyed with the idea of inviting Roy and Margaret, but decided against it. She realised it wouldn't bother her if she never saw or even heard of Roy again.

Linal Cardy was there with his wife Sue and their daughter Sandy-Jo. Also present was Theo Hasten, looking somewhat bemused by it all.

From the ceremony they went to a room in the consulate where the Cardys had very kindly laid on drinks and a buffet. Then they all drove down to Merkland Quay where Beth, Gene, Stephen and Theo Hasten embarked upon the TSS *Arconia*.

The previous days had been such a whirlwind of activity that it hadn't really sunk in for Beth that she was leaving Glasgow for good. It hit her now with sledgehammer force as she stepped on to the gangplank and realised she was technically no longer on Scottish soil. Clutching Stephen to her bosom, she hurried up the gangplank on to the deck. Gene joined her at the guard rail, and almost at once the gangplank was removed, and the various lines securing the ship to the quay were cast off.

Beth remembered then another ship setting off down the Clyde: a grey warship with Teddy Ramsay and his pals Edgar, Jacko and Ron aboard. All dead now, as was Steve. Gone for ever.

She was doing the right thing by going to Canada, she reassured herself. Nevertheless, now the actual moment of departure had arrived, how it hurt to be saying goodbye to Glasgow and Scotland.

'You OK?' Gene queried.

She tried to reply, but was unable to do so because of the lump in her throat.

'God bless you! God bless you, me darling. May St Peter and all the other blessed saints look after you and your angel son,' Mary called out, waving a hand furiously in farewell.

Cissie stood slightly apart, still as a graven statue. In her mind she was seeing Beth as a wee lassie playing with her father, and suddenly she felt old. Old, grey and finished.

'Goodbye, lass,' she whispered, through lips that fluttered briefly, then were still again.

'Will we go below?'

'Not yet,' Beth replied. With Stephen clasped tightly to her she stood there in the biting wind watching her ma till finally Cissie was lost to view.

'Land of the hills and heather, land of the shining feather . . .' someone was singing further up the ship.

Beth hooked an arm through Gene's, and they went to find their cabin.

Chapter 13

'Stewarton!' Gene proudly announced, gesturing at the cluster of buildings surrounding the railway station. He and Beth had just got off the train from Toronto. They'd disembarked from the TSS *Arconia* in Halifax, Nova Scotia, and flown from there to Toronto where they'd overnighted before journeying on. They'd left Theo Hasten behind in Toronto, where his home and business were.

A porter appeared and Gene arranged for their bags to remain behind at the railway station for the time being.

'Let's have a walk through town and I'll show you the sights,' he suggested.

'I still don't understand why you didn't telegraph to say we were arriving?'

Gene gave a lazy smile. 'It's not every day a man brings home his bride. Let's make the most of it, huh?'

'You know best.'

It was a long way from Sauchiehall Street, Beth reflected, staring down Stewarton's main artery, a straight, dusty road with two- and three-storey wooden buildings on either side. It was rather similar to many of the towns she'd seen in the movies about the wild west: wooden porches, wooden balconies that overhung the road, men with large-brimmed hats – hats that weren't quite stetsons but not far off it.

Gene took a deep breath. 'It's great to be back,' he murmured.

Beth gazed about her. It was all so strange. So alien!

'And let's hope that before long you'll also come to think of it as home,' Gene added, sensing what she was feeling.

Beth gently rocked Stephen in the crook of her arm. He was fast asleep. 'Let's hope so,' she agreed.

'I'll tell you what. As we're in town why don't we go to the store and buy what we need for that little guy?'

The idea appealed to Beth – she loved spending money. Besides, Gene was right: there were certain items that Stephen needed as soon as possible, including a cot and a pram to replace those she'd had to leave behind.

The store turned out to be a general one crammed with an incredible assortment of articles. The owner was called Mr Westlake, a small dumpy man with white hair and beard who'd have made a perfect Santa Claus.

'Hell, Gene! And how are our boys overseas?'

'Not so good, I'm afraid.' Gene gave him a short report on the Volunteers.

'Dear oh dear.' Mr Westlake frowned.

Stephen woke up and began to cry. Beth held him to her bosom and patted his back. 'He's hungry,' she said to Gene.

'And who's this little fella?' Mr Westlake enquired.

'My son.'

Mr Westlake looked stunned. 'Eh?'

Gene gave a low laugh. 'In a manner of speaking, that is. Mr Westlake, I'd like you to meet my wife Beth. Stephen is her child by a previous marriage, and now my stepson.'

'Well I'll be—' Mr Westlake exclaimed, tugging at his beard.

'Hello.' Beth smiled.

'Hello to you and welcome to Stewarton, Mrs McKay.'

'We met in Glasgow, Scotland. And it was love at first sight,' said Gene.

'Love at first sight, eh?' For the briefest of seconds there was an amused glint in Mr Westlake's eyes.

Stephen was now shrieking at the top of his lungs. 'He'll have to be fed,' Beth said anxiously.

Mr Westlake suggested Beth go into his kitchen and feed Stephen there, an offer she gratefully accepted. He took a packet of baby food from one of the shelves and led the way through a door into the rear of the store. In the kitchen he explained where everything Beth might need was to be found, and left her to it.

Ten minutes later Gene appeared in the kitchen to say he'd rung the farm and the truck was on its way to pick them up. When Stephen was fed and happy again they returned to the front of the store, where Gene had Beth choose some Levi jeans, insisting she'd need them round the farm. He also bought her a pair of fur-lined boots and several pairs of practical shoes, plus a parka for the cold weather. Finally he drew up a list of items they needed and Mr Westlake promised they'd be delivered to the farm later on that day.

The pickup arrived, driven by one of the most handsome men Beth had ever seen. He had jet-black hair, which he wore shoulder length, eyes of the same colour, and brownish, rather rough-textured skin. She guessed correctly that this was Michael Fleetfoot, the Tobacco Indian Gene had told her about.

'Hi, Michael! I'd like you to meet my wife.'

Michael stared at Beth in astonishment.

'I'm pleased to meet you,' Beth said, wondering if it would be wrong of her to shake his hand. As he didn't offer, neither did she.

Michael took off his hat. 'It's an honour to make your acquaintance, Mrs McKay,' he replied very formally.

She almost told him to call her Beth, but stopped herself in time, not sure whether that would be correct either. She'd have to consult with Gene about these things.

She decided there and then that she liked Michael Fleetfoot. There was a warmth about him, plus a sort of innocent quality, which together made an attractive combination.

Gene invited Beth to get into the cabin and told Michael to ride behind. They said goodbye to Mr Westlake and drove to the railway station, where Gene asked Michael to fetch their luggage.

'How far away is the farm?' Beth asked when they were under way again.

'The house is about six miles. Won't take us long to get there.'

Beth sat Stephen on her knee so he could stare out of the window. He stayed quiet, fascinated by the passing scene. Finally, they turned off the main road on to a rather bumpy track.

'That's the house over there,' Gene said a few minutes later, pointing ahead and to the right.

It was a big, sprawling clapboard affair that had a somewhat Gothic look about it. Smoke was curling from several of the many chimneys on its roof. There were two barns behind the house and a cigar-shaped construction that Beth later learned was called a silo. There were also some small sheds and lean-tos. Somewhere a cock was crowing, a long-drawn-out mournful sound as though it was proclaiming to the world that it wasn't at all happy with its lot. As they drew up in front of the house Beth saw that it had originally been painted white but the colour had now faded to a dirty grey. The paint was peeling badly in places.

Gene jumped from the pickup, slamming the door behind him, and strode forward a number of paces to shade his eyes and stare off into the distance. Beth was left to get herself and Stephen out.

Gene swung round to face Michael, who was standing at the rear of the pickup. 'When did Loretta start harvesting?' he demanded.

'Beginning of the week. We finished last night.'

'Son of a bitch!' Gene swore. 'I didn't want to miss that.'

'Do you want me to get Miss Loretta for you?'

'Where is she?'

'Out at west field, I believe.'

'Time enough to see her when she returns. In the meantime you can take our bags up to my bedroom.'

'Yes, sir.'

'And Michael, should you bump into Loretta before we do, not a word about Mrs McKay. That's to be my personal surprise. Understand?'

'I understand.' Michael nodded, giving Beth a glance out of the corner of his eye.

Beth followed Gene through a screen door into a large kitchen. Glancing round, she noted a pot-bellied heating stove beside which was a neatly stacked pile of cut wood, and close by a cast-iron wood-burning cooking stove. There was a sink with an ornate handpump for water and some shelves bearing an assortment of articles, while against one wall was a very old Welsh dresser displaying crockery.

'Spacious,' she murmured.

They went up some creaky stairs and along a dull passageway to more stairs. Going up these they came to Gene's bedroom on another dull and gloomy landing. The whole place desperately needed a coat of paint and a damn good spring clean, Beth thought. Loretta might be a dab hand at farming but she was certainly no housewife.

The bed was large with brass ends and sagged in the middle. Over in one corner was a washstand on which stood a pretty basin and jug. There was a moth-eaten carpet on the floor, and an oak wardrobe that had seen better days stood against a wall. The walls themselves were papered, the paper so ancient the pattern on it had faded to the extent that you had to peer closely to see there was a pattern at all. The paper had started to peel high up on one wall and there was a damp patch roughly the size of a cauliflower beside the wardrobe.

'It needs a bit of tarting up, I'm afraid,' Gene apologised. 'But now you're here I'll have the incentive to do something about it.'

Beth gave him a grateful smile.

Michael knocked the open door, then entered carrying their bags. Beth thanked him, and asked him to put them on the bed.

The room was absolutely awful, she thought in despair. The entire house was dreadful come to that. She wasn't quite sure what she'd been expecting but it was certainly something better than this. How a house could be built out in the open with only a few buildings nearby and get so little light was a mystery to her. 'Is there any chance of getting a chest of drawers in here?' she queried. 'We do need one.'

'Sure, honey. There are some drawers in my father's room. I'll bring them through right away.'

It didn't take long for Gene to bring through piecemeal his father's chest of drawers, which he quickly reassembled.

'How's that, hon?'

'Lovely,' she answered, giving him a peck on the cheek for his trouble.

Crossing to the window he stared out, seeming to become lost in thought.

'I'm sorry you missed the harvesting.'

With a grunt he roused himself from his reverie. 'How did you know I was thinking about that?'

Beth smiled. 'It wasn't too hard, believe me.'

'First one I've ever missed. That was the main reason I was so eager to catch that particular convoy – I reckoned I could still get back in time. Except the harvest was ready just that little bit earlier than I'd anticipated.'

'You don't always harvest at the same time, then?'

'Not quite. There can be several weeks' leeway either side. The determining factor is the weather. We harvest according to that.'

'As you're so pleased to be back, why don't you go out and have a nose round while I put our things away here?' she suggested.

'Good idea. Can you find your way to the kitchen again?'

'If not I'll scream for help.'

He grinned. 'You do that.'

When he was gone the smile died on her face. Sitting on the bed beside Stephen and the cases she dropped her head and cried softly for a few moments. She was so far away from Glasgow and all that she knew. It was bewildering – even terrifying.

'Come on, lass,' she chided herself. 'This won't do at all.'

Rousing herself, she started to unpack, making plans for the redecoration of the bedroom.

'How do you like Canadian coffee?' Gene asked. It was early evening of the same day and he, Beth and Stephen were in the kitchen.

'Nectar after what we've been making do with in Britain for the past few years.'

The screen door suddenly banged open and a woman strode in. She came up short when she saw the little gathering.

'Hi, El!' Gene smiled.

Loretta's startled gaze went from Gene to Beth to Stephen, then back to Gene again. 'Successful trip?' she asked.

'Very.'

Beth thought that the thing which hit you first about Gene's sister was her plainness. She was taller than Gene by several inches with a stringy muscly body that appeared completely devoid of breasts. Her nose was curved like Gene's, her eyes were small and beady, and she had extremely large teeth, hands and feet.

'Hello,' Beth said.

'Hello,' Loretta replied, a frown creasing her forehead.

It was obvious how much Gene was enjoying this moment. He was trying to keep a straight face and not succeeding. 'We arrived in a couple of hours ago,' he said.

'*We?*'

'This is Beth. We got married in Glasgow.' There was a hint of triumph in his voice.

The colour drained from Loretta's face, and she went very still.

'The baby is Beth's son Stephen by a previous marriage. My stepson now,' Gene went on.

Loretta twitched all over, the way a played-out fish might when being gaffed.

'Beth's first husband was killed while serving with the RAF. He was a war hero.'

Loretta licked her lips. Colour was gradually returning to her face. 'That was a quick romance.'

'It was love at first sight,' Gene replied, repeating what he'd told Mr Westlake.

Beth rose and extended a hand. 'I've been looking forward tremendously to our meeting. Gene's told me so much about you.'

Loretta twitched again. She shot Gene a filthy look which he pretended not to see. Then, reluctantly, she went to Beth and put her hard hand in Beth's outstretched one. 'Welcome,' she said through gritted teeth, trying to smile.

'Thank you. I know I'm going to be very happy here.'

'Now if you'll excuse me I have to go upstairs. Supper at the usual time.' And with that Loretta hurriedly left the kitchen.

What a peculiar woman! Beth thought. There again,

maybe she should have expected this. After all, how would she feel about a strange female invading her home right out of the blue!

'Don't you worry. She'll come round,' Gene said reassuringly.

'It must've been a bit of a shock for her.'

'Oh, it was. It most certainly was that!'

'Perhaps you should go after her?'

Gene shook his head.

'Well, you know your sister best.'

'I do indeed.'

'I thought she'd look a lot more like you,' Beth commented.

'We might be twins, but that doesn't mean we have to look more alike than any other brother and sister.'

'So who's the older?'

'What makes you ask that?' he said sharply.

Beth shrugged. 'I don't know. I just wondered, that's all.'

'The truth of the matter is no one rightly knows. As I told you, our mother died giving birth to us and Father was so upset he never thought to ask that question at the time. When he finally did come to wonder about it the midwife who'd attended the birth had left the country. It therefore remains a matter of speculation as to which of us is the firstborn.'

Beth sensed he didn't want to discuss the matter further. Though for the life of her she couldn't think why. But she wasn't surprised when Gene changed the subject.

Later, Beth entered the kitchen to find Loretta busy at the cooking stove, from which a marvellous smell was emanating. Gene had gone back outside to attend to something he needed to do.

'Can I help at all?'

Loretta glanced round at her, considered the offer, then shook her head.

'Smells delicious. What is it?'

'Spanish rice.'

Beth approached the stove and saw that the rice was being cooked in a very large frying pan. There were a great many bits and pieces mixed up with the yellow grains, most of which she was unfamiliar with.

'What are those?' She pointed at some red and green slivers.

'Peppers.'

'You mean pepper like salt and pepper?'

Loretta laughed. 'No. They're a . . . vegetable I suppose you'd call them. I've never really thought about it before.'

'What do they taste like?'

'Sharp and spicy. They give the rice zing.'

Beth looked up. 'I hope we're going to be friends. I'd hate for it to be otherwise.'

'A lightning romance, Gene said?' Loretta gave a thin smile.

'That's right.'

Loretta stared into the pan and slowly stirred its contents. 'Funny how you can misjudge someone, even someone you've known all your life. I just never figured Gene to be able to move so fast. It's quite out of character.'

'He's never struck me as being slow.' Beth frowned.

'You forget we're country folk. Country folk deliberate on things longer than city people, and Gene tends to deliberate longer than most. Up until he met you, that is. Now why should that be, I wonder?'

Beth flushed. 'I didn't set out to trap him if that's what you're insinuating.'

'Young widow with a baby to look after?' Loretta purred.

'It wasn't that way at all. You're distorting the facts.'

'Am I?'

'Yes you are.'

'Maybe,' said Loretta.

'What are you discussing?' Gene had silently entered the kitchen behind them.

'Nothing interesting. That right, Beth?' Loretta replied.

'Where's Stephen?' Gene asked, looking round the room.

'He's down for the night,' Beth told him.

'Shattered, eh?'

'It's been a long day.'

'If someone will put out the knives and forks supper's almost ready,' Loretta announced.

Gene smiled at Beth. 'I'll show you where they are.'

When the table was laid Gene produced a stone jar of cider, made from the farm's own apples, he informed Beth proudly. She asked if he made the cider himself, but he said that was done at a farm a few miles away where they grew apples as a main crop.

The cider was sweet on the palate, and very strong. Beth felt it going straight to her head.

'Makes your toes curl, eh?' Gene grinned.

'You can say that again with knobs on.'

'It's a lot stronger than Scotch whisky, so be careful of it.'

221

'I will,' she assured him, touching his hand affectionately.

Loretta dished up at the stove, then laid their plates in front of them. She sat down facing Beth.

'What's this?' Gene frowned.

'Spanish rice. What does it look like?'

'I know that. It's just I was expecting a T-bone on my first night home.'

'Wasn't convenient,' Loretta replied shortly, beginning to eat.

The rice was as delicious as it smelt, full and fruity, yet with a distinct sharpness to it at the same time. 'We tend to cook very plainly in Glasgow,' Beth said. 'I've got a lot to learn.'

'That's OK, hon. I'll teach you.' Gene turned to Loretta. 'What do you think about that boy upstairs? Isn't he something?'

For a second Loretta's eyes blazed fire. 'He's certainly a good-looking kid.'

'He sure is. He sure is.' Gene beamed at his sister, who stared back. 'Beth had a real easy delivery. No complications whatever. Isn't that so, Beth?'

Beth nodded, wondering why he seemed so impressed – fascinated even – by easy deliveries.

'A man would be proud to have a son like that.'

'He's only your stepson,' Loretta said quietly.

'Quite so, El. But with some luck it shouldn't be long before he has a little brother to keep him company.'

'Maybe you'll only have girls.' Loretta smiled.

'I'll tell you what. We'll have a dozen, shall we? Six of each.' Gene grinned at Beth.

'Don't you think that's a bit ambitious?'

'Hell no! Folks in these parts have a tradition of large families. Why, there was a couple out Chesley way who had twenty-two children of whom seventeen lived. What do you think of that?'

'Moo!' Beth replied.

Gene bellowed out a laugh, and even Loretta grinned. 'I like it.' He nodded. 'Great sense of humour, El. One of the things that first attracted me to her.'

'And what attracted you, Beth?'

Beth thought back. 'His being rather shy. I found that very appealing.'

'Shy!' Gene mused. 'I've never considered myself to be that.'

Beth cocked an ear, having heard a far-off sound that could be crying. Yes, it definitely was. 'If you'll excuse me, Stephen's woken up,' she said, rising from the table.

It was dark outside now, so she took a paraffin lamp with her to light the way. As she mounted the stairs the lamp cast weird, flickering shadows on the walls, shadows that twisted and turned seemingly with a life of their own.

It was chilly in their bedroom, while outside the wind was moaning. She made a mental note to ask Gene if it would be all right to have a fire here in the evening from now on, as that would not only warm the room but also make it cheery. Stephen had thrown his covers on to the floor and got cold, which was why he'd wakened and started crying. Making soothing noises Beth tucked him up again, and within seconds he was back off to sleep.

She was on the lower set of stairs leading to the ground

floor when voices raised in anger erupted from the kitchen, Loretta's strident tones rising above Gene's baritone.

She opened the kitchen door and the argument ceased immediately. Gene was red-faced and puffing slightly, Loretta pale and still. 'Coffee, anyone?' Beth asked, pretending nothing was amiss.

Gene grunted that he'd love some. Producing his pipe, he began to pack it.

'How about you, Loretta?'

'Yeah. Only make it real strong. That's how we like it.'

Beth was aware of Loretta watching her as she filled the coffee pot.

'Everyone works on a farm. What can you do?' Loretta asked suddenly.

'I know nothing at all about farming. But I'm willing to learn.'

Loretta snorted. 'You have to be born to it, as Gene and I were. How about housework?'

'I'm used to that.'

'Right. From now on the house is your province, including cooking.'

'I'm happy with that arrangement, if you are?'

'I wouldn't have suggested it if I wouldn't be happy with it,' Loretta snapped back.

This wasn't going at all the way she'd hoped, Beth thought. Loretta seemed determined to be nasty to her. Well, hopefully time would heal that. It would have to if they were all going to live together. 'I'll start first thing tomorrow,' she said.

'Breakfast is at five thirty,' Loretta said.

'What about the farmhands?'

'I'm not with you?'

'Do we give them breakfast as well? I believe that's the custom in Britain.'

'It certainly isn't here. Anyway, only one hand lives on the farm and that's Michael. He has a couple of rooms at the rear of the house where he caters for himself.'

'So it's breakfast for three and a half, then.' Beth smiled, thinking she'd have to check with Gene to find out what he and Loretta were used to having in the morning.

'Listen, I've just had the most marvellous idea!' Gene exclaimed, thumping the table with his fist.

'What's that?' Beth asked.

'The harvest is safely in and I've just returned from overseas with a brand new wife. So why don't we have a party to celebrate?'

'Are you crazy? We've never had a party here,' Loretta retorted.

'Then that's another reason for having one. What do you say, Beth?'

'I agree with you. It's a marvellous idea.'

'Tell you what. We'll butcher one of the cattle and roast it whole . . .'

'An *entire* cow?' Beth exclaimed.

'Sure. We'll barbecue out front and do a hog as well. I'll get one from Johnny Bauge. He rears the best porkers in all Ontario.'

'What's barbecue?'

'Of course, you don't have that sort of thing in Scotland. It merely means you cook outdoors instead of in. Usually hamburgers and steaks over charcoal, but in this instance it'll be a great deal bigger than that. I'll have Michael arrange it all.'

'And when are we going to have this party?' Loretta enquired.

'You don't sound too enthusiastic.'

'You spending money takes a little getting used to, that's all.'

'Huh!' Gene snorted.

Turning to Beth, Loretta went on, 'I take it by now you have discovered he's dreadfully mean?'

'That's a lie!' he retorted vehemently.

'I've never noticed Gene being tight.' Beth frowned.

Loretta pretended to think for a moment, then snapped her fingers. 'How stupid of me! Naturally he wouldn't have been that way over in Britain. Everything was being paid for by the Farmers' League.'

Gene glared at his sister, who grinned back at him. 'If I am careful with the bucks it's because of the years I had to exist on nickels and dimes.'

'It was no different for me. But I'm not mean.'

'You're confusing meanness with being careful with money. I just can't bear to see money being wasted. I suppose it's my Scottish ancestry.'

Loretta smiled. 'Bullshit!'

'I'm proposing a party. That's hardly mean, is it?' he yelled at her.

'And I'm wondering who's actually going to pay for this party. You or the Farmers' League?'

'That's a goddamn evil thing to say!'

She nodded. 'I thought so. I can see it written all over your face. It *is* the Farmers' League who's going to pick up the tab. Do you intend to include the cost in your overseas expenses? Is that how you're going to do it?' When she got no reply she laughed triumphantly. 'Bingo! Right on the old button!'

It was a revelation for Beth, who'd never had even the faintest inkling that Gene was a tightwad. But then, as Loretta had pointed out, she'd had no time to discover it. He'd been on expenses ever since they'd met. And now she came to think of it, hadn't his car been supplied by the consulate? And the steaks and champagne he'd brought to her house that night?

Gene drew on his pipe to blow smoke in a defiant stream away from him. 'Five bucks a week till I was thirty-six plus what I could earn doing carpentry work. A guy had to be careful if he wanted to keep a couple of dollars in his jeans.'

Judging from the thoughtful expression on Beth's face, Loretta reckoned she'd made her point. 'On reflection I wholeheartedly approve of the party idea. We'll invite lots of eligible bachelors. OK?'

'As the party's mainly in honour of my new bride I'll draw up the guest list.'

Loretta shook her head. 'We own this place straight down the middle. So if you want my agreement to a party then we share the guest list the same way. Half your invites, half mine.'

'That sounds fair to me,' Beth commented.

'All right,' Gene agreed reluctantly. 'That's how it'll be.'

'Let's name a date then,' Loretta suggested.

Gene sucked on his pipe. 'I'd like to wait a week or two. I feel it wouldn't be right having it immediately, while the worst of the wounded Volunteers are in the process of arriving home. They came over in the same convoy as us.'

'Were they as badly chewed up as we heard?'

'You know Bobby Sorenson?'

She nodded.

'He lost a leg.'

'Oh!' Loretta exclaimed.

'And Hank Molloy?'

'The Molloy kid with red hair?'

'That's the one. He's been blinded.'

'In both eyes?'

'Yeah.'

'Shiiit!'

'They were involved in the invasion of Sicily and really got put through the mangle. So we'll give it a couple of weeks to let the emotion of their homecoming die down a bit. During that time I'll also have to go to Hamilton for at least one night to give the report of my trip to the next full meeting of the League.'

'Let's make it three weeks this Saturday, then. That gives us plenty of time to get organised and a reasonable breathing space for the Volunteers,' Loretta proposed.

'Perfect,' Gene agreed.

Beth lit a cigarette. 'A whole cow!' she said in awe.

'*And* a pig,' Gene added with a grin.

Chapter 14

A little later Beth and Gene decided to turn in. The first thing Beth did on reaching their bedroom was to check that Stephen was still well tucked up. Then, because it was even chillier in the room than it had been earlier on, she hurriedly undressed.

'What was the argument about?' she queried as she shrugged herself into a thick flannelette nightdress.

'What argument?'

'The one you were having with Loretta when I came downstairs after being up to see wee Stephen.'

'There was no argument.'

Beth stopped en route to the bed to stare at him. 'I heard the pair of you at it, Gene.'

'You've been imagining things.'

'I was not! I distinctly heard the pair of you arguing!'

'We must just have been talking loudly. We both have a tendency to do that.'

Had she imagined it? she wondered. Had she mistaken loud talking for an argument? No, of course not. And yet what possible reason could Gene have for lying to her? Unless he was embarrassed at squabbling with his sister on his first day home? That must be it, she decided.

They got into bed at the same time. Gene put out the lamp and immediately turned and drew her close.

She was extremely tired; not at all in the mood for lovemaking. Nevertheless, she allowed him to kiss her and caress her breasts.

'Can we leave it tonight, Gene? Please?' she whispered when the kiss was over.

'I can't get enough of you,' he whispered back.

'I'm absolutely shattered, love. It's been an extremely long day.'

'But I want you.' His hand snaked down the length of her nightdress to move up again inside it.

'It's been every night since we were married. Most after-noons as well,' she pleaded.

'That's because I find you so attractive.'

'Perhaps in the morning . . .'

'The morning as well,' he said, and began tugging up her nightdress.

Anger flared in Beth. It was the first time she'd refused him and he was completely disregarding her. My God, he really was insatiable! He'd be at it morning, noon and night given half a chance.

'I don't feel like doing it one little bit,' she declared somewhat fiercely.

'It won't take long, hon. A couple of minutes, that's all,' he said huskily, pulling himself on top of her.

'I said no!'

He stared down at her, a puzzled frown creasing his face. 'What have I done?'

'Nothing.'

'Then what's wrong?'

'I simply don't feel like it, Gene. Can't you understand that?'

He didn't reply for a few moments. Then, in a strangulated voice, he said, 'I love you desperately, Beth, and want you so much.'

'I really *am* tired, though,' she persisted.

He wasn't going to be denied. He was determined not to miss a single opportunity. 'It's our first night at the farm. Our first night together in the home where we'll be spending the rest of our lives. Don't you think . . . in the circumstances . . . that it's only right and proper for us to . . . celebrate that fact?'

Damn him! she thought. He was making her feel guilty. As if *she* was in the wrong.

Grasping one of her hands, he wrapped it round himself. 'Don't ask me to roll over and try to sleep while I'm like that, baby.'

Her anger ebbed. Maybe she was being just a little unreasonable. She should be flattered that he found her so desirable. If he was being insensitive, wasn't that just typical of a man? Especially one as aroused as he was.

'Please, Beth?' he begged.

She held him off a while longer, making him pay for his insensitivity, before guiding him in.

Gene had intended to be slow, to take his time. But the sense of urgency that had built up within him had become too great to be denied. Bordering on the vicious, he thrust and thrust and thrust again.

It was a glorious orgasm: a sea of sensation crashing and thundering around inside her which finally receded and eventually disappeared back to whatever source it had exploded from.

'Goodnight, love.' She stroked his sweat-slicked body gently.

The reply was a snorting snore. He was fast asleep.

Beth came out of deep slumber with a start. Eyes still closed, she reached across to touch the reassuring form of Gene, only to remember he wasn't there. He had gone to Hamilton to give his report to the Farmers' League. He wouldn't be home again till the following night at the earliest, perhaps even the day after that.

Her nerve ends were tingling and despite being covered in heavy bedclothes she was cold all over. Snapping open her eyes, she gasped to see a figure looming over her.

'Did I startle you?' Loretta asked quietly.

'What is it? What's wrong?'

'I heard noises. Like footsteps. I thought it must be you.'

'No, it wasn't. I've been asleep.'

'Then I must've been mistaken,' Loretta said, sitting on the edge of the bed.

'Shouldn't we go and investigate?'

'I'm sure there's no need.' Loretta touched the collar of Beth's nightdress. 'That's very nice. I was admiring it earlier in the kitchen.'

'Thank you. It's not a new one. I've had it for years.'

Loretta's hand fluttered down to brush lightly against Beth's breast. Beth squirmed away, burrowing more deeply under the bedclothes. She could see Loretta's eyes were bulging slightly as she gazed down at her, and that there was a slick of sweat on her forehead.

'I find nights the hardest times of all. Don't you?' Loretta croaked.

'They can be. Especially if you've got a lot on your mind.'

'I get like a spring. All wound up.'

'I know exactly what you mean.' Beth wondered what this was all about and where it was leading to.

Loretta placed a hand on the swell of bedclothes over one of Beth's legs. 'Are you missing Gene?'

'Yes.'

Loretta nodded. 'I thought you would be.'

'Those footsteps . . .'

'I must've dreamt them. I dream a great deal. When I finally get to sleep, that is. When Gene and I were young I used to come to this room at night and talk to him if I was having trouble getting to sleep, but I haven't done so in years. It's amazing how people can live in the same house, have so much in common, yet drift so far apart. We were once very close, you know. Not any more, though.'

'I'm sorry to hear that.'

'What does he say about me?' Loretta's voice had changed, become sharp and shrewish.

'Nothing.'

'Oh, come on. He must let something drop from time to time?'

'Honestly he doesn't. If he talks about anything it's usually the farm.'

233

'Ah yes!' Loretta whispered, her eyes gleaming. 'The farm! He would talk about that.'

'Has he . . . er . . . has he come to an arrangement with you yet?'

The hand on Beth's leg tightened. 'What do you mean? What arrangement?'

'When we were in Glasgow Gene mentioned that he hoped to come to an agreement with you about the farm. Buy you out or something like that.'

There was a pregnant pause. 'So you really don't know?'

'Know what?'

The grip on Beth's leg was released as Loretta came to her feet and stood staring down at her. 'Tomorrow I'm going to cut out the beast for the barbecue. There's a job you can do for me then.'

'Always glad to be of assistance.'

Loretta smiled mysteriously. Turning, she glided from the room, snicking the door shut behind her.

Beth shivered, doubting very much that Loretta had either dreamt or imagined footsteps. So why the visit?

She glanced across to where Stephen lay asleep in his cot, and a sudden fear took hold of her. She was being ridiculous, she told herself. But the fear wouldn't go away. Getting out of bed she padded to the door, intent on locking it, only to discover there was no key in the lock.

Taking a chair, she jammed it hard against the door handle. At least no one would be able to enter the room without her hearing.

She made sure Stephen was well tucked up, then stood for a few reflective moments staring out of the window at the moon, high in a star-studded sky. In her mind she was seeing O for Oboe with Steve dressed as Biggles at the controls.

She shook her head. That was all in the past; gone for ever. Canada, Stewarton, Gene and the farm were her realities now. But she still had Stephen: a bridge between what had been and what was. And how she loved that child. Just thinking about him could bring a physical ache to her bosom.

She opened the window a few inches and inhaled the scent of the night countryside. How beautiful and clean it was, in complete contrast to Sweet Street and the Glasgow slums. She'd made the correct decision in coming to Canada, she assured herself. There could be no doubt about it.

A little later she was drifting back off to sleep again when she realised Loretta hadn't answered her question about the arrangement. She hoped she hadn't made a faux pas by saying something she shouldn't have done, and made a mental note to mention it to Gene. But by morning she had forgotten all about it.

It was a gorgeous day with just a hint of coldness in the air to herald the fast approach of autumn, or fall as the Canadians called it. Beth was in the kitchen humming to herself as she concocted a salad for lunch. Gene had telephoned an hour previously to say he'd definitely be staying over in Hamilton for another night and would be arriving home sometime the next afternoon. Stephen was lying on a blanket, gurgling and waggling his arms and legs. Every so often he flipped himself over on to his front to do some crawling till Beth returned him to the blanket where his toys were.

'Beth! Beth, are you in there?' Loretta shouted from

outside. Wiping her hands on a towel, she crossed to the screen door and threw it open.

Loretta and Michael were on horseback, and between them was a cow with a lasso round its neck. The other end of the lasso was tied to the horn of Loretta's saddle.

'It's time for that job I want you to do,' Loretta said.

'Fine. What is it?'

'Come to the smaller barn in about five minutes. You'll see then,' Loretta replied, nudging her horse forward. She and Michael made for the barn with the cow ambling along between them.

Beth finished the salad before picking Stephen up and heading for the small barn. The doors were wide open, and from inside came a plaintive mooing.

Beth came up short at the sight which greeted her when she entered. Chains had been attached to the cow's rear legs and by means of block and tackle the animal had been hoisted into the air where it now hung head down, its front legs tied together with a length of rope.

Loretta gave Beth a wicked grin as she held out an obviously well-sharpened knife. Its blade was extensively scarred from a great deal of honing.

'What do you want me to do with that?' Beth asked.

'As Gene said the barbecue's mainly in your honour, to you falls the honour of butchering the beef.'

Beth recoiled, clutching Stephen closely to her. 'What!'

'Not squeamish, are you?'

'Of course I am. I've never done anything like that before. And I don't want to.'

'It's an extremely hard life on a farm. Either you dominate it or it dominates you,' Loretta replied quietly.

Dominate. That was the key word, Beth thought. What this was all about. It was a test of wills, Loretta's against hers. It was Loretta's way of putting herself in a superior position to Beth's. Of dominating her.

Michael was looking disturbed. 'I'll do it if you like?' he offered, giving Beth a sympathetic smile.

He wasn't aware of what was actually going on, Beth realised. She wondered whether to ask him to take Stephen back to the house, but decided against it. Stephen was only ten months old; hardly likely, she hoped, to be affected in any way by what was about to happen.

'No thanks. It has to be me. But you can help by holding the baby.'

Loretta snorted. She was clearly convinced Beth wouldn't be able to bring herself to do the deed.

Beth gave Stephen to Michael and took the knife from Loretta, who treated her to another wicked grin. She was quaking inwardly as she crossed to the beast, whose mooing was more plaintive than ever.

'Don't go in too deeply or the knife will stick,' Michael advised.

Beth licked her lips, feeling she was going to be sick at any moment. Mustn't allow that to happen, she told herself. Mustn't show such an obvious sign of weakness in front of Loretta. She had to go through with it. If she didn't Loretta would have the whiphand from now on and that was something she couldn't let happen.

Beth forced herself to concentrate. She musn't make a hash of this for the beast's sake. She must do it as neatly and cleanly as possible.

She grasped the cow's throat and stretched round to

begin the cut at the far side, then drew the blade smartly towards her.

For a second or two nothing happened. Then blood welled from the cut and dripped to the floor below, while the pitifully bellowing beast began to jerk this way and that. The chains binding its rear legs rattled and clanked.

'You haven't got the artery,' Michael said quickly. Thrusting Stephen at Loretta, he hurried across to the cow and stilled it as much as he could by wrapping his arms round its haunches. 'Again. And make sure of the artery this time.'

Beth placed the tip of the knife against the far end of the cut and pushed sharply in, then dragged the knife towards her as fast as she could, using both hands.

It was like abruptly turning a tap full on. Only it wasn't water that came jetting out but bright red blood that shot for about three feet before arcing to the floor where it spattered in all directions.

Beth wanted to turn and run. Instead she willed herself to stay until the beast stopped trying to jerk and its eyes dulled into opaqueness.

'You did well for a first time,' Michael said.

Beth glanced down at her bloody hands. A voice she recognised as her own seemed to come from a long way off. 'It's amazing what you can do when you put your mind to it.' She looked up to find Loretta staring at her with new respect.

'There's more to you than I thought,' Loretta said.

Beth had won. But there was no feeling of triumph in her, only revulsion. Going over to Loretta she took Stephen and cradled the dear wee fellow in the crook of her arm. Then, forcing herself to walk straight-backed at a steady pace, she left the barn and headed for the house.

She managed to hold out until she reached her bedroom, but the moment the door was shut behind her she dissolved into floods of silent tears. Holding Stephen tightly to her, she sat on the bed and began rocking back and forth. Sensing her upset, Stephen also started to cry.

'There there. There there,' she whispered.

Gradually Stephen calmed down again. And when she returned to the kitchen a little later, showered and changed, she could smile and act as if nothing untoward had happened.

The barbecue was in full swing. Gene had appointed himself chief cook, and was sporting the most ridiculous chef's hat, which sprouted from his head like some giant white mushroom. Two pits had been dug and a spit erected over each. On the first spit was the cow's carcass, while a nice fat pig was slowly turning on the other.

With several glasses of cider under her belt Beth was thoroughly enjoying herself. All their guests were going out of their way to be pleasant to her and make her feel welcome in the area. At that moment she was chatting to Johnny Bauge, from whom Gene had bought the pig, and a young man called Hoskin McVitie.

Loretta appeared out of the throng to join them. Taking Hoskin by the arm she gave him a simpering smile. Plainly uneasy, he smiled back.

'Real nice party, Loretta.' Johnny Bauge raised his glass to her in salute.

'Why thank you, Johnny,' Loretta replied, hanging on to Hoskin's arm. What did she look like? Beth thought for the umpteenth time. Her make-up might have been applied with a spade and painter's brush, and as for her empire-line concoction dress, it made Beth think of a bell tent, with Loretta the pole holding it up.

She was after Hoskin now, Beth thought grimly. He was the fourth young man she'd seen Loretta make a play for since the start of the barbecue, and judging from Hoskin's expression she was going to have about as much luck with him as she'd had with the other three, all of whom had skedaddled out of her company as soon as possible.

'Why don't we dance?' Loretta suggested, giving Hoskin a little-girl smile.

'Why sure, Miss McKay.'

'Loretta, please. How can I dance with someone who calls me Miss McKay?'

'Let's dance then, Loretta.' He led her giggling away.

Beth glanced at Johnny Bauge, who was looking amused. 'This sort of thing is all very new to me,' she said.

'You mean the barbecue or Loretta trying to make out?'

Embarrassed, Beth pretended interest in a passing couple. 'The barbecue, of course.'

Johnny chuckled and swallowed some beer. 'Despite what people think, pigs are nice animals. Nicer than a lot of folk I could mention.'

'That's an interesting point of view,' she murmured.

Johnny drank more beer, gazing at her over the rim of

his can. 'You should've met old man McKay. Now he really was something.'

'So I've been told.'

'A real dyed in the wool son of a bitch.'

'You didn't like him, then?'

'I did. But I wouldn't have trusted him as far as I could have thrown him. He was the sort of man who every time he shook your hand you counted your fingers afterwards to make sure they were still there.'

Beth laughed. 'Bad as that?'

'Worse. Loretta takes after him. Yes siree, she do indeed. But give the old man his due, he always made this place pay. Which is very much to his credit considering its size.'

'I don't understand that last bit?'

'You mean about its size?'

Beth nodded.

'Well, let me put it this way. It's a good farm with a good potential yield return, but it's rather small.'

'It's a thousand acres. I thought that was big.'

'Maybe in Scotland where you come from but certainly not out here. By our standards it's small, and as such difficult to make a living from.'

'How can the same size farm be big in Scotland and small in Canada?'

'Different kind of dirt. Different kinds of crops. Different yield potential.' Johnny paused, then added with a twinkle in his eye, 'You've got a lot to learn about farming.'

'I've got *everything* to learn about farming,' she retorted, and they both laughed. Even as she was laughing she was thinking it strange that she'd picked up quite the wrong impression from Gene about the size and viability of the farm. She was certain he'd told her that with no trouble at all it made a handsome profit every year.

A few minutes later she and Johnny were re-joined by Hoskin, who was looking hot and flustered. 'Where's Loretta?' Beth asked.

Hoskin shook his head. 'She went off with someone else. I didn't see who.'

That was a fib. He'd ditched her, Beth thought. What she couldn't understand was why Loretta was only going after the young men. Why not the ones her own age? Then she realised that all the men of Loretta's age she'd been introduced to were married. It dawned on Beth that most men in their late thirties *were* married, which meant there were very slim pickings for Loretta within her own age group. It made sense now. Loretta was going after the younger men because they formed the bulk of the un-married males.

'Would you care to dance, Mrs McKay?' Johnny Bauge asked.

'I would. But not for the moment, if you don't mind. I'm afraid I've got raging indigestion.' She'd had it for the past five minutes or so, and put it down to the cider she'd drunk.

'Can I get you anything?' Hoskin enquired politely.

'Thank you for being concerned. I'm sure it'll pass soon of its own accord.'

It was a few minutes after that when she saw Gene have words with Loretta, who retorted angrily before flouncing off. Beth guessed Gene had been telling her to stop drinking so much, as she'd been knocking back whisky after whisky during the past half-hour. She was swaying when she walked, and her voice had become very high-pitched and raucous.

Beth excused herself, saying she had to mingle. She spoke to a farmer and his wife called Bates, then to Mr Westlake the storekeeper. Her indigestion was getting worse, and was now making her feel distinctly queasy. She considered going in and lying down for a while, but thought she could hardly retire when the barbecue was in her honour. Instead she went to check on Stephen, who was having his afternoon nap.

She was almost at the kitchen screen door again on her way back outside when she heard voices filtering through from the porch beyond. One belonged to Hoskin McVitie.

'Shiit. She's so goddamn ugly, that Loretta! It almost made me want to throw up just dancing with her.'

Beth came to a halt and listened.

'I swear I've never known a woman so desperate for a man,' Hoskin's friend replied, and they both laughed cruelly.

'I don't know why she needs a man. She's more man than many I know.'

'Ain't that the truth.'

'Has she danced with you yet?' Hoskin asked.

'Nope, thank the Lord.'

'Well, she'll get round to you, boy. You can bet your ass on that.'

'Shiiiit!' Hoskin's friend swore.

'Mind you, she does have something going for her. Like a half interest in this farm.'

'Not nearly enough to be saddled with a wife like that.

Can you imagine waking up every morning and seeing that face on the pillow next to your'n?'

Hoskin laughed. 'Now if it was Mrs McKay that would be something else entirely.'

'She wouldn't have to ask me twice, that's for sure,' Hoskin's friend enthused.

'Loretta didn't use to be like she is now. She was always ugly but she never threw herself at you as she's done since her paw died.'

'He was one real mother. When I was a kid it gave me the shivers every time I saw him. There was something about that old guy scared me shitless.'

'Yeah, I know what you mean.'

'Maybe she's just trying to make up for all the years he kept her under his thumb.'

'Maybe so.'

The two voices had started to recede. Hoskin and his friend were moving away.

'And wasn't there something funny about the will?'

'I heard that, though I couldn't tell you what it was.'

'I remember people talking at the time, but no one seemed to know the actual ins and outs of the matter.'

The voices faded into the distance, leaving Beth with a puzzled expression on her face. This was the first she'd heard of a will. Certainly Gene had never mentioned it. There again, that didn't mean anything. Why should he tell her about it, after all? It was hardly her business.

She grinned. It was bolstering to hear they found her attractive. But what they'd had to say about Loretta! Mind you, Loretta only had herself to blame. Tarting herself up as she had and behaving so tastelessly towards all the young men.

Beth went through the screen door out into the sunlight. She smiled when she realised her indigestion had gone. She decided to find Johnny Bauge and have that dance with him. She felt just in the mood for a dance now.

It was about an hour later, when everyone was eating, that Gene hurried over to Beth. 'Have you seen El?'

Beth shook her head. 'Not since you told her off. About her drinking, I take it?'

'Yeah. And I haven't clapped eyes on her since. The way I figure it either she's gone off somewhere to sulk or else she's passed out.'

'Would you like me to have a look around?' Beth asked, laying her plate to one side.

'I'd appreciate that, honey. It's just so goddamn rude of her not to be here while we have guests.'

'You hold the fort and I'll see if I can find her.'

Gene kissed Beth on the cheek. 'You're real swell, Beth. Best day's work I ever did was marrying you.'

She had started to move away when suddenly her indigestion returned with a vengeance. 'Ooohh!' she groaned, clutching her stomach and doubling over.

'Are you OK?' Gene asked anxiously.

She explained what the problem was, telling him not to worry as it was bound to pass off again just as it had previously done.

She went to the house first, but Loretta's room was empty. Stephen was awake now, so she gave him a kiss and cuddle, and asked the woman minding him to play with him outside until Beth was ready for him.

Beth went through the house from top to bottom to no avail, and then checked the garage. Neither the pickup truck nor the car was missing. From the garage she went to the large barn and the smaller one after that, drawing a blank in both. Nor was Loretta in the tiny stables hidden away behind the large barn.

Adjacent to the stables was a shed where various odds and ends of equipment were kept. Beth was passing this when she heard noises from within. The shed was very old, and several planks along one side had come adrift. Beth moved to the space thus created and peered inside.

Loretta, her dress up round her waist and her knickers round one ankle, was leaning over a barrel. Michael had removed his trousers and underpants. Neither of them noticed Beth.

Beth felt curiously light-headed as she made her way back to the barbecue, but put it down to the scene she'd just witnessed. Gene, carving the pig, gave her a wave with his knife when he spotted her making in his direction.

'Well?' he asked when she reached him.

'I haven't been able to . . .' Beth trailed off, wondering why Gene was suddenly going round and round like a top.

The next thing she knew she was in Gene's arms being carried upstairs to their bedroom. 'What happened?'

'You fainted.'

'What a silly . . .' She stopped and swallowed. 'How silly of me.'

'Doc Anderson is going to have a look at you.'

The doctor was following them up the stairs, a soft-spoken man just a little older than Gene whom she'd been introduced to earlier.

Once in the bedroom Gene gently laid her on the bed. 'Now, young lady, let's try to determine what this is all about,' said Doc Anderson, coming to sit beside her. He felt her forehead, stuck a thermometer in her mouth, and while waiting for the temperature to register rolled up her eyelids to look at the whites of her eyes.

Removing the thermometer, he studied it for a few moments. 'Tell me about the fainting.'

'I was feeling light-headed. Then suddenly everything started to go round and round.'

'Any other symptoms?'

'No . . . except for . . .'

'Except for what?' he prompted.

'Before the light-headedness I had the most awful indigestion, which I put down to the cider I'd been drinking.'

'Hmm!'

'She is OK, isn't she?' Gene asked.

'Can you undo your dress, please?' said Doc.

Beth fumbled with her buttons and the dress fell open. On Doc's instruction she pulled her slip up to expose her stomach.

'Hurt?' Doc queried, probing with a finger.

'It is a bit sensitive.'

'Excuse me,' Doc apologised, squeezing the top of a breast.

'Ouch!'

'When did you last have a period?'

'Nearly six weeks ago. I'm late.'

'Are you often overdue?'

'Very occasionally.'

Doc Anderson smiled. 'I could be wrong, but I doubt it.' Turning to Gene, he said, 'Congratulations. You're going to become a father.'

Gene's eyes lit up with intense excitement and pleasure. 'Hot damn!'

'I never fainted with my first pregnancy,' Beth said.

'No two pregnancies are alike.'

'Does that mean this might be a girl?' Gene interrupted, concern creasing his face.

Doc shook his head. 'Not at all. It's a misconception that the sex of the baby can be told from the type of pregnancy the mother has, believe me.' Going over to the jug and basin he proceeded to wash his hands. 'Now, Beth, I want you to stay in bed for the rest of the day. And I'd like a sample to take with me for verification.'

Gene took Beth's hand. 'I'm so happy, hon.'

'I'm happy too.'

'My *son*. I just can't wait.'

'It might be a girl,' Beth warned him.

'No. It'll be a boy. It has to be.'

The door was thrust open suddenly and Loretta entered the room. 'I heard Beth fainted.'

Gene sought his sister's eyes with his own, a triumphant smile lighting up his face. 'Beth's pregnant,' he announced.

Loretta was thunderstruck. 'So soon?'

'Yeah.'

Loretta whirled and fled, banging the door shut behind her.

'Jealousy, I'm afraid. She'll get over it.' Smiling, Gene lifted Beth's hand to his lips and kissed the tips of her fingers.

They were eating lunch, Gene and Loretta talking about a tractor they were having trouble with, when the telephone rang.

'I'll get it,' Gene said.

Loretta looked dreadful, Beth thought. She had done since the barbecue three days previously. There were bags under her eyes, and her skin had become blotchy. She'd taken to frowning a great deal, and was forever snapping at everyone given the slightest provocation. Often with no provocation at all.

Gene concluded his telephone conversation and hung up. 'That was Doc Anderson. The results of the tests on your sample are positive, Beth. The baby will be arriving at the end of May.'

Loretta slowly laid down her fork. 'I'll go and have another tinker at that tractor,' she announced in a strangulated voice. At the door she turned to stare at Beth, her face a mask of hate.

When Loretta was gone Beth shuddered. She was deeply disturbed by the look her sister-in-law had given her. Gene crossed to her and took her in his arms. 'I told you, she's jealous. Don't worry, it'll soon pass.'

Chapter 15

In late November the first snow came, gentle flurries of it dancing and swirling out of a leaden sky. The temperature had already fallen to finger-numbing coldness, and was dropping further with every passing day. The pot-bellied stove was on twenty-four hours a day, and fires crackled in every room, but the house remained chilled throughout. Icy draughts came in via the windows to eddy along the corridors and up and down the stairs. Outside, the landscape was harsh and bleak.

Beth had begun to put on weight, her stomach swelling and her breasts enlarging. As of yet she hadn't had the bouts of nausea and sickness she'd suffered when carrying Stephen: in their place were recurring attacks of severe indigestion. She was enjoying life on the farm but finding it quite lonely as Gene and Loretta were out of the house nearly all day long. More than once she'd thanked God she had Stephen for company.

One morning a few weeks before Christmas she noticed that the wood pile beside the pot-bellied stove needed topping up. It was Michael's job and it was very unlike him not to have attended to it, but Beth thought she would see to it herself. Stephen was happy in his cot, so she slipped into her parka and went outside, heading round behind the house to where the supply of fuel was kept.

She'd have to make several trips, she decided. Picking up four neatly cut logs, she made her way back to the kitchen and laid them on the pile. It was at the end of her third trip that she found Gene waiting for her.

'What in Christ's name do you think you're doing?' he demanded.

'I'm getting wood.'

He shook with anger. 'Of all the stupid, irresponsible . . .' He broke off to smash a clenched fist into the palm of his other hand.

'I'm being careful, Gene. I'm only carrying a few logs at a time.'

He leapt at her and grabbed the front of her parka, thrusting his face into hers so that she recoiled. His eyes were bulging and there were red anger spots on his cheeks. She'd never seen him so enraged before.

'I've told you, no heavy lifting of any kind. Nothing must go wrong. Nothing, you hear?' he hissed through gritted teeth.

She nodded. 'I'm sorry.'

'Don't be sorry. Just don't do it again.'

'All right.'

Taking the logs she was carrying from her he threw them on to the pile beside the stove. They bounced off and went flying along the floor in various directions. He inhaled deeply, running his fingers through his hair, and the fury seemed to seep out of him. 'I'm only thinking of you, hon.'

This was a new side to Gene, one she didn't like at all. Still, as he'd just said, he'd been thinking of her, which was some excuse, though hardly enough for terrifying the living daylights out of her.

'We must be careful, Beth. These things can so easily go wrong.'

'No more heavy lifting. You have my word.'

He took her in his arms and hugged her tight. 'That's my girl.'

'Excuse me,' she murmured. Disengaging herself, she made for her packet of cigarettes and lit up before removing her parka.

Gene stood very still, watching her through partially slitted lids as she busied herself at the sink. He too lit up, taking his time about packing his pipe before bringing a match to it. 'I have to go into Stewarton tomorrow, so why don't I pick up some decorating materials for our bedroom? Or better still, why don't you come with me and you can do the picking?'

'Will we be able to get what we want from Mr Westlake?'

'Sure! He's got all kinds of fancy paints and wallpapers in that store of his. Why, I'll lay a dime to a ten spot you'll be able to find just what you want. Even if you don't, his isn't the only store.'

'All right, then.'

'I'll get Michael to do the actual work for you. He's got more time on his hands than I have at the moment. And I'll tell you what else. Later on in the winter I'll dig out some wood I put by to season and make you a brand new wardrobe. Something big and grand to replace that old thing you're having to contend with at the moment. How would that be?'

'It sounds lovely.'

'It's a deal then.'

After he'd gone she slumped a little. Holding on to the edge of the sink, she took several deep breaths. Her hands were becoming rough and workworn, she noticed. When they were in Stewarton she'd pick up a jar of cream for them.

He *had* terrified her. For a few seconds there she'd felt he was quite capable of doing her actual physical harm, and indeed had come very close to doing so. It was quite bewildering, this obsession he had with the child she was carrying. Or was it? For what did she know about expectant fathers? Precious little, she had to admit. Perhaps this obsessiveness was not unusual.

She suddenly grinned. His behaviour might have been awful but she had gained from it. Ever since her arrival at the farm she'd been after him to keep his promise and do up their bedroom, only to be put off time after time with one excuse or another. Well, now it would be done, with the bonus of a brand new wardrobe to furnish it with.

Paint or paper? she wondered. For the rest of the day she debated with herself the relative merits of both.

Beth was sitting on her bed with the giant Sears and Roebuck catalogue spread open on her lap. It was the current edition, which she'd picked up in town, and she was determined to secure Gene's permission to order a number of things from it for the house.

Michael Fleetfoot was in the bedroom with her, hard at work removing the damp patch prior to getting on with redecoration. In the end Beth had decided on a combination of paint *and* paper. Warm-coloured paint for the ceiling and bright paper for the walls. It seemed the correct combination for such a naturally dull and gloomy room.

'Will you be able to fix that all right?' she asked Michael.

'Oh, yeah. A couple of clapboard panels out front have separated, which is where the water's coming in. First of all I'll do a bit of replacing in here, then fix the panels outside and Bob's your uncle! No more damp patch.'

He really was extraordinarily handsome, Beth thought. He had the face of a young god – or a film star. 'How old are you, Michael?'

'Twenty-five, Mrs McKay.'

'You look younger.'

'I'm not sure whether that's a compliment or not.' He smiled.

And what an attractive body he had, with his slim hips and well-proportioned shoulders. If he had a fault, it was that his legs were shorter than they might have been. Shorter and slightly bandy.

For some time now she'd been looking for an opportunity to speak to Michael alone. That was why she'd come up to the bedroom on the pretence of making sure he understood just how she wanted things done. She'd brought Stephen with her, and the baby was lying in the centre of the bed happily gurgling.

Reaching out, she stroked his cheek, seeing Steve in the face that swivelled round to stare at her. 'Michael, there's something that has been bothering me. Does Loretta have some sort of hold over you?'

Michael stared at Beth, his expression one of puzzlement. 'What sort of hold?'

'Is she bringing pressure to bear on you in some way?'

The penny dropped, and he realised what Beth was getting at. 'Are you asking this because you've found out about Loretta and me?'

'Yes.'

'And you think . . .' He broke off to give a soft laugh. Beth glanced away, feeling herself beginning to colour at the neck. 'I love Loretta,' Michael said simply.

Beth gaped. That idea had simply never occurred to her. 'I'm sorry. I seem to have put my foot in it.'

'What's more, Loretta loves me.'

'That can't be true!' Beth exclaimed, and immediately wanted to bite her tongue.

'It is.'

Beth pretended to play with Stephen. 'Are you certain?'

'Absolutely.'

'You love her and she loves you?'

'Yeah.'

'It seems I've made a complete fool of myself. It just never crossed my mind . . .' She shrugged. 'There's the difference in age, for a start.'

'The age difference has never mattered between us. It's simply one of those things.'

Beth was confused. It didn't add up. Not after the way Loretta had behaved at the barbecue. Trying to sort out the muddle in her mind, she remembered that when she'd originally talked to Gene about Loretta's relationship with Michael he'd told her she didn't love him. That was where the confusion had sprung from. 'If you are in love why don't you run away together?'

'Loretta might love me, but she loves the farm even more.'

'What would happen if you did marry and stay on here?'

Michael gave a thin smile. 'We'd be totally ostracised. No white person would speak to us again. More important, the same people wouldn't deal with us. The farm would go bust within a year.'

'I see.'

'Loretta wouldn't allow that to happen. As far as she's concerned, to kill the farm would be like killing herself. Which might indicate to you how deeply she feels about this place.'

'As does Gene.'

'Yeah. That's one thing they have in common.'

It was an impertinent question but Beth had to ask it. It would hardly be a revelation to Michael, as he must've seen the way Loretta had behaved at the barbecue. 'If Loretta loves you, why does she chase after every young man she meets?'

'Don't you know?'

She shook her head.

Michael stared at her for a few seconds, then turned away. 'I like the wallpaper and paint you chose, Mrs McKay. I think this room is going to look real pretty when it's finished.'

Beth took a stab in the dark. 'Is it something to do with their father's will?'

Michael busied himself with the hole in the wall, and didn't reply. It was obvious he wasn't going to.

Just what *was* in that will? Beth wondered, filled with curiosity. She knew it was really none of her business, but she decided to ask Gene about it all the same.

'Gene?'

'Yeah, hon?'

It was that night and they'd just gone to bed. Flickering shadows filled the room from the fire Beth had banked up about an hour previously.

'Do you recall telling me Loretta didn't love Michael?'

'Yeah.'

'Well, she does.'

Gene stiffened. 'Who told you that?'

'Michael. I asked him about it.'

Gene laughed. 'Either he's kidding you or she's kidding him.'

'Michael was telling me the truth. I could tell.'

'Then she's kidding him.'

'I don't think so.'

'Hot damn!' Gene swore. 'Well ain't that a turn up for the book.'

'So you *didn't* know about it?'

'No. I swear. I thought she was just using him to get her oats. I never realised . . . Don't that beat all!'

'What I can't understand is why Loretta was chasing all those young men at the barbecue?'

'She may love Michael but she sure as hell can't marry

him. I explained to you in Glasgow, white folks don't marry Indians in this neck of the woods.'

'Why does she have to get married at all? If she and Michael love one another why not just let things continue as they are? Then they could have their relationship and no one would be any the wiser.'

Gene chortled, a deep rumbling sound that had unpleasant overtones to it. 'That's certainly made my day. In fact it's made my goddamn year!'

'You haven't answered my question,' she persisted.

'How should I know!'

He was evading. Lying by default. He knew perfectly well why Loretta had been chasing those young men so shamelessly. He just wasn't letting on. 'Is it somehow connected with your father's will?'

He rounded on her with a suddenness that caused her to catch her breath. 'What do you know about my father's will? Who's been telling you things?'

'No . . . no one,' she stuttered.

'Has Michael been running off at the mouth?'

'He said nothing at all. Although I did ask him.'

'How did you hear about my father's will anyway?'

'At the barbecue. There were a couple of men out on the porch when I was in the kitchen. They mentioned it. Said there was something funny about it but neither knew what.'

Gene grunted and lay back again. 'There was nothing funny about the will. The whole thing was no more than a crazy rumour that went round town for a while, made up by some enemy of the old man's no doubt. God knows he had plenty of those.'

She knew he was lying. The lack of conviction in his voice betrayed him. 'Does your father's will concern me in any way?'

'Now how in Jesus's name could it concern you? I didn't meet you until eighteen months after we'd planted him.'

She laid a hand on his side and rubbed it. 'I didn't mean to upset you, Gene. I'm just curious, that's all.'

He snorted in precisely the same way Loretta did. 'In the light of what you've told me about El and Michael my guess is that her flirting at the barbecue was some sort of shame reaction to having fallen for an Indian. In other words, deep down she's probably pretty disgusted with herself and wants to break the tie. Throwing herself at young men was a subconscious way of trying to do so. Hell, I'm no mind doctor! I'm not sure if what I've just said makes sense to you, but it does to me.'

There was logic in it, Beth thought. But it was something he'd just made up and not what he really believed. She decided to let the matter drop for the time being.

She slid her hand down to his thigh and then to his crotch, feeling him.

'No,' he muttered, yanking her hand away.

She was pent up inside, a coiled spring dying for loving release. 'Why not?' she whispered throatily.

'Because you're pregnant.'

He hadn't touched her since the day of the barbecue. His explanation was always the same: she was pregnant. 'I'm not a piece of china, Gene. I won't break.'

'I'm not taking any risks. I don't want anything to go wrong.'

'It's quite natural, you know.'

'Sex during pregnancy can cause the loss of the child. That's a fact.'

'Possibly, yes. But it's highly unlikely. A million to one chance.'

'I don't care if it's a billion to one. I'm still not taking it,' he snapped in reply.

'Why are you so desperate for this child? And why does it matter so much that it's a boy?'

'Doesn't every man want a son?'

She felt as if there were a mass of wires inside her, all stretched to snapping point.

'I said no!' he hissed, yanking her hand away a second time.

'This is daft, Gene.'

'Perhaps. But it's the way it's going to be until after he's born. So you'd better learn to accept it.'

Sleep was long in coming. When she eventually did doze off it was to dream she was the one in the shed with Michael.

Michael brought the letter to Beth in the kitchen. Seeing it was from Cissie, Beth excitedly tore open the envelope.

Cissie was delighted to hear Beth was pregnant. My my! that certainly hadn't taken long. She was well, although troubled a wee bit with a varicose vein that had developed in her left leg.

Roy and Margaret were still the same, with no sign whatever of any forthcoming event themselves. Mrs Todd and old Mrs McGurk sent their fondest regards, as did many other neighbours too numerous to mention.

Mr Carmichael had finally given up his house. A new

family was in there now by the name of McElvey. And oh! Jeannie Beaton, whom Beth had gone to school with, had become engaged to an awful nice lad in the Navy called Harry Graham. The pair of them were planning to get married on his next home leave.

Beth read the letter through, then went back to the beginning and read it through again. When she finally looked up from the pages of cramped writing, tears were misting her eyes.

Glasgow! She could see it. Smell it, even, from the mental pictures Cissie's words had conjured up. How she missed it, that dirty awful place. For a few moments homesickness engulfed her, a great tidal wave of emotion that made her want to catch the first boat home.

For the rest of that day her mind was filled with memories. Sauchiehall Street. The Clyde. The house in King's Park she'd nearly had, the single end in Sweet Street she'd ended up with instead. The night the gasworks had gone up and Stephen was born. Mary O'Malley. Edna and Colin at the cafe. Bruce's Cave . . .

She read the letter through a dozen times that day, and when it was time for bed she slept with it under her pillow.

It was the evening of 7 February 1944. On the first of the month American forces had landed on the Marshall Islands, and a week before that there had been the landings at Anzio. The war was now running very much in favour of Britain and the Allies.

Beth and Gene followed the war news avidly. Gene was at that moment in Toronto welcoming home more

Volunteer casualties, and Beth and Loretta were sitting round the pot-bellied stove, by far the cosiest spot in the house, while Stephen was upstairs in his cot. Since Christmas Loretta had gone out of her way to be friendly to Beth and now the pair of them often sat here in the evening listening to the wireless and talking.

Beth was flushed, with a sheen of perspiration on her forehead. Every few minutes she took a deep swig from the cold can of coke she was holding.

'Why don't you move your chair back a bit? You seem to be sweltering there,' Loretta suggested.

Beth shook her head. 'It has nothing to do with the heat. It's the new pills Doc Anderson has given me for my blood pressure.' She giggled. 'They make me feel quite woozy. Just as if I was drunk.'

Loretta crossed to the window and stared out. 'It's snowing again. Blowing a real blizzard out there.'

'Do you think we're going to get cut off?'

'Could be. It's certainly showing the signs for it.'

'What about Gene?'

Loretta shrugged. 'He'll make Stewarton OK, and then he'll hire a snow plough if he has to. Don't worry. He'll get through.'

'It's a real pest he had to go away again. The League has been taking up an awful lot of his time recently.'

'That's because it's winter. The farmer's slackest season. The bulk of League business always takes place during this period.'

'How did Gene become League president anyway? I've always meant to ask him.'

Loretta lit a cigarette, having become something of a

262

chain smoker of late. 'It was one of the very few extra-curricular activities our father actually encouraged, and I suppose Gene threw himself into it because it gave him an outlet from the farm. It became a real passion with him, so I reckon it was inevitable he'd one day become president.' She stopped to cough, a dry hacking sound that was more of a bark than a cough.

'You're smoking far too much,' Beth commented.

'So what else is new?'

'I'm sorry. I was only thinking of you.'

Loretta was instantly contrite. 'No, no. It's me should be sorry for biting at you like that.'

Beth grinned at Loretta, who grinned back. 'Shall we listen to the wireless?' Beth asked.

'Naw. I'd much rather talk. Why don't you tell me more about Scotland? I really enjoy hearing about it from you.'

Beth couldn't help suspecting that Loretta's new friendliness towards her was a sham, a device to extract information which could be used against her. She thought that so far she hadn't let anything of any conse-quence slip out, but this evening, thanks to the pills Doc Anderson had given her, her guard was temporarily lowered. She felt as though she was floating along on a nice pink cloud, as if she was part of, but also slightly detached from, the proceedings.

'You met Gene in a club of some sort. Is that right?' Loretta prompted her.

'It was called Bruce's Cave after the cave where King Robert the Bruce watched the spider.' Beth giggled again. 'I always thought it was an odd name for a club catering to the American military. The Yankee Doodle Club or something like that would've been far more appropriate.'

'I like the name. It has an olde worlde charm about it.'

'That's exactly what Mr Zenth said when I mentioned it to him one night.'

'Mr Zenth?'

'He was the owner. An American with a glass eye as horrible as himself.'

'In what way was he horrible?'

Beth giggled again. 'He was a . . . lecher,' she whispered in an exaggerated manner.

Loretta's ears pricked up. What was this? 'What did he do exactly?' she asked, giving the impression that she was just dying to hear some juicy tit-bits of scandal.

Normally Beth would have realised that this was potentially dangerous ground, but tonight her judgement was completely out of kilter. 'He used to lure girls who worked for him into his office and force himself on them. If they refused to give in they got the sack.'

'No kidding!'

Beth nodded. 'As God is my judge, Loretta, that's what that awful man did. He paid fantastic wages, you see. And once you became used to that sort of money it was very difficult to say no when the alternative was to get your cards.'

Loretta's grip on Beth's arm tightened. 'Did he ever screw you?'

'He wanted to, and was working his way round to trying. Only I found out what was going on and put a spanner in his works – at least as far as I and a friend of mine called Kathleen O'Malley were concerned. I told him if he so much as laid a finger on either of us I'd tell his wife first and then the newspapers. Well, that did the trick all right. He was terrified of his wife, and if the newspapers had got hold of the story he would probably have been deported, which would have cost him dearly as the club was making a nice fat profit for him every week.'

'Sounds a real charmer.'

A little later, when Beth had gone upstairs, Loretta smiled to herself. The story Beth had told her was hardly perfect, as Beth hadn't had sex with this Zenth. But then, how was Gene to know that?

Beth woke to find herself alone in bed. A glance at the fire informed her she'd been asleep for quite some time, so where was Gene, whom she'd left talking to Loretta in the kitchen? He had arrived back from Toronto that afternoon, not needing a snow plough to get through to the farm as it had transpired.

Getting out of bed, she shrugged herself into her dressing gown and checked that Stephen was still well tucked up before making her way downstairs. Before she reached the end of the second landing she heard Gene's voice raised in anger. What on earth was going on, she wondered.

There were two large jars of Coe's cider on the kitchen table and it was obvious from the state of both Gene and Loretta that they'd drunk a fair amount of the contents. Gene was stalking Loretta, while she was retreating from him in a series of scuttling motions.

'What do the pair of you think you're doing?'

Loretta scuttled behind a chair and picked it up to hold in front of her for protection. 'There she is. There's your precious wife. Ask her to deny it!' she screamed at Gene.

'Deny what?' Beth asked sharply.

Gene turned and pointed a finger at her belly. 'Whose child is that?'

'Yours, of course.'

'That's not what she told me,' Loretta cackled.

Beth stared at her sister-in-law in amazement. 'What are you talking about?'

'The guy who owned the club you worked in. Zenth. It's his child. Not Gene's.'

Beth was astounded. 'That's not true!'

'You told me it was.'

The woman's gone mad, Beth thought. 'I never said any such thing.'

'Yes you did. The guy who owned the club was getting a piece of ass from all the females who worked for him, including you.'

'Well?' Gene demanded, swaying where he stood.

'Zenth *was* blackmailing most of the other girls into sleeping with him, but not me. I told him if he ever so much as laid a finger on me I'd expose him to his wife and the newspapers. That's what I told Loretta.'

Loretta threw back her head and laughed. The maniacal sound made Beth's flesh creep. She *is* mad, she thought.

'You happened along at just the right time for her. You imagined you were using her, but the boot was on the other foot. She was using you.' Loretta smirked at Gene.

'The child is yours. I swear it,' Beth said to Gene.

'I'll contest it,' Loretta stated smugly.

This was a nightmare, Beth told herself. An unbelievable, hellish nightmare. 'We can have a blood analysis done. That'll prove beyond doubt it's Gene's child.'

Loretta shook her head. 'Not necessarily. You see, I checked that out already.'

'There's a fifty per cent chance the baby will have Gene's blood grouping because it must have either his or mine. That's how it works.'

'Sure it does. Only he's A positive and you're O positive. The two largest blood groupings there are, which together add up to about eighty-eight per cent of the population.'

Gene frowned. 'What are you driving at?'

'Just this, brother. You can prove that the baby has A positive or O positive blood but that's no big deal as nearly everyone has. So who's to say the kid really is yours?'

'Who's to say it isn't? And how did you know I have O positive blood anyway?' Beth asked.

'I looked up your travel documents and there it was.'

Gene stumbled over to one of the stone jars and hefted it to his mouth, his Adam's apple bobbing up and down as he took several deep swallows. Then he laid the jar back on the table, belched, and wiped his lips.

Loretta inched closer to him, still holding the chair in front of her. Her eyes were wild, filled with a sort of unholy glee. 'When you put in your claim for my half of the farm I'm going to contest it on the grounds that the child isn't yours. Now, maybe I won't be able to prove that it's true but you sure as hell won't be able to prove that it isn't. Furthermore, when I let it be known she used you by foisting a bastard on to you you're going to be the laughing stock of the province.'

'What do you mean, when he puts in his claim for your part of the farm? I thought he was going to make a deal with you?' Beth said.

'Hasn't he told you about the will yet? You really should have done, Gene.'

'Shut up, you evil bitch!' he snarled.

But there was no stopping Loretta. 'That's why he married you, Beth. Because he needs an heir. A *male* heir so he can—' She broke off as Gene leapt at her to knock the chair aside. He tore it from her grasp and sent it spinning across the kitchen. Loretta's scream died in her throat as his hands wrapped themselves round her neck.

'I should've done this years ago,' he grunted, squeezing as hard as he could.

Beth stood transfixed in horror as Loretta sank slowly to her knees. Frothy spittle trickled from Gene's mouth and rolled down his chin. He grunted again and again as he maintained the pressure on Loretta's throat. Suddenly Beth snapped into action. Running to Gene, she tried to force him to break his grip, to no avail. At that moment he seemed to have the strength of ten.

There could only be seconds left, Beth told herself, seeing Loretta's eyes start to glaze over. Snatching up one of the stone jars she hit Gene hard with it on the side of the head.

He staggered under the blow, his legs buckling beneath him. He took one hand from Loretta's throat to give Beth a sideways swipe which sent her reeling.

Beth desperately fought to retain her balance and might

just have succeeded if it hadn't been for one of Stephen's toys lying on the floor. She tripped, saw the pot-bellied stove looming in front of her, and then felt her face come into sizzling contact with its surface.

For a split second there was no pain. Then it hit her. Wave after indescribable wave of it, causing her to shriek in agony. Sickness engulfed her, a nausea which made her want to void everything in her stomach. She retched repeatedly but nothing came up.

She was on hands and knees when Gene hurriedly squatted beside her. 'Let me see. Let me see.' She lifted her face to him and his features contorted. 'Oh my God!'

Loretta had flung herself into a corner of the room where she sat nursing her throat and gobbling in air.

The shock of what had happened had completely sobered Gene, who now began to shake. His nostrils were filled with the stink of burnt flesh, black and twisted before his stunned gaze.

'You must get me to the hospital,' Beth croaked, fighting the almost irresistible urge to give way to unconsciousness.

'Yeah, hon.'

'Get Michael.'

Gene rose and raced from the kitchen, leaving Beth staring across at Loretta, who was smiling wickedly at her. She most definitely is mad, Beth thought.

'Not so pretty now,' Loretta mocked.

Beth held trembling fingers up to within about an inch of the ruin which had been that side of her face. She felt the heat emanating from it, and her insides churned. But she still couldn't throw up. A solitary tear appeared in one eye.

Michael came running in, Gene behind him, and ground to a halt on seeing Beth. She pointed at Loretta. 'See to her, please, Michael. Gene, get a blanket and wrap Stephen up in it. He's coming to the hospital with us. And bring another blanket for me.'

Michael pulled Loretta to her feet and seated her in the same chair she'd used for protection against Gene. Her throat was already turning black and blue, the marks of Gene's fingers clearly distinguishable. Beth gritted her teeth as pain continued to wash over her. She willed herself to stay conscious until she reached hospital and could be certain that Stephen was in safe hands.

Gene reappeared with a bawling Stephen already wrapped in a blanket. Michael left Loretta to come and help Beth out to the car, while Gene brought Stephen.

The journey was a nightmare for Beth. Stephen, upset at having been woken and sensing there was something wrong with his mother, cried all the way, but at last they turned into the hospital driveway. As they did so the emergency doors burst open and a stretcher was wheeled out. Beth wondered how they'd known she was coming, until it dawned on her that Michael must've phoned ahead.

A white-coated doctor took Stephen from her while she was lifted bodily from the car on to the stretcher. A second blanket was thrown over her, and then the stretcher was hurriedly pushed back into the hospital. Even as the gurney came to a halt a needle was sliding into Beth's arm. 'My baby. Please look after my baby!' she cried out, trying to struggle into a sitting position.

'Don't you worry, me darling. Your babba will be just fine. I swear to you by the blessed St Peter himself.'

The voice was friendly and Irish. Just like Mary O'Malley's. 'Thank you,' Beth whispered. And then she surrendered herself to the sweet unconsciousness that had been trying to claim her since the accident occurred.

Beth came awake to find herself in a typical hospital room, with hard winter light streaming across her bed. She had a headache, a dull nagging pain seemingly originating from somewhere low down at the back of her skull. Gingerly she touched the thick pad plastered to the damaged side of her face. She shuddered from the agony even that simple touch caused her.

She felt extremely tired and strangely sore all over, as if she'd been beaten. Noticing a green button labelled *Nurse* beside her bed, she reached out and pressed it.

'And how are you today, me darling?' asked the nurse who breezed in a few seconds later.

Beth remembered the voice instantly as the one which had reminded her of Mary O'Malley. 'Where's my wee boy?'

'He's having his diaper changed. I'll bring him through just as soon as the doctor's seen you,' Nurse Shaughnessy replied with a smile.

Physically Nurse Shaughnessy wasn't at all like Mary O'Malley and was at least ten years Mary's junior. But the essence was the same and Beth warmed to her as she'd once warmed to Mary.

'Your husband's outside. The doctor said he could come in when you'd wakened.'

Beth's hand fluttered to her face. 'I must look a right sight?'

'A little pale, perhaps. But sure that only increases your female mystery.'

Beth laughed. 'You mean I'm haggard and drawn?'

'Not at all. Palely interesting I'd put it.' Nurse Shaughnessy wound Beth's bed up a little and plumped her pillows. When she was gone Beth bit her lip. She'd been desperate to ask about her burn but hadn't been able to bring herself to do so. She gulped at the prospect of being horribly scarred for life.

Gene came in looking thoroughly chastened. Scared, even. 'How are you, hon?'

'I don't really know. I've just woken up.'

He nodded to indicate that he understood. 'How can I tell you how sorry I am for what happened last night?'

'Has the doctor said anything to you about . . . about the burn?'

'Not a word. I asked several times but only got evasive replies. I waited till after midnight, and then a nurse informed me that you'd been given another shot and wouldn't be coming round till morning and I should go home. I arrived back just over an hour ago.'

There was a jug of water and tumbler on the bedside table and Beth asked Gene to pour her some as she was parched.

'The doctor will be along in a couple of minutes,' Gene said when he took the empty glass from her and returned it to the table.

'Gene . . . I think you owe me an explanation. Don't you?'

He looked away from her to stare out of the window. 'Why do you need a male heir? And how does that fit in with you putting in a claim for Loretta's half of the farm?'

Gene sighed. 'Do you remember I told you my father never knew which one of us was born first?'

'Yes.'

'Well, when he died we discovered we'd been left to run the farm jointly, each having a fifty-fifty say. That situation ends when one of us produces a male heir. The farm will then come under the sole ownership of the one to produce that heir.'

'What about the other one?'

'Nothing. Zilch. Not a red cent.'

'Why would your father do such an extraordinary thing?'

'Partly malice – he hated the pair of us and knew this would see us at each other's throats. Literally, in my case, if you think of last night. And partly as a way of keeping the farm intact. You see, he knew El and I can't really work together and would eventually fall out. Also that only half the farm isn't enough land to make a living from.'

'So this arrangement ensures that one of you gets to keep the entire shebang?'

'Precisely. It was a real cunning move of my father's, for he also knew that stuck with only half a farm we'd sell off to outsiders rather than one of us to the other. A case of if I'm not going to get it then you sure as hell aren't either.'

'Now I understand,' Beth murmured.

'The old man was a wicked son of a bitch. As his son I should have the farm. No question about it.'

'But Loretta loves the farm just as much as you do.'

'I'm the *man*. That makes a difference!' he exclaimed, glaring at her.

'I doubt if Loretta sees it like that.'

Gene snorted. 'The farm's rightfully mine, which is how it's goddamn well going to be.'

'What I'm not clear on is why you waited eighteen months to marry me? Surely there must've been local girls who would've accepted a proposal from you?'

Gene's bluster fell away, leaving him looking uncomfortable. 'You got that all wrong, hon.'

'Bullshit.'

'How can you say that?'

'The reason has something to do with Loretta. Is that it? Was Loretta somehow putting a spoke in your wheel?' When she received no reply Beth knew she'd guessed correctly. And she suspected that Gene had been doing to Loretta exactly the same as she'd been doing to him, namely sabotaging any embryonic relationships. 'So your trip overseas was a heaven-sent opportunity for you to find someone without Loretta on hand to somehow make it go wrong. And *I* was that someone.'

Gene couldn't hold her stare. Turning away, he muttered something inaudible.

'Jesus, what a pair you and your sister are,' Beth said caustically.

The doctor came in at that point. He was a middle-aged man with steely grey hair, called Arcross. 'Do you feel up to talking about your face?' he asked Beth after he'd introduced himself.

She nodded. The inside of her mouth suddenly felt very dry again.

'I won't beat about the bush then. Let it heal naturally and you'll suffer extensive scarring. On the positive side, new techniques have been evolved during the past few years. The only drawback is the expense. It costs a great deal.'

Beth looked coldly at Gene. 'So the decision is yours.'

'What sort of money are we talking?' Gene asked.

Beth gave a thin smile. Loretta had been right. Gene was mean.

'Difficult to name a figure. There are so many variable factors.'

Gene swallowed hard, then swallowed again. 'We'd better go ahead, I guess.' He was unable to keep the reluctance out of his voice.

'Good.' Arcross smiled.

'It won't affect the pregnancy, will it?' Gene asked anxiously.

Arcross turned to Beth. Very sympathetically, he said, 'I'm afraid that as a result of the shock to your system you miscarried during the night. I'm sorry. There was nothing we could do.'

Gene staggered as though he'd been hit very hard in the chest. Beth knew now why she felt sore all over.

'Was it . . . was it a boy?'

'I'm sure that—'

'Please?' Gene begged.

Arcross glanced at Beth, who nodded. 'Yes, it was.'

Gene grabbed the end of the bed to steady himself. 'A son,' he whispered.

'Mrs McKay is a healthy young woman. I'm sure there will be plenty more children.'

'Yes, of course,' Gene murmured.

'I'd like to be alone now, except for Stephen,' Beth said. 'I want him with me.'

Gene kissed her on the cheek before he went. The kiss felt cold and lifeless; his mind was clearly elsewhere.

When Stephen was brought to her, Beth cradled him in her arms, where he soon fell asleep. 'Oh, Steve, what have I done?' she choked.

But there was no reply. Only a lost feeling in her belly where up until a few hours previously there had been a baby.

Chapter 16

It was early Wednesday morning, 15 August 1945. After breakfast Beth decided to spend a couple of hours playing with Stephen, who was now nearly three years old and the spitting image of his father.

It would soon be harvest time. The harvest promised to be a particularly good one, which was just as well considering that Gene was still paying for the series of operations that had transformed Beth's face almost back to what it had been. There was a slight yellow tinge and tightness of the skin around the once damaged section, although the yellow tinge would disappear in time, Arcross had assured Beth. The tightness would remain.

Laughing, Stephen climbed into a wheelbarrow and flattened himself on the bottom, trying to hide from Beth. She pretended she didn't know where he was, and he screamed with delight when she seized the wheelbarrow's handles and started trundling it along the ground with him now clinging on to its sides.

Beth headed for the large barn, intending to dump

him out on a stack of hay she knew to be just inside the doors. Several chickens ran squawking away as she made for the barn, picking up speed as she went.

She was almost at the doors when she spotted Loretta and Michael deep in the barn, Loretta shouting angrily while waving something over her head. Beth came to a halt, wondering what was going on. Loretta had been in a foul mood over breakfast. There again, that was nothing unusual as Loretta was nearly always in a foul mood nowadays.

Loretta's hand swung down, the thing she'd been brandishing slashing into Michael's face.

My God, it's her riding crop! Beth realised. She winced when she saw blood spurt, and snatching Stephen out of the wheelbarrow she ran forward.

The crop fell a second time, and a third. Michael made no move to either take it from Loretta or defend himself in any way.

'Stop it! Stop it!' Beth yelled. Loretta swung round to glare at her. Beth held Stephen tight against her chest. 'I think you've done enough facial damage for one lifetime,' she said in a steely tone. She considered Loretta as much to blame as Gene for what had happened to her.

Michael fished in his pocket and produced a handkerchief, which he used to staunch the streaming blood. Slapping her thigh with her crop, Loretta strode from the barn. Beth went to Michael and gave him Stephen to hold while she examined the cuts on his face. 'You're lucky. They're only superficial.'

Michael grunted in reply, and set Stephen down.

'Why did you just stand there like that?'

Michael was about to answer when there came an excited shout from outside. Seconds later Gene charged in.

'It's over!' he cried.

'What's over?' Beth queried.

'The war. I just heard it on the radio. Japan has surrendered unconditionally.'

'You're certain?'

'It was on the radio, I tell you. The war is finally over!'

Beth closed her eyes. 'Thank God,' she whispered. She opened her eyes again when she felt someone tugging at her leg. Glancing down, she saw Stephen staring up at her. Falling to her knees, she took him in her arms. The war was over. *The war was over!* It was unbelievable. The long-awaited moment had finally arrived.

'Why are you crying, Mommy?' Stephen asked, his little nose wrinkled with concern.

'Because something very important has happened.'

'Something bad to make you cry?'

'No, Stephen. Something very good.'

'If it's good does that mean I can have some candy?'

She laughed through her tears. 'Today, my darling, you can have all the candy you want.'

'To hell with work. This calls for a celebration!' Gene declared. Then he noticed Michael's face for the first time. 'What happened to you?'

'I tripped and fell over,' Michael lied.

It was on the tip of Beth's tongue to contradict him but she decided not to. 'Let's all have some cider,' she said instead. And taking Stephen's hand she led the way back to the house.

* * *

279

The news spread like wildfire. By the afternoon it had been decided to hold an impromptu celebration in Stewarton's main street. Tables and chairs were put out, and people contributed generously in the way of food and drink. A local six-piece band struck up in front of Mr Westlake's store.

The farmers and their families came from all around and soon the main street was thronged. Beth and Stephen were thoroughly enjoying themselves, Stephen consuming Tootsie Roll after Tootsie Roll and Beth, for once, not counting.

It was getting on towards early evening when Beth spied Michael standing listening to the band. Seeing he was alone, she decided to ask him up for a dance. She asked a comfortable farmer's wife to look after Stephen for a few minutes, and crossed to where Michael stood. She smiled at him. 'How about giving your employer's wife a turn round the street?'

He blinked. 'You mean dance?'

'Yes.'

He glanced around. 'You've been here long enough, Mrs McKay, to know certain things just aren't acceptable. Dancing publicly with an Indian is one of them.'

'I'm aware of that. And I don't care.'

'Why cause unnecessary waves? Thank you for asking. I'm honoured you did, but I don't think we should.'

'Well I do,' she retorted. She grabbed him by the arm and dragged him into the ranks of those already dancing.

Within seconds Beth could feel eyes on her and was sure she could hear murmuring underneath the general chatter and hubbub. Murmuring about her and Michael, no doubt.

'How's the face?'

'The cuts will be gone in a couple of days. I'm a quick healer.'

'Is that because you're you or because you're an Indian?'

He thought about that, then gave a low laugh. 'I really don't know.'

Beth glanced over at Gene, who stared angrily back. He gave a sideways jerk of his head which she pretended not to notice. She was going to be in for it tonight, she told herself. 'What was all that about between you and Loretta? Or is it private?'

'It's private, but I'll tell you anyway. I've broken with her.'

'This morning?'

'No, two weeks ago. She's been at me to go back with her ever since. But I won't.'

The dance finished, and Michael made to move off, but Beth restrained him. 'Not till I hear the full story, Michael.'

'I could tell you just as easily while we stand listening to the band.'

It was true enough, but she was feeling contrary. She wanted to dance with Michael, so why not? It was ridiculous to feel she shouldn't because he was an Indian. 'I prefer to dance.'

Michael sighed. 'All right, then. As you wish.'

'You were saying about you and Loretta?' she prompted as they started to dance again.

'What do you know about the Indian religion?'

'Only that you believe in some sort of Great Spirit.'

'That's correct. He has several names amongst the tribes but I know him as Manitou.'

Beth frowned. 'I don't see the connection between Loretta and your religion.'

'I've given up Loretta because according to our belief she is a holy woman and it is forbidden to make love to a holy person.'

Loretta holy! Beth couldn't think of anyone less so. 'In what way is she holy?'

Michael gave a thin smile. 'We believe crazy people are holy. And Loretta is undoubtedly crazy.'

They danced for a few seconds in silence. 'I realised the night of my accident that she was mad. It was written all over her face,' Beth said eventually.

'I still love her, you appreciate. That hasn't changed. And I think that's why I put off accepting her condition for so long. But recently it's become so apparent that I can't continue deluding myself any longer.'

'I'm sorry you still love her.'

'I suspect deep down I've always known she had the potential to be crazy. Or, to put it another way, perhaps she's always been partially so and that is what initially attracted me. For we Indians are mystics, and attracted to anything holy as iron filings are to a magnet.'

A sudden fear gripped Beth. 'You're not thinking of leaving the farm now, are you?'

'It would be for the best. Don't you agree?'

'I . . . Yes. I'm sure it would be.'

His eyes narrowed. 'What's troubling you, Mrs McKay?'

'Loretta scares the living daylights out of me, Michael. I'm pretty certain I can take care of myself, but it's Stephen I worry about. A woman like Loretta is capable of anything.' When he didn't reply she went on, 'As it is I daren't take my eye off Stephen even for a moment. Now you two have broken up I can see her being even worse than she was before – possibly even going on the rampage. And to be truthful, Michael, you're the only one I feel I can fully trust on that farm.'

The dance stopped and this time Michael said very firmly he'd had enough. He escorted Beth over to Gene and left her.

'That was a goddamn stupid thing to do,' Gene whispered angrily as Michael disappeared back into the throng.

By the end of the day Gene had been drunk twice and sobered up twice and now he was drunk a third time. He stood in their bedroom wearing only a singlet glaring at Beth and Stephen as she tucked the wee lad, who was already asleep, up for the night. 'Don't you think it's time we put him in a bedroom of his own?'

'I want him in here,' Beth replied quietly, starting to undress.

'I'm sick to death of him crawling into bed with us. He takes up so much room I can't turn as I like to and get dreadful backache as a result.'

'I'm sorry about that. He still stays in here.'

'But why?'

'You know why. I've told you a dozen times.'

'Loretta wouldn't harm a child.'

'Maybe not. But that's something I've no intention of gambling on. Stephen will continue to sleep in here and that's all there is to it.'

'I could insist,' he threatened.

'If Stephen goes to another bedroom I go with him. The choice is yours.'

'But the little sod kicks. He puts his back against your ass and spends what's left of the night kicking me. It's nonstop once it starts, I'm telling you. Kick kick kick till I feel like screaming.'

'From now on I'll make sure he comes into my side of the bed. He won't be able to kick you from there.'

Gene snorted and ran a hand through his hair. At times like these, when she was being completely unreasonable, a terrible bubbling anger rose in him making him want to lash out at her. To hurt her. Humiliate her. Picking up his glass of whisky he drank it off, then poured himself another.

Beth never complained about his drinking, always hoping it would kill his sexual urge for that night. Sometimes it did, sometimes not.

'And what in Christ's name made you dance with Michael today? He's a sonofabitching Indian! A decent white woman doesn't dance with them. Do you want folks to talk about you?'

'I like Michael. I don't think of him as an Indian but as a man and I'll damn well dance with him if I feel like it.'

'You'll do as I say!'

'I will not.'

'I'm your husband.'

'If you want me to do as you say then don't make unreasonable requests.'

'*Me* unreasonable! You're the one who's that. And it wasn't a request. It was an order!'

'I don't take orders from anyone,' she snapped back.

His hand flashed out to grab her hair and draw her to him. 'We're part of this community and this community has its rules which you will obey. Understand?'

'That particular rule is stupid!'

'Perhaps. Only I'm not going to be spotted out because of any fancy liberal ideas my wife has. I was born and brought up round here. I like this community and want to stay part of it, which includes having all my friends remain as such. Now you won't pull any more dumb stunts. OK?'

'I'm cold,' she said curtly.

'OK?' he insisted.

She gritted her teeth as he pulled harder on her hair. She wouldn't agree, she told herself. She wouldn't!

Beth's continued defiance was fuel to the anger already bubbling inside Gene. 'Then you asked for it.' Cold, she'd said. He'd soon warm her up.

He sat heavily on the bed and pulled her down over one knee, using his other leg to hold her there. He'd teach the bitch, by Jesus Christ he would!

He pulled her nightdress up over her bottom and began to spank her, hitting the same spot time and time and time again till it felt as though steaming acid was consuming her flesh. She stuffed a fist into her mouth to stifle her sobs for fear of waking Stephen, and whispered, 'Please . . . please.' She hated herself for pleading but she couldn't take any more of this.

Suddenly the spanking stopped, and she felt his hand smoothing the fiercely burning area. Then Gene got up and went over to pour himself more whisky. 'Want some?'

'No thank you.'

'Remember, it's your side of the bed if the kid comes in. I've done with that kicking.'

Crawling between the sheets Beth closed her eyes and pretended to go to sleep. It was hours before her bottom cooled sufficiently for her to do so.

It was an evening some three weeks later. The harvest was in, and Beth was sitting darning while Gene was at the kitchen table working with plane and chisel. Beth had no idea what he was making, for he hadn't seen fit to tell her, and she hadn't enquired.

He looked up suddenly. 'Hey, I just realised something, hon!'

She wished he wouldn't call her hon or honey. To begin with she hadn't minded, but recently it had been grating on her nerves. It was so insincere. So clichéd. 'What's that?'

'You arrived just after harvesting. That means you've been here two years now.'

Two years! It seemed like twenty.

'Well, hon?'

'Yes,' she said simply, knowing what was coming next.

'You'd think you would've conceived again in that time. Huh?'

'Well it certainly isn't for lack of trying.'

He laughed. 'Hot damn. Ain't that a fact!'

The only nights he didn't insist were when she was having a period and he knew she couldn't get pregnant, and occasionally when he was incapable through drink. There were still times when he appeared during the daytime demanding sex then as well, though that wasn't so easy now Stephen was older. There had been a series of flaming rows when Gene had wanted her to go upstairs and she had refused because it meant taking Stephen with them. That just wasn't on! A sleeping Stephen in the room was one thing, a wide-awake Stephen watching some of the things Gene did to her quite another.

Of late she'd started to wake in the early hours and lie thinking about Glasgow and her friends there. But even outside these lonely reveries Glasgow had begun to figure a great deal in her thoughts. Her overriding feeling now was one of regret that she'd ever left.

She stared over at Gene, who'd gone back to working the wood, not for the first time marvelling at his artistry. He had a great talent where wood was concerned. Certainly he touched, caressed and looked at it in a way he never had with her.

Beth glanced round as the door opened and Loretta entered. Behind her was a chunky man of medium height whom Beth guessed to be in his early to mid thirties. The most noticeable thing about him was that he only had one arm.

'Hi!' Loretta greeted them, a smug expression on her face.

Gene laid down the chisel he'd been using and nodded to his sister's guest.

'This is Chuck Crerar. He fought with the Volunteers.'

'Well, come on in, Chuck.' Beth smiled and rose to gesture him further into the room.

'Chuck and I have just got engaged. We'll be getting married in a couple of months,' Loretta announced.

Gene went very still. 'Bit sudden, isn't it?'

Loretta smirked. 'Love at first sight. You and Beth know all about that sort of thing, don't you?'

'Won't you please sit down, Mr Crerar?' Beth said, indicating a chair.

'Call me Chuck,' he said, his voice a rumbling bass. 'I'd rather stand if you don't mind. I only dropped by for a few seconds as I have to get back to Stewarton more or less right away.'

'Excuse us if we appear a bit stunned, but we didn't know Loretta was seeing anyone, far less someone special,' Beth said.

'I thought it best – or should I say tactful – to keep it quiet.' Loretta smiled, staring directly at Gene.

'When, er . . . when did you meet?' Gene enquired, apparently having trouble with his breathing.

'The day of the big celebration in town. I went into this tavern for a beer, sat next to Chuck, and we haven't looked back since,' Loretta replied, her eyes flashing with triumph.

Gene turned to Chuck. 'And now you've come to ask me for El's hand in marriage?'

'We've come to *tell* you we're getting married,' Loretta told him before Chuck could do so.

'You say it's going to be in a couple of months?' Beth asked.

'Yeah. Month after next. We'll be living here, of course, as there's plenty of room.'

'Plenty.' Beth nodded.

Triumph was now oozing from Loretta. 'My ring cost a small fortune, I'll have you know.' She flashed the sapphire and diamond cluster under Beth's nose.

'Congratulations,' Beth replied, kissing Loretta on the cheek. 'Well, Gene?' she prompted.

'Congratulations, El. You too, Chuck. We'll be proud to have you in the family.'

'I think this calls for a drink. There's some whisky and gin in the cupboard,' Beth suggested.

Chuck held up a hand. 'Not for me. Like I said, I have to get straight back to Stewarton. Thank you for the offer, though.'

Gene cleared his throat. 'If you'll be living here, Chuck, does that mean you'll be grafting alongside El and me?'

'I haven't thought that far ahead yet.'

'What do you do at the moment?' Beth asked, genuinely curious.

'I'm a mechanic at Fond Du Lac garage right next door to Fiorelli's Tavern where we met.'

'I know the place, but I've never used it,' Gene said, giving Chuck a strained smile.

'He's a darned fine mechanic too. Aren't you, Chuck?' Loretta simpered.

Chuck blushed. 'I do my best.'

'He may only have one hand but you wouldn't believe how clever he is with it,' Loretta said. The double entendre was not lost on either Beth or Gene.

'Well, I hope we see you again soon,' Beth said to Chuck.

'Oh, you will. I'll make sure of it,' Loretta replied for him. 'I'll walk you to your car, honey.'

'Bye, all!' Chuck smiled, giving Beth and Gene a friendly nod of the head, and followed Loretta out of the door.

'I thought he was nice,' Beth said when she was certain they must be out of hearing range.

Gene made a fist, his face contorted with fury. 'How could she be so sneaky!'

'She's only doing what you did, after all, isn't she?'

Gene ignored the jibe. 'I know his type. White trash from way back.'

'That's unfair!'

'I'm telling you, he's good-for-nothing trash.'

'He fought for his country. Lost an arm doing so, and now holds down a job as a garage mechanic. I don't see what you can find to fault with that.'

'Are you taking her side?'

'I'm not taking anyone's side. I'm only commenting on how I see things.'

Gene stuck his face into Beth's. 'Then I suggest you don't.'

He returned to his woodwork, but misjudged a stroke of the plane and gouged a lump out of the piece of pine he'd been patiently shaping. 'Son of a bitch!' he yelled, throwing the plane at the nearest wall. It bounced off to go skidding across the floor.

It was the first time Beth had ever seen him mistreat one of his tools. It was indicative of the depth of his anger and upset.

Stephen was playing with a box of building blocks on the floor while Beth was at the sink preparing lunch. Through the window she watched Loretta squatting on the ground beside Chuck, who was underneath the pickup, which had broken down the previous day.

Loretta was radiant, and it was patently obvious to Beth that regardless of her cold-blooded reason for trapping Chuck the couple made a good pair. Since Chuck had appeared on the scene Loretta had visibly relaxed. The dangerous, ticking-time-bomb-just-waiting-to-go-off quality about her was no longer quite so apparent, although it was undeniably still there. In short, Chuck was proving extremely good for Loretta.

Beth started as a hand was placed on her waist. 'I didn't hear you come in,' she said to Gene, who was staring over her shoulder.

'November the twenty-third. That's the day they've decided on for the wedding.'

'I know. She mentioned it this morning. They want Stephen to be a page and they'd like him to wear a kilt as both she and Chuck are of Scots descent.'

Gene turned abruptly away. Bending over with his head in his hands, he started to cry.

Beth was shocked. This wasn't at all like Gene.

He looked up, his face awash with tears. He seemed more vulnerable then than Beth had ever known him or would've believed he could be. 'She's going to have a male heir before me. I can feel it in my gut.'

Beth dried her hands on a tea towel, not knowing what to do or say next.

'What wrong with Gene?' Stephen asked.

'Ssshh! He isn't well.'

Gene glanced at Stephen and the volume of his tears increased. Is he having some sort of mental breakdown? Beth wondered.

'Why can't I have a boy just like that? Is it too much

for a man to ask he has an heir?' His voice rose in pitch to border on the hysterical. 'Just one. That's all I need, for chrissake. Just one boy!'

'The boy will come in time,' Beth said softly, trying to calm him down.

Gene made a gesture which encompassed not only the kitchen but the house and beyond. 'I'd rather die than leave here, you know. I breathe this farm. I sleep and dream it. It's in my very blood. I can't and *won't* ever give it up!'

The sound of Loretta laughing came from outside and Gene made a choking sound at the back of his throat. 'It's rightfully mine. Not hers.'

Beth handed him the tea towel. 'Wipe your face. We're doing everything that can be done to have a child. You just have to let nature take its course in these things.'

When he'd finished with the tea towel Gene tossed it aside, then took several deep breaths which seemed to help pull him back together again. 'There *is* something else we can do and I should've thought of it before now. You can go and see a baby doctor.'

'Whatever for?'

'I don't know. But babies are their trade. Perhaps one can help in some way. Hurry nature along so to speak.'

Beth thought about it. 'If it's what you want.'

'It is.'

'I'll call Doc Anderson and ask him to recommend someone.'

Outside Loretta giggled again, and they heard the resonant rumble that was Chuck's laugh.

'Ring him now,' said Gene.

* * *

Ten days later, Beth was at the hospital waiting to see the specialist for the results of the tests she'd undergone the previous week.

She was feeling pleased with herself, having just bought a couple of tops she badly needed. Gene only allowed her a small amount of actual cash per month, everything else being signed for. That way he could keep tabs on not only what she spent but how she spent it. They had an account with every store and business in Stewarton, and when the invoices came in at the end of the month Gene gave her hell if she had overspent or bought something he considered unnecessary. He grudged parting with a cent more than he had to.

The reason Beth was feeling pleased with herself was because the tops had been considerably reduced. Gene nearly always approved of cut-price items, particularly when they were really needed, as these tops were.

Beth's name was called and she was ushered through to an examination room, where she found Dr Weskowski seated at a desk studying the contents of a wine-coloured folder.

He rose politely when she came in, and asked her to take a seat. Sitting down again himself, he came straight to the point.

'I'm afraid it's not good news, Mrs McKay.'

'Oh?'

'The tests on you are conclusive. You won't be able to have any more children.'

Beth was aghast. It was the last thing she'd expected to hear. 'Why not?'

'Sometime after you miscarried eighteen months ago

infection must've set in and as a result your Fallopian tubes have become sort of glued together. It's called salpingitis.'

'Sort of glued together?'

'That's correct, Mrs McKay. The egg passes along the Fallopian tubes and is often fertilised there. So when it can't get through pregnancy becomes impossible.'

'But surely something . . . an operation . . . ?'

Dr Weskowski shook his head. 'I'm afraid not. The condition is irreversible.'

'You're quite certain about that?'

'Positive. There's no known operation in this country or any other to cure salpingitis damage.'

Beth closed her eyes, then put a hand over them.

'I'm so sorry,' Weskowski murmured.

'I, er . . . it just never occurred to me there was actually something physically wrong. I only came to see you because my husband insisted. He's terribly keen for us to start a family at the earliest opportunity.'

Weskowski glanced down at the contents of the folder. 'You already have a child . . .'

'But not his. That was by my first husband,' she interrupted. Dr Weskowski made a sympathetic face. 'And the tests were conclusive?'

'Quite.'

'Then that's that.'

Outside the hospital she decided not to go home right away. She needed time to come to terms with this bombshell and think it through. At least she didn't have to worry about Stephen. Michael had taken the wee lad fishing.

She made her way to a drugstore she favoured on occasion and ordered a malted DAP – short for Drink A Plenty. Taking it to a booth, she plunked herself down.

Twenty-four years of age and unable to bear any more children. It was a tragedy. Suddenly she was frightened, little fingers of fear clawing at her insides and making her skin prickly.

Gene must never find out, she decided. This would be her secret. One she would never confide to another living soul. It terrified her to think how Gene would react should he discover what Dr Weskowski had just told her. He'd go out of his mind. Completely berserk. And she would suffer. She shivered at the thought of what he might do to her, not only in the short term but in the long run.

'What a mess,' she whispered. No, he must never find out.

Chapter 17

'Ill met by moonlight, proud Titania!' Michael declaimed, striking a pose while Stephen squealed with delight on his shoulders.

'Who's Titania?' Beth queried, going towards Michael and Stephen, who had been approaching the house as she was parking the car.

Michael assumed a pained expression. 'Don't tell me you've never read *A Midsummer Night's Dream*?'

'The school I went to didn't aspire to such heights. They thought they'd done well if you could read and write when you left.'

'Dear oh dear. How sad.'

'Mommy, Mommy. Michael caught a fish!'

'A big one?'

'A big one. It's a catfish with whiskers and it looks ever so nasty.'

Michael patted the hide bag he had slung over one shoulder. 'It'll make a beautiful supper for me.'

'Let's have a dekko, then.'

Michael set Stephen down and opened the flap of his bag so Beth could peer inside.

'Yuck. It does look nasty.'

Michael chuckled. 'Nasty but tasty. Which goes to prove you should never allow yourself to be misled by looks.'

Was that some sort of dig at her, Beth wondered.

Stephen ran ahead whooping and yelling.

'Where did you learn Shakespeare, Michael?'

'At school. It would seem I went to a better one than you did. Besides the great English poets we also read the great American ones – Emerson, Thoreau, Carl Sandburg. When you have the time you should read Sandburg's poems about Chicago. They're quite something.'

'I'd never have imagined you to be the poetry-reading type.'

'Because I'm an Indian? What do you think I do in my spare time? Sit on the floor wearing a feather bonnet puffing away on a peace pipe?'

Beth laughed. 'To tell the truth I've never thought about it. What *do* you do?'

He gave her a confidential wink. 'Despicable things that would make you blush.'

Beth remembered the time she'd seen him with Loretta in the shed adjacent to the stables. 'That I could well believe.'

'He's a good kid. Very bright and quick,' Michael said, nodding at Stephen.

'He likes you too. Far more than . . .' She stopped herself in time, having very nearly said that Stephen liked Michael far more than Gene.

'Have you ever fished?' Michael asked, tactfully changing the subject.

'No. There aren't any fish in the rivers we have in Glasgow. There were at one time but that was long ago, before the factories and works were built.'

Michael looked sad. 'Europeans have contributed a tremendous amount to the world, at the same time extracting an awful price from the world for doing so. The Indian way is to live at one with the land and the beasts on it. White men impose their will on land and beasts, ravaging both. They call it civilisation and progress. I have another name for it.'

'I don't think you like us very much,' Beth said quietly.

Michael shrugged. 'If I develop an incurable illness I don't say I don't like it. That's not only puerile but futile. I accept the fact that it's there and not going to go away.'

'Is that how you see Europeans? As an incurable illness?'

'Let me just say I can't help but believe the Indian way of life was far superior to that of the men who supplanted them. We were positive. The white man is negative.'

'Bang bang! You're dead!' Stephen shouted, using two extended fingers as a gun to shoot Michael with.

'Aaarrggh!' Michael cried. Very slowly, he toppled to the ground, where he writhed hideously before finally pretending to expire.

'Don't squash the fish.' Beth smiled.

'I was careful how I fell,' Michael replied out of the corner of his mouth, still pretending to be dead.

Stephen ran at Michael, who suddenly sat up and stabbed Stephen. 'I wasn't dead at all. It was a trick!'

'Aaarrggh!' Stephen cried, dropping to the ground and imitating Michael's death.

'The only good injun's a dead one,' Michael said solemnly.

'But I'm a cowboy!'

'Oh, sorry. I didn't realise. Released, then.'

'Released.' Stephen jumped to his feet and went galloping off, whacking the side of an imaginary horse.

'Mr McKay is in a right old mood today,' Michael commented, picking up his fishing rod from where he'd carefully tossed it when pretending to fall down dead.

'Are you surprised?'

'You mean Loretta getting married?'

Beth nodded.

'I suppose not.'

'At least she seems to have got over you.'

Michael gave her a sideways glance, but didn't reply.

'Does that mean she hasn't?'

'She and this Chuck Crerar are well suited. They should be able to make a go of it together.'

'I completely agree with you.'

They were nearly at the house. Stephen was already clattering around the porch, where he was making a great deal of noise.

'Have you made up your mind yet about what you're going to do?' Beth asked.

'You mean leave or stay?'

Beth nodded.

'I wrote to an old buddy of mine in Quebec Province who's replied saying he can get me work there any time.'

'Surely there's no problem about you staying now?

Loretta may still feel a lot for you but with every passing day she's getting more and more hooked on Chuck. So why leave a job where you're well settled when in a month or two the reason for you feeling you have to leave will no longer exist?'

'You seem very keen for me to stay.' He smiled.

'My reasons are purely selfish. The people round here are friendly enough but I haven't really got close to any of them. There's no one I can confide in the way I can with you. Life on the farm has turned out to be very lonely. Having a friend on hand makes it a little more bearable.'

Michael bit his lip. A dozen or so seconds ticked by before he finally replied. 'I'll tell you what. I'll hang about a while longer to see if things turn out the way you seem certain they're going to. If they don't, I'm off to Quebec Province. OK?'

A sudden grin split Beth's face. 'OK.'

Beth ran up on to the porch and took Stephen inside, leaving Michael staring thoughtfully after her.

Gene wasn't drunk, though he wasn't far off it. It was the evening of the day Beth had been to see Dr Weskowski and for well over an hour he'd been sitting in the kitchen morosely drinking cider. Beth had just returned to the kitchen after putting Stephen to bed and Loretta was at the table writing out wedding invitations.

Gene belched, then belched again. Using a sleeve of his shirt, he wiped his mouth.

'Pig!' Loretta muttered.

Gene glared at her. 'Who are you calling a pig?'

'You, dear brother. You not only act like one, you're also beginning to pong like one of late.'

Which was true, Beth thought. For some reason Gene had taken an aversion to bathing during the past few months.

'Are you saying I smell?' Gene replied belligerently, fingers tightening round his glass.

'Yeah.'

'That's a goddamn lie!'

'Beth?' Loretta appealed.

Beth bent over the shirt she was mending. 'Don't involve me.' If she did get drawn in she'd undoubtedly pay for it later in bed.

'OK then. In plain language, you stink,' Loretta said to Gene.

'What do you know about real men? All you know are Indians and cripples.'

Loretta paled. 'Chuck isn't a cripple.'

'There's part of him missing and that sure as hell makes him one.'

'You son of a bitch!'

'What's the matter, El? Couldn't you get a whole man? Other than an Indian, that is?'

This could very easily get out of hand, Beth thought, remaining silent. She was unwilling to get caught up in any argument, even in the role of peacemaker.

'There may be part of Chuck missing but not the part that counts. That part's there all right, and believe you me the man knows how to use it. Yes sirree! Potent is the word for him. You hear me, Gene? *Potent!*'

Gene frowned. 'What do you mean by that?'

'Have I told you he's the seventh of a family of twelve? Or that his mother came from a family of nineteen? No trouble getting children there, I'd say.'

Very conscious of the fact that she'd lied to Gene about the results of her tests, Beth averted her head so neither Gene or Loretta would see the guilty expression she knew to be on her face.

Loretta laughed, a brittle raucous sound that had the quality about it of metal being scraped against stone. She began gathering up her writing things. 'A son and *heir*. Ah, yes! That's going to shoot you right down in flames, brother of mine. Maybe sooner than you think.'

Gene started. 'What are you getting at?'

'What do you think I'm getting at?'

Gene was suddenly stricken. 'Are you telling me you're pregnant?'

Loretta swaggered to the door where she slowly turned to stare directly at him. 'I have this definite feeling. Female intuition, you might call it. I'm going to get pregnant on my wedding night. Furthermore, the baby will be "premature".' She laughed all the way upstairs to her bedroom.

'She *is* pregnant,' Gene whispered, and drained his glass.

'If she is she's only just,' Beth said, having hurriedly worked out the dates.

'But is it possible?'

'It is over a month since the celebration in town when she met Chuck, so yes. But if she is she certainly can't have had it confirmed. On the other hand, I'm told many women can tell when they're pregnant right from the word go. Perhaps she's one of those.'

Gene's face had gone quite grey, and Beth noticed for the first time how much he'd aged since their marriage. The strain of not knowing whether he was going to keep or lose the farm was taking a terrible toll on him, physically as well as mentally. He looked a wreck.

'Is there anything I can do, Gene?'

'The jar of cider's empty. Get me another,' he replied, voice and hands trembling.

Beth did as she was bid. Hours later, when she went up to bed, Gene was still steadily drinking.

Beth came slowly awake wondering what the squeaking sound was. A groping hand told her she was alone in bed.

But Gene was in the room. He was sitting in the rocking chair he'd recently brought through from his father's bedroom gently rocking back and forth. This was the noise that had wakened Beth.

She peered at him through the gloom, and saw that he was still fully dressed and drinking. However, rather than being paralytic as she would've expected, he appeared to be stone cold sober. Glancing at the bedside clock she noted that it was twenty past three.

'Are you going to stay up all night?' she asked.

He continued rocking and didn't answer.

'What are you doing?'

'Thinking.'

His voice momentarily startled her, since she hadn't really been expecting a reply. 'About what?'

'El.'

'If Loretta's pregnant there's nothing you can do about it.'

Gene lapsed back into silence, a dark brooding expression on his face as he went on slowly rocking.

When Beth awoke in the morning he was gone. His side of the bed had not been slept in, and he did not appear for breakfast.

She asked him later where he'd got to, and he told her to mind her own goddamn business.

It was an evening two weeks before the wedding and Loretta had stayed in to write thank you letters for some of the many presents she and Chuck had already received.

Gene was sitting by the pot-bellied stove puffing on his pipe. He'd been repeatedly glancing at Loretta since coming in from work and it was as though he was inwardly laughing at her. Loretta hadn't failed to notice this, and nor had Beth. But so far Loretta hadn't commented on it.

'Spending a lot of money on the wedding, is he?' Gene asked suddenly.

'A fair amount. Money you should be liable for.'

Gene shrugged. 'I'm your brother, not your father. I'm liable for diddly squat. If Chuck wants to marry you he can shell out.'

'Well, he is. Not a word of complaint from him, either. There's nothing tight-fisted about Chuck, which is more than I can say for some people not a million miles from here.'

Gene blew a smoke ring and watched it till it dissipated. 'I saw your wedding dress earlier on in the week. Very nice.'

'It's gorgeous,' Beth agreed. She thought wistfully that she'd have liked to be married in a dress as beautiful.

'Beth mentioned he's renting Cadillacs for the day. Is that right?'

Loretta nodded, wary of Gene's friendly, bantering tone. 'Yeah. One for him and the best man, the other for me and you.' She paused. 'You are still going to give me away, I take it? After all, you did agree.'

'Of course I'll give you away. I wouldn't miss it for the world.'

'What do you mean by that?' she demanded, eyes narrowing with suspicion.

'Nothing. Nothing at all.'

Loretta sat back in her chair to stare at Gene, and he smiled benignly in return. 'What are you cooking up?'

His smile widened. 'I'm not cooking anything. Neither are you.'

She frowned. 'I don't understand.'

He blew another smoke ring and watched it drift away, drawing the moment out as long as possible. 'When I say you're not cooking, I mean you're not pregnant,' he said in a lazy drawl.

'You can't know that.'

'Oh, but I can, El. I surely can.'

Beth was fascinated by the interchange. She pretended to be concentrating on what she was doing, but in fact she was hanging on every word.

'Then tell me how you think you know?'

'It was quite simple really. I didn't know your dates but what I did know was that you had your own box of sanitary towels in the bathroom. Well, after you told us you were pregnant I counted them and then waited. Yesterday the original thirteen were suddenly twelve and today it's down to seven, which can mean only one thing. You're having a period and therefore not pregnant.'

Loretta glared at her brother. 'You're disgusting.'

'I'm also right. The entire business about you being pregnant was complete and utter bullshit.' Laughing, he came to his feet and made for the door. 'Nice try, El. Nice try.' He laughed all the way upstairs, just as she'd done when she'd hinted so strongly that she was expecting. He was repaying her in kind.

And Loretta knew it. Her features contorted into a frightening expression, while one hand – fingers hooked into talons – slowly opened and shut several times. She bent again to her task of writing thank you letters, muttering vehemently to herself words Beth couldn't quite make out.

Beth left the room as quickly as she could to follow Gene upstairs. She didn't want to be alone with Loretta while Loretta was like that.

The day of the wedding was grey and overcast, reminding Beth of Glasgow weather except it didn't have the occasional tang of the sea to it. She was worried. Gene had driven off several hours previously without telling anyone where he was going and he wasn't back yet. Going to the window, she stared down at the gleaming Cadillac which had been delivered just after Gene had driven off. Of Gene there was still no sign.

She picked up Stephen and hurried downstairs to find Loretta drinking wine in the kitchen. Loretta was in her wedding dress, all set for church.

'Where is that mother!' she demanded in a strident voice.

'Don't worry. Everything will be OK. He'll be back any

moment now,' Beth replied soothingly, putting Stephen down and going to the door to stare out.

'Pretty,' Stephen said, smiling up at Loretta.

Loretta smiled back. 'Thank you, Stephen.'

The dress *had* done wonders for Loretta, Beth thought. She did look pretty in a way.

Michael came into the kitchen from the rear of the house. 'All ready to go, then?'

'No we goddamn well ain't. Gene's gone missing,' Loretta told him.

'I just can't think where he's got to,' Beth said, becoming more and more agitated.

'The son of a bitch is doing this on purpose,' Loretta muttered, and threw the contents of her glass down her throat.

'Hold on a minute!' Beth exclaimed suddenly. In the distance she could see what she now recognised to be the pickup. 'Here he comes.'

'Where have you been!' Loretta screeched when Gene entered the kitchen.

'OK, OK. No sweat! There's plenty of time yet.'

'In a pig's ass there is.'

'You have cut it awfully neat,' Beth pointed out.

'It'll only take a minute to get my glad rags on. And what does it matter if you're a little late, Loretta? It's the bride's privilege.'

'Get a move on, anyway,' Beth urged. 'Your clothes are all laid out on the bed.'

Gene nodded. 'I'm on my way, hon.' He took a few steps, and came up short as he was passing Loretta. 'You're a knockout, El. An absolute picture.'

That mollified her somewhat. 'You really think so?'

'What do you say, Michael?'

'She looks radiant.'

Loretta turned coy, just like a little girl. 'Well thank you.'

Gene turned back to Beth. 'You go ahead as planned. El and I won't be far behind.'

'Please do hurry.'

He gave her a lazy grin. 'Sure, sure. I'll be a regular Jesse Owens.'

Beth crossed to Loretta and kissed her on the cheek. 'Good luck.'

Michael gave Loretta the thumbs-up sign, and escorted Beth and Stephen outside to where the family car was parked.

'You drive,' said Beth, tossing him the key. As they got into the car she added, 'You look pretty snazzy yourself.'

'New sports coat and slacks for the occasion. I couldn't let Loretta down, now could I?'

The draped jacket was mustard-coloured, the slacks were charcoal grey verging on black. Round his neck he wore a string tie which ended in two metal bobbles, and Beth thought privately that he looked handsomer than any man had a right to be.

'I shouldn't really ask, but how do you feel about today?' she enquired as they drove into Stewarton.

'You mean about Loretta getting married?'

Beth nodded.

'I'm happy she's happy. How else could I feel?'

Beth gently touched his arm. 'You're quite a guy, Michael Fleetfoot. I like you.'

'And I like you, Mrs McKay.'

'When we're alone why don't you call me Beth? I know Gene prefers things to be on a more formal level but as far as I'm concerned you're almost family. So it's Beth when we're alone from now on. All right?'

'All right, *Beth*,' he said, clearly pleased.

When they arrived at the church Chuck's Cadillac was nowhere in evidence. It seemed he too was late. Beth peeked through the heavy wooden doors to see that the church was full. The organist was playing lustily, if with more enthusiasm and vigour than skill.

Several stragglers entered the vestibule. Beth had a few words with them before an usher led them to their seats.

'Where is Chuck!' Beth exclaimed, wondering what on earth could be holding him up.

Minutes ticked agonisingly by before a Cadillac hove into view. 'Damnation. It's Loretta!' Beth muttered. Telling Michael to keep Stephen with him, she hurried over to the kerb and indicated by frantic gestures that the car should keep going.

Loretta hastily wound down her window as the Caddy cruised slowly past. 'What's wrong?'

'Chuck isn't here yet,' Beth answered, running along-side the car.

'Shiiitt!'

The Caddy gathered speed and disappeared round a corner. Beth glanced at her watch and noted that Chuck was now well late. Where *was* the man?

She returned to Michael and Stephen and found that one of the ushers had been sent by the minister to discover what was happening. Beth explained the situation, saying she'd have the groom and best man walking down the aisle the moment they arrived.

'Here she comes again,' said Michael, nodding in the direction of Loretta's Cadillac which had turned up a second time.

Beth ran back to the pavement and waved the car on. She had a clear view of Loretta's furious face as the Caddy went by.

'She doesn't look one bit amused, and I can't blame her,' Beth said to Michael on re-joining him. Stephen was starting to fret, and Beth slipped him some sweets she'd brought along for just that eventuality.

'Do you want me to take the car and go to Chuck's place?' Michael asked.

Beth bit her lip. 'We'll give it a few more minutes yet.'

The same usher reappeared to report that the congregation were getting extremely restless. He blinked in consternation when Beth snapped that the buggers would just have to hang on.

'Loretta again.' Michael pointed.

Beth waved the car on a third time and decided that Michael should go and try to find out what the problem was. But it turned out there was no need. The twin to Loretta's Caddy suddenly came careering out of a side alley to grind to a halt in front of the church.

Jim Shallcross got out, slamming the driver's door behind him. Jim was Chuck's best man and buddy from the Volunteers. Beth ran towards him, expecting Chuck to follow him out of the car. Only he didn't. On arriving at Jim's side, she saw that the Caddy was empty.

'Where the hell is Chuck?'

'He's taken off.'

Beth stared at Jim, unable to believe what she'd just heard. 'Taken off?'

'I arrived at his apartment to pick him up as agreed and there he was packing a bag, which I thought was for the honeymoon until I remembered they weren't having one. So I asked him what he was doing and he replied getting the fuck out. We've been arguing all this while. I tried to make him change his mind but he was determined to go.'

'Oh, God!' Beth whispered. 'Why?'

Jim shook his head. 'He wouldn't let on. He just kept repeating over and over that he was going and there wasn't a damn thing I could say would make him do otherwise.'

'He had his stag last night, didn't he?'

'Yeah.'

'Was there any indication of this then?'

'Not a hint. He was one happy guy and looking forward to today. Then suddenly this morning, bang! He's off like a jack rabbit who's just realised he's got a whole bunch of guns trained on him.'

Beth glanced back at the church. All those people waiting for a man who wasn't going to appear. And what about Loretta? What an incredible slap in the face this was going to be for her.

'Do you have any idea where he's headed, Jim?'

'If I had to guess I'd say Montreal. It's a city he's been to many times and is real fond of.'

Beth and Jim had been so engrossed in their conversation that they hadn't noticed the approach of Loretta's Caddy, which now swung in behind what should've been Chuck's.

Bouquet in hand, Loretta was out the car in a flash. 'Where is he?'

Jim squirmed with embarrassment. 'You tell her,' he said to Beth.

Beth took a deep breath. Loretta looked more and more incredulous as the tale unfolded.

'I'm sorry,' Beth said when she had finished.

Loretta stood absolutely rigid. She might have been turned to stone. Clucking sympathy and shaking his head, Gene put his arm round his sister's shoulder.

Loretta's eyes suddenly blazed. 'Montreal, you reckon?' she said to Jim, who nodded. 'Then I'll go after him. And when I catch the bastard he can tell me face to face why he's run out on me.'

'Put your foot down. He can't be all that far ahead of you,' Beth advised.

Loretta's reply was to toss her bouquet aside and get back into the Cadillac, this time in the driver's seat. The car roared off, leaving a faint aroma of burning rubber behind it.

They watched the Caddy till it was out of sight. 'What do we do now?' Beth asked.

'I'll go into the church and make the announcement,' said Gene.

'Christ almighty, what a shambles!' Jim Shallcross muttered, shaking his head.

'After I've explained what's happened I'll suggest everyone goes on to the reception—'

'You can't do that!' a scandalised Beth broke in.

'Why not? There's all that food and drink which I'm certainly not going to let go to waste. Not when it's already been paid for by friend Chuck.'

'It just isn't right, Gene.'

'Of course it is. It's because of him all these people have got together so the least he can do for failing to show is give them some sort of good time out of it.'

'Well, I don't think it's right and I won't go.'

'Suit yourself, hon,' Gene said, and headed for the vestibule.

Michael brought Stephen down to where Beth was standing, and she gave him a potted version of what had occurred. Michael stared in the direction Loretta's Caddy had taken, but didn't comment. 'I'll take you and the boy home,' he said quietly.

The clock was tinging six p.m. when Gene came staggering into the kitchen carrying a cardboard box full of bottles. Beth glanced up from the floor where she was playing with Stephen. Gene was obviously drunk.

'El returned yet?'

Beth shook her head.

'You missed a fine party, hon. We sure had one swell time.'

'Is that liquor from the reception?'

'Yup.'

'But it's Chuck's. He paid for it.'

'Grow up. If I'd left it there the goddamn staff would've had it. Anyway, what good is it to Chuck? He ain't coming back.'

'Please, Gene. I wish you wouldn't swear in front of Stephen.'

'Yeah yeah, OK. Sorry about that.' Taking a bottle from the box, he poured himself a very large whisky.

313

'Do you think Loretta caught up with him?'

Gene shrugged. 'No idea. She might well have done. El can drive like a fiend when she's a mind to. I'll tell you this, though: I'm going to wait up to find out. Yes sirree!'

'Why would Chuck do such a thing? Cold feet?'

Gene grinned at her, but didn't reply.

'This suits you right down to the ground, doesn't it?'

'No pregnancy. No marriage. It couldn't be better,' he replied, and belched.

'What a humiliation for Loretta.'

'They don't come much worse,' he agreed.

'What did you tell the congregation when you spoke to them?'

'The truth. Chuck had decided he couldn't go through with it and blown town.'

'Did many go to the reception?'

'A couple dozen or so. Christ, it was a louie! I *thoroughly* enjoyed myself.'

'In the circumstances it was wrong of you to celebrate. Can't you see that, Gene?'

He wagged a finger at her. 'In the circumstances it was absolutely right for me to celebrate. With no marriage she won't be producing an heir, at least for the present. And at her age she can't have much fertile time left, whereas being a man I do.'

Beth resumed her game with Stephen while Gene lounged at the table, drinking and looking extremely pleased with himself.

When it was time to take Stephen upstairs she had trouble getting him into bed – he was playing up and being a right little so and so, and the light had faded into dusk, then darkness proper, before he eventually started to gently snore and Beth was able to tiptoe from the room.

Gene was still in the kitchen drinking, not having moved from his chair. 'You might have put on the lamps,' she admonished him, and proceeded to do so, their soft yellow glow bringing a womblike warmth to the room.

It was twenty to ten when they heard the sound of an approaching car. Gene, who'd been almost nodding off, immediately perked up again and poured himself a stiff whisky, an anticipatory smile on his face.

A car door banged and they heard footsteps on the porch. Gene sat up straighter, his smile widening.

Pinched and haggard, with her wedding dress hanging from her like a wet dishrag, Loretta came into the kitchen. She stopped just inside the door and stood slumped.

'Did you catch up with him?' Beth asked.

'No. I was almost to Toronto before I turned back. Either he didn't go to Montreal or else he went another way. The north route, perhaps, although it's much longer.'

'He's going to the States. A place called Escanaba in Michigan,' Gene stated quietly.

Beth's stomach lurched. She should've guessed.

Loretta stared at Gene. 'How do you know that?'

'He told me.'

'When?'

'This morning.'

Loretta glanced at Beth.

'I know nothing about this,' Beth said quickly.

Loretta looked back at her brother. 'So that's where you were.'

'Yup.' Gene's smile widened even further.

Loretta swallowed, then sort of staggered to the sink which she clutched at and hung on to.

'Would you like some coffee, or a drink?' Beth offered. She would never have believed she could feel so sorry for her sister-in-law.

Loretta ignored her. 'What did you do to him, Gene?'

'It was with your best interests at heart, El, I assure you. But when I found out what I did I just couldn't let my sister marry a man like that. Which is exactly what I said to him this morning.'

Tears started to roll down Loretta's face, large round drops that might have been baby pearls springing from her eyes. It was the first time Beth had ever seen her cry.

Beth glanced across at Gene, who was sipping at his drink. He was revelling in this.

'Why couldn't you let me marry him?' Loretta's voice was cracked and broken.

'Are you sure you want to know?'

'Yeah, Gene. I do.'

'He wasn't all you thought him, El. When he was abroad with the Volunteers he had a long affair.'

'None of us is exactly lily white,' Loretta said flatly.

'But his affair was with another soldier, El. Private Stanton Gourney of Walkerton. You know Walkerton? It's a real nice little town.'

'I know Walkerton,' Loretta choked.

Gene's eyes glittered as he took a draw on his cigarette, his gaze fixed firmly on Loretta.

'How did you find this out?'

'I hired a private eye. I reckoned if my sister was getting

married I should check the guy out to make sure he wasn't a bank robber or something. Well, he wasn't a bank robber, but he had been a practising homo. Sure shook me, I can tell you. I mean, who would've guessed? Him being so good between the sheets and all!'

'You . . .' Loretta trailed off, unable to think of a foul enough word to express what she thought of Gene. The tears were no longer pearls but twin opaque rivers flowing down her cheeks. 'What did you say to him?'

'I told him straight I knew about him and Stanton Gourney and that if he went ahead with the ceremony I'd just have to put it about town what I knew. Chuck was realist enough to appreciate how that would've affected him. I doubt if anyone would've spoken to him ever again. He would've been an outcast. Sent to Coventry as I believe the English call it. For they sure hate fags in these parts. Can't stand them at any price.'

Loretta sobbed, her face now creased into a tragic mask. She was shaking all over.

'How long have you known this?' Beth asked.

'A while.'

'And yet you let it get as far as it did?'

'To tell you the truth, right up until this morning I wasn't sure what I was going to do. But when it came down to the nitty gritty I realised I just had to do my duty.'

'Liar!' Loretta screamed.

'It's true about Private Gourney. Chuck would hardly have hightailed it otherwise.'

'I mean about you not making up your mind till this morning. You left it to the last moment to make me a

317

laughing stock. And you've succeeded. Jesus, how you have!'

Beth was filled with disgust. It was an awful thing for Gene to have done. To his own sister, too.

Gene decided to drop all pretence. 'There's not another man round here will entertain you now, El. Not after what's happened today. You're right – you'll be a laughing stock. There goes Loretta McKay, they'll say. All she could get was a one-armed man and he took fright, running off while she drove round and round the church waiting for him to arrive.'

Loretta slowly sank to her knees, then pitched forward till her palms were on the floor. Clenching her hands into fists, she began drumming them.

'You're no threat to me any more, El. The farm will never be yours now. I'd won from the moment I found out about your pansy friend. The private eye might have been expensive but he was worth every red cent I paid him.' Gene rose to his feet. 'Bed,' he commanded Beth, jerking a thumb in the direction of the stairs.

'Do you want me to stay with you for a while?' Beth asked Loretta, going across to kneel beside her.

'I said *bed*,' Gene repeated, a menacing tone in his voice.

Beth was prickly all over and had a dull ache in her stomach. What a nightmare situation she'd landed herself in. Who would've believed the charming chap she'd met in Bruce's Cave would turn out to be the monster who'd just reduced his sister to this devastated heap?

As they walked upstairs Beth listened to Gene's harsh breathing knowing full well what it meant. In the bedroom she gritted her teeth as he came thrusting into her. He didn't give a damn that she wasn't ready.

He woke her up twice in the night to do it again, and a fourth time in the morning just before she rose. When she hobbled down to make breakfast she felt red raw.

Nor did his mood let up. If Gene had been obsessed with sex before, he was even more so now.

Chapter 18

A week after what should have been Loretta's wedding day Gene had to go to Hamilton on Farmers' League business. His term as president had expired and he had to hand over the symbol of his office to his successor. He left saying he'd be back the day after next.

Beth waved him off with a feeling of profound relief. Forty-eight hours without sex. The prospect was heaven.

That evening after supper Loretta went immediately to her room, leaving Beth alone listening to the wireless. After a while she got bored and decided to read. She soon discovered, however, that they didn't possess a book she hadn't already read. Then she recalled the conversation she'd had with Michael about Shakespeare and the great English and American poets. She would go and borrow something from him, she decided.

'Hold on a moment!' Michael called out when she rather timorously knocked.

When he opened the door he was obviously surprised

to see her standing there. 'Why, hello, Beth. Is something wrong?'

She smiled at him. 'I was wondering if you could lend me a book? I've already read all the ones we have.'

'Why surely. Come on in.'

It was the first time she'd been in Michael's room and she was frankly dying of curiosity to see what it was like. The immediate impression was of cosiness, the next of maleness. There could be no mistaking that this was a man's room. A hand-woven Indian rug hung on one wall, and against another wall was a huge bookcase. 'I've certainly come to the right place,' she said, indicating the bookcase.

The furniture was old and exuded an aura of comfort. There was a gramophone with a few records lying beside it, and behind that an artist's easel with an unfinished canvas on it. It was so unexpected she was quite taken aback.

'I didn't know you painted, Michael.'

'I'm not particularly good, but I find it relaxing,' he replied, watching her curiously as she stared round the room.

'Sorry. Am I being nosy?'

He shrugged. 'I don't mind.'

'What sort of things do you paint?'

'Mostly Indian life as it used to be. Occasionally I do more contemporary subjects.'

'Can I see some of your work?'

'If you want.' He walked over to where about a dozen or so canvases were stacked in a corner.

He was being modest when he said he wasn't particularly

good. His talent was raw, primitive and very exciting. It seemed to leap off the canvas at you.

The first picture he showed Beth was of several Indian women going about their daily tasks. The next depicted a mounted warrior returning from the hunt with a deer slung over his pony; the third an Indian mother grieving over her dead child while the shaman looked on in defeat.

'These are marvellous,' Beth enthused when she'd been through them all.

'Do you know much about painting?'

'Not a thing. But I do know what I like and I like these.'

'You're very kind.'

'Not at all. I'm merely saying what I think, which is that these paintings have quality. At least to my eye anyway.'

'Then thank you for the encouragement. Now, what sort of book did you have in mind? I have a number of novels or, if you prefer, some excellent books of poetry.'

He crossed to the bookcase. Beth was about to follow when she noticed a canvas which he hadn't shown her, propped facing a wall and partially covered by a curtain. Unable to help herself, she went to it and turned it round.

'I wish you hadn't done that.' Michael frowned.

It was a portrait of her, not yet finished. The most striking feature of the painting was the anguish he'd captured in her eyes. 'Is that how you see me?' she asked softly.

'Of late, yes.'

'I look very sad and troubled.'

'Aren't you?'

She didn't reply, continuing instead to stare at the picture, which fascinated her. Eventually she returned it to where it had been.

'I hope you're not angry, Beth?'

'Of course not. In fact I'm flattered.'

'You have excellent bone structure. I knew when you first came here I'd have to try to paint you one day.'

She chose a novel by Edgar Rice Burroughs she thought would be entertaining and also took with her a book of poetry Michael insisted she read because he was certain she'd like it.

She was halfway back along the passage leading to the front of the house when she heard what sounded like footsteps retreating away from her.

'Loretta? Loretta, is that you?'

When there was no reply she decided it must have been her imagination.

It was ten days before Christmas and during the previous night it had snowed heavily. After breakfast Beth took Stephen outside and built him a snowman, finishing it off with an old pipe of Gene's in its mouth.

Michael appeared from the stables, where he'd been attending to the horses, en route to see Gene in the house.

'Look at my snowman! Look at my snowman!' Stephen yelled excitedly. Grabbing Michael by the hand, he dragged him over to where the snowman was.

'Very good. Did you make it all by yourself?'

Stephen nodded vigorously.

'Stephen!' Beth said warningly.

Stephen pulled a face. 'Well, I almost made him all by myself. Mommy did help just a little bit.'

'I like that! He's got a strange idea of what a little bit is.' Beth laughed.

Stephen stooped to pick up a handful of snow, which he compressed into a rather loose snowball. Michael cried out when the snowball smacked into the back of his neck.

'Ha ha ha ha!' Stephen roared.

'I'll get you for that!'

Stephen screamed and tried to hide behind his mother, screaming even louder when Michael's snowball hit him on the ear. Within seconds snowballs were flying thick and fast, Beth and Stephen joining forces against Michael. Suddenly Stephen broke away to go running towards Loretta, whom neither Beth nor Michael had seen approach.

Loretta was dark-eyed and pale, as she'd been since her disastrous wedding day. She'd been out walking alone, which had become a habit of hers since then. She often walked for many miles before finally returning to her room and continuing to brood.

'Help me, Aunt Loretta. Help me!' Stephen pleaded.

Loretta stared down at Stephen, a medley of emotions playing across her face.

'Hey, that's not fair. Three against one!' Michael protested good-humouredly.

'Come on, Loretta. Let's see what you can do,' Beth urged, making an extra large snowball with which she hit Michael square on the forehead.

Stephen shouted with glee, a shout which quickly changed to one of panic when Michael went after him.

He dodged round Loretta, Michael trying to grab him and failing to do so. Finally Stephen back-pedalled, Michael followed, and suddenly Michael was flying through the air before crashing into the snowman. Loretta had stuck out a foot and tripped him up.

Covered in snow, and sitting amongst the wreckage of what had been the snowman, Michael was a sight to behold. Loretta began to laugh. Her laughter built and built till she was bent over with it.

'I'm glad someone finds it funny,' Michael said, pretending to sulk.

Beth was pleased to see Loretta laughing. It was the first time she had done so since Chuck had run off.

'The least you can do is help me up,' Michael told her, sticking out his hand.

'OK. I guess I owe you that.'

Uttering a whoop, Michael yanked Loretta off balance and the next second she was sprawling face down in the snow. Hastily he scrambled away.

Beth fully expected Loretta to explode, but she was wrong. Sitting up, Loretta dusted herself off. 'I guess I asked for that.'

'How about some coffee? I think we could all use some after this,' Beth suggested.

'And joker for me, Mommy?' Stephen asked. Joker was what he called Coca-Cola, though Beth had never been able to find out why.

Loretta leapt to her feet and immediately grimaced with pain.

'What is it?' Michael asked.

'My ankle. I've twisted the damn thing.'

Michael squatted beside her, taking the damaged ankle in his hands and gently probing with his fingers.

'Is it bad?' Beth asked, her face filled with concern.

'Bad enough for her to see Doc Anderson, I reckon.'

'Hell's teeth!' Loretta swore.

'It was my fault, I'm afraid,' Michael apologised.

'It was nobody's fault. It was an accident, pure and simple,' said Beth.

'I'll carry you to the pickup. It'll be easier that way.' Michael lifted Loretta into his arms and strode off towards the truck, Beth and Stephen tagging along behind, to see them off. Then they returned to the house, where Stephen had his joker and Beth told Gene what had happened.

'More goddamn expense!' Gene muttered, referring to the doctor's bill that would eventually arrive.

Gene glanced up from his evening paper to cock an ear. 'Listen to that,' he said to Beth, who was preparing T-bones for supper.

Beth had been aware for the past few minutes that in another part of the house Loretta was singing. 'I've never heard her sing before. Her voice is quite pleasant.'

'Have you noticed the difference in her these past couple of hours? A complete change of mood from what she's recently been like. Why, she actually smiled at me!'

'The change has occurred since Michael took her in to the doctor's.'

A thoughtful-looking Gene scratched his chin. 'Maybe the pair of them have got together again and that's what this is all about,' he said.

The idea startled Beth. Could Michael have taken up with Loretta again? Surely not after what he'd told her.

Next morning she asked Michael about it and he assured her that Loretta was still taboo as far as he was concerned. He had certainly not given her the slightest hint or intimation during the trip to town and back that he'd changed his mind.

During the run-up to Christmas Loretta's humour got better and better. The day before Christmas Eve Beth was walking past Loretta's bedroom when from inside came the sound of Loretta laughing. There was a quality about the tone of it that made Beth's blood run cold. Laughter like that could only come from a completely deranged mind.

It had been an excellent Christmas lunch: traditional turkey and all the trimmings, including two botles of red wine, most of which had been drunk by Gene. Consequently he was fairly mellow as they moved away from the table to open the presents.

The tree was a small one, but Beth had done it up nicely. She'd hand made the paper decorations which hung from it, while little puffballs of cotton wool represented snow. She'd asked Gene if she could buy fairy lights, but he had refused, saying it was an unnecessary expense.

'The first present is for Stephen. A special one not beside the tree,' Gene announced. Beth looked at him in surprise. This was news to her. 'I'll go and get it.' He left the room.

Loretta settled herself into a chair. She wore a thin smile and her eyes were hooded. She might have been a reptile poised to strike against an unsuspecting quarry.

Less than a minute later Gene returned carrying a magnificent rocking horse. 'Here you are, boy. What do you think of this?' He placed the rocking horse in front of Stephen, whose eyes were bulging in their sockets.

It was beautifully made. Beth knew Gene had done it himself. 'Where did you find the time?' she asked.

'I've been working on it for months now – a piece here, a section there. Then I just put it all together like a giant jigsaw.'

'What do you say, Stephen?'

'Thank you very much,' Stephen whispered. With Gene's help he clambered aboard and started rocking vigorously back and forth.

'It's very kind of you to have gone to all that trouble.' Beth smiled at Gene, who shrugged, pretending it was nothing.

Beth opened a present next. Then Loretta. Then Gene. Then Stephen, still astride the rocking horse. So it went on until Gene came to his last gift, an envelope with a fancy bow tied round it.

'To my brother Gene from Loretta with all my love,' he read aloud from the attached card.

Beth was staring at the presents, thinking what a poor lot they were – apart from the rocking horse, that is. She was ashamed of the bicycle lamp she'd given Stephen, knowing he'd wanted a torch. The lamp was the cheapest she could find. But what could you expect when all she had to spend were nickels and dimes? Gene's present to her was a bottle of foul-smelling scent that couldn't have cost more than a dollar. It's the sentiment that counts, after all, not the value of the gift, she reminded herself. On her part at least that was true.

'I don't get it.' Gene was frowning, staring at the sheet of paper he'd extracted from the envelope. A single word was carefully printed on it. Loretta's still hooded eyes were fastened on Gene, her face strangely devoid of expression. 'What does *Salpingitis* mean?'

For Beth it was as though her insides had suddenly fallen out. She now knew what had been behind that maniacal laughter, and why Loretta's humour had changed since the day she'd gone to see Doc Anderson to have her twisted ankle treated.

'Doc Anderson told you, I presume?'

Loretta's gaze swung on to Beth. 'Yes,' she replied, her voice cold and hard.

'What are you two talking about?' Gene asked, completely mystified.

'Why did he tell you?' Beth asked.

'It just sort of cropped up in the conversation. He assumed I already knew.'

'Knew what?' Gene demanded, beginning to get alarmed.

Beth had considered on a number of occasions going to Doc Anderson and asking him never to divulge the results of the tests Weskowski had done on her. Each time she had decided against it, fearing that if she did so she'd bring about the opposite result. Being Gene's doctor and long-standing friend Anderson would make a point of telling him. The fear that Doc would say something to Gene had been a continual nightmare for her, and now that nightmare had become horrible reality. Only it wasn't to Gene that Anderson had blown her secret but to Loretta. And now Loretta was using it to get back at Gene.

'Wheeee!' shouted Stephen, rocking furiously back and forth.

Beth looked straight at Gene. 'After we lost the baby I had an infection in my Fallopian tubes. As a result of the infection the tubes became sort of glued together. The medical name is salpingitis.'

'How serious is that?'

'The Fallopian tubes are the passageway along which the female egg travels to the womb. If the egg can't get through it's impossible for pregnancy to take place. To put it bluntly, I can't have any more children.'

Loretta gave a long satisfied sigh.

'Is this some sort of joke?' Gene croaked. Sweat was bursting in bubbles all over his forehead.

'It's no joke, Gene. I only wish it was.'

'But . . . but why didn't you tell me? Why did you lie?'

'Frankly, I was terrified of what you might do to me.'

'There must be a cure. There has to be a doctor somewhere who can do something.'

Beth shook her head. 'The condition is irreversible. There's no doctor anywhere in the world who can make me fertile again. Salpingitis has made me barren for life.'

Loretta uncoiled from her chair and walked to the door. 'Happy Christmas, Gene,' she said, giving him a wicked, triumphant smile.

'I'm sorry,' Beth whispered when Loretta was gone. She told herself she must ensure he vented all his wrath and fury on her and none on Stephen, no matter what physical price she had to pay.

Gene was staring into space, a tortured expression on his face. His forehead was a sheen of sweat. He convulsed from within, then convulsed again, the sheet of paper fluttering from his hand.

'Why didn't the hospital pick up on the infection?'

'It probably didn't flare up until after I was discharged. Possibly even weeks afterwards. It's impossible to tell.'

'No male heir. The farm can never be mine.'

'I'm sorry. Truly I am, Gene.'

'And you're a hundred per cent certain there's no doctor anywhere can cure this sal . . . whatever you call it?'

'I'm a hundred per cent certain no doctor can make my Fallopian tubes function again.'

Stephen started to whoop and she hurriedly hushed him. Gene slowly picked up an old hunting jacket he used for work and put it on. Without another word he went outside.

Beth covered her mouth with her hand, feeling as if she wanted to be sick. Suddenly she hurried over to the rocking horse and swept Stephen off it into her arms, hugging him as tightly as she could without hurting him.

She heard the car engine burst into life, and seconds later the car peeled furiously past the house. He'll be going to get drunk, she thought. She wondered what he'd do to her when he came home.

Not for the first time she wished she could pack some clothes and run away. But that was impossible without money and she had none. She was in a trap which she didn't know how to get out of. Or, as Cissie would have put it, she'd made her bed and would now have to damn well lie in it.

Bed! The very word sent horrors coursing through her.

* * *

It was just past midnight according to the bedside clock when the car returned. She'd consumed a considerable amount of cider before coming upstairs in the hope that the alcohol would deaden whatever lay ahead of her. Stephen was fast asleep and snoring gently in his own bed just across the room. No matter what Gene did to her she mustn't yell or shout, she told herself. If she did, Stephen might wake up and his being involved was the very last thing she wanted.

Her mouth went dry when Gene entered the bedroom and stood staring at her. She'd decided not to pretend she was asleep – that would only make matters worse.

He took off his clothes and draped them over a chair. Getting into his side of the bed, he turned his back on Beth. She lay waiting, thinking that this was a ploy on his part and he was suddenly going to pounce on her when she thought herself safe.

But it wasn't a ploy. He fell asleep without touching her. Nor was there sex or retribution of any kind next morning either.

It was a Sunday afternoon in early February and the family had been to church that morning. The adults were drinking coffee in the kitchen and Stephen was playing on the floor when Michael appeared with some tiny ice skates he'd borrowed from a family he was friendly with, to ask if he could take Stephen skating.

Beth agreed. It would've been hard for her not to as Stephen was so enthusiastic.

'Take my skates and tag along. You might enjoy it,' Loretta suggested.

'Sounds like a good idea. What do you say?' Michael asked.

Beth raised an enquiring eyebrow at Gene. 'Suit yourself.' He plainly didn't care whether she went or not.

'Then I will go. But I'm warning you, I've never skated before.' She smiled at Michael.

'Then that's two pupils I've got.'

They went to Crystal Creek, which was reached through a stand of apple trees, stark and bare in winter's harsh grip.

As Loretta's feet were considerably larger than Beth's she had to wear a number of pairs of extra thick socks. Loretta's skates were figure ones, while Michael's and Stephen's borrowed ones were black and red racers.

'I'm pretty certain it's safe enough, but let me just check anyway. This creek can be treacherous at times,' Michael said. Slowly, he skated a fair way up and down the creek, and pronounced it to be solid.

The next hour was a glorious one. Stephen persevered until at last he managed to do about twenty yards under his own steam before finally toppling over.

'Well done,' Michael enthused.

Flushed with achievement and praise, Stephen scrambled back on to his feet and set off again.

'He's a trier. I like that,' Michael commented.

Beth was standing wobbling, having made nothing like the progress Stephen had. Her ankles were throbbing and her bottom was soaked from what seemed and felt like non-stop contact with the ice.

'Time for a cigarette, I think,' she proposed, grabbing Michael by the arm as she nearly fell over yet again.

There was a large boulder on the bank, and they sat on it and lit up. 'For a three-year-old he's doing exceptionally well.'

'It's the sort of thing his father would've been good at. Sport and engines. Steve had the knack for both.'

'Do you still miss Glasgow?' Michael asked, noting the wistful look in Beth's eyes.

In her mind she saw her father Andrew as he'd been when she was young. She remembered his coal cart, which she and other youngsters had often run behind. He'd sat her up on the horse once, telling her to hold on tight while the nag slowly clip-clopped down the street. Life up until the war had been good in Glasgow. Her memories of that time were nearly all fond ones.

'Oh, yes, I still miss Glasgow. Sometimes so much it's like a physical pain,' she said quietly.

Her thoughts were interrupted by a shout from Stephen, who'd just learned how to do a circle and wanted his mother to know about it.

'You should get the boy skates of his own,' Michael suggested.

Beth gave Michael a strained smile. 'I'll certainly ask Gene, though I doubt he'll agree.'

Michael didn't pursue the subject.

'How are things between you and Loretta now Chuck Crerar isn't on the scene any more?'

'Fine. No problems at all. I was certain that with him gone it would turn sour between us as it did before, but thankfully it hasn't.'

'So you will definitely stay on and forget all that nonsense about Quebec Province?'

Michael nodded.

'I'm so pleased about that. I can't tell you how much.'

'Do you mind if I say something, Beth?' Michael asked a little hesitantly.

'Go right ahead.'

'I'm an only child and ever since I can remember I wanted a sister. Not a brother as you might think but a sister. I hope you're not offended, with me being an Indian, but I've come to consider you the sister I never had and always wanted.'

Beth was bowled over. Taking his hand, she gave it a squeeze. 'I'm proud you think of me like that. I have a brother whom I used to respect but haven't for a long time. From now on I shall think of you as my brother.'

'You do me honour,' Michael declared, bowing his head.

Beth took a deep breath, suddenly feeling clean and fresh inside. The feeling was a good one.

Michael's head jerked up, his eyes narrowing.

'What is it?'

He came to his feet to stand staring up the creek. 'I heard movement of some kind.'

'I didn't.'

'It's best I take a look. Just to be on the safe side.'

'Stephen, come here!' Beth called out.

'Oh, Mom . . .'

'This instant!' she snapped, waving him to her.

'I was enjoying myself,' Stephen pouted when he was by her side.

'I didn't say it was finished. I just want you here beside me for a moment or two.' She was watching Michael, who'd knelt by a log protruding from behind a bank of earth. Dropping into a crouching position he snaked round the log and behind the bank to disappear from view. A few minutes later he reappeared to beckon Beth over to the log.

'There was someone here all right,' he said pointing to smudged footprints in the earth.

'A man or a woman, do you think?'

Michael squatted down to stare at the footprints. 'Impossible to tell, really. Either the sex or the age group.'

Beth gazed along the length of the bank to the apple trees in the distance, starting slightly when a crow suddenly cried raucously overhead.

'I want to skate some more. You promised I could,' Stephen complained, tugging at Beth's hand.

'On you go, then.'

'I'll go with him,' Michael said.

Beth stared at his retreating back. It was a great relief that he was definitely staying on. His friendship was a big comfort to her. She felt safe when he was about.

She thought about the footprints. Probably just some kid mucking about, she thought. Who else would it have been?

The following Saturday Beth took Stephen into Stewarton to buy some badly needed items, including half a dozen bales of wire from Mr Westlake's store. Mr Westlake said that if she'd park the pickup at the rear he'd load it for her, and it was agreed that she'd call back in thirty minutes.

She and Stephen strolled down the main street and stopped outside Stewarton's only beauty parlour, where she regarded herself in the first of its two large windows.

Self-consciously she touched her hair. What a mess, she thought. Split ends everywhere. She sighed. There was no point mooning over something she couldn't get. As always she'd have to do her hair herself. Gene would have a canary if she had it done professionally.

'How about a joker?' she said to Stephen, who whooped his agreement.

At the drugstore she ordered a large Coke for Stephen and a DAP for herself. They had just settled into their booth when a man who'd followed them in came over and smiled down at her.

'Hello, Beth. Mind if I join you?'

His face was familiar, but for the moment she couldn't place it.

'I know I've changed. Surely not that much, though?'

It dawned on her that his voice was Glaswegian. And . . . Her mind went numb with shock as she recognised him. The colour drained completely from her cheeks.

'You're dead,' she whispered.

He placed his hand on the back of her wrist, his flesh warm against her suddenly chill skin.

'I'm as alive as you are, Beth,' said Teddy Ramsay.

Chapter 19

Teddy sat beside Beth and stared across the table at Stephen, who was regarding him curiously. 'So you're Steve's son,' he said.

'You know that, then?' said Beth.

'Your mother told me when I went to see her.'

'She never mentioned it in any of her letters. And she writes regularly.'

'I asked her not to. At the time I wasn't sure whether it would be a good thing or not.'

Beth took a deep breath, then ran a hand over her face. 'Excuse me. I'll be OK in a minute. You must appreciate what a shock this has been for me.'

'You've put on weight. Or is it my memory that's faulty?' Teddy asked, giving Beth an awkward smile.

'No, you're right. I put it on when I became pregnant a second time and have never been able to lose it.'

'So there's another child?'

Beth shook her head. 'We lost him before he was born.'

'I'm sorry.'

'I have so many questions! I simply don't know where to start.'

'He's the spit of his father,' Teddy commented, nodding at Stephen.

'Did you know my paw?' Stephen queried.

'Yes, I did. I knew him very well indeed.'

'This is your father's brother. Your uncle,' Beth explained.

Stephen's eyes opened wide. 'From Scotland?'

'From Scotland,' Teddy confirmed.

Beth cleared her throat. 'Did you get my letter? *The* one?'

'And Steve's. They were the last I received before the Japs came at us.'

'When did you find out about Steve?'

'End of last September when I got back to Glasgow.'

Tears welled up in Beth's eyes. 'He was killed a week before we were . . .' She trailed off, realising that Stephen believed that she and his father had been married. She flicked her gaze from Teddy to Stephen, then back again. Teddy got the message.

'Your mother explained the situation to me,' he said.

'What I don't understand is if you were taken prisoner why were your parents never told you were still alive?'

'For the simple reason I was never taken prisoner. Thank God! I saw Changi prison and many of the poor blighters who'd been in there. They weren't a pretty sight.'

'Did you fight the Japs, then?' Stephen asked eagerly.

'Yes, son.'

'Did you kill many?'

'Quite a number, I suppose.'

Beth frowned. 'If you weren't taken prisoner, what happened to you?'

Teddy's eyes took on a faraway look. When he next spoke it was with pain in his voice. 'The regiment was up country when the Nips invaded and we took the brunt of it. The regiment was overwhelmed, but not before they'd given a damn good account of themselves. I remember one incident where ten or eleven of us ran across a clearing – or tried to, anyway. When we got to the other side there were only two of us left alive. Lance Corporal McMahon and myself. He was killed a few minutes later.'

'How awful.' Beth shook her head.

Teddy sipped his coffee before going on. 'I met up with a chap called Lanky Lisle and together the pair of us hid out for the night. At daybreak three more Royals stumbled on to us. Two days later we numbered fifteen, including Colour Sergeant Abercrombie. The colour sergeant took command and it was his decision we follow on behind the Nips. Their advance line had swept over us by then, you see. We intended to join up again with our main force wherever and whenever we could. Only we never did. For Singapore and what was left of the main force surrendered before we could re-establish contact. When we found out about Singapore from a radio we captured we thought that was it. We would have to surrender as well. Then we started finding the bodies of other soldiers who'd surrendered only to be slaughtered for their pains.'

'Steve and I heard about the crucifixions.'

Teddy nodded. 'We saw plenty of those. And other things I can't mention in front of the boy here.'

'So what did you do then?'

'Travelling by night, we slowly made our way back up country till we came to the outskirts of a small town called Mersing where we stole a banyan boat. Then we headed out to sea towards some uninhabited islands Abercrombie knew of about ten miles offshore. As luck would have it a storm blew up during which we lost a man overboard. The boat was wrecked on the beach of one of the islands, and we stayed there for a year.'

'And it *was* uninhabited?'

'Oh, yes. Although we did find a crudely built house there – no more than a shack really. From some of the things inside we gathered it had belonged to an Australian based in Singapore who'd used it as a sort of occasional residence.'

'So you lived in the house?'

'Far too risky, Beth. About once a month the Japs would land on the island and check it over, presumably for people like ourselves. So we daren't leave any clues about that we were there and staying in the house would've been exactly that.'

'Where did you live, then?'

'Part of the island was fairly dense with jungle, so that was where we set up shop. It wasn't a bad life. Certainly far better than we'd have had in Changi. There were fish in the sea and coconuts on the trees, and seabirds that tasted delicious when we devised a way of catching them. Plus lots and lots of fruit.'

'What happened after the year?'

'Abercrombie said we shouldn't just be sitting idly by but should be doing something active against the Japs.

His plan was to return to the mainland where we would operate as a guerrilla squad harrying the Nips wherever possible. A vote was taken and it was fourteen for, none against.'

'So how did you get back from the island without a boat?'

Teddy smiled briefly. 'We had two choices. Either make a boat ourselves or else take the Japs' when they next came calling. We took the Japs'.'

'How did you do that?'

'The Japs always treated coming ashore as a bit of a lark. I think they thought of it more as a recreational thing than anything else. So the sentries left aboard were pretty lax. Abercrombie and two others swam out to the boat, hauled themselves on deck and knifed the sentries. The rest of us went out on the dinghy the Nips had left on the beach and once aboard settled down to await their return.'

'They must've realised something was wrong when they saw the dinghy was back at the boat, surely?'

'Why should they? It wasn't a particularly big dinghy so every time they went in and out they had to make several trips. As they didn't all arrive back at the beach at once those assembling presumed a party had already been taken out.'

'What did you do?'

'When about eighteen of the couple of dozen who'd gone ashore had foregathered Abercrombie stepped up behind the boat's machine gun and let them have it.'

'God,' Beth whispered, shuddering.

'We landed that night in a secluded mainland cove,

scuttled the boat, and headed inland. We ranged up and down the length and breadth of the country until the Japs finally surrendered. Of the fourteen of us who came off that island six survived, which is fairly good considering some of the things we did and the fact that the Japs were always on our tail.

'The British repossessed Singapore on September the fifth and the six of us were having a drink in Raffles Hotel on the fourteenth. On the twenty-sixth we arrived back in Britain. The following day I was home in Glasgow and learned that my family were dead.'

'I know – I'm so sorry. My mother wrote and told me your parents had passed on, and I thought how sad it was that they'd never seen Stephen – never even knew they had a grandson. It seemed right to spare them the extra worry at the time, but I regret it now, for their sakes. It must have been dreadful for you to find they were gone, and Steve too.'

'I didn't even have the house to stay in. Another family had taken it over after Ma died so I had to take lodgings with a neighbour.'

Teddy stirred what remained of his coffee. 'All those years in the jungle I dreamt of Glasgow. Taking up again where I'd left off. But it wasn't the same. Glasgow had changed. I had changed. And it didn't take long to realise my dream had been without substance. The real Glasgow seemed dirty and smelly after what I'd become used to – everything grey and drab, and lacking in colour. It might have been different if Mother and Father had still been alive. I'd have had something then to hold me. But they weren't and there was nothing. The upshot was I decided to travel.'

'But why Canada?' Beth asked.

Teddy reached over and ruffled Stephen's hair. 'This young man here is all that's left of my family. Well, a link anyway. And I wanted to see him, if only once.'

'Where are you staying?'

'In Toronto. I have a job there with a firm called Black, Block and Bloomingdale. The Three Bs, they're known as. They're a firm of quantity surveyors, which you might recall was what I was studying before the war. It's not much of a job but it pays reasonably well. When I've saved up enough I'll move on.'

'Where to, Teddy?'

He shook his head. 'I haven't made up my mind yet. I suppose I'll go where the mood takes me.'

'It's marvellous seeing you again. Knowing you're alive.'

He stared at her for a moment, then looked away. 'I thought about contacting you at your home address. I decided against it in case it might cause problems.'

'Why do you say that?' she asked sharply.

'No reason. Just that I don't know what your husband is like and he might be the type who objects to an old flame looking up his wife. Particularly an old flame whose brother his wife has a child by.'

'You're right. Gene is exactly that type,' she admitted.

'I don't work weekends, so I thought my best plan would be to come to Stewarton every Saturday and keep an eye out for you. There was bound to be one Saturday when I could catch you and the boy here alone together.'

'How many times have you been to Stewarton, then?'

'This is my fourth visit. I did spot you the Saturday

before last but you were with a man. A rather swarthy young chap. So I kept my distance.'

'That wasn't Gene. It was Michael, an Indian who helps at the farm.'

Teddy pointed to her face. 'Excuse me for asking, but what happened there?'

Beth reached up to touch where the plastic surgery had been performed. Teddy listened intently while she told him that she'd accidentally fallen against a pot-bellied stove and had undergone surgery as a result.

'Can I have another joker?' Stephen asked when Beth came to the end of her recitation.

'Joker?' Teddy queried.

Beth laughed. 'He means Coke,' she explained.

'Let me buy it for him. Please?' said Teddy.

Beth nodded her consent. Teddy went up to the counter where he bought Stephen not only a jumbo-sized Coke but two jam doughnuts to go with it. When he was back at the table again Teddy indicated Stephen, now wolfing down a doughnut. 'He speaks very well. How old is he?'

'Three last December.'

'Then he's very advanced, I'd say.'

Beth tapped her forehead. 'Bright and quick like Steve used to be.'

'Dear old Biggles,' Teddy murmured.

'You must've hated us after getting those letters?'

He gave her a strained smile. 'I will admit to being somewhat aggrieved. There again, I was used to losing out to Steve. It had been happening for as long as I could remember.'

'We both felt terrible about it. Feeling we'd stabbed

you in the back. It's difficult to explain, Teddy. Neither of us set out to fall in love with the other. It just happened.'

'Your mother told me about Roy throwing you out of the house.'

'That didn't make things any easier, I can assure you.'

'You worked in some sort of club, I believe?'

'For American servicemen. I met Gene there when he was over in Glasgow on business in connection with the Ontarian Farmers' League, of which he was president at the time.'

'You're happy then, I take it?'

Beth put on a false smile. 'Extremely so. I find the outdoor life suits me and of course it's perfect for Stephen.'

'I'm pleased for you. For the pair of you,' Teddy replied slowly.

Beth was aching to confide in Teddy but couldn't bring herself to do so. After all, when you got right down to it, what right did she have to complain? Hadn't she been using Gene when she married him? So she had no reason to object when she discovered that he'd been using her as well. As for Loretta, how did you explain the fear that such a person generated? Being so level-headed himself, Teddy would probably think she was exaggerating where Loretta was concerned.

'I'm learning to ice skate, but my stepfather won't buy me skates,' Stephen suddenly announced.

'Michael has started to teach him and says that given a season or two he could be very good,' said Beth.

'Steve used to ice skate.'

Beth raised her eyebrows in surprise. 'I didn't know that?'

'We both did when we were young – out at Crossmyloof ice rink. For three or four years we went every Saturday morning. Steve was a real speed king while I was slightly more pedestrian. He was older than me, mind. It always upset me all the same that I could never go as fast as him.'

'And now he's dead,' Beth whispered, bowing her head.

'We had our differences, Steve and I. Fought like cat and dog. But I loved that man. I'd give my right arm here and now if it would bring him back.'

'He thought very highly of you. Always said you were the brains in the family and one day would go far.'

Teddy gave a dry laugh. 'It's amazing how war changes things. I had ambition at one time, but not any more. You can't go through what I did overseas and come out the other end wanting to get ahead. You see it all in perspective, I suppose. Getting ahead and being ambitious just don't rate very highly at all. They've been demoted to a very low position on life's totem pole.' He paused. 'Do you realise it's five years next month since we met? I worked it out the first time I came to Stewarton. It seems a lifetime at least.'

'How old are you now?'

'Twenty-six. You?'

'Twenty-four.'

'Steve would've been twenty-nine in a couple of months had he lived.'

'Mommy, you're crying,' Stephen said, peering into her face.

'Sorry,' she whispered, picking up a paper napkin and dabbing her eyes.

'There's a ladies' room in the back. Why don't you go and sort yourself out while Stephen and I get to know one another better?' Teddy suggested.

'Does that mean I can have another joker?'

'He shouldn't really. Though it is a special occasion, I suppose,' Beth muttered.

Stephen clapped his hands. 'And lots of crushed ice, please.'

'I'll make absolutely certain of it,' Teddy assured him, winking at Beth.

When Beth returned from the Ladies, Stephen and Teddy were chatting away as though they'd known one another for ever. 'I'm sorry to say it, Teddy, but we really must go.'

'Aaawww!' Stephen moaned, hurriedly slurping down what remained of his drink.

Outside the drugstore they halted. 'Will we see you again?' Beth asked.

Teddy stared at her, then glanced away. 'I don't think so.'

Suddenly it was awkward between them. 'Well, goodbye. Thanks for looking us up.'

'I've bought an old Hudson. It's parked this way.' Teddy pointed down the street.

'We're in the other direction.'

'That's it then.' He smiled.

'God bless you, Teddy,' Beth whispered, feeling tears coming back into her eyes. She kissed him very quickly on the cheek, then, taking Stephen by the hand, strode off towards Mr Westlake's store.

At the corner she glanced back. Teddy had already disappeared from view.

On the way home, Beth drew into the side of the road and parked on the hard shoulder.

'Why have we stopped, Mom?'

'We have to talk.'

Stephen groped in a pocket to produce a twenty-dollar bill which he held up for Beth to see. 'Uncle Teddy gave me this to buy skates with.'

Beth took the bill and stared at it for a couple of seconds before replying. 'We mustn't let your stepfather know where you got this. He just wouldn't understand. I'll hang on to it for now and when I've thought up some way of explaining it we'll come back to Stewarton and get the skates. OK?'

Stephen nodded. 'OK.'

'The other thing is this. I don't want you to mention Uncle Teddy to your stepfather either. It's difficult for me to explain to you, so just accept it would upset him. I don't want that to happen.'

'Why?'

'Why would it upset him?'

Stephen nodded again.

'It just would. Grown-ups can be very sensitive about such things. Particularly men.'

'I wish we were seeing Uncle Teddy again. I thought he was smashing.'

'I wish so too. But it's not to be, I'm afraid.'

'Why?'

'He's very restless and when you're like that you want to keep on the move.' Beth reached over and touched Stephen's cheek. 'So you won't mention anything about us meeting Uncle Teddy, will you? It'll be our secret.'

'I promise. And as we've stopped, can I have a wee?'

All that Coke! Beth thought.

The farmhouse came in sight and the first thing Beth saw was smoke belching from her partially open bedroom window. She stuck her foot down and the pickup leapt forward.

She screeched to a halt in front of the house and dashed inside to find Gene working on some mechanical parts on top of the table. 'The bedroom's on fire,' she shouted to him as she raced for the stairs.

He looked after her uncomprehendingly.

'The bloody bedroom's on fire!' she repeated.

Gene passed her on the stairs, taking them three at a time.

'There's smoke pouring from the window. I saw it as I drove up,' she called out to his back.

Gene opened the bedroom door and black, acrid smoke enveloped him. Coughing, he went inside to reappear seconds later with the wash jug. 'Fill that,' he barked at Beth.

When she joined him in the bedroom she discovered him beating at the wardrobe he'd made for her with a blanket. The fire, which was smaller than she'd imagined, was located in a bottom shelf.

Gene snatched the jug from her and threw its contents over the blaze. It crackled and sputtered but didn't go out.

'More water,' he said tersely, thrusting the jug back into her hands.

Michael appeared at the door and seemed to take in the situation at a glance. Hurrying over to the window, he opened it fully. Immediately, fresh air gusted in and a great deal of the smoke that had been building up in the room was displaced.

Beth set off at a run and soon returned with the jug brimming over, to find Stephen standing outside the door watching the proceedings wide-eyed.

This time all the flames were extinguished. Gene and Michael smothered the sizzling embers with the blanket and a pillow.

'What's going on?' Loretta demanded, standing in the doorway with a hand on Stephen's shoulder.

'We're cooking waffles. What does it look like!' Gene snapped in reply.

'No need to get humpty about it.'

Michael pulled out the clothes hanging in the wardrobe. Many of them were still smouldering, and he tossed them through the window on to the snow outside.

'Hey, wait up, We might be able to salvage some of that lot!' Gene exclaimed.

'I'll have a look at them later and see if anything can be worn again,' Beth said.

Gene shook his head. 'What an expense! I daren't think what it's going to cost to buy new.'

'We're insured,' Beth reminded him, and his face brightened immediately.

'That's not so bad then.'

Michael rummaged amongst the items at the bottom of the wardrobe and produced a charred object which Beth instantly recognised. Uttering a desolate cry, she ran to Michael and took what remained of One-eyed Suzie from him, remembering that the scraps she'd treasured all these years had also been at the bottom of the wardrobe. A cursory examination confirmed the scraps were no more, and she burst into tears.

'We'll replace it all,' Gene promised her.

'Suzie and my scraps *can't* be replaced.'

'They were only kids' things anyway. No great loss.'

Beth glanced at Michael and saw he understood how dear these 'kids' things had been to her. To Gene she said, 'My da gave me Suzie on my seventh birthday. He brought her home wrapped in brown paper and I thought her the bestest doll ever. She lost an eye when I dropped her out of a tree, which is when she became known as One-eyed Suzie. All these years I've loved Suzie as though she was my own child. You saying she was just a kids' thing shows how incredibly insensitive and stupid you really are.'

Gene's face tightened with anger. Michael looked away, pretending not to have heard, while Loretta smiled.

He's going to hit me, Beth thought, bracing herself for the blow.

Gene exhaled, long and slowly, then nodded. 'I forgot for the moment how important it was to you. I'm sorry.'

Beth sagged a little from relief. 'I spoke a bit out of turn myself, but I'm very upset. Suzie and the scraps were the last link I had with Da.'

'How in hell did the fire start anyway?' Gene exclaimed, bending to examine the charred mess at the bottom of the wardrobe.

'One of you two probably left matches in a pocket,' Loretta suggested.

'Sounds unlikely. Matches nowadays don't just ignite

for no reason at all. They're specially treated to prevent precisely that happening,' Michael said.

'Can you repair the wardrobe, Gene?' Beth asked. It was a handsome one, and like all Gene's woodwork terribly well made.

'I'll have to make a whole new bottom, but that won't be too difficult.'

'It's a mystery,' Michael commented, squatting beside Gene.

'Certainly got me beat,' Gene muttered. He had sifted through all the ash and debris and found nothing which might give a clue as to how the fire had started.

'Act of God?' Loretta suggested, raising an eyebrow.

What remained of Suzie came apart in Beth's hands.

Since Gene had found out that Beth couldn't have any more children he'd gone from one sexual extreme to the other. From that day forward he hadn't made love to her.

Beth didn't mind this lack of sexual activity in the least. After so long it was a great relief not to have to put up with his demands any more. Her body was gradually beginning to feel as if it was her own personal property again.

On the night of the fire in the wardrobe she lay awake for a while, thinking, and then turned her head. 'Are you still awake, Gene?'

'Uh-huh.'

'I think Loretta set that fire today.'

There was a few seconds' pause. 'What makes you say that?'

'Well, you couldn't find any reason for it to have started

353

by itself. And it certainly wasn't an act of God. So *someone* must've started it. That's the only logical answer.'

'Because I couldn't find a reason doesn't mean there wasn't one.'

'All right. Did you have any combustibles in your pockets? Lighter fluid perhaps?'

'You know I keep that downstairs in the kitchen.'

'But you might have bought a small phial and forgotten about it?'

'No.'

'Are you certain?'

'I'm very careful about that sort of thing. There was nothing in any of *my* pockets. Besides, the fire started at the bottom of the wardrome amongst the bits and pieces there.'

'Some scarves . . . gloves . . . a couple of old ties. Several cushions, and a dress I intended to remake sometime. Plus Suzie and the scraps. Nothing there that should suddenly burst into flame.'

'But why would Loretta want to set fire to the bottom of our wardrobe?'

'It wasn't the wardrobe she was setting on fire but Suzie and my scraps. She knows how I treasured them because I recall quite clearly telling her once. She was deliberately destroying Suzie and the scraps to get at me.'

'Go on.'

'She's hated me since the moment I first arrived and it's getting worse. I've felt that quite distinctly of late. I suspect it's in her mind to hurt me by whatever means she can.'

Gene chuckled in the darkness.

Beth went cold all over when she heard that chuckle. Her skin blossomed with gooseflesh at the sudden realisation that it would be very much to Gene's advantage if Loretta were to do away with her.

Don't be ridiculous! she told herself. It was an awfully big jump from setting fire to the contents of a wardrobe to murder. Anyway, her death might be to Gene's advantage but it certainly wouldn't be to Loretta's. Loretta would want Gene to continue being married to a woman who couldn't give him an heir.

She was just dropping off to sleep when a new throught struck her. What if Gene was somehow manipulating Loretta? What if he'd found a way to convince her that Loretta herself would benefit by her death?

Outside, the wind was howling eerily. You're spooking yourself, she thought. Seeing ghosts and gremlins where there's nothing more than shadows.

Still, the fact remained that the wardrobe had been set alight. And Loretta *was* crazy. She might not be certified but she was undoubtedly insane. And both Loretta and Gene would do anything to acquire sole title to the farm.

She edged as far away from Gene as the bed would allow.

Chapter 20

Next morning Beth saddled a horse and with Stephen perched in front of her rode to the north part of the farm where Michael was tending the cattle in their covered winter premises.

The small herd of cattle was even smaller than it had been, Gene having had a third of them butchered earlier on in the winter. The herd had long been a bone of contention between Gene and Loretta. He wanted them all to go; she was determined that they would stay. It now appeared that Gene had won this particular argument, for the remainder of the herd were scheduled for the abattoir in the spring, after which the entire farm acreage would be given over to crop raising.

Michael had been shovelling cow cake from a large storage bin, but was now leaning on his shovel thinking about what Beth had just said. Stephen was peering through some wooden slats at a group of shuffling cattle. 'I don't think you're being over-melodramatic at all, Beth. What you're suggesting is within the realms of possibility, in my opinion.'

'But murder! It seems so far-fetched.'

'There must've been many victims in this poor benighted world who've died thinking that.'

'If he is manipulating Loretta, why not just divorce me and save himself the trouble, I asked myself this morning. My first answer was the time element. Divorce takes time. More important, I'm sure he wouldn't want to risk the settlement I would undoubtedly get, which must include a portion of his half of the farm.'

'You could waive that, of course.'

'Certainly I could. Though I doubt very much whether Gene would believe I would. When it comes to the farm his mind is every bit as twisted as Loretta's.'

'Your argument is that if Loretta were to murder you she'd either be executed or else be put away for so long she'd stop being a threat to Gene. Meanwhile Gene could marry again almost at once to sire that desperately needed heir.'

'That's how I worked it out,' Beth agreed.

'OK. Except supposing Gene had nothing to do with Loretta's recent behaviour, then might it be that she has plans to do to him what you were suggesting he might be trying to do to her? In other words, murder you and somehow put the blame on to him so that it's Gene who's either executed or put away?'

Beth shook her head. 'I hadn't thought of it that way round.'

'There again, both hypotheses might be no more than a load of imagined bullshit. Of which there's a great deal of the real McCoy not a million miles away.'

Beth grinned. Bull and cow muck there certainly was in abundance. Piles of it everywhere, their combined stench making the head reel. 'So what do you think I should do, Michael?'

'You want my honest opinion?'

She nodded.

'I take it you don't love him?'

Beth blushed. 'That obvious, eh?'

'The signs are certainly all there, as I've often observed. Well?'

'I don't love him and never have. When I met him I was in a bit of a jam. He seemed a nice chap and a way out for me. I may never have loved him but I have done my damnedest to make him a good wife, except I can't give him the one thing he wants. A child.'

'Don't get too close there!' Michael warned Stephen, who was trying to clamber through the slats. Stephen extricated himself and sat down to build a castle from some straw. He was soon totally absorbed.

Michael brought his attention back to Beth. 'Why don't you do what I was going to until you convinced me otherwise? Cut your losses and clear out?'

Beth gave a small smile. 'I've thought about that, but it's impossible. I've no money. He only gives me a few dollars a week. I don't know whether or not it was intentional on his part but depriving me of cash means I'm virtually trapped here.'

'Nothing you can sell? Jewellery perhaps?'

'No.'

'I see.'

Beth stroked the flank of her horse, a gentle beast called Doris Mae.

'Doesn't he keep petty cash lying around the house?

Couldn't you lay your hands on some of that?' Michael queried.

'Not enough to make any difference. How far would I get on twenty or thirty bucks? With the exception of harvest time I've never known him have more than that at home.'

'If you had the money, would you go?'

'I've got to the stage where I'm fearing for my life and that of my child. There's no question I wouldn't go.'

Michael stared at Stephen, still playing happily with the straw. 'I told you I've come to think of you as a sister, so I'm going to treat you as one. I have a little over twelve hundred dollars saved up – the money that was to take me to Quebec Province and get me started there. I'm going to give you a thousand of it.'

'You can't do that!' Beth exclaimed.

'Why not? What's a thousand dollars against a human life? Or two human lives, come to that?'

'Oh, Michael!' Beth whispered, moisture glistening in her eyes.

'Furthermore, if I were you I'd go next week. Isn't Gene off to Hamilton on League business for several days?'

'I'll accept the money, but only as a loan. I don't know how yet but I will pay you back. And you're right, Gene is away next week, which makes it the perfect time for me to do a disappearing act.'

'I'll pick the cash up on Saturday from the bank and slip it to you the day you go into Stewarton for the last time. I'd suggest you give considerable thought to where you're going – work out your plans beforehand, in other words.'

'I'll do that. You're marvellous, Michael. I'll never forget you, brother.' She went to him and lightly kissed him on the cheek.

'Very cosy I must say,' Loretta commented coldly.

Beth and Michael swung round to see Loretta astride a horse gazing at them. Neither had heard her approach.

'You come to help?' Michael asked.

'No. I'm on my way to inspect a section of the north fence which has been worrying me. I'm certain it won't last the winter.'

'Stephen and I were out for a ride. I just stopped by to chat,' said Beth. It was the truth, if not the full truth.

Loretta gave her a razored smile. 'Of course. Why shouldn't you? It is a free country, after all. Isn't it, Michael?'

He didn't reply.

Loretta's horse was a magnificent bay of seventeen hands, one of several she regularly rode. 'I think there's something wrong with Tigre. Nothing I can put my finger on, just a feeling, that's all. Will you have a look at him sometime?' Michael was excellent with all animals, horses in particular.

'Sure.'

'OK then.'

After Loretta left, Beth called to Stephen that it was time to go. 'I'll never be able to thank you enough for lending me the money, Michael. What you've done is open a door for me through which I can escape the terrible nightmare my life has become,' Beth said when she'd remounted and lifted Stephen to sit in front of her.

'I'm going to miss you, sister,' he replied, sadness in his voice.

'And I'll miss you, brother.'

Outside it had started to snow, large flakes swirling

down out of an ice-blue sky. Beth was so relieved that she sang all the way back to the farm.

Beth lay in bed staring at the ceiling, excitement throbbing inside her. Gene had left that afternoon and wouldn't be home again till late the day after next. She and Stephen were making a seemingly innocent journey into Stewarton in the morning where they'd be boarding the Toronto-bound train.

She intended to return to Glasgow and her own people, though she had no idea what she'd do when she got there. That was a bridge she'd cross when she came to it.

She glanced across to where Stephen lay sleeping in the darkness, a great lump of emotion rising in her throat. The sooner he was away from this awful place the better.

Now she was leaving she'd been looking at the farm with new eyes. She'd become used to how run down it was. Despite many initial urgings on her part Gene had never got round to having the house painted and generally done up, the sole exception being their bedroom.

He was so damn mean, she thought. Short-sighted to boot, for eventually he'd have to have the house redecorated, and when he did it would inevitably cost him a great deal more than if he'd kept up with the decoration and running repairs.

She had no compunction whatever about leaving him. He'd become as a stranger to her of late. They might not have been married but merely two people sharing the same accommodation. Being away from here would be like shedding a great load she'd been carrying for too long, which had become heavier and heavier as time went by. She wasn't a wife any more, but a pawn in a game waged incessantly between Gene and Loretta. A game in which she'd come to fear for her life.

Her thoughts were interrupted by the sound of horses whinnying. What on earth had upset them at this time of night? They must've smelt a rat – that always set them off. They'd soon settle down again.

But they didn't. The whinnying became louder and more urgent, a note of panic setting in. My God! she suddenly thought. Maybe the stables are on fire!

Throwing back the bedclothes she leapt out of bed and started dressing as quickly as she could. Stephen was fast asleep with a finger in his mouth. Beth rushed from the room and made her way downstairs, where she snatched up her parka as she went through the kitchen.

Outside it was bitter cold. Within seconds her face was numb.

The horses were still whinnying, and intermingled with the noise was a new sound: that of drumming hooves. The horse doing the drumming would be El Gato Grande, she guessed, the big stallion only Gene rode. Even Loretta was wary of El Gato Grande, describing him once as the meanest son of a bitching horse they'd ever owned at the farm.

There were no flames in evidence, certainly none that could be seen from outside. The stables' doors were partially ajar to reveal lamplight within.

El Gato Grande was in a right state, eyes rolling and head tossing as he continued to drum his hooves on his stall floor. Tigre was plunging in her stall while even dear old Doris Mae was shuffling excitedly around. The other three horses in the stables were also disturbed, one whinnying seemingly non-stop.

There was definitely no fire, which was a great relief. So it must've been a rat – or a squad of the buggers, considering how alarmed the horses were.

'Hush up now, all of you. Hush up,' she said in soothing tones, wishing Michael were there to help her. He'd have been able to calm them down in moments flat.

Suddenly it struck her that as two of the paraffin lamps were lit somebody must be about. 'Michael, are you here somewhere?' she called out. 'Loretta, is that you?'

Now El Gato Grande was banging his stall door with his rear feet. Beth stared at the big stallion. She didn't want to get too close to him as he frightened her, a fact she made no bones about.

'Come on, everyone. Beth's here. No need to keep making such a fuss,' she said in as calm and authoritative a voice as she could manage.

She started when a gust of wind whistled in the doors, causing one of the lamps to swing on the nail from which it was hanging. She jumped a second time when there was a sort of grunting noise from a stall she'd thought to be empty. 'Who's that?'

A hand covered in blood appeared over the stall, followed by Michael's blood-streaked face.

'Oh!' Beth exclaimed, covering her mouth.

Michael stumbled from the stall to stand swaying. He was naked from the waist down, and his crotch was a mess of congealing blood.

Beth was transfixed. She wanted to run to him, but her feet were rooted to the spot. She watched in horror as his eyes dulled as if a light in them had been switched off. Slowly, he crumpled to the ground.

He was dead. Beth knew it without having to examine him. The light had gone out in his eyes at the moment of death. At the back of her mind she thought that it hadn't been rats that had set the horses off, it had been the smell of blood.

It took a supreme effort but somehow she crossed over to kneel beside him.

Michael had been castrated. Nor was the mess of congealing blood round his crotch his only wound. The left side of his head had been caved in, leaving a deep depression through which slivers of bone protruded.

Bile rose in her throat in a foul-tasting flood. Turning her head aside, she vomited.

When she had finished she wiped her mouth. Her hands were shaking and cold sweat ran the length of her back and buttocks. Unaware that she was doing so, she started to rock to and fro.

'What's wrong with these goddamn horses!' Loretta exclaimed angrily, striding into the stables. She came up short on seeing Michael's body.

'He's dead,' Beth choked.

Loretta uttered a heart-rending cry, then ran forward to throw herself over the corpse. She began to wail, tears streaming down her cheeks. Hauling Michael up by the shoulders, she thrust his face into her bosom and hugged him tightly.

Beth came to her feet. 'I'll go and ring the police.'

Loretta was covered with Michael's blood, her entire front sticky with gore. 'Ask for Sergeant Ed Slattery. Tell Ed we need him here,' she moaned.

Halfway back to the house Beth stopped and threw up again.

Sergeant Ed Slattery was a tall thin man with foxy features whom Beth judged to be in his early fifties. With Slattery was Constable Dodds, about twenty years younger than Slattery and very dour.

It was almost an hour since Beth had got out of bed to go over to the stables; forty minutes since Slattery and Dodds had arrived. Dodds had put through a call for an ambulance and one was now parked outside the stables.

Loretta was a woman beside herself. At one point she'd become so hysterical that Slattery had been forced to slap her to bring her back to her senses. She was sitting now by the pot-bellied stove cradling a mug of coffee Beth had made her.

Beth stared into space. Surely this was all some horrible dream and soon she'd wake up to find Michael still alive. But it wasn't a dream. She was awake. And her friend Michael was dead. Beth felt as if she might choke on the painful lump in her throat which accompanied that thought.

The door banged open and Ed Slattery came in, to carefully lay a wad of bills on the kitchen table. 'A thousand bucks in all. Found them in the deceased's room. Now ain't that a helluva thing!'

Beth gazed at the money Michael had promised to give her in the morning. Now it too was gone. Like Michael.

'I wonder how he came by this? It sure is an awful lot of dough for an Indian to have lying around. You know anything about it, Loretta?'

Loretta shook her head.

'You, Mrs McKay?'

'No, Sergeant,' Beth lied.

Constable Dodds came in to say that the body was now loaded aboard the ambulance and would be taken away in a few minutes.

Loretta seemed to crumple in on herself. She was obviously distraught with grief and her body heaved as she gave a muted sob.

'Why would they do what they did to him?' Beth asked Slattery.

'You mean cut his cock off?'

Beth blanched. The sergeant needn't have been so crude about it. She decided she didn't like the man. There was something inherently dirty and vulgar about him that repulsed her. 'Yes,' she muttered in reply.

Slattery shook his head. 'No idea, Mrs McKay. Although it's my educated guess that it was done by another Indian. Either that or a nutso perv of some kind. But I'd lay my week's salary on its being an Indian. They do some of the weirdest things for the weirdest reasons. Maybe another buck had a grudge against Fleetfoot and waylaid him. There again, there's this money here. Perhaps that's got something to do with it.'

'What about tracks round the stables? Any luck there?'

'Naw. I know there was a fall of snow today but that entire area round the stables has been real chewed up since then. I will come back tomorrow and have another look in the light, but I'm not really hopeful, no sirree!'

'I still can't believe it,' Beth murmured.

'Do either of you know why he was in the stables at that time of night?' Dodds queried.

'I spoke to him earlier about having a look at my horse Tigre. That's probably what he was doing when the attack took place,' Loretta replied.

Beth shuddered, then automatically glanced at the outside door as the ambulance siren rent the air. Part of her listened to the siren as it faded into the distance, taking Michael's mutilated body with it, while another part listened for Stephen in case the siren had wakened him.

'I think it best I take your statements from you in the morning,' said Slattery, gathering up the wad of bills.

It was a macabre question to ask, but Beth wanted to know. 'Did you find the bit of Michael that was cut off?'

'Yeah. In the stall where he'd been lying. It had been thrown to one side.'

'It's gone in the ambulance with him,' Dodds added.

'What a terrible thing to do to a man,' Beth whispered.

'You don't think . . . whoever did it might still be around?' Loretta asked.

'I doubt it. But just to be on the safe side I'd sleep with a gun close at hand tonight,' Slattery replied.

Loretta nodded. 'I'll do that.'

'I'll ring Gene. He ought to know about this,' Beth said. But when she tried to do so it was only to be told by the clerk at the hotel where he was staying that he'd gone out early that evening and hadn't yet returned. She decided to go to bed and try again in the morning.

She looked out Gene's hunting rifle, loaded it with a round, and took it up to the bedroom with her. She placed it on the side of the bed where Gene normally slept and lay sandy-eyed in the darkness, thinking about Michael. In the time she had known him he had indeed become as close as a brother to her and she grieved for him now in a way she knew she never would for Roy.

A fierce wind rattled the window panes, and the house creaked. Outside it had started to snow again. This night was to have been her last on the farm, but everything had changed now.

She felt desperately lost, alone and scared. Silently, she began to weep.

Beth opened the door to Michael's room and stared about her. It was just as she remembered from her previous visits. No, that wasn't quite true, she told herself. On the surface it appeared the same but the life force had gone out of it. That intangible thing that was Michael was no longer present. The room was now merely a room. Inanimate.

The funeral had taken place that afternoon, a quiet affair with a round dozen mourners present. His parents had been there, an elderly couple seemingly quite stoical about the death of their son. His mother was called Wanda. A strange name for an Indian, Beth had thought. She had promised to pack Michael's belongings and send them on to his parents' address, which Wanda had scrawled on a piece of paper.

She was in Michael's room now to make a start on the packing, and try to judge how many boxes would be required.

Gazing round, she saw that his many books were going to be the biggest and most expensive item to send. Damn the expense! she thought. Gene would just have to fork out. Michael had been a loyal employee, after all, murdered in the performance of his duties.

Beth had talked to Sergeant Slattery before the funeral. The only progress he'd made had been to confirm that the thousand dollars had actually belonged to Michael. Michael had drawn it from the bank the previous Saturday. Slattery was still convinced that he had been killed by another Indian, although he had no idea why. He wanted to interview a man by the name of Dominic Yellowtrees who was known to be an enemy of Michael's, but so far Yellowtrees hadn't been located.

Crossing to the bookcase, Beth fondly ran a hand over a line of books. She would keep several of them as mementos, she thought. Something to remember Michael by. Then she recalled the painting of her he'd been working on. She would keep that also. She made her way over to where a stack of paintings were standing against the far wall.

Her portrait was the first in the stack, and, like Michael, had been mutilated. With a hammering heart she lifted it and set it upright on a nearby chair, where she could get a better look at it.

A knife or sharp instrument of some kind had been used to score and slash the canvas, and a brown substance smeared and streaked over the scarred surface. Beth bent to the canvas and sniffed, then recoiled in disgust. The brown substance was human excrement.

Her mind was whirling as she gazed at the damaged painting. What sort of person would do a thing like that? Suddenly she knew. The same person who'd murdered Michael.

The destruction of the canvas had to have been done since the night Michael was killed, for Slattery and Dodds had visited this room that night and the following day. They would have seen the canvas and would've at the very least commented on the state of it. Therefore the damage had been inflicted since then, which meant it had been done by either Gene or Loretta.

Beth lit a cigarette, forcing herself to think; to try to reason out which one of them it was. Although she and Michael had talked about murder it had been her life and Stephen's she'd been afraid for. So when he'd been killed she'd believed the crime to have been committed by a person or persons unknown.

Loretta's reaction had been so utterly convincing that it had never crossed her mind that she could be implicated. If it had been a performance then it had been an outstanding one. And Gene had been in Hamilton. Except . . . when she'd rung to tell him about Michael's death he hadn't been available. Could he have left the hotel that evening to murder Michael, then returned to Hamilton? It was certainly possible. Hamilton wasn't that far away, after all.

But why had Michael been killed? That was what she couldn't understand. There was no sense to it, or at least none that she could see.

She started to shake, feeling as though she was going to come apart at the seams. It was a completely selfish thought, but if only the killer had waited another day, she and Stephen would've been out of it. On their way home to Glasgow. 'Oh, Ma, I don't know what to do!' she whispered.

She considered going to see Sergeant Slattery but dismissed that idea out of hand. Stewarton was a small community of which the McKays were long-standing members, while she on the other hand was a newcomer and foreigner. If she was to accuse Gene or Loretta it had to be with absolute proof, which she didn't have. An accusation under any other circumstances would mean a closing of ranks with heaven alone knew what repercussions for her.

Gene or Loretta. Which one? she agonised.

She was soon to find out.

That night after supper Beth returned to the kitchen after putting Stephen to bed to find Gene morosely drinking cider and Loretta doing a crossword puzzle. Loretta was still wearing the black dress she'd worn to Michael's funeral. As Beth entered the room, she glanced up from her crossword and gave Gene a dazzling smile. 'Did you know, brother dear, your wife was being laid by Michael? By an Indian?'

Beth went rigid, then turned to stare incredulously at Loretta. 'I beg your pardon?'

Loretta ignored Beth, her gaze riveted on Gene, who was gawping at her. 'You've always considered Indians to be dirty, haven't you, Gene? You thought it disgusting when I had an affair with him. How could I? you asked me more than once. An Indian! Saying it as though an Indian was on the same level as vermin. Well, one of those vermin has been having your wife.'

'It's a lie. Michael never laid a finger on me,' Beth burst out.

'You're the one who's lying. Didn't you use to go to his room when Gene was away?'

'I . . . I did go on several occasions. But only to borrow and return some books.'

'The day he was killed I rode to the cattle shed and found you necking with him. You can't deny it. I saw it with my own two eyes.'

'You misinterpreted what you saw, Loretta. I wasn't necking with him. I gave him a peck on the cheek, that's all.'

'Oh yeah? Well, what about the time I saw you holding hands down at Crystal Creek?'

'Holding hands?' Beth echoed, bewildered.

'He heard me and came looking. But I was too smart for him. I got clean away.'

Beth recalled the incident now. 'We weren't holding hands. He'd said something rather sweet to me and I squeezed his hand in appreciation. I can assure you it was a gesture of friendliness. Nothing more.'

Loretta turned to Gene, whose eyes were bulging in their sockets. 'You believe that and you'll believe hogs can fly.'

'You've got it all wrong,' Beth protested.

'Not me. When I put two and two together I don't come up with five, honey.'

'Well you have this time.'

'The hell I have!'

'You and Michael,' Gene choked.

'We were friends. Only that. I swear.'

'I never could understand why he gave me up,' Loretta went on. 'There was some dumb-ass excuse that didn't make any sense. Then gradually I came to realise it was because he'd got the hots for my sister-in-law.'

'It's simply not true!' Beth exclaimed, beginning to get scared now.

'Baloney it isn't!'

Beth stared into Loretta's face and in that moment knew that it was Loretta who'd murdered Michael. Furthermore, the castration was explained. It was Loretta's revenge on him for supposedly having an affair with her.

'Indians are . . . unclean,' Gene jerked out.

Loretta's eyes were burning brightly with a combination of hate and insanity. 'And one of them has had his hands all over your wife. Touching and feeling her most intimate parts. Parts that should only be touched and felt by you. Not only that, Gene, he's been inside her. Inside what should be your sole preserve. And when he'd finished you'd come along for your turn. Putting yours where his had just been. How she must've laughed at you, brother. How they both must've laughed.'

Sweat had appeared on Gene's forehead. Loretta bore on, her voice dripping malicious venom. 'What I can't help wondering is how you and he compared, because Michael was excellent in the sack. I can sure confirm that. So how did you rate against him? Against that dirty Indian?'

'Stop it!' Beth screamed.

Gene came to his feet, his chair tipping backwards and crashing to the floor. His face was puce with anger, his breathing laboured and harsh.

'Can't you see what she's doing!' Beth yelled.

'Every night you've been away. And until you gave up the presidency you were away a lot. She's been with him. Being laid by him,' Loretta taunted him.

'I noticed how close the pair of you were. But it never entered my head that you—'

'We weren't!' Beth cried.

'Disease carriers. That's what Indians are. Disease carriers. I always had all my shots when he was getting his piece of tail from me. Have you been getting your shots, Beth? For if you haven't you could've passed that disease on to Gene.'

Gene was shaking all over.

'Michael wasn't diseased. He never gave anything to me because he never had the opportunity. And I certainly couldn't have passed it on to Gene even if he had done.'

'So!' Loretta smirked.

Gene started to advance on Beth. She backed away.

'I'd like to know sometime how Gene compared against Michael. I enjoy a good laugh,' Loretta said as she headed for the door.

'An Indian with my wife. It makes me want to upchuck,' Gene snarled.

'He never was, Gene. On my life.'

Gene's reply was a cruel, vicious smile.

Beth grabbed a kitchen knife and held it in front of her. 'Don't come any closer.'

Gene continued to advance. With a soft laugh Loretta left them, snicking the door shut behind her.

Gene reached out for Beth and she slashed at his hand. He cursed when an inch-long gap was ripped open at the base of his thumb.

This is precisely what Loretta wants, Beth suddenly realised. She wants him to kill me. Or me him.

Beth grunted as the knife was swept aside and a balled

fist sank into her stomach. Oh, my baby! Who's going to look after Stephen! she thought in wild despair as she dropped to the floor.

Gene kicked her in the ribs, then kicked her again. Reaching down, he grabbed hold of her hair and yanked her into a sitting position. His open hand smashed time and again into her face.

This is it, she thought. Any moment now.

'Indian fucker . . . Indian fucker . . .' he repeated over and over.

There was the salt taste of blood in her mouth. Her face felt as though it had been set on fire.

She slid sideways and banged her head against the floor. Her senses reeled. When she glanced up at Gene he appeared distorted.

She tensed as his hands encircled her throat. Strong hands, used to physical work. Knotty and calloused, and filled with power.

Please let it be quick, Lord, she prayed. She waited for the hands to tighten.

They didn't. Gene surprised her by pulling her back into a sitting position. His breath rasping in his throat, he slid his hands up and down her neck. Then, with a quick movement, he thrust her face into his crotch and pushed her head from side to side. With his other hand he fumbled with his trousers and they dropped away. He fumbled again to release himself.

'Open!' he commanded, tugging at her hair. When she complied he rammed himself home.

Thinking if he came it might defuse the situation she did what he wanted. It was something she'd never done before and found disgusting, but she didn't care what he subjected her to as long as it saved her life. For Stephen's sake.

'This is all you're good for, Indian fucker. I'll never do it properly to you again. Not where an Indian's been,' Gene croaked, digging his nails into the scalp at the back of her head.

It seemed to go on forever. Then suddenly, mercifully, it was all over.

He put himself away to stare down at her, his gaze hard and unforgiving.

'I never slept with Michael. We were just good friends.'

He continued to stare at her before abruptly walking out of the kitchen to go through to the front of the house.

Beth sagged with relief and for the space of a few seconds closed her eyes while she offered up a silent prayer. Then, coming to her feet, she staggered over to the sink and pumped water into the bowl. The water was ice cold, tangy and deliciously fresh. But it didn't remove the foulness from her mouth.

She'd been within an inch of death, she knew. If beating her up hadn't made him sexually aroused he would've gone on to strangle her. She was as certain of that as she was of the fact that Loretta had killed Michael.

It came to Beth then that there was still one avenue of escape left to her. Still a friend she could turn to. What was that name again? B something . . . Yes, that was it. The Three Bs . . . Black . . . Black, Block and . . . Black, Block and Bloomingdale.

She'd ring Teddy in the morning.

Chapter 21

Their rendezvous had been for eleven a.m. and it was now sixteen minutes past. He isn't going to come after all, Beth thought in black despair. And then the drugstore doors swung open and in walked Teddy.

'Sorry I'm late, but a tyre blew and I had to stop and change it.' He smiled down at her.

She bit her lip. 'You've no idea how good it is to see you again.'

'Where's Stephen?'

'He's with neighbours who have a little boy the same age. I wanted us to be alone when we talked.'

He gave her a quizzical look, then jerked a thumb at her empty cup. 'More coffee?'

'Please.'

She lit a cigarette while he was at the counter, absent-mindedly noting that she'd almost gone through a pack since getting up that morning. Her fingers were stained yellow with nicotine.

Teddy sat in the booth facing her and slid her fresh

coffee across. 'Now what's this all about? You sounded almost hysterical on the telephone.'

He listened in horror as she related her story, interrupting several times when he wanted her to clarify or expand on a point. His gaze never left hers for an instant.

'That's it. Right up to date,' she finished.

'This Gene sounds . . . awful. If you don't mind me saying so.'

'He is. And Loretta's even worse. Only I'm not married to her.'

'How can I help?' Teddy asked quietly.

'Lend me some money. As much as you can. I must get Stephen and myself away from Stewarton.'

Teddy sighed. 'If only you'd asked me last week.'

'How do you mean?' Beth lit yet another cigarette. The inside of her mouth was thick and tacky but she could still taste Gene from the night of the funeral. She wondered how long it was going to take before the foulness was gone.

'Naturally I'll give you all the money I've saved. Only at the moment I don't have it because I've loaned it to a pal at work.'

Depression and a new wave of fear settled on Beth. The cigarette trembled between her fingers as she brought it to her mouth.

'I'll have it back in five weeks. There's three hundred and fifty dollars, which isn't enough to get you and the lad to Glasgow but certainly sufficient to set the pair of you up in Toronto.'

Beth gave a cynical smile. 'My luck gets better and better. Who is this person you've loaned your savings to anyway?'

'Dan works for the Three Bs and he and his wife Libba

have been exceptionally kind to me since I joined the company. I'd only been there a few days when they invited me over for a meal and the friendship's been going from strength to strength ever since. A property came on the market they were terribly keen on but they needed an immediate cash down payment and they were a bit short. When I found out I offered my three hundred and fifty until Dan made all the necessary financial arrangements. When he has, that money's yours.'

Beth reached across the table and squeezed his hand. 'You're a brick, Teddy. I knew I could rely on you. But five more weeks! My God, it seems like an eternity away. All I want to do is pack a case and run as fast and far as I can right now.'

Teddy looked thoughtful as he sipped his coffee. 'Tell you what. Would it help if I gave up my job in Toronto and moved here to Stewarton? I could find a room somewhere and a casual job. Anything would do as long as it paid enough for me to get by on. The thing is, Beth, being in Stewarton I'd be around should you need me.'

'Teddy, no. It's wonderful of you to offer, but I couldn't allow you to do that. It's the job you've wanted all your life – the work you studied for for all those years. Stephen and I will be fine.'

Embarrassed, Teddy glanced away. 'As a matter of fact I'm not sure that it's what I want to do. Maybe the war changed me, or something, but I think I need to spread my wings a little before I settle down for good. Maybe try the west coast or the United States. And I have a responsibility towards Stephen, don't forget. I am his uncle, after all.'

That disappointed her. Even hurt her a little. But he

was right: his nephew was his first concern. She'd renounced all claims to his affections when she'd taken up with Steve. Still, he needn't have been so bald about it.

'And you'll go back to Glasgow when you can?' he went on.

'Yes. I've had a great yearning for that dirty old place of late.'

Teddy's eyes took on a haunted look. 'When I was there after the war I'd walk down the streets and they were filled with ghosts. Folk I'd known. Grown up with. Loved. All dead. Remember when you were at school if you made a mistake in your exercise copy book you'd use your eraser to rub it out, and the indentation the erasure always left? Well that's what I saw in Glasgow. The indentations of people who'd been rubbed out. They were everywhere.'

'Oh, Teddy,' Beth whispered.

'Do you know what I mean?'

She nodded. 'Up until the miracle of your reappearance you were one of my indentations.'

They stared at one another, each acutely aware of how much the other had changed since the days when they'd gone out together. Beth could read no clue to Teddy's feelings in his face, but for her own part she was aware that she found this new, maturer Teddy every bit as appealing as the young man she had fancied herself in love with all those years ago.

'What's all this then?'

Beth glanced up and gawped. Gene was standing by the booth glaring down at her. 'I thought you were at the farm,' she stuttered.

'I'd forgotten I'd arranged a meeting in town this

morning. When I saw the pickup parked outside I thought I'd look in to see if you were here.'

Beth's brain had seized solid. She couldn't think of even the beginnings of an explanation for Teddy's presence.

Teddy wriggled out from the booth and stood facing Gene. He'd realised this had to be Beth's husband from the consternation on her face. 'I take it you're Mr McKay?'

'I am.'

'I've come to Stewarton from Toronto looking for farm work and learned earlier on today that you lost a man last week. Mrs McKay was pointed out to me and when I was told she was Scots like myself I followed her in here to ask if she'd be interested in helping a fellow country-man by giving him a job. She told me I'd have to see you.' It wasn't a particularly well put together lie but Teddy thought it not bad considering it had been completely off the cuff.

'Have you done farm work before?' Gene asked, regarding Teddy through partially slitted eyes.

'No. But I *am* used to working with my hands.'

'What do you do in Toronto?'

'I'm with a quantity surveyor and I want to leave because there's too much sitting at a desk involved. I spent most of the war out of doors and I'm now happiest there.'

Interest flickered across Gene's face. 'Where was this "out of doors"?'

'Malaya.'

'But wasn't that controlled by the Japanese?'

'I was with an independent guerrilla squad after Singapore fell.'

Gene was clearly impressed. 'Which part of Scotland are you from?'

'Glasgow. Same as your wife. We've just been talking about some of the places we know in common.'

'I've been there myself. In fact that's where we met.'

'So your wife said, Mr McKay.'

'What brings you to Canada, then?'

Teddy shrugged. 'The war made me restless. I went back to Glasgow but couldn't stick it so decided to see more of the world. I chose Canada because I've always fancied coming here.'

'What do you think, hon?' Gene asked.

Don't seem too eager, she warned herself. 'We do need someone to fill Michael's place,' she replied in a non-committal tone.

'My last live-in hand was an Indian and I was intending to replace him with another Indian. The pay's slightly less for them. How do you react to that?'

Oh, you mean bastard! Beth thought. That was just typical of Gene. Still, in this instance it could work to her and Teddy's advantage.

'As I'd be learning the work that seems a fair enough deal to me,' Teddy answered cunningly.

'In that case I'm certainly willing to try you out. But you'll also have to be given the green light by my sister. All the decisions we make are joint ones.'

'Fair enough.'

They drove to the farm in convoy, Gene leading with Beth in the pickup behind him while Teddy brought up the rear. When they arrived they found Loretta in the stables grooming Tigre.

Teddy repeated his story. Loretta listened intently, every few seconds her gaze flicking in Gene's direction.

She thinks this is some sort of plant on Gene's part and therefore isn't going to agree, Beth realised, correctly reading what lay behind Loretta's stony expression.

Teddy for his part was trying not to stare too hard at Loretta. He kept remembering what Beth had said about Michael's being hit on the head and castrated. The war had made him well used to violent death, even mutilation. But what he had seen had been done by Japanese. First, men; second, an alien culture. A white woman capable of the same violence was new to his experience.

Loretta shook her head. 'You'd be a liability, I reckon. We need someone who knows the ropes, not a beginner.'

'I learn quickly.'

'For a start I don't suppose you can even ride?'

'No, Miss McKay. Though I don't think it would take me very long to pick it up. As I said, I learn quickly.'

'You're certainly full of confidence, I'll give you that.'

'He's willing to work for the same wages as Michael,' Gene said.

Loretta looked at Gene, then back to Teddy. A thin smile twisted her lips. 'I'll tell you what. Why don't I saddle up one of these horses for you? It would help us judge whether you're going to learn as quickly as you say.'

'He can have Doris Mae,' Beth suggested quickly.

'I'll do the choosing.'

Beth knew what Loretta was up to. 'Not El Gato Grande. That's too much to ask.'

'Does the big horse scare you, Scotsman?' Loretta grinned, indicating El Gato Grande. On cue, he snickered, showing huge yellow teeth.

'He's got a deal of spirit,' Gene said.

'Yes, I can see that.' Teddy had also cottoned on to Loretta's game. He could see from her eyes that if he backed down now he definitely wouldn't get the job. Those eyes disturbed him. They reminded him of ones he'd seen in the jungle. Predator's eyes.

'Why not Tigre? Surely he's handful enough,' Beth said.

'Yeah. I think Tigre,' Gene agreed.

That settled it for Loretta. Now it had to be El Gato Grande. 'Well?' she demanded, rounding on Teddy. Her voice cracked like a whiplash.

'Saddle the beast and I'll have a go.'

'This is silly,' Beth protested. Teddy could be seriously injured. Killed, even.

'In here or outside?' Teddy asked.

'Outside.' Loretta began saddling the big horse.

Beth's stomach was churning with apprehension when they all moved out of the stables. She saw that Teddy's brow was furrowed in thought.

El Gato began noisily blowing through his nostrils. 'He's real frisky today,' Loretta informed Teddy with a nasty smile.

He returned the smile, not showing any of the fear he felt. He had long since learned to master his emotions when in a tight spot.

'I believe it's the left side you mount from?' he said.

'This is silly,' Beth repeated. Loretta was a sadistic bitch.

Teddy put a foot in the stirrup. El Gato Grande shuffled away and Teddy hopped after him.

'If it isn't Hopalong Cassidy,' Loretta smirked.

Teddy grabbed the pommel and hauled himself up into the saddle, instantly aware of the power of the animal beneath him. His right foot hurriedly sought the other stirrup.

El Gato Grande snorted and pawed the ground. He moved his rear round to the left, then to the right.

'Let's see what you can do, cowboy.' Loretta whacked El Gato Grande viciously on the rump.

The big horse reared on to his hind legs and whinnied, his front legs stabbing the air. Teddy managed to retain his seat, though only just.

'Yahooo!' Loretta yelled, waving her arms. Very excited now, El Gato Grande galloped away, Teddy clinging precariously to the reins.

'If there are any vet's bills, you personally pay for them,' Gene said to his sister.

El Gato Grande wheeled in front of the house to make for the large barn, and disappeared round the far side of it. For the space of several minutes which to Beth seemed like hours the big horse careered about with Teddy on his back. Eventually the inevitable happened. Teddy came off.

'Shit,' Beth swore as Teddy went sailing through the air to land with a bone-jarring thump on a small pile of bricks Gene was going to use to repair a wall. She ran up to where Teddy lay on the bricks, conscious but with the wind completely knocked out of him. 'Are you all right?'

Teddy sat up slowly and gulped in deep breath after

breath. A quick examination confirmed he hadn't broken anything, though he was going to be badly bruised on his arms and pelvis, which had taken the brunt of his landing.

Beth exclaimed when she saw there was blood seeping through his clothes from his chest.

Teddy gazed inside his shirt. 'Scrapes and scratches. Nothing to worry about.'

Beth glanced over at Gene, who'd caught El Gato Grande and was trying to soothe the horse. Loretta was standing with hands on hips staring at her and Teddy. Beth experienced an almost overwhelming desire to go across and claw her sister-in-law's face to shreds. She turned again to Teddy. 'I want to put iodine on your front.'

He came to his feet and dusted himself off. 'No. That's too much trouble for you, Mrs McKay.'

'I won't have you getting infected on my account,' she said quietly.

Loretta sauntered over. 'Not at all bad. You managed to stay on longer than I expected.'

'Do I get the job then?'

With a smile twisting her lips, Loretta slowly shook her head.

A flame of anger erupted in Beth. 'That's despicable!'

'Isn't it just.'

There was no point in arguing. Beth knew she'd never get Loretta to change her mind. Nor was there any point in appealing to Gene. As he'd said, farm decisions had to be joint ones. If Loretta vetoed Teddy then that was that.

'Come into the house and I'll get you sorted out,' she said to Teddy.

'I really don't feel—'

'Come into the goddamn house!' she exploded.

Once in the kitchen Beth put a pan of water on to boil then told Teddy to strip to the waist. She'd give him a clean shirt of Gene's to go away in as his own was all bloody.

Loretta had followed them in and shortly afterwards Gene appeared. 'I could use a cup of coffee,' he said.

'After I've attended to this man here,' Beth replied firmly.

For a second or two it seemed Gene might make an issue of it, but he didn't. Instead he sat down facing Teddy.

'I asked you to take your shirt off,' Beth said, rummaging for the iodine bottle.

Still Teddy hesitated.

'Embarrassed, are we?' Loretta smirked, raising an eyebrow.

'If you want to know, yes, I am.'

'A grown man like you!'

Teddy stared at her. Then he stood up and began to remove his shirt.

'I've just stuck El Gato Grande back in his stall. When he's calm again you can go unsaddle him and give him a good rub down,' Gene said to Loretta.

'He's your horse. *You* rub him down.'

'It's your fault he's in a lather. You'll do it.'

Brother and sister glared at one another. No love lost there, Teddy thought, removing his vest.

Beth, having found the iodine bottle, turned to Teddy. Her mouth fell open when she saw his chest. 'God in heaven!' she exclaimed.

Loretta and Gene glanced over, and they too registered shock at what they saw.

Beth crossed to Teddy and slowly walked round him. All the exposed flesh below his neck was covered in a multitude of tiny scars. Literally thousands of them. 'How did you get those?'

'In the war.'

'But how?'

Teddy stared at the floor. 'The Japanese.'

'What did they do to you?' Gene demanded.

Teddy brought his attention to bear on Gene and explained in a matter-of-fact tone, 'I told you I was part of a guerrilla squad. Well at one stage a Nip platoon captured me and took me back to their camp. Since they hadn't killed me outright I assumed they had something special in mind and I was right. They stripped me naked, wrapped a roll of barbed wire round me, then suspended me from a tree branch so I could be blown about by the wind. It was monsoon time. I hung there for three days until the lads came to the rescue. Needless to say, there weren't any Japanese survivors.'

'Jesus!' Gene murmured, shaking his head.

Beth felt quite faint. Wrapped in barbed wire and hung from a tree! The concept was positively mediaeval. 'Did it take you long to heal?'

'Everything takes a long time to heal in the jungle. Even the most minor cut drags on and on. But I did eventually.'

Beth wanted to hold him, to lay his head on her breast, to stroke and comfort him. She cleared her throat. 'I'll wash that blood off then get some of this iodine on you.'

Loretta was fascinated by Teddy's story. Her mouth was slightly open and the tip of her tongue trembled like that of a snake poised ready to strike. She turned abruptly away. At the kitchen door she said casually to Teddy, 'By the way, if you still want that job it's yours.'

'I want it.'

Loretta's eyes glittered. 'Good.' And with that she left the room.

'When can you begin?' Gene asked, pleased to be getting a white man for an Indian's wages.

'I can be back here with my things by tomorrow night.'

'Then it's a Monday morning start. By the way, I still don't know your name.'

'Teddy Ramsay.'

'Ramsay? That was my wife's first husband's name. He was a pilot killed in the war.'

'It's a fairly common name in Scotland. Particularly in Glasgow,' Teddy lied. It wasn't a common name at all, and there certainly weren't any more Ramsays in Glasgow than in other major Scottish cities. But Gene wasn't to know that.

The following night at suppertime Beth announced that she was taking some food to Teddy, who'd arrived about an hour previously. 'Just this once, to make him feel welcome,' she said, heaping stew on to a plate.

'Give him a glass of cider as well. He'll probably like that,' Loretta suggested.

She fancied him. The signs were unmistakable, Beth thought as she made her way downstairs. Teddy answered her tap on the door and ushered her inside.

'Safe to talk?' he whispered.

'Yes.'

'I've been worrying about Stephen—'

'I've already attended to that,' Beth cut in. 'I explained when I picked him up yesterday that you were coming to work here and he mustn't let on who you really were or that he'd met you before.'

'Will he be able to manage that?'

'He's a bright child. He'll be all right. I'll just have to keep reminding him, that's all.'

Teddy accepted the food and cider and laid them on the table.

'The cider was Loretta's idea. You watch her like a hawk, Teddy. I'm certain she has designs on you.'

'You've got to be joking! Don't worry, I'll be careful!'

'What happened about your job in Toronto?'

'I've arranged for my friend Dan to break the news to them tomorrow. He'll explain that it was of the utmost importance that I left Toronto as abruptly as I did.'

'And the money Dan owes you?'

'I gave him this address and he'll forward it on the moment he has it. So it's a case of just marking time for the next five weeks until it arrives.'

Beth laid a hand on his arm. 'I can't even begin to tell you what a relief it is to have you here. I'm still scared, but not nearly as much as I was.'

'How about your husband walking into the drugstore like that!' Teddy grinned.

'At least you turned it to our advantage. It was very quick thinking on your part. I was impressed.'

'I'll enjoy being round the boy for a while. It'll give me the chance to get to know him.'

She removed her hand. It seemed to her it wasn't entirely

welcome there. 'He misses Michael, you know. They were great pals.'

'What did you tell him about Michael?'

'That he was killed in an accident. Poor Stephen. He cried his wee eyes out.'

Teddy looked grim, but didn't reply.

'I want to show you something. Remember the portrait I told you about?'

Teddy nodded.

'Well, it's still here. I haven't had the chance to get rid of it yet – I'll have to do it when Gene's away. If he knew Michael had painted me he'd no doubt see it as some sort of confirmation that Michael and I *were* having an affair.'

She went to a walk-in cupboard at the rear of which various boxes plus other odds and ends were stacked, and extricated her portrait from behind them. Teddy gave a soft whistle when she set the mutilated canvas up for him to look at.

'I wouldn't be at all surprised if she used the same knife on this that she used on Michael.'

'It's frightening.'

'I couldn't agree more. I'm showing you this because I want you to realise just how careful you must be. I've already lost you once. I couldn't bear to do so a second time.'

He stared at her for a few moments. Then, picking up the portrait, he returned it to where it had been. 'I'll be very careful, Beth. You have my word on that.'

Suddenly she felt shy in his presence. Almost ill at ease. 'I'll see you in the morning, then.'

'Yes. You'd better get back or they'll be wondering what's happened to you. And thanks for the meal.'

Returning to the kitchen, Beth was aware that her cheeks were burning. That wasn't like her at all.

Beth was outside talking to Hoskin McVitie while Stephen played on the toboggan Teddy had done up for him, painting it red with black stripes and polishing the runners till they shone like new. It was an old one Gene had produced a few days previously, saying it had been his when he was a kid.

Hoskin was at the farm to collect a bull Gene was selling him. Loretta was bringing it down now from the covered premises where it had been spending the winter.

'Here she comes,' Beth said, pointing. The bull had a rope through its nose ring, and Loretta, mounted on Tigre, was holding the end. The bull was ambling along amiably enough, seemingly quite content to follow Loretta.

'He sure drives a hard bargain, your husband,' Hoskin said.

'It couldn't have been that hard a bargain or you wouldn't have agreed to buy,' Beth teased him.

'There are more ways than one of looking at things.'

'In other words you're both satisfied with the deal.'

Hoskin grinned as he lit a stogie.

Beth glanced over to where Teddy was forking cattle feed on to a cart. He'd taken to farm work like the proverbial duck to water. Even Gene hadn't a word to say against him, and Gene was the most demanding of taskmasters.

Hoskin had brought an old horse box to transport the bull in. He started to open its rear and put the loading ramp into place.

Getting off the toboggan, Stephen ran towards Teddy. The pair of them had become firm friends and were almost inseparable. Teddy paused to wave at Stephen, then returned to wielding the heavy pitchfork he was using.

Gene drove round the corner of the house in the pickup. He bumped in the direction of the horse box and had almost reached it when suddenly his exhaust backfired. Bang! It was like a small cannon going off. Bang! Bang! Bang! the exhaust went in rapid succession.

The bull reacted instantly, its placid demeanour vanishing to be replaced by rage brought on by fright and alarm. A jerk of its head sent the end of the rope spinning from Loretta's hand. Tigre screamed with pain as the bull's short horns jabbed into his belly.

'Oh, Christ!' Beth exclaimed as Loretta and Tigre went crashing to the ground. Fortunately, Loretta had the presence of mind to kick herself free of the stirrups to go rolling away so she wasn't trapped beneath the fallen horse. Tigre's leg was obviously broken, judging from the angle it was twisted round at. The horse was desperately trying to rise, but was unable to do so. Loretta lay flat, mesmerised by the advancing bull. She was saved by a final bang from the exhaust, which diverted the bull's attention.

Wild-eyed and trembling all over, the beast broke into a trot. It was heading straight for Stephen, who'd stopped running when the commotion started and now seemed rooted to the spot. Beth screamed, and Teddy acted. Running at the bull, he raised the pitchfork over his shoulder as though it was a spear. With a sort of coughing grunt, he hurled the pichfork with all the strength he could muster.

The pitchfork took the bull in the centre of its body, all five prongs sinking deep into its flesh before the weight of the handle dragged them clear. With a bellow of anger the bull changed direction again, snow churning beneath its feet as it charged Teddy.

Hoskin dashed forward and snatched up a terrified Stephen. Racing back to Beth, he grabbed her too and pulled her behind the horse box.

Loretta was back on her feet, watching as the bull chased Teddy, who was making for the large barn, the closest building to him. He vanished inside with the bull in hot pursuit, and glanced swiftly about him for any possible means of escape.

A chain dangled from the hay loft. Teddy ran for it, and jumped as high up its length as he could manage, swinging out of the way as the bull thundered past. He started to climb, but the chain wasn't securely attached at the top and slithered from its fixture point, sending him crashing to the ground below.

'Hi! hi! hi!' yelled Hoskin, who had picked up the pitchfork and now waved it at the turning bull to take its attention away from Teddy. But the bull was having none of it. With blowing nostrils it glared at Teddy, the one who'd hurt him. Teddy threw himself to one side as the beast drummed by once more.

By this time Beth, carrying Stephen, and Loretta were at the barn entrance. Beth's heart leapt into her mouth when she saw the predicament Teddy was in, but Loretta's eyes gleamed as she watched the unfolding drama.

Hoskin advanced with the pitchfork. Despite the cold,

his face was covered in running sweat. 'Come on, you mother!' he muttered, jabbing at the bull's rear.

What happened next was extremely quick. The bull wheeled and flicked one of its short stubby horns. Hoskin was thrown to the ground, gashed in the neck, and the bull brought its attention back to Teddy.

Beth glanced round to see that Gene was still in the pickup. 'Get a gun, for chrissake!' she shouted. Stephen began to wail; reaction to his narrow escape.

Teddy rolled behind a bale of hay and felt his buttocks bang into something metal. His groping fingers found the head of a sledgehammer.

The bull pawed the dirt with its right hoof. Slowly it lowered its head, aiming its horns at the prostrate Teddy.

In one fluid motion Teddy came to his feet with the sledge grasped firmly in his hands. He waited patiently, content to let the bull make the next move. He was no stranger to confrontation situations, having been in so many while in the jungle, and was prepared to stand there for as long as it took for the bull to commit itself.

It wasn't long. With a sudden bellow the bull charged again, more than a ton of irate bone, muscle and sinew bearing down on Teddy. Teddy knew that if he misjudged the first blow there wouldn't be a second. The sledge swung in an overhand arc and took the bull square between the eyes.

The effect of the strike was instantaneous. The bull stopped dead in its tracks, as if it had run into a brick wall. It shook its head, gave a soft grunt, and sank slowly to its knees. Teddy hefted the sledge in preparation for another blow should it be necessary, but it wasn't. The bull was quite stunned.

Blood pouring from the gash in his neck, Hoskin looked at Teddy in wonder. 'That was the most goddamnedest thing I ever did see.'

'Give him a minute to recover a bit and then we'll get him into the horse box,' Teddy said, dropping the sledge to the ground.

Gene appeared, carrying his hunting rifle. 'You're a bit late. It's already been taken care of,' Loretta said scathingly.

There were tears in Beth's eyes and her heart was thumping nineteen to the dozen. Like a film loop, all she could visualise in her mind was the bull bearing down on Stephen. If Teddy hadn't reacted as quickly as he had the wee fella would've been killed, or at the very least badly hurt. She hugged Stephen tight while the tears coursed down her cheeks.

'I'm sorry about that. I didn't realise the pickup needed a service so badly,' Gene apologised.

Loretta stared at him, knowing that to be a lie. Beth knew it too. Gene had remarked to her only the other day that he would have to take the pickup into the garage as amongst other things it was backfiring badly in certain circumstances. Gene had deliberately arranged for Loretta to collect the bull, and then had driven up in the hope that the animal, which was well known for its nervousness, would react in the way it had. What had just passed had been an attempt on Loretta's life.

Hoskin picked up a length of rope and hobbled the bull's back feet. 'Just to be on the safe side,' he said to Teddy.

'Go and thank Teddy for what he did,' Beth said huskily, setting Stephen down. Still crying, the boy rushed into

Teddy's outstretched arms, and Teddy hugged him as tightly as Beth had done.

The bull gave a plaintive bellow, then came upright again. Hoskin began to lead it from the barn, the bull following him willingly enough, having had all the fight knocked out of it.

Teddy released Stephen, who ran back to Beth. Turning, he found Loretta behind him.

'I must say I was very impressed,' she said.

'Are you all right?'

'Oh, fine. Although for a little while back there I surely thought my time had come.'

Teddy glanced over at Stephen, still anxious for the lad.

'You like kids. That's something I admire in a man. At your age you should be settled down with a mess of your own. You'd be a great father, I can see,' Loretta said.

'The war put paid to a lot of things that might've been.'

'But the war's over now. Those who came through it must pick up what pieces they can and get going with their lives again. Yeah, you should have kids of your own. Long overdue, I'd say.'

Eyes hooded, Gene had been listening to this dialogue. 'There's a horse outside with a broken leg, Loretta. You want to finish the beast or will I?' he said.

'I'll do it,' she replied, taking the rifle from him.

For a moment brother and sister were motionless. Beth had a sudden wild idea that Loretta was going to turn the rifle on him; then Loretta gave a thin slash of a smile before striding from the barn. Gene swivelled round to stare at Teddy, a perplexed frown on his face.

Gene was still staring at Teddy when a shot rang out.

Chapter 22

Late that night Beth was woken by Stephen, crawling into bed beside her. It was a habit she'd almost broken him of, but she decided that after his fright earlier on she'd make this time an exception to the rule and not say anything. To be truthful, she gained just as much comfort from his presence as he obviously did from hers.

Settling Stephen down, she realised Gene's half of the bed was empty, and wondered where he was. Stephen dropped back off to sleep almost instantly, his body pressed hard against Beth's. She heard a floorboard squeak out in the corridor, and then the door opened to re-admit Gene.

'What have you been up to?' she queried in a whisper.

He threw his dressing gown over a chair and slithered beneath the bedclothes. 'I heard a noise so went to investigate.'

'What was it?'

'El going downstairs. I followed her to find out what she was up to.' A match flared in the darkness as Gene lit a cigarette. Typically, he didn't offer Beth one.

'And what was she up to at this time of night?'

'Can't you guess?'

Beth had suspected this might happen. She had seen the way Loretta had been looking at Teddy after he'd stunned the bull: a look of frank admiration, not to mention lust. Something inside her jumped at the thought of Loretta and Teddy together.

It was a good hour later when Loretta finally returned to her own room. Beth was awake, listening for her, as was Gene. Beth sensed him tense when Loretta padded past their door, his breathing changing to become tight and strained.

'It's started to thaw out,' he said for no apparent reason.

'That's good.'

'Won't be too long now before I can drill the seed. My favourite time of year, that.'

Loretta and Teddy. The image conjured up in Beth's mind made her want to be sick.

After a while Beth went back to sleep, but Gene remained awake. He lay very still, his face creased in thought.

Beth knocked the window and gestured for Teddy to come into the kitchen. It was mid-morning the following day and she'd been trying to catch him on his own since Gene and Loretta had left after breakfast.

'I thought you might like some coffee,' she said when he entered.

'It's thawing like billy-o out there.'

'That a fact?' She banged the cups down on the table, and glanced over at Stephen playing happily in a corner.

He had a couple of small cardboard boxes and the cardboard insides from several toilet rolls, and was putting them together to make a Crusader fort. The Crusaders themselves were wooden laundry pegs.

The coffee was ready, so she slopped it into their cups, then slopped milk in after it.

'Help yourself to sugar,' she snapped.

'Is something wrong, Beth?'

'Depends what you call wrong.'

He nodded. 'Loretta told you about last night. Is that it?'

'She didn't have to. Gene heard her go down to you. I woke up and he told me.'

Teddy sat on the edge of the table and sipped his coffee. It amused him to see Beth so angry. And jealous? Yes, she was, he decided, and wondered about that.

'I imagine she's very good in bed. Michael certainly seemed to think so,' Beth sniffed.

Teddy neither reacted nor replied.

'Oh, how could you? With a woman like that, who . . . who did what she did to poor lovely Michael. Didn't your flesh crawl?'

'No.'

'I suppose she threatened you. Said you'd lose your job if you didn't service her?'

'That's an awful word, Beth. I'm surprised at you.'

'But it's the right word as far as she's concerned, isn't it? I suppose she thinks because you've taken Michael's job you're also going to take his one-time place between her legs?'

Teddy was amazed at this outburst. It was so unlike the Beth he knew.

Beth tried to light a cigarette but her hand was shaking

so much she couldn't. Teddy came over and helped her by holding the hand steady.

'I could've managed,' she hissed, and flounced across to Stephen, pretending to check he was all right, although it was obvious he was.

Teddy regarded her quizzically. 'I must admit that when she appeared with a bottle of wine last night I did fear the worst. But what actually happened was the complete opposite.'

'Oh?'

'She asked if she could come in, saying she wanted to talk to me. I opened the wine. We drank and chatted. She's a highly intelligent woman with quite a sense of humour. She also has tremendous charisma when she wants to use it. I was impressed.'

'So it would seem.'

'You said Michael was in love with her?'

'He said he was.'

'Well, from what you've told me about Michael I can understand how he'd be attracted to a woman like Loretta, and vice versa. The usual run of males round Stewarton can't really appeal all that much to her. She's extremely knowledgeable about all manner of things, you know.'

'Sounds to me like she made a conquest.'

Teddy laughed. 'No fears. She's about as much my type as Olive Oyl, to whom she bears more than a passing resemblance.'

Beth laughed with him. It was true now she came to think of it. 'So nothing happened, then?'

He ran a finger in several directions over his chest. 'Cross my heart and hope to die.'

Beth sighed. It was an enormous relief. 'I was very worried for you.'

'I appreciate that.'

Suddenly Beth was at a loss for words. Feeling rather foolish, she collected up their empty cups and took them to the sink where she busied herself washing them.

Teddy stared at her back for a few seconds. 'I'd better return to work. Himself wants me to get the seed ready for drilling, which he says will probably be in a few weeks' time. Sooner if this thaw continues the way it has.'

'Bye, Teddy!' Stephen called out from where he was playing.

'Bye, son,' Teddy replied, his voice filled with warmth and affection which Beth didn't fail to note.

'Take care of yourself, mind,' she whispered without turning round from the sink where she was now only pretending to be busy.

She watched him through the window till he was out of sight.

That evening after supper Gene went over to sit by the pot-bellied stove and started in on some cider, knocking back two large glasses of the stuff in rapid succession.

'Quite a thaw, this. I've never known one like it,' Loretta said casually.

Gene grunted.

'The temperature just keeps climbing and climbing. Last look I had at the thermometer it was ten degrees higher than the same time yesterday.'

Gene swigged down more cider, then belched.

Beth winced. God, he could be such a pig. She hardly recognised the Gene now facing her as the man she'd met at Bruce's Cave. Talk about Jekyll and Hyde!

'I'm worried about the cattle,' Loretta went on.

Gene glanced across at her. 'Why?'

'This thaw's a real freak. Who knows what could happen up where they are?'

'Like what, for instance?'

'There's the danger of flooding, for a start. And cattle get spooked very easily when the weather's strange. When they're nervous they're liable to do anything.'

Gene thought about what she'd said. 'Could be you're right. The sooner we sell them off the better. They're nothing but a pain in the ass anyway.'

The cider was already getting to him, Beth could tell from his querulous tone. He would start to get quarrelsome soon if he continued to drink, which was more than likely. She dreaded the belligerent stage, shuddering to think that he might get aroused and make her give him oral sex again. The memory of the one time she'd been forced to do that still filled her with revulsion and made her skin creep. Thank the Lord there was only a fortnight left till Teddy's money arrived. She was literally counting the remaining days, ticking them off in a calendar she kept in her head.

'Until we do sell the cattle they represent a capital investment for us and I like to guard my investments,' Loretta said.

'That's fair enough.'

'With that in mind I think I'll spend the night up there with them to keep an eye on things.'

'I've no objection.'

'I'll take a bedroll, and I'd be obliged if you'd fill a vacuum flask for me,' she said to Beth.

'I'll get it ready right away. Some sandwiches too, in case you get hungry while you're there?'

'Thanks. And I think I'll get Teddy to come along with me. Just to be on the safe side.'

Beth stiffened. So that's what this was really all about. It had nothing to do with the cattle whatsoever. The bitch wanted to spend the night alone with Teddy.

'I'll go and tell him to get ready,' Loretta said, and left the kitchen.

When she was gone Gene swore vehemently. 'He's another goddamn Chuck Crerar. She's got plans for him and I know exactly what those plans are.'

A few minutes later Loretta returned to say that she and Teddy would be leaving shortly and they'd be going on horseback. 'I don't want to risk problems with the pickup in its present mechanical state,' she added, giving Gene a double-edged smile as she spoke.

After Loretta had run upstairs to pack a few items Gene sat glowering at Beth as she cut the sandwiches. 'I'm snookered because of a wife who can't have any more children,' he growled.

'You found a way round Chuck Crerar. No doubt you'll be able to do the same with this one given time,' Beth replied tartly, thinking that Gene wouldn't be able to dig anything up against Teddy in the space of a fortnight. No, Loretta was the one Teddy had to worry about. But he could look after himself. He'd find a way of playing her along for two weeks.

Gene poured more cider, switching the focus of his glowering from Beth to the contents of his glass. Beth continued to make sandwiches, giving the majority of them a date filling because Teddy loved dates and Loretta hated them.

Early next morning when Beth got up the temperature was higher than ever. A glance out of the window revealed that the snow close to the house had gone. The ground must be sodden, she thought.

Halfway through breakfast Gene was called to the telephone. While he spoke, Beth fussed over Stephen, whom she'd recently been having trouble getting to eat.

'A nice boiled egg and soldiers. What more could you ask for?'

Stephen pulled a face. 'I'm not hungry.'

'If you don't eat you won't grow big and strong.'

'I don't like white. I only like yellow.'

'Eat the yellow then.'

'But I'm not hungry,' he repeated.

Beth sighed. There were times when she could've cheerfully picked up his meal and crowned the little bugger with it, and this was one of them. Where were Teddy and Loretta? They should've been back by now.

'Eat some of the soldiers then,' she cajoled.

'Soldiers is a stupid name to call slices of toast.'

'It's traditional.'

'What's traditional, Mommy?'

She leaned across and tweaked his ear. 'You won't catch me with that trick, young man,' she said, knowing he was trying to divert her attention from his not eating.

'That was Johnny Bauge,' Gene announced, sitting back down at the table.

Beth liked Johnny. 'What did he want?'

'He didn't want anything. He called to tell me Crystal Creek is in bad spate. A regular torrent, according to him. I'd better go and have a look to see if it's causing any damage.'

He sipped some of his coffee, regarding Beth over the rim of his cup. With a sudden smile, he went on, 'Say, I've just had a dandy idea. Why don't you and the boy come with me? I'm sure he'd love to see the creek in spate. It should be quite a sight.'

Beth wasn't at all keen. She wanted to see Teddy and assure herself that he was safe – and find out what had gone on between him and Loretta during the night.

'I was only thinking of Stephen. You're always complaining I don't do enough with him,' Gene said plaintively, realising Beth was going to turn down his suggestion.

That was true, though only to a degree. It had been a long time now since she'd encouraged Gene to get more involved with her son.

'What's a spate?' Stephen asked.

'It means the creek's in flood. A lot of the snow that's melted has found its way into the creek and it's swollen to river size,' Gene explained.

'I'd like to see that,' Stephen enthused.

'You can come with me on your own then.'

That settled it for Beth. Her policy was never to allow Stephen to be alone with either Gene or Loretta. 'We'll both come with you. When will we leave?'

'Right away.'

Stephen immediately slipped from his chair. 'I'll put my coat and wellingtons on and wait outside.'

Beth was stacking dishes in the sink when it suddenly dawned on her that Stephen had managed it after all. He'd got Gene talking about what spate meant and as a consequence had got away without finishing his breakfast. Fly wee monkey, she thought.

Beth and Gene joined Stephen outside a few minutes later. 'We'll drive there. I reckon that's the best plan,' Gene said.

'Pickup or car?'

Gene gave her a wicked grin. 'Tell you what, let's take Teddy's Hudson. Those old Hudsons are built like Sherman tanks and can cope with almost anything. I don't want to risk either of my two vehicles getting stuck in a quagmire.'

What a mean thing to do, Beth thought. Just typical of Gene. She tried to protest but Gene would have none of it. He clambered into the Hudson and started the engine, Teddy having left the key on the dash as he always did when parked at the house.

Away from the farm buildings there were still large mounds and patches of snow left and in places areas of slush. Beth sat with Stephen on her knee as Gene headed the Hudson in a straight line towards the creek.

Loretta and Teddy had decided to return to the house in a roundabout way, which was why Gene never saw them. But they saw him – or the Hudson, at least. They didn't know Gene had borrowed it.

'That's my bloody car!' Teddy exclaimed, standing in his stirrups and pointing.

Loretta glanced over to the house, where the pickup and family car were plainly visible. So who was in the Hudson?

'Someone trying to steal it?' Teddy queried.

'It seems unlikely. But what other explanation is there? Gene must be out somewhere and Beth couldn't have heard it being taken. Or if she did she must've thought it was Gene driving off in one of ours.'

Teddy swore. He had become extremely fond of the Hudson. 'Whoever's in it must hit Crystal Creek that way. Right?'

Loretta nodded.

'Which means I may have a chance to catch up to find out just what's what.'

'Let's go then,' Loretta replied, heeling her horse into a trot.

When they arrived at Crystal Creek Gene parked the Hudson under a tree and they all got out. Beth was carrying Stephen, as she didn't want him running around in what must be a dangerous spot. And how dangerous it was they soon saw. The creek was at least ten times its normal width and considerably deeper.

'Dearie me!' Beth exclaimed, staring at it in amazement. The water was muddy brown in colour, in complete contrast to the normal clarity which had given it its name. Pieces of debris floated by, including several broken branches, a plank of wood, a half-submerged mattress and a swept-away fence post.

'Let's move a bit closer,' Gene suggested, taking Beth by the arm and guiding her to a small knoll which jutted out slightly over the fast-moving water. It was a moment before he spoke again, and when he did his voice was strained.

'Michael never mattered to me because El could never have married him. But this Teddy Ramsay is different. He's a white man.'

Beth turned to stare at Gene. What had suddenly brought this on?

'I need to have an heir before she gets one. It's as clear-cut and simple as that. Which makes you a liability, Beth. A liability I have to get rid of.'

Fear clutched at her insides. 'I'll go away—'

'That's no use,' he interrupted. 'Too much time would be involved and that's just something I don't have to spare.'

She clutched Stephen tightly to her. The boy was gazing out over the creek in fascination, not realising the danger he was in.

Beth cursed herself for walking blindly into Gene's trap. She should've realised something was amiss when he suggested they all do something together. He would only have done so with an ulterior motive in mind.

She tried to edge round him with the intention of making a dash for it, only to be blocked by his arm.

'The farm's going to be mine. Not El's. I won't mourn long, Beth. I've already got someone picked out to replace you. Someone who'll have no trouble bearing me an heir.'

Beth cried out as Gene gave her a sudden shove. Stephen yelped as he found himself toppling towards the water he'd been so avidly watching. Mustn't let Stephen go, Beth told herself as the brown sludge closed over her head.

The water was fairly warm, which surprised her. Then

she was kicking for all she was worth, forcing her way back to the surface, with Stephen struggling frantically in her arms. There was a tremendous undertow trying to suck them down again. Stephen was lead in her embrace; far heavier than he normally was. She remembered then that he was wearing wellingtons which would be filled with water, causing the additional weight.

She clawed at the little boots and succeeded in getting one off, but the other defied all her efforts. She finally gave up on it when she and Stephen went under again, since she needed her one free hand to battle back to the surface.

At that point Teddy and Loretta came trotting up and saw Beth and Stephen being swept downstream. Teddy immediately leapt from Doris Mae and went chasing after them, only to come up short when Gene stepped aggressively into his path. Using the side of his hand Teddy felled Gene with a savage blow to the base of the throat, and jumped over him to continue running along the bank after the bobbing Beth and Stephen. A little further on was an acute bend in the creek where the current slowed. Reaching the bend at the same time as the pair in the water, Teddy started to wade out after them.

A heavy branch careered into Beth, tearing Stephen from her grasp. She gave a great wail of anguish as that dear sweet face vanished under the branch.

Swimming furiously now, Teddy saw Stephen disappear. He changed direction fractionally and headed for the branch, diving the moment he reached it. It was impossible to see anything beneath the surface, so it was sheer luck that his groping fingers closed over Stephen's collar.

He tried to yank the child upwards but Stephen was stuck. The smaller branches of the large branch, Teddy thought. Sure enough, several had become entangled in the boy's clothing. They refused to snap, being far too pliable, so Teddy placed his feet against the underside of the large branch and pulled with all his might. Stephen was ripped free.

Teddy surfaced a few feet away from Beth, who looked almost spent and about to give up.

'Head for the bank. Make yourself do it, woman. Make yourself!' Teddy commanded her in his most authoritative manner.

Beth's response was to flail one tired arm in front of the other. Slowly she began cutting through the water. With Stephen in tow Teddy reached the bank ahead of Beth, to find Gene waiting for them. Loretta stood beside him, her face a study of mixed emotions.

'Oh no you don't,' Gene muttered as Teddy tried to clamber ashore. Putting an open hand in Teddy's face, he pushed. Teddy and Stephen splashed back into the water.

Loretta's half-crazed confusion suddenly resolved itself into one blinding principle. The farm ought to be hers, and, since she had pinned her prospects of acquiring it firmly on Teddy, she mustn't lose him now. Dimly, she also realised that it would be to her advantage if Beth didn't drown. She leapt into action.

Fingers of both hands dug into the soft mud of the bank, Beth was hanging on grimly, waiting to recover enough strength to be able to haul herself further up on to dry land. From the corner of her eye she could see Teddy making a second attempt to pull himself and Stephen ashore.

Between them, Gene was punching Loretta as if she was another man, and she was slugging him back as if she really was. He wrapped his arms round her in a bear hug and the pair of them staggered from side to side like a couple of drunken sailors. Gene's arms were still wrapped round Loretta when he lost his footing in the slippery mud and they plunged sideways into the creek.

As they went in, Teddy dragged himself and Stephen out. Leaving Stephen he crawled across to where Beth was still grimly hanging on, and slithered her up on to the bank.

On hands and knees, Beth made her way over to Stephen. 'I think he's dead,' she whispered to Teddy when he joined her.

Stephen's eyes were closed, his skin pale as ivory. Teddy lifted an eyelid but there was no sign of life underneath; nor was there a heartbeat when Teddy put his ear to Stephen's chest.

'Oh, God!' Sitting, Beth dropped her head in total despair.

Teddy flipped Stephen over on to his front, and began rhythmically pumping Stephen's arms the way the army had taught him. Dribble after dribble of brown water trickled from Stephen's mouth.

It was something Teddy had learned in the jungle. He didn't know how it worked, only that it sometimes did. Focusing his mind on Stephen, he willed the boy to live, feeling his own life force go forth to envelop Stephen as he went on pumping.

Stephen's left eye flickered first. Then his cheek twitched. With a cough, he started to breathe again.

'Oh!' Beth exclaimed very softly.

Stephen's eyes opened to stare at Beth. 'Mommy,' he whispered.

Beth gathered him to her, tears streaming down her face, and began to rock to and fro.

Teddy sat back on his haunches and breathed a profound sigh of relief. The mind was a great mystery, he mused; capable of many strange things in moments of extreme stress. A doctor would no doubt have said his pumping had revived Stephen, but he knew better. The pumping on its own hadn't been enough.

Coming to his feet, Teddy ran to the Hudson for the old tartan travelling rug he knew to be on the rear seat. Bringing it back to Beth and Stephen, he draped it round them.

'What about Gene and Loretta?' Beth whispered.

In the drama of resuscitating the boy, Teddy had completely forgotten about them. He glanced out over the creek but there was no sign of them.

'Can you stand?' he asked Beth, who nodded.

He helped her to her feet and told her to get into the car and turn the heating on. He'd return shortly. Then he pulled himself into Doris Mae's saddle and kneed the placid horse into a walk, guiding her past the bend in the creek to head downstream.

Despite the waves of hot air blasting out of the Hudson's heater both Beth and Stephen were shivering when Teddy rejoined them. Teddy reckoned it was more from reaction than from cold.

'Well?' Beth said.

Teddy slid into the driver's seat. He had tied Doris

Mae and Loretta's mount to a nearby tree, intending to pick them up later. He shook his head.

Beth stared at Teddy. 'What do you think?'

'Beyond the bend the current really picks up speed and there are a great many whirls and eddies.'

Beth turned from Teddy to gaze out over the swollen creek, her lips moving in silent prayer. 'Loretta's a witch and Gene is too rotten to drown. They'll turn up,' she said, and shuddered.

'When we get back to the house we'd better ring the police anyway. We'll tell them you and the boy fell in and they were swept away in the rescue attempt. Whatever the outcome of all this, I think that's best. Don't you?'

Beth nodded.

Four days later Crystal Creek finally began to subside and two days after that Sergeant Ed Slattery presented himself at the house. 'Constable Dodds and his party have just called in. They've found Gene and Loretta down at Scotch Mill, almost buried in a wall of mud.'

Elation leapt in Beth. Her almost constant prayers of the past six days had been answered. 'Is Constable Dodds certain it's them?'

'He says there's no doubt about it. Although a formal identification will have to be made, of course.'

'Of course,' Beth echoed. She staggered and had to grab at the wall for support. It was *confirmed*. They were both dead! Out of her and Stephen's life for ever.

Teddy, who'd been sitting at the table drinking coffee, came to her. 'Is there anything you want?'

Beth shook her head.

Slattery played with his hat, which he was holding in front of him. 'I'm real sorry, Mrs McKay. Real sorry. Gene was a fine upstanding man who'll be sorely missed in this community, I can tell you. Particularly in the League.' He paused. Played with his hat a little more. Then added, 'Constable Dodds says they were entangled together. As though they'd been trying to save one another.'

Drown one another more likely, Beth thought.

'In a way it seems kind of fitting that they should die together, having been born together like,' Slattery went on.

Beth took a deep breath. 'Thank you for coming over in person and as soon as you did, Sergeant. I'll make the necessary arrangements for the funeral now.'

'Could you come in tomorrow and formally identify the bodies? I'll make sure Mr Desiato the mortician has them nice and cleaned up for you by then.'

Teddy winced. That had about as much subtlety as the sledgehammer he'd used on the bull.

'I'll be there,' Beth promised.

Slattery put his hat back on, relieved he'd got that over and done with. 'Ma'am!' he said, touching his hat brim. Teddy walked him to the door.

When Teddy came back Beth wasn't there. Stephen was having a nap in her bedroom and she'd gone to sit with him, wanting to be alone with her son to think things through.

Teddy decided to ride up and feed the cattle. He also had some thinking to do.

It was a big funeral with nearly all of Stewarton attending. The minister spoke of tragedy and heroes, and dying in a noble cause. Good riddance to bad rubbish was what Beth thought as she threw a handful of dirt down on to Gene's coffin. And I hope you're frying in hell for what you did to poor Michael, she added when she did the same to Loretta's casket.

Because she didn't cry, the mourners present presumed she was putting an extremely brave face on it. In fact the only tears she could've shed were ones of relief and joy. She knew she should've invited some of the folk back to the house but couldn't bring herself to be that much of a hypocrite, so she put it about that she would've found it far too distressing.

Home from the funeral, Beth opened a king-sized bottle of Coke for Stephen, telling him to drink as much joker as he wanted. The penny-pinching days were over. Then she cracked a bottle of Scotch and poured out two huge measures.

'What happens now?' Teddy asked, sipping the whisky she'd handed him.

'It's ironic the lengths Gene and Loretta went to to try to get the farm for themselves, and in the end neither of them got it. I did.'

'So what'll you do with it?'

'I shall sell. There's bound to be at least one of the neighbours whose land borders this who'll want to increase their acreage. I should realise a tidy sum. Enough to take care of Stephen and me for a good few years.'

'It's an ill wind,' Teddy commented, finishing his whisky.

Beth immediately poured him another hefty measure. 'There's one other thing. I'm going to sell the cattle off separately. Hoskin McVitie will help me there. I want you to have the money they bring in.'

Teddy stared at her in astonishment. 'I couldn't accept it, Beth!' he protested.

'Yes you can. It's the very least I can do. Besides, I want you to have it. I insist.'

'I don't know what to say,' he replied after a lengthy pause.

'You don't have to say anything. Just that you'll take it.'

'I'd prefer Stephen—'

'I told you. Stephen and I will both be well taken care of out of the farm proceeds,' she interjected. 'So there's no need to worry about him.'

Teddy glanced across to where Stephen was drinking Coke, his heart going out to the wee fellow. What a wrench it was going to be when he said goodbye. 'All right then. Thank you.'

'Thank *you*. If it hadn't been for you it would've been our funeral today.'

He stared at her, opening his mouth to speak. Then he changed his mind and drank some whisky instead.

'Is it still the west coast or the States for you, Teddy?'

'There's nothing to keep me here now, is there?'

'No.' She turned away from him so he couldn't see her expression.

'And you'll go back to Glasgow as you'd intended when you were going to get Michael's money?'

'Yes.'

Teddy realised he wasn't enjoying the whisky. It was lying heavy and sour on his stomach. He ran a hand across his face. He'd been dreaming of the war the previous night, an old nightmare that the Japs had got hold of him again. As always happened when he reflected on that recurring nightmare, the myriad scars covering his body started to itch. 'I think I'll go over to the small barn. Some work needs doing there.'

'Can I come?' Stephen asked.

'Of course you can, son.'

With a whoop Stephen finished off his Coke and jumped down from his chair, taking Teddy by the hand as they went out of the door.

Beth poured herself another large whisky, noticing that she was already giddy. She wasn't normally much of a drinker but right now she intended to get drunk as the proverbial skunk. After all she'd been through with Gene and Loretta she reckoned she'd earned the right. Stephen would be entirely safe with Teddy.

Two and a half weeks later Beth switched off the pickup's engine outside the back of the house and glanced across to where Teddy was playing with Stephen. The snow and slush had long since given way to spring. Overhead, rooks were cawing loudly, while in various patches of garden round the house clumps of flowers had burst into bloom.

Beth touched the envelope in her lap and her spirits sank. Stephen had grown so fond of Teddy, as indeed had she. Suddenly, quite illogically, she was angry.

Getting out of the pickup she banged the door shut behind her and strode over to where Teddy and Stephen were to hand Teddy the envelope. 'That's the money from the sale of the cattle. I thought it best you had it in cash. We don't want everyone knowing our business.'

Teddy opened the envelope and riffled through the thick wad of bills it contained. He was about to make some jocular remark when he became aware that a stricken Stephen was staring up at him.

'As what your friend Dan owed you has already come in, I suppose you'll be moving on now,' Beth said, her voice hard and cold.

'I suppose so.'

'When will you go?'

'The end of the week, I think.'

'You're not really going to leave us, are you?' Stephen asked, a tremor in his voice.

'I'm afraid so, son.'

'But why?'

'I only came here to help you and your mummy out. Now I've done that it's time to move on.'

'But I don't want you to go,' Stephen wailed, grabbing hold of Teddy's trouser leg and clutching it.

'There's no point in me staying. Your mummy is selling this place and you'll soon be going back to Glasgow,' Teddy explained.

'Can't you come with us?'

Teddy shot Beth a glance that said he wanted her to help him out in this difficult situation. She stared through him as though he wasn't there.

'It's sad but true that all good things usually come to an end. That's something you have to learn in growing up.'

Tears filled Stephen's eyes. Letting go of Teddy's trouser leg, he turned and fled in the direction of the stables.

'Now look what you've done!' Beth snapped. Brushing

past Teddy she ran after Stephen. Perplexed and mysti-fied by her hostile attitude, Teddy stared after the pair of them.

Late that night Beth came abruptly out of a deep sleep. An alarm bell had gone off in the recesses of her brain. Something was wrong.

Her first thought was for Stephen. A quick grope told her he wasn't alongside her, so she got up and padded over to his bed. She drew in a sharp breath when she saw that it was empty.

A dozen different thoughts rushed through her mind as she threw on her dressing gown and hurried out into the corridor. A few minutes later she was in the kitchen, having hastily checked every room in between. Stephen wasn't there either. And now panic was really beginning to set in. She must go and rouse Teddy. He would help her find him.

Light was showing underneath the door, which surprised her. She would've thought Teddy would have been fast asleep by now.

'Come in!' he called out when she rapped.

Teddy was sitting in a chair with Stephen sobbing on his lap, the wee boy's eyes awash with tears. 'He appeared about ten minutes ago,' Teddy explained.

Beth took a deep breath. She opened her mouth to tell Stephen off, then decided against it as he was already distressed enough. Kneeling beside him, she curled a hand round his. 'Why did you come here?'

'I don't want Teddy to leave,' Stephen choked.

'He came down all those stairs and along that

passageway in the dark. I think that was awfully brave of him.' Teddy smiled and stroked the side of Stephen's face.

'So do I,' Beth agreed.

'Why don't you make a cup of coffee and we'll both have a cigarette?'

She nodded. That was a good idea. Stephen needed time to calm down before she took him back to bed.

'There are biscuits in a tin over there.'

'Can I have a cookie?' Stephen asked, brightening a little.

'There are several chocolate ones. You can have those.'

'And some coffee?'

Teddy looked at Beth, who nodded. 'All right. But lots of milk in it, mind.'

He's a natural father, Beth reflected, marvelling at how close a bond had grown up between those two in such a short time.

As they drank their coffee and ate the biscuits, Teddy chatted on to Stephen about this and that; nothing of consequence, although you wouldn't have thought it from the way Stephen hung on every word. After a while the boy's hands fell sideways and his head drooped as he dropped off to sleep.

'He's absolutely shattered. I bet he was lying awake fretting for ages before coming down,' Teddy said.

'Give him a couple of minutes to get properly under and then I'll take him upstairs.'

Teddy drew nervously on his cigarette. 'I've decided where I'm going from here and it's not the west coast or the States.'

'Oh?'

'I'm returning to Malaya. I miss it dreadfully, which I suppose is surprising considering all the hardship I went through there. But a place can get into your blood – become part of you without you realising it, which is what's happened to me. All the time I was there I dreamed of going home to Glasgow, yet when I finally got there I no longer belonged. I was a stranger in my own land, if you like. I now realise that where I *do* belong is Malaya. That's where my roots have gone down and where I want to settle.'

'Are you sure?'

He nodded. 'Absolutely.'

'What will you do there?'

'Being on this farm has given me the answer to that. I've found I enjoy working with my hands and that the outdoor life suits me, so I shall use the cattle money to buy a partnership in one of the smaller rubber plantations.'

'Oh, Teddy. I hope it works out for you.'

'It will. I *know* it will.'

Beth stubbed out her cigarette. She was envious of him. Envious that he'd found his niche.

'Beth?'

She glanced up. 'Yes?'

'If I don't say this right now I never will. All the time I was in Malaya I dreamt not only of Glasgow but also of you. Often when things were really bad I'm convinced it was only the memory of you that brought me through. Oh, I knew you'd never be mine. That you'd chosen Steve. But even knowing that I couldn't forget you. I lied when I told you I only came to Canada to see Stephen. I also came to see you.'

He paused. Then he went on, his voice now tight and

strained. 'Beth, I still love you as much as I've always done and I think we could make a damn good go of it together. Will you marry me and come to Malaya?'

At that moment her life, which had seemed so out of sync, suddenly clicked back into place. There was a rightness about marrying Teddy – an inevitability even. He made her feel safe, secure and happy. What more could a woman ask for? 'I'll add what I get for the farm to your cattle money and then perhaps we can buy that small plantation outright.'

A smile split his face.

Beth glanced at Stephen snuggled in Teddy's arms and a new-found joy welled through her like a warm bubbling stream. 'We've both come a long way from that air raid shelter where we first met.'

'Far more than just miles,' he whispered in reply.

Other bestselling titles available by mail:

☐	Twilight Times	Emma Blair	£6.99
☐	Little White Lies	Emma Blair	£6.99
☐	Three Bites of the Cherry	Emma Blair	£6.99
☐	Sweethearts	Emma Blair	£6.99

The prices shown above are correct at time of going to press. However, the publishers reserve the right to increase prices on covers from those previously advertised, without further notice.

——————————— sphere ———————————

Please allow for postage and packing: **Free UK delivery.**
Europe; add 25% of retail price; Rest of World; 45% of retail price.

To order any of the above or any other Sphere titles, please call our credit card orderline or fill in this coupon and send/fax it to:

Sphere, P.O. Box 121, Kettering, Northants NN14 4ZQ
Fax: 01832 733076   Tel: 01832 737526
Email: aspenhouse@FSBDial.co.uk

☐ I enclose a UK bank cheque made payable to Sphere for £ . . . .
☐ Please charge £ . . . . . . to my Visa, Delta, Maestro.

☐☐☐☐☐☐☐☐☐☐☐☐☐☐☐☐☐-☐

Expiry Date ☐☐☐☐   Maestro Issue No. ☐☐

NAME (BLOCK LETTERS please) . . . .

ADDRESS . . . .

. . . .

. . . .

Postcode . . . . Telephone . . . .

Signature . . . .

Please allow 28 days for delivery within the UK. Offer subject to price and availability.